PRAISE FOR THE NOVELS
OF KAREN WHITE

The Girl on Legare Street

"Karen White delivers the thrills of perilous romance and the chills of ghostly suspense, all presented with Southern wit and charm."
—*New York Times* bestselling author Kerrelyn Sparks

"If you have ever been fascinated by things that go bump in the night, then this is a bonus book for you . . . will have her faithful fans gasping."
—The Huffington Post

"In *The Girl on Legare Street*, Karen embraces Charleston's mystical lore, its history, its architecture, its ambience, and its ghosts."
—*Lowcountry Weekly* (SC)

"Elements of history, romance, and humor. I couldn't wait to see what was going to happen next."
—BellaOnline

"Beautifully written with interesting, intelligent characters and a touch of the paranormal. The story is dark [and] ofttimes scary."
—Fresh Fiction

The House on Tradd Street

"Engaging . . . a fun and satisfying read."
—*Publishers Weekly*

"*The House on Tradd Street* has it all: mystery, romance, and the paranormal, including ghosts with quirky personalities."
—BookLoons

"White delivers funny characters, a solid plot, and an interesting twist in this novel about the South and its antebellum history."
—*Romantic Times*

continued . . .

D0038498

"Has all the elements that have made Karen White's books fan favorites: a Southern setting, a deeply emotional tale, and engaging characters."
—A Romance Review

"If you enjoy ghost stories with some mystery thrown into the mix, you are going to love this . . . wonderful, mysterious, and ghostly tale."
—Romance Reviews Today

"Brilliant and engrossing . . . a rare gem . . . exquisitely told."
—The Book Connection

"An extremely talented and colorful writer with tons of imagination."
—Fresh Fiction

The Memory of Water

"Beautifully written and as lyrical as the tides. *The Memory of Water* speaks directly to the heart and will linger in yours long after you've read the final page. I loved this book!" —Susan Crandall, author of *Pitch Black*

"Karen White delivers a powerfully emotional blend of family secrets, Low-country lore, and love in *The Memory of Water*—who could ask for more?"
—Barbara Bretton, author of *Just Desserts*

Learning to Breathe

"White creates a heartfelt story full of vibrant characters and emotion that leaves the reader satisfied yet hungry for more from this talented author."
—*Booklist*

"One of those stories where you savor every single word . . . a perfect 10."
—Romance Reviews Today

Pieces of the Heart

"Heartwarming and intense . . . a tale that resonates with the meaning of unconditional love." —*Romantic Times* (4 stars)

"A terrific, insightful character study." —*Midwest Book Review*

The Color of Light

"A story as rich as a coastal summer . . . dark secrets, heartache, a magnificent South Carolina setting, and a great love story."
— *New York Times* bestselling author Deborah Smith

"As lush as the Lowcountry . . . unexpected and magical."
— Patti Callahan Henry, author of *Between the Tides*

MORE PRAISE FOR THE NOVELS OF KAREN WHITE

"The fresh voice of Karen White intrigues and delights."
— Sandra Chastain, contributor to *At Home in Mossy Creek*

"Warmly Southern and deeply moving."
— *New York Times* bestselling author Deborah Smith

"Karen White writes with passion and poignancy."
— Deb Stover, award-winning author of *Mulligan Magic*

"[A] sweet book . . . highly recommended."   — *Booklist*

"Karen White is one author you won't forget. . . . This is a masterpiece in the study of relationships. Brava!"   — Reader to Reader Reviews

"This is not only romance at its best—this is a fully realized view of life at its fullest."   — Readers & Writers, Ink

"*After the Rain* is an elegantly enchanting Southern novel. . . . Fans will recognize the beauty of White's evocative prose."   — WordWeaving.com

"In the tradition of Catherine Anderson and Deborah Smith, Karen White's *After the Rain* is an incredibly poignant contemporary bursting with Southern charm."   — Patricia Rouse, Rouse's Romance Readers Groups

"Don't miss this book!"   — *Rendezvous*

THE STRANGERS ON
MONTAGU STREET

KAREN WHITE

New American Library

New American Library
Published by New American Library, a division of
Penguin Group (USA) Inc., 375 Hudson Street,
New York, New York 10014, USA
Penguin Group (Canada), 90 Eglinton Avenue East, Suite 700, Toronto,
Ontario M4P 2Y3, Canada (a division of Pearson Penguin Canada Inc.)
Penguin Books Ltd., 80 Strand, London WC2R 0RL, England
Penguin Ireland, 25 St. Stephen's Green, Dublin 2,
Ireland (a division of Penguin Books Ltd.)
Penguin Group (Australia), 250 Camberwell Road, Camberwell, Victoria 3124,
Australia (a division of Pearson Australia Group Pty. Ltd.)
Penguin Books India Pvt. Ltd., 11 Community Centre, Panchsheel Park,
New Delhi - 110 017, India
Penguin Group (NZ), 67 Apollo Drive, Rosedale, Auckland 0632,
New Zealand (a division of Pearson New Zealand Ltd.)
Penguin Books (South Africa) (Pty.) Ltd., 24 Sturdee Avenue,
Rosebank, Johannesburg 2196, South Africa

Penguin Books Ltd., Registered Offices:
80 Strand, London WC2R 0RL, England

First published by New American Library,
a division of Penguin Group (USA) Inc.

First Printing, November 2011
10 9 8 7 6 5 4 3 2 1

 REGISTERED TRADEMARK—MARCA REGISTRADA

Library of Congress Cataloging-in-Publication Data:

White, Karen (Karen S.)
The strangers on Montagu Street/Karen White.
p. cm.
ISBN 978-0-451-23526-8 (pbk.)
1. Women real estate agents—Fiction. 2. Women psychics—Fiction. 3. Ghosts—Fiction.
4. Charleston (S.C.)—Fiction. I. Title.
PS3623.H5776S77 2011
813'.6—dc22   2011026916

Set in Bembo STD
Designed by Alissa Amell

Printed in the United States of America

To my readers, whose enthusiasm for the first two books about Melanie and Jack inspired this one.

Acknowledgments

Thanks again to the usual suspects: Wendy Wax, Susan Crandall, and my long-suffering family, who, although only vaguely aware that I do something with my spare time besides laundry, make all of this possible.

Thanks, too, to the awesome talent at Penguin Group and New American Library: my editor, Cindy Hwang; the entire art department (who are responsible for my gorgeous covers); the resourceful sales and marketing teams; and my publicity team (thank you, Craig and Heidi!). And thanks to the truly remarkable publishing team without whom my books would still only be ideas knocking around in my brain: Leslie Gelbman, Kara Welsh, and Claire Zion. To my agent, Karen Solem, a huge thanks for sticking with me since the beginning.

Any book set in Charleston requires plenty of visits for "research," so I must acknowledge the warm and gracious citizens of the Holy City for always welcoming me with their trademark hospitality and fabulous cuisine. I look forward to my next "research" trip for the fourth book in the Tradd Street series.

THE STRANGERS ON
MONTAGU STREET

CHAPTER 1

The phone rang out in the night-shrouded house, shrill and insistent, bringing me abruptly out of an odd dream that somehow involved me, Jack, a shovel, and something dark and undulating buried beneath the black earth. But when Jack opened his mouth to speak, I heard only the ringing of the telephone, jerking me upright in the bed and sending General Lee scampering to the floor with an irritated bark. I reached for the phone, remembering too late that the cord had been pulled from the wall, and held it to my ear before I recognized the pinpricks of warning on the nape of my neck.

Melanie.

I listened for the words that weren't really words, more like sounds punctuated with static that only I could hear. "Grandmother?"

Melanie, I heard again, the sound soft and melodic. I felt no fear, although I suppose a phone call from the dead would alarm most people. But I was used to it.

"Grandmother?" I asked again, hearing only the staccato pop of static. I closed my eyes as my mother had taught me, and focused on the sound, trying to make words form in my mind.

Don't be afraid.

I resisted rolling my eyes and tried hard to push aside my impatience, wondering once again why ghosts couldn't just come right out and say what they wanted. My life was like one long B movie, with me as the lone member of the audience shouting at the screen, "Just tell her already!"

Refocusing again, I closed my eyes tighter and listened while trying to ignore General Lee's pawing at my leg in an attempt to get my attention.

Don't be afraid. And listen to your heart for a change.

My eyes popped open as I suddenly realized that Jack had been telling me the same thing in my dream. The dial tone sounded in my ear and I quickly hung up the phone. General Lee whined and pressed his paw against my nightgown. I looked down at the small black-and-white fur ball, reluctantly inherited along with the housekeeper, Mrs. Houlihan, and the historic house on Tradd Street where I now lived. The same house that was apparently crumbling beneath my feet and sucking money from my bank account at an alarming rate.

I bent to pick up the neglected dog, but he escaped my grasp and instead ran to the dressing table and began pawing at one of the drawer handles, making the brass clang against the dark polished mahogany.

"What?" I asked, following him and wondering why I actually expected an answer. General Lee was only slightly less communicative than the ghosts I'd been speaking with since I was very small and hadn't yet learned to keep such "skills" to myself.

With only the light from an outside streetlamp to guide me, I crossed the room to the dresser and was about to repeat my question when I spotted what looked like a wallet lying on the middle of the dresser top nestled between my La Mer night cream and the folded spreadsheet I used each day to allocate my—and sometimes other people's—time.

I flipped on a small crystal lamp, then blinked until my eyes became accustomed to the light. Because I was convinced that wearing my glasses would officially make me old, they were hidden in my nightstand drawer, so I had to squint to see. I stared hard at the object I was positive hadn't been there when I went to bed. It was definitely a wallet, and a familiar one at that. I picked it up and flipped it open, not at all surprised that I recognized the face on the South Carolina driver's license. Jack Trenholm, six-foot-two, one eighty-five, black hair, blue eyes. After glancing in the bills section and noticing he had two twenties and a ten tucked inside, I snapped it shut with disgust. Nobody had a decent driver's license photo; my own closely resembled one of those fuzzy photos taken of Bigfoot. But Jack's, of course, was almost as good as the publicity photo that appeared on the back cover of his books. As a bestselling author of true-crime historical mystery novels, he had no right to look like a *GQ* model. It was irritating and not a little unnerving.

I frowned down at General Lee. "How did this get here?" The more appropriate question should have been, "Why?" but I'd long since learned unusual things happened around me a lot, and always for a reason—but never for a reason that was easily explained. Besides, I was talking to a dog, and the subtleties of my question would surely be lost on him.

I rubbed my hand against the soft leather while I thought. I hadn't seen Jack for about two weeks—not since the disastrous afternoon when a heretofore unknown teenage girl had shown up on my front porch and called him "Daddy." I'd happily stepped back to allow Jack, his parents, and Jack's girlfriend (my very distant cousin Rebecca Edgerton) to take care of that little problem. I had plenty of issues of my own to deal with—the least of which being the diagnosis of a cracked foundation on my very old historic albatross of a house. And my inability to ignore my unreasonable attraction to Jack Trenholm.

I looked at the clock on my bedside table, and while I was wondering whether five fifteen was too early to call Jack, the doorbell rang. General Lee and I looked at each other and I thought I saw him frown, but that could have been my poor eyesight. I quickly slid my feet into my slippers, slipped a robe over my nightgown, and put the wallet in the robe's pocket. After scooping up the dog, I descended the staircase to the main hall, sincerely hoping that my visitor was the living, breathing kind.

The front door lights had been left on, illuminating the piazza of my Charleston single house and making it easy to recognize the familiar outline of my visitor through the glass sidelights on either side of the door. After punching in the code to disarm the alarm—A-B-B-A, for my favorite musical group—I unlocked the dead bolts and opened the door.

"Jack," I said calmly, my voice completely belying the jumpy, skippy thing my heart seemed to be doing. "I hope you have a really good reason for waking me up and darkening my doorstep at this hour."

He smiled the smile that had cut down swaths of women in his wake since he'd been a toddler. "Now, Mellie—I saw a light in your window, so I know you were awake. What were you doing? Organizing your closet alphabetically by designer?"

While I tried to think of a response that didn't include the embarrassing fact that I'd already done that, I saw his gaze traveling from the toes of my slippers up to the high neck of my nightgown that peeked out of the top of my oversize and very thick robe. Despite its being late spring, I was dressed for winter, since I was notoriously cold-natured.

I frowned at him, taking in his khaki pants, loafers without socks, and white button-down shirt with rolled-up sleeves. I also noticed the messy hair, the unshaven jaw, and circles under his eyes that, unfortunately, did nothing to lessen his appeal.

Before I could say anything, he said, "I don't remember seeing that in the Victoria's Secret catalog. Is it new?"

"What do you want, Jack? I have far more important things to do than hang around my front door chatting with you."

His smile slipped just enough for me to notice. He looked behind him to glance at a darkened spot on the piazza before turning back to me. His smile now resembled a grimace, and I felt the first tremors of unease. "I need to ask a favor."

I crossed my arms, relieved. Obviously, this was some kind of a joke. Jack never asked for favors. His usual MO was to ply his victim with charm so that she never knew she was doing exactly what he wanted her to do. "Will this involve getting me on my back? Or maybe just getting me drunk so that I embarrass myself?" He hadn't technically done either thing, but I liked to pretend that those two instances had been both deliberate and his fault.

Instead of the snarky comment I expected, he frowned and gave a quick shake of his head. Too late, I realized that he wasn't alone on the piazza, as the young girl I'd met only once before emerged from the shadows behind him. Jack stopped slouching against the doorjamb and straightened, allowing the girl to move into the foyer ahead of him. She eyed me in very much the same way her father just had, but with a far more critical eye and accompanied by the loud smacking of chewing gum.

"Nice slippers." She blew a large purple bubble with her gum, then snapped it back into her mouth.

I looked down at my feet. My slippers had been a gift from my best friend, Dr. Sophie Wallen, a professor of historical preservation at the College of Charleston, and I rather liked them. I kept telling myself it was because they kept my feet warm and not because they resembled General Lee, since I wasn't really a dog person. Especially at this moment, as I watched my fickle dog move from my side to sit at the girl's feet and nuzzle her leg.

Jack moved into the foyer, closing the door behind them, and I could see the lines of strain around his mouth, even though he was trying very hard to keep his smile in place. "Melanie, since I didn't get the chance to formally introduce you the last time we were here, I'd like you to meet Emmaline Amelia Pettigrew. Emmaline, I'd like you to meet my . . ."

He paused, as if unsure what to call me, and I couldn't blame him. "Friend," I interjected, feeling the unusual need to help him. It was very clear to me that Jack was completely out of his league with this woman-child.

"Melanie Middleton," I added, and stuck out my hand, because I couldn't think of anything else to do.

The girl stepped under the foyer chandelier and I got a better look at her. Despite the heavy black eyeliner, bright red lipstick, teeny-tiny denim skirt, and pink Converse high-top sneakers, I could tell she was very young, maybe thirteen or fourteen. She also had beautiful black, wavy hair and startling blue eyes that left no doubt as to her relationship to Jack.

Ignoring my hand, she snapped another bubble with her gum. "Nola," she said. "My real name's Nola."

I dropped my hand and looked at Jack.

"We just received her birth certificate from California, and it seems she was officially named Emmaline Amelia. Apparently she's always been called by a nickname."

Nola crossed her arms across her chest and she wore an expression that was somewhere between a smile and a smirk, and I knew enough to brace myself. "Mom always called me Nola because I was conceived in New Orleans, Louisiana, when she and this guy were drunk off their asses."

Jack spoke through gritted teeth and I had the fleeting thought that I should be enjoying this a lot more than I was. "Like I said, her name is Emmaline Amelia and she's been living for the last thirteen and a half years with her mother in Los Angeles."

I raised my eyebrows at him. There was a whole story behind those words that he'd have to share with me eventually. But not now. An almost imperceptible tremor shook the girl, and her knuckles were nearly white where her hands gripped a ratty backpack. And there was something in her take-no-prisoners stance, in her bravado, that didn't ring true. Something sad and lonely and scared. Something that re-minded me of the young abandoned girl I had once been.

I didn't know a lot about teenage girls, despite having once been one, but I knew that assigning a new name to her right now wasn't a good idea. I also knew that the girl standing in front of me wasn't an Emmaline or an Amelia.

Directing a warning glance to Jack to remain silent, I said, "Nice to meet you, Nola. I think that name suits you."

With a triumphant look that was meant for her dad, she said, "So, are you sleeping with him?"

"Absolutely not," I said at the same time Jack said, "Not for lack of trying."

Nola rolled her eyes. "I told him that I would only consider staying with you if the two of you weren't hooking up or anything."

Or anything. I wasn't sure what that last part encompassed, but I knew for sure that whatever Jack and I had going on, it certainly couldn't be classified as "hooking up."

"Stay with me?" I turned a sharp look at Jack.

"Yeah. That's the favor I was going to ask."

"What about Rebecca?" I asked, feeling light-headed. I already had a pretty jam-packed schedule, and I couldn't envision making room on my spreadsheet for one more thing, much less a troubled teenager.

Nola made a gagging sound as she leaned against my Chippendale console table, causing the Dresden figurine on top to wobble but, for-tunately, remain in place. "Oh, please. Don't make me puke. All that sugary pink fakeness would make me want to strangle her, and I don't want to spend time in juvie."

I raised my eyebrows, although I was in complete agreement with her assessment of Rebecca. Forcing my voice to remain calm, I suggested to Jack, "And your parents?"

"They've already downsized to a one-bedroom condo. They'd put it up for sale today and buy a new house to make room for Emma . . . Nola, but I don't want them to do that. Besides, we, ah, kinda need something now."

"And she can't stay with you because . . . ?"

Jack clenched his teeth. "Because . . ." He shrugged, either because he couldn't think of a good enough answer or because he didn't want Nola to hear it.

Nola piped up. "Because he doesn't want me. He never has."

Jack took a step toward her, his hands palms out. "That's not true, Nola. I've told you that. I don't know why you won't listen."

Nola's voice rose a notch. "You're the one who won't listen." Nola's face reddened beneath her makeup, but it was more than just anger or hurt, and it suddenly occurred to me that I knew nothing about the circumstances that had brought her to Jack. Something had wounded Nola in a much more profound way than she wanted anyone to know, and it was apparent even to me that Jack really didn't have a clue.

My neck started to feel a little clammy. "Maybe I can just be your intermediary whenever you two have an argument. Sort of like a referee. I'll even do house calls." I smiled at them hopefully.

They both looked at me with identical expressions of disdain, two pairs of matching blue eyes making me feel very, very small and hardhearted. Some part of me even enjoyed watching them spar like a normal father and teenage daughter. I'd never fought with my parents, but only because I'd never been given the chance; my mother had left when I was six and my father had usually been too drunk to care. Despite my relationships with both parents having vastly improved over the last year, I still felt a huge void in my growing-up years. Not that I wanted to revisit them. I was thirty-nine years old, after all. Way too old to be dealing with teenage angst. Or to be single, but that was another matter altogether.

Grasping at my final straw, I said, "But she doesn't even know me."

Nola's look was so searing that I expected to see smoke rising from my terry-cloth robe. "It would be better than staying with him." She jerked her chin in Jack's direction. "Or living on the street." Her look indicated that the latter choice was only marginally worse than living with me.

Jack put his hand on my arm and turned the full force of his considerable charm on me, starting with a penetrating look from his very, very blue eyes. "We're here at this ungodly hour because we were arguing up until midnight, when I called a truce just to get some sleep. That's when I caught her trying to sneak out. I made her sit with me on the living room couch until I thought you'd be up." He shook his head. "Please, Mellie," he said, using the nickname that I barely tolerated, although both he and my mother delighted in using it—my mother because it had been my childhood name, and Jack because he enjoyed irritating me. He continued. "It will only be for a little while, until we can figure this all out with cool heads—something we apparently can't have while living under the same roof."

In a last-ditch effort to avoid disaster I said, "What about school? Doesn't she need to be registered where she lives?"

Nola rolled her eyes. "School's lame."

Jack looked like he wanted to say something to her but thought better of it. Instead he said, "I already got her transcripts and she's a straight-A student. I'm going to try to get her involved with a home-schooling group to finish up the year. In the meantime, my mother's trying to get her into Ashley Hall, her alma mater and your mother's, too. I'm hoping their combined efforts can get her a spot in the fall."

I knew what an Ashley Hall girl looked like—smooth hair, lacrosse stick, fresh-faced—and I couldn't imagine Nola fitting in there any more than I would have at her age. But I bit my tongue. It had nothing to do with me.

Jack added helpfully, "So basically Nola has the whole summer to get acclimated to Charleston."

I looked at both of them as they stared at me expectantly, Jack hopeful and Nola resigned. I wanted to shout out an immediate "no." I had my own life to live, unfettered by husband or children or any other responsibilities that didn't include making my sales quota for Henderson House Realty. Or continuing the restoration of my beautiful yet money-sucking house. But when I looked at Nola, I saw again a scared and abandoned child who, except for the telltale trembling, was trying very hard to appear brave and strong. Unfortunately for both of us I saw not just her trembling; I saw myself.

"Fine," I said carefully, wanting to end Nola's misery and not willing to set her up for more rejection. "She's welcome to stay here for a bit. The guest room has clean sheets on the bed, and there are clean towels in the hall bath. I'll make sure Nola feels at home for as long as she needs to stay here." I shot a questioning glance at Jack in the hopes that he'd be able to give me not only a finite time period, but some kind of encouragement, too.

Instead, the only look I got from him was one of extreme relief. For all of the emotional trauma he'd caused me in the last year, I should have been gloating. Instead, I could only feel sorry for him and for Nola, their estranged relationship so much like the one between my father and me up until recently, when he'd finally decided to become sober.

"Thank you," he said, and all I could do was smile.

Jack walked to the door and pulled it open. "I know Nola doesn't want to forget this." He reached for something on the piazza and pulled inside the house a beat-up guitar case, scuffed and scratched, the original black of the case nearly completely hidden by stickers, most of them illegible. On the top near one of the latches was a small white rectangle with the faded black words I LOVE N'AWLINS. NOLA.

He set it down by the foyer table and I stared at it for a moment, feeling the telltale pinpricks of gooseflesh on the back of my neck for the second time that night. I looked around, expecting to see . . . something. The temperature seemed to drop by a few degrees, and I watched Nola rub her arms. And then I heard what sounded like very quiet music. I glanced at Jack and Nola to see if they were hearing it, too, but they were concentrating on trying to figure out how to say good-bye without physical contact.

I strained to hear better, but the melody was so light that it was almost beyond my hearing range. The notes were strummed on an acoustic guitar, the tune hauntingly beautiful.

"So, Nola," Jack was saying. "You have my cell phone. Call me if you need anything. Anything," he emphasized.

She nodded, her jaw sticking out in the same way Jack's did when he was upset and trying not to show it.

I turned to Nola. "I want to speak with your dad for a quick moment. Why don't you go ahead up to your room—at the top of the stairs turn left. It's the third door on the right, and the bathroom's right next door to it. Make yourself at home and I'll be right there."

With a heavy sigh, Nola picked up her guitar and slung her ratty backpack over her shoulder, the unzipped corner exposing the well-worn face of a nearly threadbare teddy bear. It surprised me to see it, and it told me more about Nola than all of her heavy makeup and belligerent attitude. It also reminded me that Nola was only thirteen years old, and very alone. Well, almost. General Lee, the little traitor, happily followed at her heels, content to be led away by a perfect stranger.

As she headed up the stairs, I called after her, "Nola, I have to go into my office early in the morning, but I'll tell my housekeeper, Mrs. Houlihan, to look after you and get you anything you need. I'll have her make you breakfast, so tell me what you want and I'll make sure we've got it."

She turned around and with a sullen expression said, "I don't like to wake up before noon, and I only eat vegan and organic." Without waiting for a response, she turned around and headed up the stairs, one slowly exaggerated step at a time.

I faced Jack again, seeing a faint glimmer in his eyes. "That could be a problem for you, Mellie, seeing how you only eat processed baked goods and animal protein. I guess I should have warned you."

"About a lot of things, apparently." I crossed my arms over my chest. "You've got a lot of things you need to tell me, starting with where her mother is."

His face sobered as he sent a quick glance up the stairs. "She's dead."

Jack's words didn't surprise me; I suppose I had known from the first moment I'd seen Nola. But a lifelong attempt at trying to bury my sixth sense made me extremely obtuse sometimes.

He placed his hands on my arms and pulled me closer to the door. Quietly, he added, "Nola's probably listening, so I don't want to talk about it now, but meet me at eight o'clock at Fast and French for coffee and I'll tell you everything."

I sighed. "You really owe me."

With a low voice, he said, "I know." He didn't drop his hands from my arms as he continued to look at me, and for an odd moment I thought he might kiss me, and I even thought that I might want him to. But the time for that was long gone, buried too deep beneath all sorts of reasons why Jack and I were wrong for each other—not including the fact that he had a girlfriend and now a teenage daughter.

He let his hands slip from my arms. "That wasn't an almost-kiss, was it?"

"No," I said, a little too quickly.

"Good. Because I think I've lost count," he said, referring to his annoying habit of reminding me each time he almost kissed me. But that all seemed like such a long time ago. He stepped out onto the piazza. "I'll see you at eight then."

"I'll be there," I said, before I closed the door and latched it, then set the alarm. As I began turning off the lights and heading back upstairs, I heard the music again, so faint that I couldn't be sure I was hearing it at all, and I found myself turning my head like an antenna trying to pick up a better signal.

It seemed to get louder as I reached the top of the stairs and headed for Nola's room, where I found General Lee sleeping outside her closed door. I raised my hand to knock and held it there while I listened as the music faded and was replaced by the sound of sobbing coming from the other side of the door. I lowered my hand, then quietly backed away and headed toward my room, leaving the hall light on and my door cracked open. I slid out of my robe, and as I began to get ready for work, I couldn't help but wonder how many ghosts this lost and lonely girl had brought into my life.

CHAPTER 2

I had just finished writing the note of warning to Mrs. Houlihan to let her know that a teenage girl was sleeping upstairs and would expect to be fed something vegan for breakfast when she woke around noon. I'd hoped to make it out the door before the housekeeper got there, because I was sure there were going to be way more questions than I could answer. I'd left my business card and a note under Nola's door telling her to call me when she got up so we could figure out the rest of her day. Hopefully, my breakfast with Jack would answer at least part of that question.

I scratched General Lee behind the ear, then gave him a treat, because I just couldn't stand that forlorn look he gave me each time I left him behind. As I shut the kitchen door behind me I heard voices from the back garden. I froze for a moment as I always did when I heard voices in my house, remembering the ghosts who'd inhabited it when I moved in. Most of them were gone, the ones remaining unobtrusive and with a mutual understanding that we not get in one another's way.

Carefully negotiating the flagstone path my father had installed for me as part of his garden restoration, I followed it by the side of the house to the garden, where the voices mingled with the sound of the burbling fountain of the peeing boy. I stopped and stared, not sure whether I should frown or laugh.

Sophie, never a candidate for a magazine cover, except for maybe *National Geographic,* wore what looked like a pair of oversize jeans split in the middle and then connected with quilted patches to make a sort of long skirt. She had on her ubiquitous Birkenstocks, her toenails each painted a different color, a tie-dyed tank top, and her long, curly black hair barely tamed by a lime green scrunchy. She was in stark contrast to the man in the plaid shirt and jeans standing next to her, my plumber, Rich Kobylt. His tool belt hung heavy on his hips, leaving the jeans a little lower in the back than I would have liked. They were both staring at the brick foundation of my house and shaking their heads. It couldn't be good if Sophie, an expert in the field of historical restoration, was shaking her head while staring at my very old house.

With more good cheer than I felt, I called out, "Good morning." I walked closer to them, and the spike of my high-heeled shoe stuck between two flagstones into the soft grass, sucking my shoe into the clinging mud and bringing to mind how this whole house had sort of done the same thing to my life.

"Good morning," they both said in unison, much the same way I would imagine an undertaker would greet his subject.

"What's wrong now?" I asked as I stopped in front of Sophie and followed her gaze to the rather large crack that wound its way through the brick from the ground to the first floor. "I already know about the cracked foundation. Please tell me it's not more serious than that."

Rich and Sophie glanced at each other before the plumber turned back to me and spoke. "Actually, Miz Middleton, except for a hurricane, things don't get much worse for an old house like this than a cracked foundation. And this one's as bad as it gets."

I nodded slowly as I listened, hearing the familiar sound of a cash register ringing in my brain. "How bad is bad?"

"Well." He drew the word out. "Looks like your bond courses are broken. Don't much know why, except the house is old. Maybe the roots of that old oak tree have stretched a little too far. It's anybody's guess, really. You're in danger of a wall collapse, since this is a structural wall—"

He'd lost me at "bond courses." My eyes must have glazed over, because Sophie interrupted him.

"What he's trying to say, Melanie, is that it's only going to get much, much worse if we don't take care of this right away. It's going to be pretty major—lifting the house from the existing foundation, then building a new one. It's the only way to do it right."

I stood blinking in the bright morning sunlight, my dream of finally settling into my house and resuming my ordinary, quiet life suddenly as foreign to me as wearing one of Sophie's outfits. I turned to Rich. "Aren't you a plumber?"

"Yes, ma'am. I'm also a certified technician in foundation repair, and co-own Hard Rock Foundations with my son, Brian. We offer a lifetime transferable warranty, and we're listed in the BBB, too. Plus Dr. Wallen here has used me on many of her restoration projects and can speak for us."

Resignation filled just about every muscle fiber in my body. "How much will it cost?" I asked, then quickly held up my hand. "No, don't tell me. I'll call you later to discuss it in detail and after I've had a glass of wine." Or two. "Just tell the workmen not to start before six o'clock in the morning, because I don't want to be awakened before I have to." I thought briefly of Nola and her weird sleep habits but didn't say anything. She wouldn't be staying with me long enough for it to matter. "Sophie, just let my dad know so he can write the checks." My father was the trustee for the estate I'd inherited and in charge of all the expenses relating to the house's restoration. I wondered briefly how much a detonator and TNT would cost.

"Actually," Sophie began as she and Rich exchanged another glance between them.

"Well, see now, Miz Middleton, what Dr. Wallen's trying to say is that the house won't be livable while we're workin' on it. You'll need to move out for a spell."

I considered throwing myself onto the grass and having a tantrum, complete with banging fists and kicking feet. But that would have taken much more energy than I had.

"For how long?" I ventured, trying to keep my smile from turning into a feral grin. "I only just moved back in after having all the floors stripped and redone, for crying out loud. And I've just retrieved all of the furniture from storage." I raised my hands, palms up. "And what will General Lee think, being thrown out of his house again?"

Sophie looked hard at me for a long moment before responding. "I'm sure you and General Lee will cope just fine at your mother's. And I'm thinking three months—tops. Depending on the weather, of course."

I opened and closed my mouth several times, feeling like a drowning fish. Giving up on words, I simply nodded, then turned on my muddy heel and nearly ran right into Nola. The first thing I noticed was that she was wearing the same clothes I'd seen her in the previous evening, and they looked like she'd slept in them. The second thing I noticed was that she didn't look very happy.

"What the hell?" she shouted at me, her fists on her hips. "Why would you open my window when it's, like, a thousand degrees out here? And why was my guitar in the bed with me? What in the hell were you even doing in my room?"

Before I could think of something to say, Sophie stepped forward. Sticking her hand out, she said, "You must be Nola. I'm Sophie Wallen, a friend of Melanie's. And can I say I just love your nail polish—the black polish I use doesn't have that kind of shine."

After a moment, Nola raised her hand and allowed Sophie to pump it a few times before letting go. Her gaze swept Sophie's outfit from head to toe and I stiffened, prepared to defend my best friend, regardless of how much I might agree with Nola's assessment.

"Nice skirt," she said, completely devoid of sarcasm. "My mom made me one just like it, but I had to leave it behind in California because it didn't fit in my backpack."

I glanced over at the plumber/foundation repair specialist and assumed his horrified look matched my own.

Nola crossed her arms over her chest. "How did you know who I was?"

I waited for Sophie to answer, having been just about to ask the same question.

Sophie beamed, an expression honed by years of teaching college students and coercing them to see her as a person of authority despite being half their size. "Oh, sugar," she drawled, despite the fact that she'd been born and raised far north of the Mason-Dixon Line, "your daddy and I are good friends and we chat quite a bit. I was the one who suggested he bring you here when he mentioned you weren't comfortable staying with him."

I raised my eyebrows at Sophie so she'd know that we'd be having a discussion later.

"Not that here is any better," Nola remarked, glaring at me. "I'm not used to getting up at the break of dawn. I mean, what the f—"

Before she could say the final word, I tried to draw her back down the pathway to the kitchen. "I think I heard Mrs. Houlihan's car. Why don't we go get you some breakfast? I'm sure you'll feel better about things once you've eaten."

Nola remained rigid. "Right. I already checked your kitchen. Just a lot of dead animal meat and a bunch of processed and high-gluten doughnuts. Ugh. Who eats that crap? I guess my dad just wanted me to starve to death."

With a warning glance at me not to say anything, Sophie took Nola's arm. "I know what you mean. I can't believe she eats that stuff, either. Why don't you run upstairs and get changed and then I'll take you to my favorite place to eat breakfast. They've got awesome tofu muffins and eggless eggs. You'll love it."

I stifled a shudder as I watched Sophie lead Nola back into the house. "Drop her at my office when you're done, all right?"

Without turning back, Sophie shot me a thumbs-up. As they disappeared around the corner of the house, I heard Nola say, "But who opened my windows?"

Sophie's reply carried clearly to us in the back garden. "It's an old house, sugar. Things happen here that wouldn't ordinarily happen anywhere else."

I avoided looking at Rich, knowing he'd had several "experiences" while working on the house; I just wasn't going to go there.

Instead, I began walking down the path, raising my hand in farewell. "Thanks, Rich. Just let me know when you're ready to start work so I can empty the house. Again. You know how to reach me."

I walked to my car, parked in the old carriage house in the back of the property that had been converted to a garage. After closing the door, I sat inside it for a long time before starting the engine, wondering yet again how my once-controlled life had spun off the tracks like a train in a hurricane without my having had to do a single thing.

∝

There was already a small crowd waiting at Fast & French on Broad Street when I walked up to the door at exactly five minutes past eight o'clock. I was punctual to a fault and considered myself late if I wasn't at least ten minutes early. I hoped this wasn't a harbinger for the rest of my day.

I glanced through the crowd, not really expecting to see Jack, as he wasn't the early-to-rise sort, and I figured he'd probably gone back to sleep after he'd left my house earlier that morning. And if he was here already, it must be because what he wanted to discuss was very important to him.

My phone beeped, alerting me to a text message. It was from Jack, letting me know he was seated at the counter in the back room. Excusing myself as I moved by people to get through the door, I tried not to feel nervous as I made my way past the hostess and to my seat next to Jack, two menus already waiting on the counter.

Fast & French, otherwise known as Gaulart et Maliclet to non-Charlestonians, was a personal favorite. I loved the artsy interior, with murals and other artwork displayed on just about every flat surface. I found the juxtaposition of the modern artwork set against the classical old-house woodwork of the fireplace and cornices charming. Not wanting to be accused of actually liking or appreciating old architecture, I kept that little observation to myself.

"Good morning," I said warily. "Have you been sleeping outside on the sidewalk since you left my house waiting for them to open?" He still had the five-o'clock shadow, but his clothes were cleaned and pressed and he smelled faintly of soap. Still, I couldn't resist the dig. Except for this morning, I'd never seen Jack out of bed earlier than ten o'clock. Or in it, either, but that was yet another path I'd rather leave undiscovered.

"Good morning," he replied cheerily, his dimple showing through the scruff on his cheek. "And no, I didn't sleep here. I just didn't want to be late since I know how much that irritates you." His dimple deepened.

A young and perky waitress stood in front of us on the other side of the counter. "Are y'all ready to order?"

Without looking at the menu, I said, "Two chocolate-filled croissants and a cappuccino with double cream, please."

"Will that be all for the two of you?" she asked, looking at Jack and giving him a big smile. I wouldn't have been surprised if she'd written down her phone number and reached over to slide it in his pocket. It had happened more than once.

Jack cleared his throat. "Actually, that's all for her. I'm just having coffee. Black, please."

The girl raised her eyebrows as she wrote down our order and picked up our menus. I shrugged. Of all of the inherited traits from my mother's Prioleau side of the family, a high metabolism was a bonus. I considered it a fair trade-off for the other, much more annoying trait of being able to talk with dead people.

"One day you're going to wake up fat, Mellie, and it will serve you right."

I'd always been taller and thinner than girls my age, and nothing had changed in the last thirty-nine years. Despite the lack of any bust to speak of, I did appreciate the ability to eat what I wanted and still fit into my pants.

I snorted, taking a spoonful of cream off the top of the cappuccino that had been set in front of me. "You'll be the first person I'll tell when that happens, Jack," I said as I closed my eyes, savoring the sweet taste on my tongue.

"So, how did it go after I left?" Jack asked as the waitress poured coffee into his mug.

"As well as could be expected, I guess. She'd just been dropped off at a stranger's house by her father, after all. When I went up to her room after you left to see if she needed anything, she was crying pretty hard. I didn't go in. I remember being that age, and knew that intruding wouldn't have been the right thing to do."

Jack nodded contemplatively. "That's why I figured leaving her with you was the right thing. I would have barged right in and asked what was wrong."

"Because you're a guy." I took a sip from my cup. "Still, I would think that all your experiences with women would have taught you how to handle it better."

"She's only thirteen, Mellie. And my daughter. Believe me, when I was a thirteen-year-old boy, girls my age were from a different planet. Apparently, they still are."

I surreptitiously studied him as I took another sip, imagining that he'd been no less devastating at thirteen than he was now at thirty-five. "Have you sought any professional help?"

He nodded. "Yeah. We went to see a child psychologist, who told me that Emma! . . . Nola is surprisingly well-adjusted, considering what she's been through, and the best thing I can do right now is to integrate her into my life." He snorted. "We can't even live under the same roof, so I'm not sure how I'm going to manage that."

"You'll figure it out," I said, patting him on the arm, my words more confident than I felt as I remembered the bewildered girl he'd dropped off on my doorstep.

We waited while the waitress placed my croissants on the counter between us and added an extra fork. I slid the plate in front of me, along with both forks, then took my first bite. After chewing and swallowing, I said, "You'd better start from the beginning—like who Nola's mother was, and why I've never heard of her or her daughter."

Jack began to trace circles with his finger on the counter as he spoke. "It's not what you think, Mellie. I dated Bonnie Pettigrew—Nola's mother—my senior year in college. She was from Columbus, Georgia—a real sweet Southern girl. I wouldn't say she was the love of my life, but we had a good time together. We made each other laugh. I was the starting quarterback at South Carolina, but you probably already know that."

I kept a blank look on my face as I stood by my insistence that I had never Googled him. He regarded me steadily for a long moment to see if I'd crack, and when I didn't, he continued. "Bonnie was a cheerleader, so we had that in common, too. It was almost sort of expected that we'd date, you know?"

I nodded, even though I didn't know. My four years in college had been more academic than social, and I could count on one hand the number of football games I'd attended while at South Carolina. And on three fingers the number of dates I'd had.

Jack continued. "Bonnie was pretty musical, too. Used to write songs all the time and play them for me on her guitar. She was good. Real good. Wanted to write music and planned to head out to California just as soon as she graduated. Said it was a great place to be an artist, and the scenery would inspire her. It was pretty much understood that we would part ways then, and I was okay with that."

"And then there was that trip to New Orleans for Mardi Gras," I said, unable to keep the sarcasm out of my voice.

"Yeah. There was that," he said, his voice flat. "We had a good time. I wasn't a raging alcoholic then, but definitely working on it. We partied a lot. Drank a lot."

"And apparently didn't use protection."

Jack signaled for the waitress to bring him more coffee. "Apparently not. I was young and very stupid. Although I was probably too out of it to even realize, because it never occurred to me that Bonnie might have gotten pregnant. She never even said anything at all. I just remember that about a month before graduation she told me she decided it was time for her to go, that she didn't need a degree to do what she wanted to do with her life, and that she was moving to California. She just forgot to mention that she was pregnant."

"And after she had the baby, she never contacted you?"

He shook his head. "Not once. And I had no idea how to get in touch with her—not that we'd really ever planned to do that, anyway. I did write to her mother in Columbus once—her dad had died when she was a baby, and all she had was her mother. Bonnie had never been that close with her mom, and the only thing she could tell me was that Bonnie had made it to California and she hadn't heard from her since or expected to. It was sad, really, but I figured Bonnie was doing what she wanted to do."

"So you forgot about her."

With a hard look at me he said, "I didn't say that. I just moved on. But I never forgot her."

I pressed my fork into the remaining crumbs on my plate. "Why do you think she didn't tell you about the baby?"

He stared down at his cup for a long moment. "Because she knew that I would have wanted us to get married, to raise the child together. And Bonnie would never have settled for that. She would have been miserable being stuck in South Carolina and forced to leave all of her dreams behind. She probably figured she could handle being a single mother if it meant she could pursue her dreams."

A surprising wave of relief swept over me. The Jack I knew, even though he wasn't without faults, would never have knowingly abandoned his own child. I drained my cup, leaving it up to my face longer than necessary so that he couldn't read my expression. He was too good already at reading my mind. Putting my cup down, I asked, "So what happened to Bonnie?"

Jack motioned to the waitress for another refill and I did the same. "She killed herself."

I coughed on the final mouthful of crumbs. I hadn't expected to hear that. "Intentionally?"

"It appears so. It's what's on the coroner's report, anyway. Drug overdose, although from what I've learned from the police detective assigned to the case, she wasn't a stranger to OD'ing. She'd been rushed to the hospital at least three times in the last two years for taking various cocktails of prescription and street drugs."

"Poor Nola," I said, remembering her expression when I'd met her, of loss and grief and something else that had been unnameable at the time. But now I understood what it was, because I'd seen it for so long in my own reflection: abandonment. "Who would take care of her when her mother was sick?"

"No one, as far as I can figure out. Bonnie had had a long string of live-in boyfriends, and the latest one, Rick something-or-other, had been there for about two years. But I imagine Nola would have taken care of herself. She doesn't seem the sort to want to have to ask for help."

"No." I shook my head, in complete agreement with him for once. "She doesn't." I swallowed. "So how did she find her way to you?"

"Bonnie left her an envelope—one of those 'open only in the event of my death' kind of things—and in it was my name, the name of my parents' store on King Street, and a one-way Greyhound bus ticket to Charleston."

I raised my eyebrows. "She traveled cross-country on a bus all by herself? I can't even imagine what kind of guts that took. She looks much older, but she's only thirteen, for crying out loud." I shook my head.

"She hid at a friend's house and then slept on a park bench for a night to evade child services before deciding that finding me might be a better option." Jack kept his voice level, but I could tell it was hard for him.

"Why didn't she call you first to let you know she was coming?"

Jack pushed away his empty mug. "Nola's not very talkative about a lot of things—especially about her mother's death—but she was very clear about this one thing: Bonnie had always told her that I knew about the pregnancy but chose to give them both up." He looked up at the ceiling and blinked hard, and all I could do was place my hand on his arm and squeeze. After a moment, he said, "I believe she did that so Nola would never be tempted to leave her. And from what little I can get out of Nola, they had a good relationship when Bonnie was clean. Bonnie even taught Nola how to play the guitar, and they'd play together sometimes for extra change. Not that Nola will let me hear her play. She dragged that beat-up guitar all the way from Los Angeles and yet refuses to play a note."

I remembered how I'd developed an aversion to opera music after my own mother, a famous opera diva, left my father and me. "She needs time," I said, hoping that she would require less than the thirty-three years it had taken me to get over it, and then only because my mother was still alive to explain that she'd left me to save my life. With Bonnie's death, her reasons would always remain unspoken.

"I know. That's why I had to bring her to you. Sophie said you'd understand." He gave me an apologetic smile. "No matter how many times I tell Nola that I didn't even know she existed until I saw her on your front porch, she won't believe me. And we can't forge a relationship until she accepts that—which she won't if we're living under the same roof and continually banging heads."

I frowned. "There's only one problem. I'm happy for her to stay with me as long as you think this will take, but I'm about to be kicked out of my house again."

Jack quirked an eyebrow.

"Sophie and the plumber were yammering about it this morning, but it all comes down to a cracked foundation. I haven't asked my mother yet, but it looks like I'll be moving in with her for about three months. I'm sure she'd love to have Nola, too, but I'll need to check with her. She's always going on and on about someday having a grandchild, so maybe having her best friend's granddaughter living with her might cure her of that for a while."

"Or cure her of ever wanting one of her own," Jack said with a strained look. "Teenagers aren't for wussies."

"Then it's a good thing my mother and I aren't."

The waitress brought our checks and I could see her straining to see if Jack wore a ring on his left hand. She sent me a smug glance when she caught me watching her. Jack shoved his hand in one pocket of his jeans and then the other. "That's odd. My wallet's missing."

Calmly, I reached into my purse and pulled out the wallet General Lee had found on my dresser. I'd left it on the hall table and had picked it up on my way out of the house that morning. "Is this it?"

He took it from me and flipped it open. "It's definitely mine. Where'd you find it?"

"In my bedroom."

He furrowed his brow. "Not to be coy, but if my wallet was in your bedroom, wouldn't I have had to have been there, too? And believe me, I would have remembered that."

I swatted his sleeve. "I have no idea. All I know is that I got one of my calls from a disconnected phone right before I found it. I'm sure they're related."

"Your grandmother again?"

Jack was one of the few people who knew about my sixth sense. Although it had been a closely guarded secret for most of my childhood and adult years, the idea that it was more of a gift than a curse was gradually growing on me at my mother's urging. But only gradually.

I nodded.

"Did she say anything?"

I thought about her words—*listen to your heart for a change*—and knew better than to tell Jack. He'd find some way to embarrass me or bribe me later if he knew. "Not really," I said. "You know it's never clear."

"True, but we've also learned that there's no such thing as a coincidence. If she's responsible for my wallet being in your room, then she wants to tell you something about me."

I dug into my own wallet to hide the color rushing to my face. "Maybe. Like 'don't answer the door.' If only I'd listened." I smiled up at him but he wasn't looking. Instead he was looking inside his very empty wallet.

"I had fifty dollars in here. Any idea what might have happened to it?"

I shook my head. "It was there when I found it last night. I didn't check it again before I slid it into my purse before coming here."

Our eyes met as a mutual understanding dawned. "Don't jump to conclusions, Jack," I said. "I'm sure there's a logical explanation. Maybe it fell out and it's still on the table. I'll ask Mrs. Houlihan as soon as I get home. Just don't do anything until you hear from me, okay?"

He pressed his lips together, then relaxed. "Fine. But I want you to call me the second you find out."

"I will." I stood and picked up his ticket. "My treat. You can get the next one."

"Already asking me for the next date. That's sweet, Mellie."

Before I had a chance to respond his cell phone rang, but when he looked at it he just frowned and turned off the ringer.

"Bill collector?" I asked as I pushed open the door.

"Rebecca, actually," he said, following me out of the café.

I wanted to ask him why he wasn't taking her call, but I held back. I didn't want him to think that I cared. As I slid on my sunglasses I said, "There's something you should know, Jack."

He folded his arms and gave me his famous half grin. "I already know you think I'm pretty hot, Mellie. Tell me something I don't know."

This time I gave in to the temptation to roll my eyes. "Nola didn't come alone, if you know what I mean."

He straightened, his face serious. "Bonnie?"

"I have no idea. Whoever it is stuck the guitar in Nola's bed last night and opened her window. All I know is that it wasn't me or General Lee."

"Did you tell Nola?"

I shook my head. "She's already having a hard enough time adjusting, so I don't think it would be a good idea right now—or ever. At best it would freak her out, and at worst she'd never believe another word I said to her. Which could be a problem if you're using me to help build her trust."

"True. We'll just play it by ear, then."

"Fine." I fumbled in my purse for my car keys. "Look, why don't you give her a couple of days and then come to dinner Friday night? We can do a cookout. Burgers, hot dogs, cole slaw—that kind of thing. Sophie and Nola kind of hit it off this morning, so I'll invite Sophie and Chad, too. It might help move things along." I frowned up at him. "Nola's really vulnerable right now, Jack. As difficult as she's bound to be, we need to give her a little slack."

Surprising me, Jack pulled me forward in a close embrace, and after a moment of trying to figure out where my own arms should go, I let them fall around his broad shoulders.

"Thanks, Mellie. I knew you were the right person to come to."

I patted his back, wondering whether he'd drag out that awful "friend" word, but enjoying being held in his arms anyway. Finally, I pulled back, ending the embrace, if only because it reminded me too much of what I'd willingly given up. "You're welcome. I'm glad I can help." Clearing my throat of something I couldn't identify, I added, "And don't think I won't expect some kind of payment in the future."

His face brightened. "Is that an invitation, Mellie?"

Looking up to heaven and shaking my head, I turned and started walking down Broad. "Grow up, Jack," I called over my shoulder, then listened to his laughter until I turned the corner onto King Street.

CHAPTER 3

I stood with Nola outside Trenholm's Antiques on King Street and paused. I didn't like being around old furniture any more than I liked being in hospitals or cemeteries; it made it far too easy for lost souls to find me. I caught sight of our reflection in the large plate-glass window: me in my sharp navy D&G suit and heels, and Nola dressed like Sophie's protégé in worn Converse sneakers, striped leggings, and a short floral dress. And there, right behind Nola's left shoulder, was the face of a woman that disappeared almost as soon as I saw it. So quickly that for a moment I thought I'd imagined it, except for the lingering aura of sadness that permeated the air and pressed against my chest.

Taking a deep breath, I pulled open the door and held it open for Nola before following her into the store. Jack's parents had owned Trenholm's Antiques since before he was born, and it was not only a fixture in Charleston, but also known and respected worldwide for its high quality and oftentimes rare furniture and objets d'art. Even as a child, I'd admired the store, but only from the sidewalk and from what I could see through the large front windows. As it was, I already heard the rustling of old skirts and the murmurings of soft voices as I stood inside the door, waiting for my eyes to become accustomed to the dark interior.

"Melanie, Nola. What a lovely surprise." Impeccably dressed as always in a St. John cream-colored suit, Jack's mother, Amelia, approached from the rear of the store, where she'd been arranging delphiniums and foxgloves in a very large blue-and-white Meissen urn. She appeared to be as delicate and rare as the porcelain, but I knew better. Anybody who'd raised Jack Trenholm and lived to tell about it had to have been made of stronger stuff.

She enveloped me in a whiff of Chanel No. 5 as she kissed both cheeks before turning to Nola. Nola conveniently crossed her arms in a successful attempt to avert a hug or any kind of physical contact.

Amelia looked confused for a moment but quickly regained her equilibrium. "I was doing some shopping yesterday on King Street and I saw something in a window that I couldn't resist. I hope you like it." She walked quickly to an Italian marquetry desk in the corner and reached behind it.

When I saw the shopping bag from Palm Avenue, I cringed a little. I *loved* Palm Avenue: What's not to love about pink and green and Lilly Pulitzer prints? But I somehow couldn't quite picture Nola in a cotton piqué polo shirt, or in any color that might be called pastel.

Amelia continued. "Your daddy said Miss Middleton is having a little cookout on Friday, so I thought you might like something new to wear. I had to guess at your size, but I think I got it right—I'm a bit of a pro at shopping." She gave a little laugh and I was surprised to hear nervousness in it. "I hope you like it." She held out the shopping bag to Nola like a queen bestowing a knighthood.

Nola took the bag, frowning into the pastel-colored tissue depths, and I knew an immediate intercession was necessary. "Here," I said, taking the bag. "Let me put this by the door so we don't forget it on the way out." I smiled broadly as I placed it by the door and returned, hoping they couldn't tell I was gritting my teeth.

We both watched as Nola turned to study an intricately carved cheval mirror. A thick fog had begun to form around Nola's reflection in the mirror, although nothing was visible in the store. I looked at Nola and Amelia to see whether they'd noticed anything, relieved when it appeared that they hadn't. The whispered voices around me seemed to get louder, and I recognized my name spoken several times from more than one voice. As I'd learned to do since I was a child, I began humming to myself to drown out the noise and let the spirits know that I didn't want them speaking to me.

I stopped suddenly when I realized that both Amelia and Nola were staring at me.

Nola frowned. "Was that supposed to be music?"

I gave her the look I normally reserved for Realtors who'd just given me a less than favorable counteroffer. "Of course. 'Fernando' was one of ABBA's greatest-selling singles."

Nola snorted. "ABBA? As in the guys who wrote the music for that lame musical *Mamma Mia!?* What are you—like a member of their fan club or something?"

I was spared from answering by Amelia. "Why don't you look around, Nola? Miss Middleton and I have a little business to talk about. I promise it won't take long, and then maybe we can go have lunch. Do you like pizza?"

I took Amelia's arm and began to lead her back to the desk. "Only if it's made of grass and tastes like cardboard."

Amelia sent me a questioning look.

"I'll explain later," I said as we each took a seat at her desk. I reached into my purse and pulled out the spreadsheet I'd made of my home's inventory, separated by room. There were columns for the approximate year each piece was built and its value, along with a column for my thoughts about each piece and whether or not I liked it. I wasn't really sure of the reason for this last column, only that an inventory seemed incomplete without it. I spread it out on Amelia's desk and turned it to face her.

"Sophie said it would be a good idea to empty the house before they begin working on the foundation. I figure I could either put it all in storage, or you and Sophie could find several house museums that would be interested in hosting an entire room from my home for a short period of time. It just all needs to be gone as soon as possible."

Amelia slipped on her reading glasses and stared down at the spreadsheet. "What's this?" she asked, indicating a column head.

"That's the amount of time it would take to bring each piece down and up the steps based on its weight and how many men it would take to carry it."

Her eyes were wide and blue over the tops of her glasses as she regarded me. After a while, she returned to the spreadsheet. The manicured nail of her index finger indicated another column. "What does this say?"

I squinted, not having brought my own glasses, then sat back, embarrassed. "Nothing. Just my personal thoughts about a piece of furniture."

"Isn't that Jack's name?" She adjusted her glasses on her nose. "The print's so tiny—I guess you were trying to make sure it fit in the box. It has to do with the grandfather clock in the front parlor."

I stared at the indicated box, squinting and trying to pretend I couldn't read it.

"I'm pretty sure that's Jack's name," she said, turning it around to face me. "In fact, I'm sure that's it—isn't it?"

Resigned, I nodded. "It says, 'Reminds me of Jack.' That's the clock where we found the Confederate diamonds."

She was looking up at me, a small smile on her lips. "I see," she said, and I was afraid that she actually did.

We went through the entire list, and as we were finishing up I realized that I'd lost track of Nola. I stood suddenly, wondering whether she might have sneaked out, but saw her in the back corner of the showroom, her back to me. She seemed mesmerized by whatever she was staring at, and I moved to stand next to her, Amelia behind me.

"I just got that in and stuck it back here while I try to figure out the best way to display it," Amelia said. "John thought the front window would work best."

Nola took a step back and I got a better view of the enormous dollhouse that sat on the ground yet whose turreted roof was visible behind Nola. It was a Victorian with lacy fretwork, decorative brackets and spindle work, and a large circular turret that claimed one corner of the house and culminated in a mansard-style roof.

"It's beautiful, isn't it?" Amelia asked as she moved to stand next to Nola.

Nola just shrugged as if uninterested, but her gaze was fixed on the house. Mine was, too, but I guessed not for the reason hers was. The edges of the house seemed smudged to me, like the surface of a highway in the midday sun, and when I stepped closer to try to see more clearly, my skin felt singed.

Amelia continued. "We think it's about seventy years old, but I'm not sure yet. I'm still tracking down its provenance—something Jack has always helped me with. I purchased it here in Charleston, but it's had lots of owners. For some reason, people don't like hanging on to it for very long."

I watched as the house's edges continued to undulate, the air heated and suffocating along its periphery. I took a step back. "So you don't know anything about the original owners?"

Amelia shook her head. "Not yet. I do know that the most recent owners had had it less than a year and were eager to sell it. The price they were selling it for was so low I almost feel as if I should send them an additional check."

My gaze shifted to Nola, who was now using her index finger to delicately trace the scrollwork on the front porch balustrades. My skin felt burned just watching her, but she didn't even flinch.

"Did you have a dollhouse like this when you were little?" I asked Nola, eager to draw her out of the trance she seemed to be in. The blurred edges around the house were now becoming blackened, like the way approaching night throws everything in shadows. I wanted to grab her arm and pull her back, but I hesitated, not wanting to have to explain myself.

Nola's black-rimmed eyes met mine as she dropped her hand. "No," she said, the word short and harsh. Amelia looked at me and I could tell that she'd heard the hollowness, too. Nola turned her back on the dollhouse and crossed her arms. "It's just a stupid kid's toy. I'm glad my mom never wasted her money on something like that."

The words hit Amelia like raindrops, so that she seemed to droop under the weight of them. I imagined she was thinking of all the years her granddaughter had grown up without her, without all the love Amelia would have showered on Jack's only child. She managed to hold on to her smile. "You're probably right, Nola. I imagine this dollhouse has been passed around so much because little girls grow tired of it fairly quickly and don't want it taking up so much space in their bedrooms."

I looked back at the dollhouse, where the spindles and brackets had now all turned black, and knew that whether or not Amelia really believed what she was saying, she was wrong: Apparently there was another compelling reason why little girls didn't want that dollhouse in their bedrooms.

The rustle of long skirts brought my attention to a woman in an Empire-style gown with a high waistline and ruffled sleeves sitting at an eighteenth-century dressing table with a marble top and three-way mirror. The green of her gown was marred only by the red stain spread across the bodice of her dress. I looked away as soon as she stood and began walking toward me.

"We need to take a rain check on lunch, Amelia. I just remembered an appointment," I said as I took hold of Nola's arm and began leading her toward the door. "Thanks so much for your help. I'll see you and John at the barbecue." I stopped for a moment and faced her, seeing the woman in the green dress coming toward me again and hearing the rise and fall of more voices. "You know you're welcome to drop by anytime to see Nola."

Amelia smiled at me gratefully. "I know." She turned to her grand-daughter. "I hope that's all right with you. I want us to get to know each other better." She stepped forward as if to embrace Nola, but Nola quickly turned, pretending not to see.

I spotted the shopping bag by the door and thrust it into Nola's hands. "Thanks, Amelia, for the clothes. I'm sure Nola will love them." I opened the door for Nola and she started to go through it before she stopped and turned back to Amelia.

"Thanks," she said slowly. "For the clothes." She gave Amelia a brief smile before ducking through the door.

The light in Amelia's eyes brightened. "You're welcome," she said, but Nola had already moved down to the front window, where she'd pressed her forehead against the glass and was staring at the dollhouse again while pretending not to.

⚭

I began to walk down King Street toward Market, and Nola followed. I had almost two hours before my next appointment, and even though I liked to spend my mornings coordinating my BlackBerry with my other two calendars I kept for backup, I figured a chat with Nola was overdue.

I turned to her. "I've got a little time right now, so I figured I'd show you a bit of Charleston. If you don't mind the walk, I thought we'd go to the open-air market. It's kind of touristy this time of year, but there are some pretty neat local vendors and handcrafted items you might enjoy."

Nola shrugged and I took that as a yes. We continued walking past the windows of the small boutiques and chain stores along King Street, but I kept my gaze focused straight ahead. I didn't want to be distracted by the tempting displays or from my real reason for taking a long walk with Nola.

Although the temperature was only in the high seventies, the humidity hovered around ninety percent, and I could feel it in the way my skirt was beginning to stick to my legs. I glanced over at Nola and saw beads of perspiration on her upper lip, her heavy makeup beginning to run. I reached into my purse and pulled out a neatly folded tissue before handing it to her. Frowning, she stared at it for a moment before taking it and pressing it against her cheeks. "It's so frigging hot here," she said.

I refrained from mentioning that it wasn't even summer yet, or that she wore too many clothes for the climate. I also didn't comment on her choice of words. I figured all that could wait for later. Instead I said, "I know you took the money from your father's wallet."

Her steps didn't falter and she didn't look at me, but I saw her shoulders go back as if preparing for an assault. "So?"

At least she hadn't denied it. Still, I hadn't been raised by an army father for nothing. Despite his battles with alcohol, I'd been raised by the strict military code and still adhered to it. "It's stealing. There are two things I won't tolerate and that's stealing and lying. Don't do it again. Do you understand?"

She didn't say anything, and when I stopped walking, she stopped, too. "Do you understand?" I asked again.

She met my eyes—something I hadn't expected—and replied, "Yeah. I get it." There was still defiance in her words, but there was relief there, too. "It's stuffed under my pillow. I'll give it back."

I thought for a moment that she wanted to say something else, but when she didn't I said, "Good," and continued walking. "I'm glad we understand each other." I knew the conversation wasn't over, but I also knew that she wasn't ready to continue just yet. And if I wanted to get to the bottom of why she'd taken the money in the first place, I'd have to bide my time. There was more than just stealing involved, something I'd been convinced of when she'd met my eyes and told the truth. Her resemblance then to the young me had been uncanny, and I couldn't help but want to give her a second chance.

We reached the covered open-air market that stretched between Meeting and East Bay streets, where long tables were set up displaying wares for the throngs of tourists in their kaleidoscope-colored T-shirts. The pungent scents of horses, from the nearby tourist carriage barns, and cooking food mingled in the air like new neighbors still trying to get to know each other.

The rumor was that the market had once been a slave auction house, but that was just something made up for the tourists. The land had actually been donated in the late eighteenth century for a food market, and while its wares had changed over the years, its purpose had not. I generally avoided it because, slave market or not, it was filled with the spirits of Charlestonians both past and present.

We strolled slowly through the crowds of people until Nola paused by a table displaying the traditional sweetgrass baskets. A woman whose black skin had been baked by the sun into the color of dark coal sat in a chair behind the table weaving a basket in the time-honored tradition passed down by the generations of women in her family. A middle-aged woman sat next to her, watching carefully as Nola picked up a tiny basket only slightly larger than my hand. She held it up to get a better look, studying the intricately woven blades of sweetgrass done with such skill that the beginning and end of each blade disappeared into a seamless weave.

I smiled at both women before turning to Nola. "It's beautiful, isn't it? These baskets are part of the local Gullah history brought over with slaves from West Africa. Dr. Wallen takes some of her classes on a field trip to Edisto Island to see how they're made. She says there's a direct correlation between the making of these baskets and the restoration of the old houses here in the city. I have no idea what she's talking about, but I do love these baskets."

Reluctantly, Nola put the basket down and prepared to move on. I noticed again the ratty condition of her backpack and the frayed rubber of her Converse sneakers and made the educated guess that she didn't have much spending money. In a move that I can only call impulsive, since I rarely did anything without advance planning, I picked up the basket and held it out to the younger woman. "How much is this one?"

"Seventy-five dollars," she said as she stood and moved to the edge of the table to face me. "All made by hand."

The price was high, and I could tell by Nola's quick intake of breath that she thought so, too. But I figured any kid who'd had the guts to get on a bus and take it to the other side of the country to live with strangers needed a little something to call her own.

"I'll take it," I said, drawing my wallet from my purse. The woman quickly processed the transaction and placed the basket in a plain white paper bag before handing it to Nola.

Nola kept her arms crossed in front of her, pressing the Palm Avenue shopping bag against her chest. "It's not mine," she protested.

"I got it for you," I said, taking the bag and pressing it into Nola's hand. "It's a welcome to the Lowcountry. Besides," I added, as I drew her away from the table, "I'm going to make your dad pay me back." I winked at her, eliciting a small smile, and began walking again.

We passed tables of beaded jewelry and homemade perfumes, wreaths made of twigs and dried marsh grass, and individually wrapped bags of candied pecans and peanut brittle. Never one to pass up sugar, I bought one of each and held one up to Nola.

She shook her head. "No, thanks. It's probably made with real eggs and lots of sugar."

I took a bite of peanut brittle, savoring the burst of sweetness on my tongue. "I certainly hope so."

"How can you put that stuff into your body?" she asked with disgust as I took another bite.

I swallowed with a smile. "Very easily, thank you."

As Nola paused at a booth selling hand-carved wooden animals, I broached the next question. Gently, I asked, "Why did you take the money from the wallet?"

She picked up a statue of a sleeping cat and moved it up to her face to study it closely. "I needed to buy something."

"You do know that you can ask your dad for money, right? Don't tell him I said this, but I think he's a pretty reasonable and fair-minded guy. I don't think he'd be a pushover, but he'd listen."

She continued to study the cat, turning it over and running her fingers over the smooth, dark wood. "I know." She placed the cat gently on the table, keeping her eyes averted. "That's not the problem."

I frowned, not understanding until I saw the stain of pink rise on her cheeks. "Oh," I said, unsure how to continue. "You needed . . . female things?"

She gave a short nod, followed by a shrug.

I placed my hand on her arm and gently led her away from the table. "I think he could handle it, Nola. He's not as clueless as he looks."

That brought another slight upward turn to her lips. Still, she wouldn't meet my eyes as she turned to walk back in the direction we'd come.

I followed. "He's your father, Nola. No matter how embarrassing you think it would have been to ask him, it would have been better than stealing the money."

She stopped so suddenly that I nearly ran into her back.

The hand clutching the two shopping bags turned nearly white. "My mom never had money for that stuff, so once a month I took a bus to a different town and stole what we needed. I figured paying money for it would be better." She turned and continued walking.

It took a moment for her words to sink in, and then I had to jog in my high heels to catch up. "Look, Nola. Let's go to Trellis Pharmacy and we'll get you everything you need, okay? Even makeup. But don't ask me to buy you any black eyeliner. You've got the most beautiful blue eyes, and nobody can see them with all that black goo smeared around them."

Her eyes narrowed and her mouth puckered in a look I was already beginning to recognize as defiance, and I cut her off before she could speak. "You can keep the red lipstick for now if you like. Just get rid of the black eyeliner." I'd work on ditching the lipstick and multiple earrings later.

Her expression didn't change as she spoke. "If you're not trying to hook up with Jack, then why are you being so nice to me?"

Her question brought all kinds of thoughts to mind—like why she was referring to her father by his first name, and how somebody so young could know so much about circumspect adult behavior.

I took a deep breath and met her eyes. "Because you remind me a lot of somebody I used to know." Before she could ask any more questions, I started walking. "Come on; the store's not too far."

She shrugged and fell into step beside me, and we walked in silence for several blocks before she spoke again. "Mellie?"

I didn't register surprise that she was not only calling me by my first name, but that she was using my nickname, because it occurred to me that it was the first time she'd addressed me directly.

"Yes?" I replied, keeping my gaze focused straight ahead.

"Thanks."

"You're welcome," I said, forcing my smile to remain small. And as I turned to look at her I caught our reflections in the front window of a store as we passed by, seeing the unmistakable image of a third woman following closely at our heels. I stopped, turning abruptly, and found myself staring at nothing at all.

CHAPTER 4

I had just finished discussing the menu for that night's barbecue with Mrs. Houlihan—which included tofu burgers and baconless baked beans served on a separate table so unsuspecting guests wouldn't accidentally eat any—when I heard a tapping on the back kitchen door.

I stood to let my mother in, along with a blast of hot air. Despite the heat, my mother barely glowed with perspiration and carried with her the scent of flowers. She closely resembled a more refined, albeit brunette, version of Dolly Parton, with the same enviable proportions. If not for the fact that I closely resembled her in almost every other way, including our ability to communicate with those no longer living, I would have demanded my DNA be checked.

She kissed me on both cheeks and that's when I noticed the yellow rose in her hair.

"Nice flower," I said as I closed the door, then led her out of the kitchen. Mrs. Houlihan was very protective of her domain, and when it was time to get to work you didn't want to get in her way. General Lee remained on his bed in the corner, his eyes trained on the housekeeper, hoping to catch a stray scrap.

"Thank you. An early-morning gift from your father and his garden."

I didn't bother to ask her what my father was doing at her house in the early morning, because I really didn't want to know. Although they'd been divorced and estranged for over thirty years, their budding romance might have actually been sweet if it weren't for the fact that they were my parents.

As my mother followed me into the front parlor, she asked, "Are you expecting the ladies from the Historical Society for tea or something?"

I sat down on the sofa while my mother took the Queen Anne chair opposite. "No, why do you ask?" I began to pour coffee from the tray Mrs. Houlihan had brought in earlier while I'd been doing paperwork at my grandmother's desk. Amelia had found the desk at an estate auction, and my mother had given it to me. It gave me no small comfort to sit at it to go through mail or pay bills and feel my beloved grandmother with me, despite the fact that with her phone calls I never felt that she was that far from me anyway.

My mother made a point of studying my heels, white linen dress, and Grandmother's pearls before responding. "Are you wearing that for a barbecue?"

I handed my mother a cup of black coffee on a saucer while I filled my own cup with four sugar cubes before filling it, making sure to leave enough room for cream.

"What's wrong with what I'm wearing? The hem's not hanging out, is it?"

She closed her eyes and shook her head. "Don't you have, oh, I don't know, a pair of skinny jeans or something? Something that would make you look young and hip, maybe a little sexy?"

I tried to pretend that my mother hadn't just used the word "sexy" in a sentence directed at me. A thumping beat began to reverberate throughout the house, followed shortly by two slamming doors and then the sound of water being forced through old pipes.

I raised my voice slightly so I could be heard over the noise. "Why would I want to look sexy in my own backyard?"

She lifted both eyebrows.

"What?" I really had no idea what she was getting at.

"Isn't Jack coming tonight?"

I pretended that my pulse hadn't just skittered at the mention of his name. "Of course. The party's for his daughter. But what's that got to do with what I'm wearing?"

She closed her eyes again, as if summoning divine strength. "Mellie, sweetheart, I think that Jack would appreciate seeing you in a nice pair of well-fitting jeans. Especially if he's bringing Rebecca to the barbecue."

My hand stilled with the coffee cup halfway to my mouth, and I could see little ripples in the surface caused by the thumping noise from upstairs. Carefully, I replaced the cup in its saucer and sat back. "Mother, in case you haven't noticed, Jack's seeing Rebecca. Not me."

"Yes, well, we all know the words to that song 'Love the One You're With.' If you ask me, she's his second choice, because you're too high-strung to let yourself go and see that the two of you were made for each other. Really, Mellie. It's time you listened to your heart for a change."

I stared at her for a long moment. "Have you been speaking with Grandmother?"

"No, why?"

"Because she called earlier this week and told me the same thing." I decided not to mention that I'd been dreaming about Jack right before the phone rang.

"Good. Then maybe you'll listen."

"Mother, you know as well as I do that Jack and I couldn't be together for any length of time before one of us killed the other." The thumping sound from upstairs reminded me of another reason. Before she could say anything else, I said, "I asked you over this morning because I have a favor to ask." I smiled benignly. "I have to move out for about three months while my foundation is being repaired, and I was hoping that I could move in with you."

She actually looked genuinely pleased. "Sweetheart, you know you don't even have to ask. Your father and I would love to have you."

I skipped over the "father and I" part and went straight for the next part of the favor. "I won't be alone. I hope that's not a problem."

"Well, of course you'll need to bring your adorable General Lee. He's part of the family."

I kept smiling as the noise from upstairs escalated. The bathroom door and then the bedroom door were thrown open, followed by a slam.

"What *is* that, Mellie?"

My smile didn't falter, but I was surprised my teeth didn't rattle. Living with a teenage girl for three days had left me feeling as if I'd been run over by a truck and then left in the middle of the road. We'd moved past the point of polite strangers and were now testing boundaries like a pin to a balloon. "That's Emmaline Amelia Pettigrew. Otherwise known as Nola, Jack's daughter."

Her left eyebrow rose, Scarlett style. "I see. Amelia's been telling me about her. And she's living with you because . . ."

"Because she and Jack keep butting heads. Apparently Nola's mother told her that Jack abandoned them both and she believed her." I glanced toward the foyer, afraid that Nola would sneak up and overhear. "I'll tell you everything later. But for now Nola's with me, and where I go, she goes." I perked up. "Besides, you always say how you regret not being there for my teenage years. Here's your chance."

My mother dabbed at the corners of her mouth with one of the linen napkins and stood. "You and I have dealt with evil spirits and vengeful ghosts. Surely we can handle one teenage girl."

We heard doors open again and the sound of a hair dryer turning on. I quickly walked to the foyer and called up the stairs. Raising my voice, I called out, "The fuses are a little delicate. You might want to turn off the stereo. . . ."

The lights flickered once, then went out completely, along with, fortunately, the noise that had been coming from the stereo. Even though I'd just purchased it for Nola, I had a small spark of hope that it had been ruined beyond repair.

"Shit! What the . . ."

"Nola!" I shouted back. "We have company."

My mother, to her credit, didn't flinch. Instead she moved past me and stood on the bottom step. "Nola? Hello. This is Mrs. Middleton, Melanie's mother. I'm looking forward to meeting you when you're in a better mood. In the meantime, why don't you make yourself decent and come on down so Melanie can show you how to change a fuse. I have a feeling it will be a skill you'll come to appreciate."

With a satisfied smile, she stepped down into the foyer as Mrs. Houlihan stuck her head out of the kitchen door. "Somebody blew a fuse and I lost my power. Do you want me to change it?"

"Thanks," I said, "but I've got it covered."

"Just make it quick," the old housekeeper said. "These baked beans won't bake on their own."

I faced my mother again, but her attention was focused on something behind me. I turned, too, and saw Nola's guitar case leaning against the newel post, where I could have sworn it hadn't been earlier.

"What's that?"

I spotted the N'awlins sticker on the case, not like I needed further ID. "It used to be Bonnie's—Nola's mother—but it's now Nola's. Although according to Jack, she won't play a note."

Two furrows formed between her eyebrows. "Then what's it doing here?"

"Nola and I would like to know the same thing. Sometimes she wakes up with it in her bed; other times it just appears at random locations throughout the house, as if it wants to be seen."

"Maybe Bonnie is trying to tell you something."

"Could be," I said, not meeting her eyes. "I haven't tried to contact her so I'm not sure, but it seems likely." Unlike my mother, I preferred to let sleeping spirits lie. I wasn't one to jostle them awake and ask them to move to the light already. I'd spent a childhood being ridiculed for my particular "gift" and an adulthood trying to hide it. And at the age of thirty-nine, I saw no reason to change my MO. Changing it just made life messy.

My mother's eyes were understanding as she met mine. "You haven't told her yet, have you?"

I sighed. "About her mother possibly still being here or my ability to have a conversation with her?" I shook my head. "I don't think she's ready to hear either. She already has trust issues, and I can't see her believing anything else I say if I started out with, 'Hi, Nola. I see dead people.'"

"You're probably right, but eventually you're going to have to tell her. And you'll have to find a way to talk with Bonnie—or whoever it is—to figure out why she's still here." She took a step closer to the guitar case. "I could place my hands on it if you think it would help."

I gripped her forearm, holding her back. My mother had the ability to communicate with spirits by touching objects associated with them, sometimes with disastrous results. I liked to think of it as only a last-ditch measure. "I don't think that's necessary. Bonnie could just be hanging around to make sure Nola gets settled. Why don't we wait and see?"

She gave me her knowing look, the look mothers most likely acquire during the birthing process, and I tried very hard not to squirm in my Valentino heels.

"After the barbecue tonight, I'm heading over to Caroline Lane's. Her sister passed last fall and left some unfinished business that Mrs. Lane would like to settle so her sister can rest in peace. You're welcome to come along."

"Mother, please. You know how I feel about performing like a circus seal. And what would my clients think if it got out? I'd never be taken seriously again."

A shriek sounded from upstairs, rapidly followed by stomping footsteps and a door being thrown open. Again. "Stop moving my damned guitar! Where'd you put it?"

Hating to shout in my own house, I moved to the base of the stairs again. "I'll give it to you after you help me change the fuse."

The door slammed in response.

"Somebody needs to talk with her about that language."

"I know, Mother. I just can't do it yet—she's still too raw from the trauma of the last month. We'll figure it out."

I walked with my mother to the front door, and she paused on the threshold. "I've got a few errands to run, and I know you've probably got something to organize, so why don't we plan on your picking me up at my house at one?"

I frowned. "What for?"

"To take you shopping for a nice pair of jeans. Bring Nola, too. Amelia told me she'd purchased some things for her at Palm Avenue, and it doesn't take any psychic powers to guess that Nola wouldn't wear most of it. We can return what doesn't work and hopefully find something else we can all agree on. Amelia will understand."

Knowing it was futile to argue, I said, "Whatever." I cringed at how much I was starting to sound like Nola after only three days. I wondered whether, after three months of living with her, I'd be cursing and admiring Sophie's fashion sense. I shuddered at the thought.

"Great. I'll see you both at one." She kissed me on both cheeks, then walked down the piazza, her heels clicking across the black-and-white marble tiles.

I was in the process of walking with a pot of real baked beans toward one of the tables set up in the garden when a low wolf whistle came from behind me. I turned to see Jack lounging in a chair with a nonalcoholic beer resting beside him on the wrought-iron table. Turning my back on him, I set the pot down and began to arrange the flowers my father had provided for the occasion. "What? You've never seen baked beans before?"

He shook his head slowly. "Not escorted by such a fine pair of blue jeans, that's for sure."

His expression sobered quickly as the kitchen door opened behind me and Rebecca Edgerton appeared, a vision in pink shorts, a matching pink sweater set, and a pink headband resting on her blond head, a mutinous-looking Nola following close behind.

Jack stood and smiled warily at his daughter and Rebecca, no doubt wondering whether he should gird his loins. I stared at Nola for a moment, trying to reconcile what I was seeing with what I knew of the girl. She wore her Converse sneakers with green neon laces, and matching socks that went to almost midcalf on her long, gangly legs. Her skirt was denim, one I recognized from our shopping trip that afternoon, but with a shredded hem that I was sure hadn't been on it when it was purchased. Her new, crisp white Lilly Pulitzer blouse looked like it had been mistaken for a subway wall by a graffiti artist with a penchant for peace signs, and although her eyeliner had been applied with a lighter touch, the red lipstick had not been. But the most notable part of it all was the pink headband, remarkably like Rebecca's, that pushed back her dark hair, showing off her beautiful bone structure and features, and highlighting the scowl on her face.

Sophie turned from where she'd been working on displaying her eggless, sugarless, and tasteless lemon bars on a tray. "That's just wrong," she said under her breath.

Nola stopped in front of her father, crossed her arms over her chest, and glowered in his direction. Rebecca put an arm around Jack's waist. "Doesn't she look precious? Pink is really her color—don't you agree?"

"Just precious," Jack answered as he avoided Rebecca's kiss by offering his cheek instead. "Is that a gift from you?"

Nola shot him a "you're the most oblivious man on the planet" look, and I was starting to prepare for violence when Sophie walked toward them. "Hey, Nola. You've got to try one of my lemon bars. They're completely vegan, and very tasty, if I may say so myself." She gently put her arm across Nola's shoulders. As she passed me I heard her add, "As soon as she's not looking, you can toss that thing into the fountain."

A real smile erupted on Nola's face. I was mouthing the words "thank you" to Sophie when I caught sight of her left hand on Nola's shoulder. The little sparkling diamond on her fourth finger, to be more specific.

"Sophie? What's that ring?" My voice was a lot louder than I'd intended, effectively ending all conversation.

Chad, Sophie's colleague at the College of Charleston and what I thought of as her platonic roommate, looked up from where he'd been tossing a tennis ball with General Lee, his eyes wide and innocent. Not so platonic after all, I guessed.

Sophie clasped her hands behind her back but it was too late. My mother rushed forward and past me, her hands reaching for Sophie's. "Let me see it; let me see it!"

"You're engaged?" I asked, surprised and not a little hurt that she hadn't confided in me. I considered Sophie Wallen to be my best friend, and as such I would have expected her to tell me first.

She shot me an apologetic look as she held up her left hand to show my mother the round diamond in an antique platinum setting. It was a little more traditional than I thought Sophie would have wanted, but it was lovely. And sparkly. And completely and totally unexpected. I was happy for her—I was. It was only that I couldn't yet wrap my mind around the fact that it would be Sophie and Chad from now on, and not just Sophie and me.

Chad joined his fiancée as everyone crowded around the happy couple, and I found myself being forced back as I listened to how he'd proposed while they were sharing a shift checking the loggerhead turtle nests on Isle of Palms.

"It's like they were made for each other," a voice said beside me.

Startled, I looked up to see the dark and handsome face of Marc Longo. We had dated for a short while the year before, until I'd learned that he'd lied to me to gain access to Confederate diamonds hidden in my inherited house on Tradd Street. Although he'd since apologized and made attempts to amend our relationship—no doubt helped along by a single blow to the jaw offered by Jack—I doubted that I could ever really trust him again, regardless of how sincere he seemed. It didn't help that Jack loathed him and used every opportunity to let Marc know it. The feeling was mutual.

"Marc," I said, offering my cheek for a kiss. "It's so good to see you." I stared up at him, wondering how to ask him why he was there. He'd definitely not been on my small family-only invite list.

As if reading my mind, he offered, "Your mother invited me. Said something about there being too many females and she needed me to even things out."

I shot a look over at my mother, who was pretending not to notice Marc or me and instead was making a good show of listening as Sophie and Chad told everyone about their ideas for the wedding. I caught the words "barefoot" and "hemp," but was too distracted by Marc's hand, which was now squeezing mine in an earnest grip.

"So does that sound like something you'd like to do?"

I glanced back at Marc, realizing he'd been talking to me. "I'm sorry; what did you say?"

"I said that I'm planning on having a party at my beach house to celebrate Carolina Day. I was hoping you'd come and play hostess."

"I'm pretty sure she's busy that night," Jack said, coming up behind me. "Or she will be, seeing as her birthday is the same day." He offered a big smile and a hand toward Marc. "Matthew, right?"

To my surprise, Marc took the offered hand and shook it. "Ah, the famous Jack Trenholm. A pleasure, as always."

I studied Marc's face, confused by the look I saw there. It was similar to the look I imagined a cat wore while standing next to the empty bowl of cream.

"Why, thank you, Matt. Can't say I feel likewise, but the sentiment's appreciated just the same." He glanced down at Marc's impeccably tailored shirt and pants, the dark brown Italian loafers. "Just stopping by on the way to the opera? We don't want to make you late."

"Actually, no. I'm here for the duration. I was invited by Mrs. Middleton, although I'd like to think Melanie and I are good enough friends that I wouldn't need an invitation." He squeezed my hand, doing nothing to make the situation less awkward.

I was thankful when Marc let go of my hand. "So when's the next international bestseller coming out, Jack, or is that a closely guarded secret?"

Again, I couldn't decipher Marc's expression. Usually I felt the need to stand in between Marc and Jack to prevent any blows, but Marc actually seemed genuinely interested in Jack's answer. Surely he couldn't know what a sore subject it was for Jack. Although originally enthusiastic about Jack's book about the hidden Confederate diamonds and the disappearance of a former resident of my house on Tradd Street, his editor and agent had suddenly stopped taking his phone calls.

"Thanks for asking, Matt. But I rarely mix business with pleasure, so I'm going to spare Melanie the boring details and instead escort her over to Nola, who wants to know whether the cake is vegan and when she can have a piece."

Jack tugged on my arm, leaving me no choice but to follow. I waved, and from the corner of my eye I watched Rebecca approach Marc, her gaze directed at Jack and me.

"Remind me to have a word with your mother," Jack said in my ear. "My daughter's here and I don't want her to be exposed to lower life-forms like that."

We both looked over to where Nola was standing between Sophie and Chad. The pink headband was long since discarded—most likely in the fountain behind her—and Sophie and Chad were wearing matching quilted vests and single braids, a collection of hemp necklaces around their necks. If I hadn't known the three of them and happened to come across them in a dark alley, I'd probably head the other way. "Yeah, I know what you mean," I said, but the sarcasm, for once, seemed lost on Jack.

I looked around the small gathering. "Where are your parents? They said they'd be here."

It took Jack a moment to register that I was speaking to him. He shrugged. "I don't know. I'm sure they're on their way. My mother mentioned something about a gift for Nola. Maybe that's what's holding them up."

A cold breeze swept across my back like icy fingers, making me shiver despite the heat. I looked up at Jack to see whether he'd noticed it, but he was too busy staring at Marc and Rebecca with a concentrated frown. Marc looked up and saw us, then smiled an unnatural smile again. Jack tensed beside me.

"Melanie?" I turned at Sophie's voice.

I faced her, a smile plastered on my face. "Congratulations on your engagement," I said, trying very hard to keep the ice out of my voice. "When were you planning on telling me? After the third baby was born?"

"Look, Melanie, I'm really sorry about that. I wasn't sure how you'd take it, so I was working on a way to tell you when I was sort of found out tonight."

"Then maybe you shouldn't have worn your ring."

"Why not?" piped up Nola, who seemed to have appeared beside Sophie like a new appendage. They even wore matching braids now.

"Because," I explained, "best friends tell each other stuff first."

Nola looked up at the sky as if seeking guidance on how to address incredibly stupid adults. "Yeah, but she probably felt bad about telling you that she was going to get married, seeing as how you're old and not married and don't even have a boyfriend."

It took me a moment to mentally chip the ice from my lips. "Thank you, Nola, for that observation. I'm only thirty-nine, for your information. That's hardly nursing home material."

Nola screeched and threw her hands over her mouth. "OMG! I didn't know you were *that* old! You're practically dead."

Unable to find a response that wouldn't require my getting physical, I abruptly turned around, only to run into my mother. "Mellie, just the person I was looking for. What do you say we do your fortieth birthday party here? Your garden is just perfect for entertaining, and your father said he can start working on plans right away."

I felt the embarrassing and completely unexpected prickle of tears behind my eyelids. I wasn't sure whether it was from what Nola had said—which I somehow thought might have a glimmer of truth—or the fact that my mother seemed to be in collaboration with Sophie, Nola, and apparently the rest of the world on making me feel old and permanently single. I wanted to tell her that it was all her fault, that abandoning me was what had sent me down this path of approaching spinsterhood, but I held back, afraid that if I opened my mouth I'd start crying.

A commotion at the garden gate made me turn away, and I stared in surprise as two men wearing Trenholm Antiques hats and matching uniform shirts slowly stepped their way down the brick path through the gate, carrying a pallet with something tall and bulky hidden under a quilted tarp.

Behind them came Amelia and John Trenholm, Jack's parents, both grinning broadly. I approached and gave them each a kiss on the cheek. "Wow—I can't imagine what that could be."

The words dried in my throat as I smelled singed tar and ashes, the edges of the tarp seeming to melt into rubbery, reaching fingers. I watched the men lower the pallet to the ground, then slowly remove the tarp. *Don't!* someone shouted, but the voice came from inside my head and nobody else heard. I opened my mouth to make the men stop, but it was too late. The turret of the dollhouse had already been revealed, the tarp slowly being pulled away inch by inch, like some bizarre burlesque show.

"It's exquisite," Sophie whispered beside me, but I hardly heard her. I was too busy trying not to choke on the stench of burning tar.

"The house looks so familiar," she continued. "I wonder whether it was built as a replica of a real house."

Amelia shook her head. "I have no idea. It's had a lot of owners, so chances are it might not even be originally from Charleston. I'm sure we can find out. Jack's pretty good at that."

Everyone who'd gathered around the dollhouse to admire it now stepped back as Jack approached with Nola. I could tell that she was trying very hard to pretend that she didn't particularly care that at the advanced age of thirteen she'd been given the first dollhouse she'd ever owned, or that it was probably one of the few gifts she'd ever received. Because I could see her eyes, and they were the eyes of a girl who never expected anything good to happen to her and had just realized that it could.

I felt my mother watching me and I turned my head. Her eyes were narrowed in concentration, and I knew she could smell the acrid scent heavy in the early-summer night. She stepped forward, and before I could stop her she reached out her hand to touch the curling eave of the old dollhouse, and the air screamed.

CHAPTER 5

I stood in the doorway to Nola's room and watched as she carefully unwrapped each doll figure from old newspaper, standing them on the wraparound porch of the dollhouse one by one. There was a father, a mother, an older brother, and a younger sister. They were all blond and blue eyed, except for the daughter, whose chestnut hair hung down her back, and wire-framed glasses hid dark brown eyes. There was even a dog, a shaggy-looking mix between a golden retriever and a sheepdog. Each human figure was carved from wood and dressed in Victorian clothing, their stares vacant. I only hoped that the voices I'd begun to hear right after my mother fainted were a temporary thing.

"Are you sure you want the dollhouse in your bedroom?" I asked, remembering the acrid scent of smoke and my mother's reaction to it when she touched it. She'd actually fainted, right there in my garden, and I had to tell everybody that she had low blood sugar. My father had taken her home immediately, but before she'd left she'd told me that she'd seen only a bright flash of white light.

Nola looked at me long enough for me to see her roll her eyes. "I don't want to hurt Amelia's feelings. She's pretty nice, even if she is old." She carefully moved the dog to be beside the boy, and I had the oddest sensation that that was where it belonged. "I mean, how clueless do you have to be to give a teenager a dollhouse?"

I noticed how she called everybody by their first name, as if she were afraid to acknowledge any familial relationships such as "father" or "grandmother."

I pressed on, not completely sure that the dollhouse should be in her bedroom, especially at night while Nola slept. "But if you wanted it in the living room, I wouldn't have a problem with it, and I'm sure your grandmother wouldn't mind. Might even give you more room up here. I was thinking about maybe putting in a little music corner here, with a great chair for guitar playing, and a place for your music and your mother's guitar. . . ."

The look she gave me wasn't as hostile as I'd been expecting. It was more bleak, as if she'd rehearsed this conversation to keep the emotion out of it. "I don't like to play the guitar. I just keep all that crap because it was hers."

A cold breeze rippled a pile of sheet music Nola had stacked next to her bed. "Air-conditioning," I said quickly in response to her questioning look. The vent was directly over my head and wasn't currently blowing anything. I hoped Nola wouldn't notice.

I thought I saw something move on the dollhouse, but when I turned to look I was met with five blank, staring gazes. I rubbed my hands over my arms, feeling chilled. "Well, let me know if you change your mind."

"Whatever," she said as she moved to the open back of the house and began arranging the miniature furniture.

"Don't stay up too late." Without waiting for an answer, I backed out of the room, not sure whom or what I didn't want to turn my back on, then headed down the stairs. Jack sat on a Chinese Chippendale chair in the foyer, but when I opened my mouth to greet him, he put a finger to his lips and motioned for me to follow him onto the front piazza. Curious, I followed, flipping on the outside lights against the gathering gloom, then took a seat in one of the wicker rocking chairs. He leaned against the porch railing and casually crossed his ankles, but his tense jaw and shoulders belied his relaxed pose.

"Where's Rebecca?"

"I needed to speak with you, but Rebecca needed to get home, so Marc drove her."

I studied him in the dim light, wondering whether anything he'd just said hit him as awkwardly as it had me. But from the engrossed look on his face, it looked like his thoughts were elsewhere.

Clearing his throat, he said, "I wanted to talk to you about Nola, but didn't want her to overhear."

"Good move," I said. "Although she seems pretty preoccupied with her new toy."

"Yeah." He shook his head. "What was my mother thinking? I don't know about you, but I think that dollhouse is pretty creepy."

I raised my eyebrows but didn't say anything, wondering whether the signals the dollhouse was sending out were so strong that somebody with a thick skull like Jack could pick up on it.

He placed both palms on the railing and leaned toward me. "Is there something I should know about that dollhouse?"

I shrugged, not sure how to answer. "I don't know. Yet. I'm not crazy about it being in Nola's room, but she was really insistent. I'll keep an eye on things, though." I paused for a moment. "Could you tell me what Bonnie looked like?"

He tilted his head. "She was tall and slender—like Nola. But her hair was long, and she always wore it straight. She liked to wear loose-fitting clothes, like Sophie, but with a little more style." He smiled softly. "Why?"

"I told you that I thought Nola hadn't come alone—and your description of Bonnie matches that of a woman I've seen a few times. Since Bonnie's guitar keeps finding its way into Nola's bed or other strange places, I just wanted to make sure it was her doing it." I shrugged. "Maybe the dollhouse spirits can keep Bonnie company."

Jack narrowed his eyes at me. "Do ghosts really do that? Make friends, I mean?"

"I have no idea. I try not to hang around them too much. Most of the ghosts I've known are sort of the loner types."

His gaze was focused on the black and white tiles of the piazza floor. "Has Bonnie . . . said anything to you?"

I shook my head. "Not yet. She seems kind of shy. But as I said, she keeps moving her guitar—which makes Nola mad at me, since she thinks I'm doing it—and just now she rustled some sheet music. Maybe she simply wants Nola to take guitar lessons."

I studied Jack for a long moment, smelling the fragrant oleander from the garden, which would always make me think of him, probably because like the beautiful and sweet-smelling flower, Jack was an irritant and quite possibly fatal to my well-being. His hair was still dark, his shoulders broad, his waist trim. He was devastating at thirty-five. I couldn't help but wonder what he'd looked like as a college football quarterback. "You need to tell me more about Bonnie so that I can try to reach her. Did she have any success as a songwriter? Did she ever marry? That kind of thing."

He looked stricken, as if I'd just told him that the tooth fairy wasn't real. "I have no idea. I can't believe that I don't know anything about her life after we broke up. Or that I had a daughter. Somehow I think I should have known."

I clasped my hands to keep them from reaching out to him. This was dangerous territory, and I wasn't completely sure that I would survive the journey unscathed. Besides, comforting him was Rebecca's job now. "Don't beat yourself up, Jack. Bonnie didn't want you to know. That's why she lied to Nola about you. She was hell-bent on cutting ties with her past, and she was very successful at it."

He rubbed his hands over his face. "Has Nola opened up to you at all? Anything about her mother? About her growing up?"

I shook my head. "Not a thing. I've tried to start conversations to get her talking about it, but let's just say that teenagers aren't the best conversationalists. Especially those who feel like they've been exiled into hostile territory." I considered him for a moment. "As crazy as this sounds, I think your mother did the right thing giving Nola that doll-house. Seeing her with it was the first time I ever saw her face go soft. Like a kid's should be. It's strange seeing such a grown-up face on a thirteen-year-old. Maybe this is the beginning."

He was regarding me closely with what I secretly called his "Jack look," and I shifted uncomfortably. Usually when Jack Trenholm wanted something, it was only a matter of time before he found even unwilling subjects bending backward to do what he wanted.

"What?" I asked, running my tongue over my teeth to make sure I didn't have food stuck between them.

"Does Nola have a diary?"

Warily, I said, "I have no idea. Why?"

"I'm just thinking that if she won't open up to us, maybe we should try to find her diary to see in her own words what's going on in her head. There might even be stuff in there about Bonnie."

I started shaking my head before he'd even finished speaking. "No way. Uh-uh. Even if she does have a diary, it's off-limits to you, or to me, or anybody but Nola." I thought of my own teenage diary and how humiliated I would have been for anybody to have read it, but not for the reasons one might imagine. My diary during those awkward teenage years (and even beyond, if I wanted to be honest) consisted solely of lists of what I'd worn each day, to make sure I wouldn't repeat an outfit in a certain period of time. I was so hopeless and pathetic there wasn't even one remark about a crush on a particular boy or hating my parents.

He at least had the decency to look abashed. "Yeah, you're right. I'm a guy, you know? I don't always consider all angles before I speak."

I cleared my throat. "You know, Jack, for someone with such a long track record with women as you claim to have, you're a little clueless about the younger versions."

A wicked grin spread across his face. "Tell that to Mary Beth Maybank, who sat in front of me in math class in seventh grade."

I raised an eyebrow and Jack shrugged. "She was an early developer. I could unhook her bra through her sweater in five seconds flat. Made me a hero with the other guys when she had to get up to go to the girls' room to fix it."

"That's different. This is your daughter. Imagine some teenage boy doing that to Nola."

His face changed immediately and I have to admit to being a little scared. "I'd kill him."

"Exactly. This is uncharted territory for you, Jack. For both of us, really. But at least I have faint memories of actually being a teenage girl once upon a time so that maybe I can relate a little. From what I remember about my own thought processes back then, I think the only choice you have is to be patient and to keep trying to get through to her. And not be too upset at the repeated rejections. She'll come around as soon as she realizes that she's safe here and that she's got a family who loves her, bad fashion sense and all." I kept to myself how Jack's concern for his daughter was a completely unexpected—and totally appealing—quality. Maybe a little too appealing.

"Still," he said, straightening, "I'm going to try to find out as much about Bonnie as possible. Maybe there's something that can help me bond with Nola. I've got nothing else, so I might as well start there."

I was about to tell him that being a concerned and present father was the best place to start—something I did happen to know about—and that he'd already covered that, but my phone rang. I slid it out of my pocket and looked at the number.

"It's my mother," I said to Jack, then held the phone to my ear. "Hello?"

"Your father's sleeping, so I thought now would be a good time to speak to you about that dollhouse."

My father, a lifelong disbeliever in all things that went bump in the night, had recently seen his first ghost, the long-dead Hessian soldier who'd resided in my mother's ancestral home for a couple of centuries. Although he still denied their existence, explaining what he'd seen as a trick of the light or my own projected imagination, his resistance wasn't nearly as adamant as it had once been.

"What about it? You said all you could see was a bright white light." She was silent for a moment. "At first, yes. But . . ."

"But what?" I prodded.

"There was something behind the light. Something . . . bad. But somebody, some*thing,* was preventing me from seeing it. To protect me or them, I don't know. Whatever you do, don't put it in Nola's room until we can find out for sure what it's all about."

I frowned into the phone. "It's a little late for that." I glanced at Jack and he was frowning, too.

I listened to my mother breathe into the phone. "Then be very, very careful. Keep an eye on Nola and her behavior. Let me know if you see her acting strangely, or becoming overly negative."

"Really, Mother? Like how could I tell the difference?"

"Never mind. You'll be moving here within the week, so I'll be able to keep an eye on her, too. Maybe even suggest she keep the thing downstairs."

"Good luck with that. She's very pigheaded about what she wants. She gets it from her father." I glanced at Jack to see him scowling at me.

"Be that as it may, keep a close eye on her, and let me know when I can expect you."

"It might be another week. Amelia and I are still trying to coordinate where all the big pieces of furniture are going. I don't suppose I need to be here for that. And I—"

My words were cut off by a muffled scream from inside the house. Before I could tell my mother I'd call her back, Jack was already inside and sprinting up the stairs. I reached Nola's room right behind him and had to stop for a moment to register what I was seeing.

General Lee, a dog more closely resembling a teddy bear than a wolf, had his teeth bared and he was snarling in the direction of the dollhouse, where Nola stood glowering at him. I was sure that if she could curl her lips above her teeth, she'd be snarling, too.

"What happened?" Jack demanded, his voice a lot calmer than how I knew we both felt.

Nola's hair was soaking wet and dripping on the rug and wood floors, but I didn't think it was a good time to point it out. "I went to take a shower and when I got back the dog must have been messing with my dollhouse, because all the people are moved. And look—the head's broken." She held out a shaking hand where the figure of the boy, its head at an awkward angle, lay.

General Lee whimpered, so I bent down to scoop him up. But when I took a step toward the dollhouse, he wiggled out of my arms and ran as fast as he could out of the room. My eyes met Jack's for a moment before we both turned to get a closer look at the dollhouse.

The entire dollhouse family, except for the boy and dog, was crowded in the high turret window as if trying to see something outside. I swallowed thickly. "Where's the dog?" I asked.

"Right here." She tapped a spot on the floor in front of the dollhouse with a black-painted toenail.

The head of the dog figure was cracked in half, the body almost hidden under the bed, as if it had been thrown with a good deal of force.

"And where was the boy?"

"Same place." Nola's face reddened. "I want you to keep that damned dog out of my room, okay? He's just going to wreck everything."

I was sure that General Lee would ignore any kind of restraining order, just as I was sure that he'd had nothing to do with rearranging the dollhouse figures—and not just because he didn't possess the opposable thumbs required to do that kind of manipulation. Luckily, Nola was either unaware of dog anatomy or was too upset about the broken figures to really care.

"Look," I said, trying to force a calm reason I wasn't feeling, "I've got some superglue downstairs. I'm sure I won't have any problem making this look brand-new again, okay?" I held out my hand to Nola.

With a sniff, she dumped the boy into my hand. "Fine. But I'm keeping my door closed. I know this is your house and all, but I really don't like you and your dog messing with my stuff."

I glanced at the bed, noticing for the first time that Bonnie's guitar was propped up on the pillows. "I'll remember that," I said as I began backing out of the room.

"Are you going to be okay in here?" Jack asked. "You can always come back with me, you know."

Nola's voice dripped with an equal measure of angst and sarcasm. "Right. That would solve everything."

"Just checking. You have my number if you need me. Anytime."

I waited in the hallway for Jack to close Nola's door.

"What was that all about?" he asked quietly as we headed for the stairs.

"I'm not sure—and neither is my mother. And it might not even be about the house at all. All my life I've done a lot of reading on the subject of spirits and the like—just so that I'd know that I wasn't crazy and that other people had the same kind of experiences that I always have. Anyway, Nola's at that emotional, hormonal age where they sort of attract energies wherever they are." We reached the foyer and I stopped to face him. "But there's one more thing you can research while you're looking into Bonnie's past."

He raised his eyebrows.

"The dollhouse's provenance. Just in case."

"Just in case what?" he asked slowly.

"To find out exactly what came with the dollhouse besides just furniture and dolls."

His eyes met mine for a moment before I turned away and led him toward the front door.

"And if something did?" he asked.

I paused just for a moment. "We could give it away. To Rebecca."

Jack's head tilted. "Why Rebecca?"

"Because the spirits would take one look at the pink haven she calls her bedroom and they'd be tripping over themselves to get to the light."

I could tell he was trying very hard not to laugh. "Good night, Mellie."

"Good night, Jack."

I'd already closed the door behind him before I thought to remind him again not to call me Mellie.

CHAPTER 6

For the second time in less than a year, I found myself on my mother's doorstep with stuffed suitcases, except this time I also came with a recalcitrant teenager. I was almost looking forward to the stay, if only so I'd have an ally in the war against the sullen surliness I was now experiencing on an almost hourly basis. I knew it was mostly because objects in Nola's room refused to stay put and she believed that I was responsible, but I somehow felt that it was easier accepting the blame than telling her the truth.

Nola looked up at the square, brick Georgian house with the two-tiered portico, her mouth open. Even the late-spring garden was opulent in its display of colors and scents, and a new trellis arbor—courtesy of my father—showed off its stunning crimson offering of butterfly roses. My mother had grown up in this house, and I'd spent the first six years of my life visiting my grandmother here. I suppose that was why I never noticed the grandness of it or how imposing it might seem to a stranger who'd never experienced the love and warmth inside. Or its ghosts.

"Holy shit," she said.

I frowned at Nola, recalling something my mother had once said when I was still young enough to listen, after I'd repeated something my father had said when he thought I was out of hearing. I could still taste the Dial soap on my tongue. Speaking softly, I said, "Ladies don't use foul language. And if my mother hears any, she'll wash your mouth out with soap."

Nola's eyes widened with what I thought to be worry, so I took the opportunity to press on. "And I won't stop her, either."

Nola took a step back from me, making me feel as if my words had made an impression. But I was too horrified at realizing that I was becoming my mother to appreciate any victory. We both turned toward the door at the sound of approaching footsteps.

"Mellie, Nola!" my mother sang as she flung open the door before ushering us into the foyer of her Legare Street home. She enveloped us in successive hugs scented with Chanel No. 5 and wrapped in silk. I had once hated that particular perfume, as it always reminded me of the mother who'd abandoned me when I was six, but it was beginning to grow on me again, just like my burgeoning interest in opera and sharing shoes. The whole "mother-daughter" thing was a lot like moving to another part of the world where nobody spoke your language, and with the addition of Nola to the mix, I had a feeling it was about to get a lot more interesting.

"Hello, Mother. Thanks again for letting us stay."

"Don't be silly, Mellie. You're my daughter and I want you to think of my home as yours. And you, too, Nola. I've even had house keys made for both of you so you can come and go as you please. Mrs. Houlihan has already set herself up in the kitchen with General Lee, so it will be just like home."

Nola groaned. "Why does the dog have to come, too?"

Not that long ago, I would have agreed with her. Moving from military base to military base with my father, I wouldn't have been allowed to have a pet even if I'd wanted one. But then I'd inherited General Lee from the late Mr. Vanderhorst and I'd found myself a pet owner, if one could call me that. I was more like General Lee's companion and sleeping buddy, source of food and treats, and a warm lap. Not wanting to display weakness, I thought I'd done a pretty good job of hiding my growing fondness for the furry little guy.

I frowned at Nola—something I found myself doing a lot lately, and if I wasn't careful, it would give me wrinkles. "If you say one more mean thing about my dog, you're going back to your father's." I picked up my suitcases and headed past them toward the stairs. "I'm assuming I have my old room?"

There was a brief silence as Nola and my mother contemplated each other as my last words sank in. "Yes, dear, and Nola has the room across from you. The bathroom, luckily, has been redone, but I'm afraid the bedroom hasn't been tackled yet. I've been too busy with the rest of the house and didn't anticipate having a guest so soon." She began walking toward the stairs as she spoke to Nola. "Colonel Middleton will be here shortly and can carry the rest of your things if you just want to grab your backpack and guitar for now."

I staggered under the weight of my own suitcases, and wondered why she hadn't mentioned that to me.

She continued speaking to Nola. "But the mattress is new and the sheets are clean, so I'm sure you'll be comfortable."

"As long as there's room for my dollhouse, it should work."

I turned and met my mother's gaze. Jack and Chad were supposed to bring the dollhouse over later, and I'd hoped that by the time it showed up my mother and I would have had time to convince her to keep it anywhere other than her room.

I stumbled into my bedroom and dumped my suitcases before joining Nola and my mother. Like the rest of the rooms in the house, Nola's room was large and airy, with tall windows and ceilings, the requisite deep crown moldings and medallions. But what this room lacked was my mother's and Amelia's keen eye for interior design. The previous owners—scrap-metal millionaires from Texas—had, unfortunately, left their mark on this room, making me think of that line from *Macbeth* about all of Neptune's ocean scrubbing something clean. As I examined the room's color palette, I doubted that an entire ocean would be enough.

Black foiled wallpaper with hand-painted and oversize neon orange daisies sprouted on all four walls from floor to ceiling in an apparent attempt to re-create a drug-induced alternate reality. A puce velour rug covered up the beautiful hardwood floors, but not enough to completely disguise the purple-dotted decals that were affixed to the wooden boards in a random pattern, like vomit from a similarly hued leopard. Long strings of miniature pom-poms in an assortment of colors even Crayola wouldn't claim hung from each window as some sort of space-age curtain. My stomach heaved a little from staring at it.

"This is awesome!" Nola exclaimed as she dropped her guitar and backpack in a corner, the teddy bear's face poking out of the opened zipper. I felt sorry for his eyes that lacked lids to block out the horror. "I thought you said you hadn't had a chance to decorate it yet."

"Um, er, not exactly," stammered my mother. "The previous own-ers left it this way."

"Wow. You got lucky. You don't have to change a thing, huh?"

My mother and I traded glances again and I was sure her horrified expression matched my own. Swallowing heavily, I said, "We're thrilled you like it."

Walking to the far side of the room, my mother pushed open a door. "And you have your own private bathroom."

Nola stuck her head inside the newly remodeled space, taking in the tasteful neutrals, the black-and-white marble, the delicate faux paint pattern on the wall. "Too bad they didn't fix the bathroom, too."

I stood in the middle of the room near the large tester bed that my mother had covered in a simple white chenille bedspread she'd found in the attic. I stared at the expanse of white like a person stares at the stationary horizon to quell carsickness. The room held only the bed, a dressing table, a dresser, and a low chest of drawers that my mother planned to convert into a TV table for the small flat-screen that would be arriving later. The furniture had been culled from the attic, my house, and Trenholm's Antiques, and I was just realizing that we should have crammed more furniture into the room. As we'd left it, there was plenty of room for one large dollhouse in any of the four corners.

"I love how airy you've made the room, Mother. Lots of good, empty space. I wouldn't add a thing." I smiled hopefully at Nola as she emerged from her bathroom.

"Except for the dollhouse," she said as she stomped across the room in her military-style boots, something I wouldn't necessarily call a fash-ion accessory or wear in public with striped leggings and a short, ruffled skirt. "I think it would be perfect here," she said, indicating the corner to the left of the headboard. "Don't you think so, Mellie?"

I was too busy scrounging around for reasons why the dollhouse shouldn't go anywhere in a thirty-foot radius of her to correct her use of that dreaded nickname.

"Actually, Nola," my mother said, "we were thinking that the empty room down the hall would be the perfect spot for it. That way you can put it in the middle of the room and see it from all angles instead of against a wall. I could even find a large table to put it on so everything's more or less eye level. What do you think?"

Nola's lower jaw stuck out just enough to remind me of her father when he made up his mind. And if blood were indeed thicker than water, I knew that we had as much hope of persuading her to change her mind as we had of convincing the Architectural Board of Review to allow me to paint my Tradd Street house purple.

"I think it would be perfect in that corner." She moved to the bed and stepped up on the little stool beside it to plop down on the bed-spread. "Maybe we can find another bedspread that goes with the room, something with a little more color. I mean, if it's not too expensive."

I tried to think of a tactful way to tell her that if she wanted to find something that matched the room's decor, she'd have to be prepared to Dumpster-dive behind Goodwill, where I'm sure they discarded those items that would never sell. As if reading my mind, my mother sent me a look of warning, so I kept my mouth shut.

The doorbell rang. Turning to Nola, my mother said, "That must be your grandmother. We'll leave you here to freshen up and get ready for lunch. We have to be at Alluette's Café at noon, so we'll need to leave in about half an hour."

A crease formed between Nola's eyebrows. "Why are we going again?"

"We wanted you to meet Alston Ravenel and her mother, Cecily. They're cousins of yours—third cousins, once removed on your grand-mother's side." She began listing Nola's family tree, as all Charlestonians are wont to do, until Nola's eyes began to glaze over.

My mother noticed and stopped with the genealogy lesson. "Any-way, you and Alston are the same age and both entering the eighth grade. Alston is already enrolled at Ashley Hall, your grandmother's alma mater—and mine, too—so we thought this would be a good way to find out more about the school before your admission interview."

"Admission interview?"

There was a hint of panic in Nola's voice, and I instinctively took a step toward her, remembering my own sense of panic each time my father had announced yet another move to a different army base. "Didn't Amelia tell you about this?"

"Yeah, I guess." Nola shrugged. More quietly, she said, "I didn't think I'd still be here to deal with it."

I stilled. "Where did you think you might be?"

She shrugged again, avoiding my eyes. "Anywhere but here."

I saw my mother open her mouth but I quickly shook my head. Turning back to Nola, I asked, "What made you change your mind?"

With her gaze glued to the floor, she mumbled, "Mrs. Houlihan makes good tofu burgers."

I bit the inside of my cheek. "I'll take your word on that." I found myself clenching my hands together, my nails biting into the skin as I tried to find the right words that would tell her I understood without sounding too emotional. The one thing I'd learned about Nola was that she didn't allow emotions to guide her in any decision, and it bothered me to consider what she'd gone through in her short thirteen years to make her that way. I'd at least had thirty-three years of maternal abandonment as my excuse.

I recalled watching part of a music video on MTV when the cable guy had come to install my DVR. It was a live concert where kids were throwing themselves into a crowd with raised arms, trusting that somebody would be there to catch them. I'd found myself holding my breath, sensing the danger, but feeling somehow bereft, too, knowing that I'd never known that kind of security, especially not as a teenager. Taking a deep breath, I said, "You must feel like you're jumping into a mosh pit at a Slipshod concert, not really sure where you'll land or who will catch you."

She lifted her eyes to mine and her expression could only be called a scowl, but I saw the brightness in her eyes again, and I couldn't help but feel I'd hit the mark. "The band is Slipknot, Mellie. Nice try."

My mother took my elbow. "Come on. Let's not keep Amelia waiting. Come down when you're ready, Nola."

Twenty minutes later, the three of us turned from where we were sitting in the parlor when we heard loud clumping coming down the stairs, then watched with matching stunned expressions as Nola appeared wearing the same outfit she'd been wearing earlier—complete with combat boots and short, ruffled skirt.

Amelia quickly stood and gave Nola a hug. "You certainly have a sense of style, dear, and one that even your old grandmother can appreciate." She left her arm around Nola and faced us, the older, elegant woman in the St. John knit suit and Ferragamo pumps next to the beautiful teenager dressed in an outfit that looked like it came out of a rag-bag. I had the absurd impulse to jump up and high-five Amelia for knowing the right thing to say.

My mother and I stood and gathered our purses. As I held open the front door for everyone as they exited, Nola said, "I hope this stupid café has food I can eat."

Amelia didn't bat an eye. "Alluette's is known for its organic and vegan menu. That's why I chose it."

And another point for you, Amelia, I thought as I locked the door behind me. Aloud I said, "I hope they have food for the rest of us."

My mother sent me a look that I'm sure was meant to remind me of my manners. I rolled my eyes in response as I dropped the keys into my purse, then followed them to Amelia's car.

I sat in the back of the Lincoln with Nola, Amelia and my mother up front. I'd never ridden in a car with Amelia Trenholm before, but for the first time in our acquaintance I began to understand where Jack got his penchant for driving at breakneck speeds down narrow, tourist-filled streets. I clutched at the door handle with my left hand and braced my right on the headrest of the driver's seat in front of me.

Nola kept her gaze focused outside her window, apparently oblivious to everything except her own thoughts. My mother didn't seem to notice as she and Amelia chatted away as if driving like a Formula 1 driver through the streets of Charleston were an everyday occurrence. The radio was set at a very low volume to an oldies station. I thought I recognized the song they were playing but couldn't hear it clearly enough to know for sure. Hoping that music might distract me from the knowledge that I was most likely hurtling toward certain death in a car driven by a woman I'd never have thought had homicidal tendencies, I tapped my mother on the shoulder.

"Can you turn up the radio, please?"

Without pausing in her conversation, she reached over to the volume control and turned it up. I relaxed somewhat against the cream leather upholstery as I recognized the familiar strains of ABBA's "The

Winner Takes It All." Closing my eyes, I began to sing quietly to myself about a heartbroken lover who's desperate enough to ask her ex if his new lover kisses like she did. My eyes jerked open as I realized what I was singing aloud, and found Nola staring closely at me with Jack's blue eyes.

"Do you know who sings that song?" she asked.

Smugly, I said, "Of course. ABBA."

"Great. Let's keep it that way." She sat back in her seat and pretended to stick her finger down her throat. "As if listening to ABBA wasn't nauseating enough to begin with." She leaned forward and tapped her grandmother on the shoulder. "Can you change the station, please? I think I'm getting carsick."

Without a pause in the conversation, Amelia switched the channel to an alternative rock station where they were playing the recent hit of a new and up-and-coming star, Jimmy Gordon. He had more of a bluesy sound than a rock sound, but his voice dripped honey, and he wasn't too hard on the eyes, either. The song "I'm Just Getting Started" was haunting and melodic, with just enough of a beat to give it airtime on more mainstream stations.

I turned to Nola to ask her what she thought of the song, but stopped in midsentence. Her skin was even paler than usual, her fingers like claws digging into the tops of her thighs through the striped tights.

"Are you all right?" I asked, wondering whether she'd been serious about being carsick.

"Change the station," she said with a strangled voice, but loud enough for both women in the front seat to hear. My mother turned her head to ask why, but when she caught sight of Nola's expression, she reached over and pushed a button. "What's wrong?" she asked.

Nola sat back, her face cold and immobile. "I hate that song. And I hate Jimmy Gordon."

"I don't think he's that bad. I actually like him—" I began.

Nola cut me off. "I've met him. And I don't like him."

The icy tone of Nola's voice must have captured Amelia's attention. "Who's Jimmy Gordon?" she asked, looking at us in the rearview mirror.

Nola stared out her window, her shoulders curved into a perfect letter "C" as if to shut out even the light, effectively letting us know that the conversation was over.

"Apparently not one of Nola's favorite recording stars," I said. "Why don't you turn the radio off? We're almost there anyway."

With a frown in my direction, my mother shut off the radio without question. I wondered if she'd have been so understanding with me at that age, or if all the absent years and the separation of a generation was all that was needed to bridge the mother-daughter abyss. If I ever had children—which was highly doubtful, seeing as how I was thirty-nine and perpetually single—I decided that I'd drop them off on my mother's doorstep when they reached ten and retrieve them again once they were in their twenties.

Amelia found garage parking on Meeting Street and then we walked a couple of blocks to Reid Street, where Alluette's Café was located. The coral-colored restaurant appeared casual yet charming, with a rustic counter bar and a square pass-through behind it to the kitchen, where several people were busily preparing for the lunchtime rush. Above the pass-through was a chalkboard with the day's specials, along with the words HOLISTIC SOUL FOOD AND VEGANS WELCOME. Despite the warning, the list of specials included fresh local fried shrimp that's along with the savory scent of cooking food, made my mouth begin to water. Three large glass canisters filled with what appeared to be chocolate-chip cookies sat on the bar. Organic or not, they looked moist and delicious, and I knew I'd be leaving with at least two to tide me over until dinner.

I turned to see my mother and Amelia greeting a tall, slender blond woman dressed sharply in a navy twill pants outfit with an Hermès scarf knotted around her neck and a younger version of herself standing just inside the doorway.

My mother motioned for Nola and me to approach. Not sure why I was doing so, I put my arm around Nola's shoulders and led her forward. I shook hands with both Cecily and Alston Ravenel, then introduced Nola by gently propelling her in front of me. I watched as both Ravenels took in Nola's boots and choice of clothing, my fists clenching.

Cecily smiled and reached out her hand to Nola. "You are the spitting image of your father, but I'm sure you've heard that."

I looked closely at her, trying to judge her age, which I assumed was probably a few years younger than my own, and wondered whether she'd dated Jack. Most of the female population of Charleston seemed at one time or another to have had some sort of relationship with him. My fingernails were now biting into my palms, and I had to force myself to unclench my hands.

"Your grandmother and Mrs. Middleton have been telling me so much about you that I can't wait to get to know you better." Her smile was warm, her words genuine, and I found myself relaxing. She was either an authentic Charleston lady who kept any negative thoughts to herself, or she really was looking forward to getting to know Nola. Or she'd dated Jack and still had fond memories. I felt like mentally slapping myself to get the image out of my head.

Nola's smile was guarded as she shook Cecily's hand. "It's a pleasure to meet you."

I looked on with surprise, realizing I'd been holding my breath to see how Nola would respond. Obviously, her mama hadn't forgotten her Southern roots, regardless of how far she'd left them behind.

Reaching behind her to grab the blond girl's elbow, Cecily said, "And this is my Alston, who, as I'm sure you've already learned, will be starting eighth grade at Ashley Hall this fall."

Alston reached out a slender, manicured hand, a pearl bracelet circling her wrist. "Hello," she said, her voice so soft that I had to lean forward to hear her. "It's nice to meet you."

As with her mother, there was nothing underlying her comments, and I looked on closely as Nola took Alston's hand and shook it. "Likewise," she said slowly, as if waiting for Alston to pull something out of her Coach bag and hit her on the head with it.

Alston withdrew her hand. "I like your boots," she said softly, and I realized two things right then about Alston Ravenel: She was very shy, and she was also very kind. Or, despite her tailored appearance, had really bad taste in clothing.

"Thanks," said Nola, taking in Alston's Lilly Pulitzer skirt, blouse, and pale yellow cardigan tossed over her shoulders. Even the girl's headband boasted a Lilly print. I was about to pat myself on the back for a successful meet-and-greet when Nola leaned forward. "What kind of name is Alston?"

I held my breath, waiting for Alston's answer. She looked surprised, like nobody had asked her that question before. And, I realized, living in Charleston where everybody recognized the name, they probably hadn't.

Matter-of-factly, she said, "It's a family name on my daddy's side. His great-grandmother was an Alston and I guess he wants everybody to know it. What about Nola? Is that a family name?"

Nola smirked, and I forced myself to keep my hand by my side instead of clamped over Nola's mouth. "Nope. It's a nickname. It stands for New Orleans, Louisiana."

Good, I thought. *Time to stop there.* I watched as the older women began to move away toward our table, hopefully out of earshot.

"That's where I was conceived," Nola continued.

Cecily looked a little shocked, but Alston threw back her head and let out a decidedly unladylike laugh. "That's the funniest thing I've heard in, like, forever." We began to move to our table, the two girls following me. In a quieter voice, Alston said to Nola, "I guess it's a good thing I'm named Alston, because otherwise they might be calling me Four-poster."

Nola let out a loud laugh, causing heads to turn, but I didn't care. It was the first time I'd ever heard her laugh, and I couldn't wait to tell Jack. As I settled in my chair, I felt the old familiar tingling on the back of my neck. Turning my head slightly so no one else would notice, I stared at the front window, where a woman with a sad face was peering into the restaurant. She wore a flowing skirt and a T-shirt, her blond hair long and parted in the middle like a seventies hippie. She was so solid that I'd started to think she was real. But then somebody on the sidewalk walked right through her and she vanished, leaving only a lingering feeling of despair.

I turned back to the table and saw Nola watching me closely, and as we ate our meal, I couldn't help but wonder whether Nola had felt it, too.

CHAPTER 7

I backed myself through the front door of Henderson House Realty, balancing my briefcase and my usual breakfast of a latte with extra whipped cream and bag of chocolate-covered doughnuts. I'd worked at Henderson House for over a decade as a Realtor specializing in historic Charleston real estate, despite the fact that I held firmly to the belief that old houses were little more than money-sucking holes in the middle of an otherwise great lot, and usually filled with enough spirits to keep a person up all night. Assuming you were unlucky enough to have been born with the ability to hear them.

But I was good at what I did, and it paid the bills and kept me in my Louboutins, so I couldn't complain too much. Except when the spirits of the dead got tired of me ignoring them and decided they needed to get my attention.

I carefully made my way through the reception area, intent on making it to my office in the back without spilling anything, when I made an abrupt halt. Slowly retracing my steps, I stopped in front of the receptionist's desk, where the intrepid Nancy Flaherty, receptionist and wannabe golf pro, had sat ever since I'd come to work at Henderson's. There was her golf ball paperweight, golf club bookends, St. Andrews course mouse pad, and T-shaped paper clips all on her desktop, but no sign of Nancy. Instead, in front of the desk on what appeared to be a bright orange yoga mat, sat an attractive woman in her late fifties or early sixties, with white-blond hair and sparkling blue eyes. She sat in an extremely uncomfortable-looking pose, with her legs crossed and her feet on top of the opposite inner thighs and her hands folded as if in prayer.

"Namaste," she said in such a thick Southern accent that I had to think for a long moment before I understood what she'd said.

"Good morning," I said hesitantly. "Where's Nancy?"

The woman unfolded herself from her pose and rose to her full height, which hardly seemed to be much over five feet, if that. "Hi, there," she said, offering her bejeweled hand. "I'm Charlene Rose, and I'm a friend of Nancy's. Yesterday we were playing golf and I accidentally pinged her on the head with a badly timed shot. The doctors say she'll be fine once the stitches come out."

"Stitches? Was she hurt badly?"

"Just three stitches, and I said I'd pay for any plastic surgery if so much as a mark is left on her forehead. But she's okay. I booked her into the Charleston Place hotel and spa for a week so she can recover."

"Great," I said, staring closely at the woman. "Have we met before?" I asked, still wondering why she was there on a yoga mat in the reception area.

She brightened. "I was in a movie once with Demi Moore. I was an extra, actually, but I had a speaking part. They cut all of those scenes out, but I was in a crowd scene at the end. Maybe that's where you saw me."

"Maybe," I said, pausing long enough for her to explain why she was there. And why there was a yoga mat on the floor.

Her gaze traveled to my latte with the towering dollop of cream and the bakery bag with the grease spots on the bottom. "You must be Melanie Middleton."

"Good guess," I said, realizing that if Nancy had felt well enough to prep Charlene, then she must really be okay.

Charlene frowned. "That stuff isn't good for you, you know."

Catching myself before I rolled my eyes, I said, "Why are you here? And why are you doing yoga in the reception area?"

Charlene's bright smile didn't dim a single watt. "I like getting up early to exercise, and Nancy promised me that nobody gets here before nine except for you, and that you didn't mind her chipping practice." She patted the phone that I noticed had been moved to the edge of the desk. "I made sure I could reach it."

I restrained myself from stamping my foot. "But why are you *here?*"

"Oh, I guess I should have explained myself. I'm here as a substitute for Nancy while she's out. She knew I'd be perfect for the job, because she talks about all y'all a lot, so I feel as if we've practically known each other for years. And don't worry about training me. Nancy's already told me everything and I'm a quick study. Plus, I've got Nancy's number on speed dial in case I run into any trouble."

"Well, it's a pleasure to meet you," I said slowly as I began to make my way back to my office. "I don't like . . ."

". . . to be disturbed before nine o'clock, because you need this time to organize your day and your calendars, although I can't see why a person would need more than one. And I'll be happy to pick up your breakfast on the way in each morning. Maybe something healthier. You've got a cute figure now and all, but with what you're eating and your age, you can't expect that to go on forever."

I gritted my teeth and walked a little faster so I wouldn't be forced to dump a hot latte on her.

I was just washing down my last doughnut when my BlackBerry buzzed on my desk. I glanced at the screen and saw Jack's name and cell phone number. I flipped it over so I wouldn't be tempted to answer. I needed to separate myself from him, and speaking with him first thing in the morning was a guaranteed way to make me think about him all day. I'd call him back at one minute past noon, so then I'd have the morning free from thoughts of Jack.

I'd just started my spreadsheet of the day with all of my appointments and bathroom breaks when the office phone on the corner of my desk rang. I hit the speaker button. "Yes, Charlene?"

"It's Jack Trenholm on line one."

My jaw clenched. "I thought you knew that I don't take phone calls before nine."

"But this is Jack. Nancy said that you always take his calls."

I took a calming breath. "No, she's mistaken. I'd really rather not talk to him at all, but especially not first . . ."

I looked up to see Jack standing in the doorway of my office. Speaking into his cell phone, he said, "Thank you, Charlene. You don't need to patch me through. And did I mention how pretty you look in blue?"

I hit the disconnect button at the same time Jack shoved his phone in a back pocket. He looked better than the last time I'd seen him, and

I wondered whether it was because he didn't have the daily stress of dealing with a teenager to age him. Still, there was something in his eyes that didn't quite match his usual self-assured Jack-ness.

Sitting back in my chair, I slid my reading glasses off my desk and into the top drawer. I didn't think I could take one more reference to my age. "Hello, Jack. Lovely to see you, as always."

Without being asked, he came inside and sat down on one of the two comfortable armchairs I had placed in front of my desk for clients. "Likewise. Although I will admit to feeling a little hurt that you've been screening my phone calls."

"Sorry. But some of us have actual jobs that require us to work." I scrutinized him, taking in his chin stubble, his wet hair, his slightly rumpled appearance that I found oddly attractive. "And it's rare to see you awake and mobile at this hour of the morning."

"Maybe I never went to sleep." His eyebrows lifted slightly. I felt a little stir somewhere in the pit of my stomach that I attributed to too much sugar.

I forced myself not to blink. "You must want something if you're here instead of in bed."

He paused just long enough to make sure that my use of the words "bed" and "you" in the same sentence had not gone unnoticed. "I'm on the way to the airport, but I wanted to stop by and show you something first."

"Shouldn't you save all your personal viewings for the TSA guys?"

His only response was another quick raise of his eyebrows before he leaned over to the backpack he'd set on the floor beside him. He unzipped the top, then reached inside to retrieve a small object before placing it in the middle of my desk. I stared at the miniature piece of furniture, so exquisite in its detailing that it looked like the full-size version had been miraculously shrunk.

"What is that?" I asked, resting my chin on the desk so I could examine it more closely.

"When Chad and I moved the dollhouse to your mother's, I noticed this miniature sideboard in the dining room. It looked really familiar, so I borrowed it to show my mother, and I was right."

"About what?"

He pointed at the diamond-shaped inlays on the double-tier top of what appeared to be mahogany wood. "This inlay design is characteristic of Robert Walker. He was a cabinetmaker from Scotland who had a shop here in Charleston. His furniture is very rare and valuable now, and my mother had a very similar piece in her store a few years ago."

I sat back in my chair. "Meaning . . . ?"

"Meaning that if what we're assuming is correct—that the house and its contents were modeled after a real home—then the house was mostly likely in Charleston, and might even still be. That should help us find the original owners and find out whether any of them are still hanging on in the miniature version."

"So no luck tracing previous owners?"

"Not much. Following the sales records, all I've been able to determine so far is that it's been all over the South and spent a year at a house in Boston. The dollhouse doesn't seem to be a favorite with any owner. The longest it's lasted at the same location is a year and a half."

I thought for a moment, remembering the figure of the boy and the broken dog, and could pretty much figure out why nobody wanted to keep the dollhouse for very long. "But if the house it's modeled on is still here, why wouldn't Sophie or I recognize it? Between the two of us, we know every single historic house in Charleston, at least by sight. But not this one."

"Well, assuming it wasn't torn down before the Preservation Society got its teeth into the area, it could be disguised. Over the years owners made changes to make a house seem more modern. We've seen Greek Revivals remade into Victorians and vice versa, depending on the current day's style. Our house could be hiding behind a Georgian pediment, for all we know." He slid the sideboard toward me. "I'll let you have this now so you can put it back before Nola sees that it's missing."

"Good idea," I said. "And speaking of Nola, I learned something interesting this week. We were in the car and that new hit by Jimmy Gordon, 'I'm Just Getting Started,' came on the radio, and Nola got pretty upset. Had us change the station even. Said that she'd met him and she didn't like him."

Jack leaned back in his chair. "Did she say anything more? Like how she'd met him?"

"No, actually. She made it very clear that it was a subject she didn't want to pursue."

He tapped his fingers against the desktop. "She and I need to spend more time together. Maybe while I'm gone you can think of something that a father and daughter could do together that would be fun."

I didn't think it would be helpful to point out to him that I had no frame of reference for that sort of thing. My childhood with my father consisted of me trying to keep him sober, or making sure he at least appeared that way.

Jack continued to look at me, but I could tell that he wasn't really seeing me, and I wondered whether he was thinking about Bonnie. Finally, he said, "In the meantime, I'll do a little checking on Jimmy Gordon. Could be he and Nola met through Bonnie, since she was a songwriter. Would make sense, I guess. It's worth checking out, anyway. Anything to get through to Nola would be a help at this point, since nothing else is working."

His voice sounded full of defeat. I didn't want to, but I found myself feeling sorry for him. "How long will you be gone?" I asked gently.

His eyes brightened, and I could tell that the old Jack was back. "Why? Are you planning on missing me?"

I sighed, all sympathy vanished. "No. I just wanted to know whether I should be the one to check back with your mother about the piece of furniture. If you're off somewhere having fun, I wasn't sure you'd remember to call."

He rested his elbows on the chair arms, steepling his hands in front of him. "I'm going to New York, but not for fun. Unless you'd like to come with me."

Again, something stirred in the general region of my abdomen, and I made a mental note to skip the double cream in my latte next time. "I believe I mentioned that some of us are required to work. And have a teenager at home." I sent him a pointed look as I sat up. I spread my hands on my calendar as an indication that I was ready to get back to work instead of ready to drop everything and join him. Which all of a sudden didn't seem like such a bad idea. "Besides, I don't think Rebecca would like it if you and I took a trip together."

His eyes didn't leave my face. "I said nothing about a romantic getaway with you, Mellie. I was merely implying that you could use some fun, and New York with me would be a great way to experience it. I didn't for one moment believe that you would assume we'd be sharing a room and all that comes with it."

I knew there were flaws in his logic, but I was too busy feeling flustered, because that was *exactly* what I'd been thinking and he knew it. Without dropping my gaze, I reached out to the phone and pressed a button for the receptionist's desk. "Can you get me somebody on the phone? Anybody. It doesn't matter."

Jack smirked as he stood. "Don't worry; I'm leaving. I've already spoken to Nola, so she knows where I am and how to reach me. And you know that I appreciate you taking her in and keeping an eye on her." He lifted his backpack onto his shoulder. "Just let me know if my mother turns up anything."

My boss's voice interrupted my mental struggle to come up with a parting shot at Jack's back. "Melanie? Is that you? I don't really think it's my job to be placing phone calls for you."

I froze, staring at the phone as I realized I'd hit the wrong button. "Sorry, Dave, my mistake," I said in a voice I hoped sounded as groveling as possible. I looked up and saw that Jack had already left, but the sound of his laughter carried down the hall and through my open door.

⤜

I recognized Sophie's new white Prius parked in front of my mother's house on Legare Street. She sat on a curved iron bench in my grandmother's rose garden with her left hand held out in front of her as if catching the sparkle of sunlight through her new ring. An unexpected pang of . . . something hit me hard as I watched her. It wasn't jealousy, I knew. I was truly happy for her and Chad and really only wondered what had taken them so long to figure out how perfect they were for each other. I walked quicker, not wanting to have the time to examine my feelings more closely, afraid that the source might be more about lost opportunities and the passing of time.

"Hi, Sophie. Were we supposed to be meeting? I don't remember seeing it on my calendars."

She quickly placed her hand in her lap, then shook her head, her wild, unruly curls held off of her face at random intervals with several multihued scrunchies. "Nope. Was driving by and decided to stop in and see if you were home. Your mom and dad said I could wait. They were on their way to SNOB for dinner and then a movie, and told me to tell you that you don't have to wait up."

"Where's Nola?"

"With her grandparents. They were invited to a Lowcountry boil at the Ravenels' house out on Sullivan's Island, and their granddaughter, Alston, invited Nola. They'll bring her back, but it will be late. I have no idea who any of these people are—I'm just repeating what your mother told me. Said it would save her a phone call to you, since she was already running late for her date." Sophie's eyes widened. "I didn't know a woman in her sixties could get away with a plunging neckline, but your mother sure can carry it off."

I didn't want to think about my mother dressing up for a man—my father, no less—so I quickly changed the subject. "Can I sit?"

She moved over to her side of the bench and I settled myself next to her, dropping my briefcase on the ground. "So what did you want to see me about?"

She held up her left hand, the sun making the diamond on her fourth finger shoot sparks of light through all of its prisms. "This."

"Oh." I smiled. "It's beautiful."

"Amelia helped Chad pick it out. You know how big he is on recycling, and he thought an estate piece made more sense than buying something new." She stared down at the antique setting in the platinum band, the intricate design around the round diamond unusual and marking the piece as an antique. "I think it's beautiful just because it's mine, but I'm not really good at being able to tell if something's *actually* beautiful, you know?"

I tried to reply with a straight face. "Yeah, I've noticed." I took her hand to move the ring in the light. "But it really is stunning. Chad— and Amelia—did a fabulous job."

She placed her other hand over mine and squeezed. "I'm sorry I didn't tell you before. I really did want you to be the first to know. Things just sort of . . . got out of hand."

"Yeah, I figured. I'm not upset—not anymore."

Sophie sat back and looked at me. "Really? Because you still have that pinched look around your mouth."

"That what?"

"You know, that look you get when you have an unexpected visitor you hadn't planned on, or some task on your spreadsheet takes longer than it should and messes up everything that follows. Or when you see Jack and Rebecca together. That look."

I concentrated on making my face neutral. "I'm sure I don't know what you're talking about. But I *am* happy for you and Chad. I knew you were made for each other the minute I saw him. I mean, you're both vegans, and he likes the way you dress. Believe me, he's one of a kind."

Sophie elbowed me. "Yeah, I know." Serious again, she said, "I'm glad you're okay with it, because I wanted to ask you if you'd be my maid of honor."

The unmistakable pinpricks of tears threatened my eyes. I blinked hard and forced myself to look stern. "That would depend."

"On what?" Sophie said, her expression guarded.

"On who's picking out the bridesmaids' dresses."

She tossed back her head and laughed. "Oh, gosh, Melanie. You had me worried there for a moment. Like that would matter."

"I'm serious. I won't wear gauze, or tie-dye, or anything with beading. And definitely no hemp."

Sophie threw her arms around me in a tight hug. "You're the best, Melanie. I'm sure we can find something we both like. But just so you understand, we want it to be outside so everybody can come barefoot."

I nodded slowly, holding back from saying what I really thought of the idea. It was Sophie's wedding, after all, and if she wanted me to walk down an aisle barefoot and swinging incense, it was her call. And if I ever got married, I would simply pay her back by making her wear a hoop-skirted taffeta confection with her hair tucked into a neat chignon.

"Sure. Whatever you want. It's your wedding. Let me know if you need any help. I'm pretty good at organizing things."

Her eyes widened, and it took her a moment before she could come up with an answer. "Thanks, Melanie. I'll keep that in mind. Although

I don't think I'll need much organizing. It's going to be a small wedding—just family and friends. But I'll be sure to let you know if we need any spreadsheets."

I patted her knee and stood. "You do that." I looked up at the empty house. Not that long ago, I had relished my solitary existence: coming and going as I wanted, enjoying the quiet and solitude of an empty house. Now it just seemed . . . well . . . lonely. I looked down at Sophie. "Want to come watch *Glee* with me? I've seen a few episodes with Nola, because she made me, and it's kind of addictive."

Sophie stood, too. "Thanks, but Chad's cooking a vegan lasagna tonight. You could join us, but I know you'd go home hungry and have to raid Mrs. Houlihan's pantry."

"Yeah. That's all right. Maybe General Lee will watch with me."

Impulsively, Sophie hugged me again. "Thanks for agreeing to be my maid of honor. You know I'd do the same for you."

"Don't hold your breath," I said as I pulled away and headed for the front steps under the imposing double-tiered portico.

I could hear the smile in Sophie's voice. "And I promise not to tell anybody you watch *Glee*. I think that would turn off more prospective clients than telling them you see dead people."

I smirked at her retreating back, watching her for a moment as she approached her car, probably already anticipating her romantic evening with Chad and vegan lasagna. I almost called back to her that I'd changed my mind, but stopped myself. They were engaged and probably wouldn't welcome a third wheel, regardless of how much they said they wouldn't mind.

I entered the foyer and breathed in the old-house smell that I'd grown to love, along with the smell of boxwoods and lemon oil. They were comforting scents that must have been familiar to the generations of my family who'd lived in this house before me. The scents no longer brought to mind the alarming sound of money being sucked out the windows and chimneys. Lately I'd discovered that instead they made me think of how lucky I really was. Not that I would ever admit that out loud, of course.

After kicking off my heels and placing them neatly on the steps to carry upstairs when I went, I placed my briefcase next to my grandmother's desk in the parlor. I was halfway through the foyer on the way to the kitchen when I heard an odd whimpering, followed by a scratching sound. I paused, wondering whether I'd imagined it, then heard it again. *General Lee.*

In my bare feet I raced up the stairs, taking them two at a time, automatically heading down the hall in the direction of Nola's bedroom. I found the dog standing in front of the closed door, his plumed tail—usually curled above his back—now tucked between his hind legs. As I approached, he whimpered again, then raised a front paw and scratched at the door.

I knelt down and he leaped into my outstretched arms. I hugged him to me, surprised at my relief at finding him safe. I did *not* like dogs. I wasn't prepared to take the first step on the road to becoming one of those old spinster women who lived alone but with a thousand pets.

I buried my face in his soft fur. "Are you okay, sweetness? Mommy's here." I looked around, just to make sure nobody was listening. I turned my attention to the door, wondering whether the strip of light beneath the door had become brighter.

The doorknob turned in my hand, and I pushed the door open, staying safely in the hallway. I listened as the door struck the doorstop on the wall behind it, icy cold air hitting my face.

The large windows on the facing wall were all thrown wide-open, allowing inside the warm late-afternoon air. Buttery light from the lowering sun crept like long fingers across the wood floor and four-poster bed, across the putrid rug, and toward the dollhouse that now dominated the far corner of the room.

Once again the dollhouse family, minus the son and the dog, stood crowded at the turret window. I stepped forward and General Lee began to whimper again. I put my hand on the back of his head so he wouldn't jump out of my arms and hurt himself. And personally, I didn't really want to be alone at that moment.

I looked around the floor for the two missing figures, even knelt down to see whether either one had rolled under Nola's bed. I was just about to shut the windows when I spotted them. They were standing on the antique captain's chest that was used as a bench seat under the windows. I could see the lines of dried glue where I'd reattached both sides of the dog's skull and fixed the boy's neck.

A strong breeze blew into the windows, although the trees outside weren't moving. Then, one by one, each window shut as if a person moved down the line, closing them in succession.

I swallowed. It was always easier when they approached me first. And if they didn't, I ignored them and then they usually went away. But this was Nola's room, and I had no idea who this spirit or spirits were. I couldn't just let them be.

"Hello?" I said, my voice cracking. "Hello?" I said again, more forcefully. I could see my breath as I spoke, my lips and teeth cold.

I heard the flutter of paper and turned around to where Bonnie's guitar case had fallen open, a stack of sheet music in a heap on the floor in front of it. The pages shook and shimmied as if somebody were thumbing through them.

"Bonnie?"

The rustling stopped just as the radio on the night table turned on, the volume set as loud as it could go. I recognized Jimmy Gordon's "I'm Just Getting Started." I quickly walked toward the bed and flipped off the radio, the sound of my thudding heart filling the void.

"Bonnie?" I said again, but the room had already begun to warm up again and I knew that she was gone.

General Lee managed to leap from my arms to the bed, and then off the bed and out the door as fast as he could go.

I stared at the kaleidoscope of colors in the room, the contrast with the nineteenth-century furniture, and felt the press of years enveloped in the room push down on me. A heavy sigh filled the space as I backed myself toward the doorway, and I wasn't sure whether it was mine. "Never mind," I said to the empty room, then closed the door on its ghosts.

CHAPTER 8

My eyes flickered open. A narrow strip of gray eked its way through the tall, dark drapes and I lay still, wondering why I wasn't in my bedroom in my house on Tradd Street. Then I remembered the crumbling foundation and yet another forced evacuation, and I allowed my eyes to flutter closed again. Until I realized that General Lee wasn't on the pillow next to me, and that the noise I'd heard that must have awakened me was the sound of footsteps outside my door.

I bolted upright, straining to hear anything out of the ordinary. Not that there was a lot on that list under the "historic Charleston home" heading. If your house didn't pop, groan, creak, or moan, it just wasn't old enough. I grabbed my robe from the foot of the bed, then slid my feet into the fluffy slippers and made my way into the darkened hallway.

Nola's door was open, and when I peeked inside I saw that the room was empty and, fortunately, quiet, with all windows shut. Even the guitar was behaving itself and resting silently in the corner like a guitar should be. I squelched a gnawing worry as I headed for the stairs, noticing my mother's bedroom door was closed at the same time I caught the scent of my father's cologne. I focused on not tripping on my robe as I descended the stairs, wondering what was the least awful thought to contemplate—a missing teenager or one's parents sharing a bed. As I pushed open the kitchen door, I still wasn't sure.

Like the rest of the house, the kitchen was dark, with lonely shards of light from the outside streetlamps stealing inside the tall windows. Slivered fingers of gray touched the stainless-steel appliances and the newly restored mantel of the fireplace that had hidden a room behind it for two centuries. The room was emptied now of all its secrets and, I had thought, its ghosts.

I heard a slight rustling sound and my eyes scanned the far wall. "Wilhelm?" I whispered the name of my protector, a Hessian soldier whom I thought I'd sent to the light a month before. I sniffed the air, expecting to smell the unmistakable scent of gunpowder that surrounded his apparition. I stopped abruptly, recognizing a completely different smell instead. *Sugar?*

Without turning around, I stuck my hand out behind me and flipped on the light switch. The overhead canned lights and pendants over the island shone brightly, illuminating the granite countertops, polished floors, and Nola and General Lee sitting on the floor in front of the pantry door with a package of powdered doughnuts opened between them. Both wore identical guilty expressions and equally matching patches of powdered sugar on their faces.

Relief at finding them both safe overrode my surprise. I knelt on the floor and patted my knees for General Lee to come to me. With a reluctant look back at Nola, he slowly walked over to me and allowed me to pick him up. As I brushed the powdered sugar off of his muzzle, I looked more closely at Nola and saw tearstains on her cheeks, leaking into the sugar encrusted on her lips and chin.

As a child the one thing I'd hated the most was to be caught crying. If I'd wanted people to see my tears and ask me what was bothering me, I would have stood in the middle of the street and screamed out how unfair it was to have a mother who didn't want me.

"Don't worry; I won't tell anybody you're eating refined sugar," I said, scratching General Lee under his chin. Lowering my voice as if I were speaking in a confessional, I added, "I actually had some of Chad's vegan lasagna that Sophie brought over for you, and it was pretty good. But I will deny it with my last breath if you tell them."

I turned around and put General Lee on the floor. "But before you put those doughnuts back in the pantry, take a couple out and sit down at the table."

With a loud groan, Nola slid up the refrigerator to a stand and did as I asked and plopped two doughnuts on a clean plate Mrs. Houlihan had left in the dish drain. I took two glasses out of a glass-fronted cabinet, then removed two cartons of milk from the fridge—one soy and one regular—and filled each glass nearly to the brim.

I put a glass in front of Nola at the table, then sat across from her, reaching for my doughnut at the same time. I took a bite and chewed slowly, hopefully giving Nola a chance to talk. But she said nothing. Taking a chance, I said, "The house makes a lot of noises at night, doesn't it? I hope it's not keeping you awake."

She shrugged, and I noticed her oversize T-shirt from a Rush concert in 1993. *Bonnie.* I knew then that her sitting on the floor in a dark kitchen and crying wasn't because of something like being scared in an old house or being lonely or misunderstood. Her mother had abandoned her in the most permanent, irrevocable way possible. It was hard to accept and understand that from the perspective of a grown woman, and I couldn't begin to understand how a thirteen-year-old would try to wrap her head around it. I kept remembering the glimpses I'd had of Bonnie, and the lingering despair she left behind, and I knew there was much more to her story.

"Are you missing your mom?" I ventured.

Nola slid her plate across the table, her doughnut untouched, and looked away, but not before I saw her lower lip trembling. I almost told her then: that I kept seeing her mother and that if I kept trying, I might be able to get her to talk to me. But reason intervened; it was still too early, and if I ever wanted her to trust me, now didn't seem to be the time to make her think that I might be mentally unstable and delusional.

Her voice was so quiet that when she did speak I thought for a moment that I was imagining it. "I sometimes hear her playing her songs on her guitar, like she's still here. Do you think that means I'm crazy?"

I tried not to shake my head too vigorously. "No. Not at all." I thought for a moment, wondering whether I'd ever seen eyes that sad before. "I think it means that you miss her, and you're holding on to the thing you both loved—the music. You know, Ashley Hall has a wonderful music program. Maybe if you got involved . . ." I stopped, the thunderous look on her face telling me I'd gone too far.

General Lee walked over to Nola's chair and hoisted himself up on his hind legs, placing his front paws on her leg. His face had that pathetic-cute expression he must spend hours practicing in a mirror that's impossible to deny. I watched as Nola scowled at him before emitting a put-upon sigh and picking him up. She cradled him in her arms, and I saw some of the tension leave her shoulders. I'd give the dog an extra treat later.

With her face buried in his fur, she said, "My mom didn't want me, and neither does my dad."

I was completely out of my league here; this wasn't a real estate negotiation, or an exclusive listing, or a counteroffer—all things I was competent at. All things that required hard bottom lines and no emotions. I was as out of place and unprepared here at my mother's kitchen table as I would have been taking over for the pope in Rome.

I closed my eyes, wishing Sophie were there. She always knew the right thing to say. Instead I found myself channeling my mother and repeating something she had said to me, a truth I was still discovering, tasting it slowly like a long-simmered soup. "Sometimes we have to do the right thing even if it means letting go of the one thing we love most in the world."

Nola looked up at me with red-rimmed eyes. "Are you saying she was right to kill herself?"

I shook my head, still not fully understanding my mother's words, but at least knowing what they *hadn't* meant. "No." I tried hard to visualize this conversation as a list of to-do items, making sure that nothing was left off. It's how I got through my life, and I had no other resource. "I'm saying she must have thought she had no other choice." Again, my thoughts wandered to my own mother's explanation of why she'd left me all those years ago. Feeling relief and gratitude toward her for this unexpected guidance, I said, "She must have believed somehow that you would be better off without her."

Nola ducked her head back into the dog's neck. "Then why would she leave me with . . . him?" She spit out the last word, not even willing to say Jack's name.

I found myself in the unusual position of having to defend Jack. But I felt I was on solid ground here with my advice, because my father and

I had gone through the same awkward dance when he recently decided to become a part of my life after decades of emotional absence. "He's a good person, Nola. And I know he loves you. He just has no idea how to be a father right now—you need to give each other time as you get used to this situation."

"He abandoned us. My mother told me that. That he knew about me, and still didn't want me."

If a heart could physically break, I was pretty sure mine would be lying on the kitchen table in a thousand pieces. I gave up on my mental spreadsheet and list, knowing they would be of no help to me here, and instead leaned back in my chair. At least I had the truth on my side, and that was something.

"I don't know why your mother said that, and I'm sure she had her reasons. But your father would never have abandoned you if he'd known about you. And he wants to do the right thing now, if you'd just give him a chance. He's annoying and pigheaded, sure, and used to getting his way."

I was rewarded with a small twitch of her lips.

"But," I continued, "he's also kind and caring. And he understands his responsibilities." I narrowed my eyes at her. "And if you tell him I said those nice things about him, I will force you to wear a lime green skort and lacy white blouse. With matching green Keds. I have that exact outfit in my closet, so it wouldn't be that hard."

She pretended to shudder. "My mother wouldn't lie to me. She wouldn't."

Despite the determination in her words, I heard the question in them, too, and I felt encouraged enough to press forward. "He wants to do something fun—like a father-daughter outing. So you can get to know each other. I was thinking maybe a kayaking excursion in Charleston Harbor. There's an outfit on Shem Creek that takes groups and does a saltwater tour."

She contemplated the ceiling for a long moment. Finally, she said, "Whatever. But can I bring a friend?"

I knew that wasn't what Jack had intended, but at least it was a place to start. "Sure," I said. "Which friend?"

She gave me a look apparently meant to make me feel like the stupidest person on the planet. She succeeded. "I've only got one. Alston Ravenel."

I remembered the shy Alston with the infectious laugh and good sense of humor. Smiling, I said, "Sure. Give her call. Your dad gets back from New York tomorrow, so how about Saturday?"

Nola sighed heavily, as if speaking to me were taking a great effort. "Nobody calls anybody anymore. They text, or Facebook, but they definitely don't call. That's so 2000."

I contemplated her for a long moment, wondering how many blows my ego could take before holding up a white flag. "I didn't know you had a cell phone."

"I don't." She looked pointedly at me.

Feeling a little more secure in adult territory, I said, "I'll be happy to talk to your dad about it—that's his decision, not mine. In the meantime, you can use the good old-fashioned house phone. Call your grandmother if you don't have the number."

"Whatever," she said again, but made no move to get up. She chewed on her lower lip while I waited, hoping whatever it was she had to say wouldn't make me feel any more inadequate. Finally, she said, "Does Jack drink?"

Her question took me by surprise. Jack was a recovering alcoholic, and had, in fact, been my father's AA sponsor the previous year. But I thought Jack should be the one to tell Nola. "Not anymore," I answered, hoping that would be the end of it.

"Because when I was staying with him, he bought a six-pack of beer and then the next day I saw him smash each of the full bottles in the sink. He'd been leaving messages for somebody all day—I think somebody in New York—and nobody was calling him back, so I think he was pretty pissed." She paused, as if deciding whether she should tell me more. Slowly, she said, "My mom's boyfriend—two boyfriends ago—used to smash the bottles when my mom brought home booze. He was trying to keep her clean. I think that's why she broke up with him."

Something hard and heavy formed in the pit of my stomach, but I forced my expression to remain neutral. I was worried about Jack, and what would have made him buy beer after he'd been sober for so long. But the sick feeling came from listening to Nola, and how easily she used words like "keeping clean" and "booze." She was only thirteen years old, but as I stared at her across the kitchen table with her face scrubbed clean and the multiple earrings removed from her ears—something Sophie, of all people, had suggested—Nola looked like what she was: a scared and lonely child.

"I appreciate your telling me." I took a deep breath. "I think your dad's going through a tough time right now, but I'll make sure that he won't go it alone, okay?" I had no idea what I was actually promising, but I knew I had to reassure her that at least one parent would be a stable anchor for her.

I watched as the sky through the window behind her began to pinken. "Why don't you try to go back to bed? I'm going to go ahead and get dressed and get to the office early. I think my mother said something about taking you in for a haircut. . . ." My words trailed off as I heard the distinct sound of a man speaking quietly.

With my fingers held to my lips, I stood and darted for the light switch, then turned off the overhead lights.

"Good night, Ginny," came the loud and definitely masculine whisper from the foyer.

"Sh!" came an equally loud reply from upstairs. "Don't wake up Mellie or Nola. You'll know we'll never hear the end of it."

"Sorry. I just think I'm a little too old to be sneaking around like a teenager in heat."

Something clattered on the marble floor.

"Ouch! What was that for?" My father's annoyed whisper was louder than his usual speaking voice.

"You forgot your belt. I don't want Mellie finding it in my room. Now go before the sun is up and the neighbors see you."

"Can I see you tonight?"

"Only if you leave right now."

"Ginny?"

"Yes?"

"I still love you."

"Go."

There was a long silence, followed eventually by the sound of the dead bolt on the front door turning, and then the door closing softly.

I looked at Nola in the brightening gloom, her cheeks red, her eyes sparkling. "Ew," she said.

"Ew," I spit out, before we both dissolved into smothered laughter that erased, at least for a while, all the sadness the predawn hours had laid open.

CHAPTER 9

I paused outside my bedroom door, still wrestling with the clasp on my necklace, listening to the faint sound of music. At first I thought I was hearing the radio, until I realized the sound was coming from the bathroom, with the hum of water from the shower as the backdrop. Nola's bathroom had another entrance into the hallway, and I moved to stand in front of it to listen more closely.

I noticed the melody of the song first, haunting and lyrical, one of those songs that stays with you long after it's over. Then I noticed the voice singing it. If I hadn't known who was behind the door, I would have thought an angel had somehow decided to take up residence in my mother's house.

Leaning against the doorjamb, I closed my eyes and allowed the notes and the words to fill my head. The doorbell rang and I jerked myself away from the door, embarrassed to find my eyes moist, the heartbreak in Nola's voice real enough for me to feel it. Glancing at my watch, I realized that it must be Alston, and she was exactly five minutes early. I knew there was a reason I liked the girl.

I opened the front door and Alston stood there wearing cute plaid walking shorts, a pale pink polo shirt, pearls around her neck, and her hair in a high ponytail. "Good morning, Miss Middleton. I hope I'm not too early. It's a bad habit, but I hate being late."

Her smile faded a bit as she took in my own outfit. Thinking I might have dropped powdered sugar down the front of my shirt, I looked down and cringed. We wore nearly identical outfits, right down to the white Keds and plaid shorts, except my plaid was in darker hues of green and blue, whereas hers were in pale yellows and pinks. I laughed as I opened the door a little wider and ushered her inside. "I guess we both got the same memo, didn't we?"

"That's for sure." She looked around. "Is Nola ready?"

"No. And Mr. Trenholm isn't here yet, either. Can I get you something to eat or drink while we wait?"

"Actually, I wanted to see Nola's dollhouse. She keeps telling me about it and I've been dying to see it."

"Sure," I said, leading her toward the stairs. "She's still in the bathroom getting ready, so we won't be in her way."

I tapped on the bedroom door and, when I didn't hear anything, turned the handle and stuck my head inside to find the room empty. Turning back to Alston, I said, "Give me just a minute to make sure the coast's clear." I picked my way across the floor to the connecting bathroom door and knocked. "Nola?"

The shower stopped. "What?"

"Alston's here and she wants to see the dollhouse. Is it okay if I bring her in?"

"Whatever. I have all my stuff in here. Just don't mess anything up."

I looked behind me. Nola didn't have a lot, but what she did have was strewn from one end of her room to the other, as if the laundry basket in her closet, or drawers and hangers, didn't exist. "All right," I said. "But hurry up. You have reservations at nine and the excursion won't wait."

As I made my way back to the bedroom door, I kicked clothes to the side to create a walking path to the dollhouse. "The coast's clear," I called out to Alston.

At first glance, everything appeared to be normal, assuming "normal" was a word that could be used to describe this particular dollhouse. The girl figure was poised at an upstairs window with a miniature telescope, the father at a desk in the library. I had to look hard to find the boy, eventually locating him in what appeared to be an upstairs nursery, sitting on the floor in front of a mini replica of the dollhouse. A china-faced doll sat on the floor beside him, and a tiny silver tea set was on a table nearby.

A quiet voice came from behind me. "Did you and Mrs. Middleton decorate Nola's room?" Alston asked, a polite smile stuck to her face.

I thought for a moment to torment her and tell her that it was our pride and joy, but I just wasn't that convincing as a liar. "Oh, gosh, no. We just haven't had the chance to redo it yet. But Nola seems to like it."

Relief passed over her delicate features. "It's not my taste, but I can see why it appeals to Nola. She likes a lot of bright colors, doesn't she? Probably because she grew up in LA. From what I've heard, things are a lot more colorful there."

I was about to suggest a future career in diplomacy when Alston reached inside the dollhouse to the parents' bedroom. "Why is the mother facedown in the bed and covered up like that?" she asked as she pulled the mother out and sat her in the wing-backed chair by the fireplace.

"Maybe she was tired," I said, striving for a light tone.

Alston picked up the dog that had been hiding behind a sofa in the front parlor and brought him up to the mother to place him at her feet. "Nola said that sometimes she dreams about these people, but they're real in her dreams. And they tell her where they want to be placed in the house."

I looked at her with alarm, wondering whether she and Nola understood just how odd that was. "Must be that vegan diet," I said, interjecting a hollow laugh.

"Maybe." She stood and frowned. "I really want to see the front. Nola said it looks like a real house."

I stood, too. "It's too heavy for us to move, but there should be enough room for you to slip between it and the wall to get a good look."

With her back to the wall, Alston slid behind the house. "This is amazing," she said, her eyes brightening. "I thought the rooms and the furniture looked real—but this is awesome." A light crease formed between her eyebrows. "Actually, there's something really familiar about it."

"Really?" I said. "You recognize it?"

She shook her head. "Not exactly. But still . . . I don't know. It's like I know this house from somewhere, but not this exact thing, you know?"

I tried to keep my voice steady. "If you think of it, would you let me know? I'm . . . curious who these people might have been and who the dollhouse belonged to."

"Sure," she said, giving me an odd look. She slid out from behind the house just as Nola opened the bathroom door. She'd apparently had a hairstyling lesson from Sophie, and her beautiful dark waves were bound on top of her head with an assortment of brightly hued barrettes. She had been paring down her makeup little by little and now wore only a bit of eyeliner—in brown, not black—and mascara. I'd like to think that it was because she was learning from my mother and me how to properly accentuate one's features with makeup instead of obliterating them, but I think it had more to do with using the time to sleep. She kept on insisting that she was meant to sleep until noon, no matter how many times I had to pull her out of bed several hours earlier than her target.

Her clothes were still a hodgepodge of mismatched styles, colors, and patterns, and I kept waiting for her to tone that down, too. Surely it was only a matter of time before she realized that she wasn't doing herself any favors. Then again, there was Sophie. Her inability to dress appropriately hadn't seemed to hold her back any. Today Nola had chosen a simple torn white T-shirt and long, ripped denim shorts to go kayaking in. Her feet were bare, so there was still hope she'd wear something other than combat boots or high-top Converse sneakers.

"Hi, Alston." She gave a small wave to her friend. She stopped when she spotted me, her eyes going from me to Alston, then back again. "Really? What did you two do—rob a J.Crew store?"

The doorbell rang. "That must be your dad," I said. "I'll go down to let him in while you finish getting dressed, then come down. You don't want to be late."

As I turned to leave the room, I noticed that the dollhouse mother had somehow returned to her bed and was lying facedown in her sheets. I glanced at Alston, hoping she wouldn't notice.

Jack appeared the same as he had the last time I'd seen him, except he was freshly shaved and was wearing khaki shorts and a collared golf shirt. His bare feet were clad in Top-Siders. I looked behind him on the porch. "Where's Rebecca?"

"Don't get me started," he said, brushing past me. "She said I'd promised to take her furniture shopping, but I thought she'd understand that an outing with Nola might be more important."

"Sorry to borrow a word from your daughter, but 'duh.' Of course it is."

His eyes darkened as he regarded me. Quietly, he said, "I knew you'd say that."

I swallowed thickly. "But those are two-person kayaks, and Alston's already here."

He looked pointedly at me. "Do you have plans this morning?"

I'd anticipated a quiet morning to organize my closet, something I hadn't had a chance to do yet since moving in. And the grout in my bathroom wasn't as white as I'd like, and I'd planned to attack it with an old toothbrush and bleach. Neither of which would constitute "plans" to Jack.

"Not really," I said. "But I don't like deep water."

"You'll be wearing a life jacket."

"But what if it falls off?"

He grinned his trademark grin, as effective as him picking me up and putting me in the kayak. "I'll be there to save you."

I was working on my next protest when Nola and Alston came down the stairs, their physical appearances as different from each other as possible, but both of them moving with the same lanky stroll, with arms and legs that seemed too long for them.

"Good morning, Nola." Jack smiled, a different smile from what I was used to. It was a genuine smile not intended to charm or coerce—I could tell by the way the corners of his eyes wrinkled—but there was uncertainty in it, too. And that was one thing I'd never seen.

Alston stepped forward and offered her hand. I wanted to say that I'd never seen such a mature teenager, but I knew I had been just like that at an even earlier age. At least in my case it was because I knew at least one person in my family needed to be an adult.

"Good morning, Mr. Trenholm. I'm Alston Ravenel. My mother told me to say hi. We both love your books."

"Your mother?"

"Cecily Ravenel, but you probably knew her when she was still Cecily Gibbes."

Both eyebrows rose as a secret grin crossed his face. "Ah, yes. CeCe Gibbes. I remember her well." He paused, my imagination filling in the empty space. "Please give her my best. And before you go home this afternoon, remind me to send you back with an autographed copy of my latest book."

"Oh, we already have that one—the one about Napoleon, right? We're waiting for the new one. When will that be out?"

Jack's face hardened almost imperceptibly. "That would be the million-dollar question. I've just come back from New York asking the same thing. Unfortunately, I still don't have an answer, but I promise you that as soon as it comes out, I'll send over a copy."

Alston beamed. "Thanks, Mr. Trenholm. I can't wait to tell my mother."

Jack turned his attention to his daughter. "I'm looking forward to today. It'll be fun." He looked at her pale arms, exposed in the white T-shirt with the torn-off sleeves. "Do you have sunscreen? It'll be hot out on the water, and the reflection will make you burn that much faster."

She looked up at the ceiling as if asking for divine guidance. "It's a little too late for trying to play daddy, don't you think?"

Before he had to come up with a response, I walked over to an insulated bag I'd prepared and left on a hall chair. "I've got sunscreen and some snacks in here, so not to worry. I'm sure Nola knows she needs to protect her skin. I also stuck in two golf visors Nancy gave me to shade their faces."

Nola looked at me in horror. "Not the ones with 'Fighting Cocks' on them, right? There's no *way* I'm wearing that word on my head."

I looked pointedly at the T-shirt she wore, with a disembodied fist making the horn sign demonstrating that she couldn't be *that* particular about signage on her clothing.

Jack looked offended. "Everybody here knows the University of South Carolina's Fighting Cocks. Now, I wouldn't go to New York or Los Angeles wearing that on your head, but here it's pretty much mandatory. Even your mom had a T-shirt or two."

Nola scowled. "And look where that got her." She brushed past us and out the door.

Jack stared after her for a long moment, and I figured he must have been trying to get the look of desperation out of his eyes, because only a little bit remained when he turned back to me. "We'll wait out on the porch while you're getting changed."

"Actually, I'm ready to go."

"Like that?"

I tucked in my chin. "What's wrong with what I'm wearing?"

I knew he wanted to make a comment about my shorts not being short enough, but there were two minors within earshot, luckily. Instead, he said, "You're wearing pearls."

Indicating Alston, I pointed out, "She's wearing them, too."

Alston nodded. "Mama says that a lady doesn't wear diamonds until after five o'clock unless it's her engagement ring. It's still morning. Besides, a lady's perspiration actually polishes the pearls, so it's good for them."

We both looked at Jack as if that should be enough of an explanation.

When it appeared that he couldn't argue with that sound bit of logic, I hoisted the insulated bag and put the strap over my shoulder. "I put a few extra pairs of those pedicure flip-flops in the bag just in case anybody needed waterproof footwear or if they got their sneakers wet."

I was relieved to see a flash of humor return to Jack's eyes. "You're like a soccer mom. It's kinda scary."

"I like being organized and prepared. Wish there were more people like me."

"God forbid," Jack muttered as he took the insulated bag and held open the door for Alston and me.

~

We stood on the dock behind the kayak rental at Shem Creek with white streaks of sunscreen striping our cheeks and arms. Alston had been the one to convince Nola that she needed it, and I'd had to do the same thing with Jack. I pointed out that he should be a good example to Nola, and that was all the coercing I'd needed to do. Apparently the apple didn't fall far from the Trenholm family tree.

The man assigned as our guide, Lew, began handing out the bright orange life vests to the people on the dock, assessing the kayakers for size with practiced eyes. There were several groups bunched together to get outfitted before going on their respective tours, and I had somehow managed to end up at the rear of the line. When Lew reached me, he paused. "We're out of adult vests, but I think this children's one should fit you."

I heard a snort behind me, and I turned to find both Nola and Jack smirking at me. Alston had the decency to look away as if she hadn't just overheard that humiliating exchange. I grabbed the offensive life jacket and put it on, trying to remember what Lew had told us about how to fasten all the straps correctly.

"Can I help?"

Even though Jack's eyes were partially hidden behind sunglasses, I imagined I could see them laughing. "No. I think I'd rather it fall off and me drown, thanks."

"Suit yourself." He moved over to Alston and Nola, who'd done a pretty good job of strapping themselves in, and Jack just had to tighten and test the snugness and fastenings. When he turned back to me, I'd managed to converge all the straps into the front in one massive knot.

"Still don't want my help?"

I looked around for Lew, but he was busy with a couple of newlyweds who'd somehow managed—intentionally or not—to attach their life jackets together. Giving one last ineffectual tug at the knot, I said, "Go ahead. But if it falls off I'm claiming in the lawsuit that it was intentional."

Softly, so I was the only one who could hear him, he said, "It's not a life jacket I'd want to make fall off, Mellie. Now come stand a little closer so I can fix this for you. I promise I won't bite."

We stood facing each other, practically nose-to-nose, as he fiddled with the straps on my jacket. I could feel his breath on my face, and the heat of his body, and for an awful moment thought that I might actually swoon. As soon as he was finished I backed away, wondering whether I might already be in menopause to at least explain the powerful hot flash I'd just experienced.

"Thanks," I said quickly, as I began to make my way to the line where everybody was being handed oars. I stood next to Alston. "So I guess it's you and me, since it's two to a boat."

"No way," said Nola. "I'm going with Alston. You get to go with my dad."

I sneaked a sidewise glance at Jack to see whether he looked hurt, but his expression remained relaxed. I assumed his military training had prepared him for dealing with a teenager assault.

"Fine," he said with a smile. "Your loss. It's a well-known fact that I can't go anywhere on the water without dolphins swimming right up to me. Apparently they love me."

"Really?" Alston asked as she prepared to get into their kayak.

Nola sent her friend a disdainful look. "Please. My mom told me that men will make up anything to impress you." She accepted the guide's hand and stepped into the back of the kayak.

Alston looked at Jack, who just shrugged, as she sat on the front seat and gripped her oar.

Jack took my arm and led me to the next-loading boat. "You sit up front. Just be careful getting in. I wouldn't want you to fall in the water, because I can't swim."

I looked back at him in alarm, only to see him grinning broadly. Wanting to wipe it off his face, I said, "I hope my oar doesn't accidentally slip out of the water and knock you overboard. I'd never see your body floating away."

There were only four kayaks in our small group, one with the guide and the last one with the newlyweds, who seemed oblivious to everything but each other. We headed out into Charleston Harbor, where we could see Fort Sumter looming like a mirage off in the distance.

"What's that?" Nola asked, pointing to the Civil War landmark.

Jack answered. "That's Fort Sumter, where the first shots of the War of Northern Aggression were fired."

"The what?"

Alston tried to hide her smile as Jack explained. "It's what the rest of the world calls the Civil War. In polite Charleston society, it can also be called 'the Late Unpleasantness.'"

Nola frowned until Alston said, "He's joking, Nola. We haven't called it that for at least fifteen years."

Nola rolled her eyes and firmly gripped her oar. The girls struggled a bit at first, unsure as to how much strength each one was putting into each stroke of the oar, or what direction they needed to turn. They ended up ramming into our kayak a couple of times, and I couldn't tell whether it was intentional or not. They hit the newlyweds and the guide only once each. But each time, Jack calmly offered suggestions, coaching them in a gentle and helpful way that even I couldn't find fault with. After the first few scowls, Nola began to accept her father's instructions, and soon the girls were commanding their kayak on their own with very few mishaps.

Watching their struggles made me notice how easily Jack and I controlled our own kayak. We slid smoothly through the water, instinctively knowing when and how much to push, when to turn right or left, when to speed up or slow down. I only hoped Jack hadn't noticed it, too.

"We've got a great rhythm going on, Mellie. Like we've been doing this forever."

"Hm," I said, paying great interest to Lew as we drew up to a rookery where hundreds of birds, including blue herons and brown pelicans, speckled the sky and took turns huddling and flying, squawking in alarm as we approached. The smell of all those bird droppings nearly made me gag, and I wanted to tell the birds that their squawks were completely unnecessary, as the smell alone would keep me—and most other sane humans—away.

Jack continued, his voice low so the other kayakers couldn't hear us. "It's like our bodies can communicate telepathically to move in the right direction for optimum momentum. We're like two spoons in a drawer."

"More like two negative ends on separate magnets," I muttered as I stabbed an oar into the water and let it drag, effectively making us turn in a circle. I faced him. "Do you talk like this to Rebecca?"

His eyes were cool behind his sunglasses. "Actually, no."

Flustered, I turned around and saw that the three other kayaks had moved beyond us, closer to the rookery.

"I miss you, Mellie."

I began paddling, feeling a heavy drag, and knew he was letting me go it alone. "I'm right here, Jack. And we see each other all the time."

"That's not what I mean and you know it. We're not through, you know."

"I don't think Rebecca would be happy to hear that."

He didn't respond, and I didn't turn around to see his expression. I startled as a sleek gray body glided by just under the surface of the water, parallel to our kayak.

"Is that a dolphin?" I asked, incredulous.

Jack's dimple showed as he grinned. "Yep."

I shook my head, staring into the dark gray waves as tiny bubbles rushed to the surface. "I bet she's female," I muttered.

"Nola! Alston!" Jack called, getting the girls' attention, then motioning for them to come closer.

Nola looked skeptical as she glanced at me, so I mouthed the word "dolphin" so she'd understand. They began to paddle closer to us; then Jack held up his hand when their kayak was about twenty feet from us, the spot where I'd first seen the dolphin between us.

"Come on, baby," Jack said quietly, his eyes searching the water. Five seconds later, not more than four feet from the front of Nola's kayak, two sleek gray backs with dorsal fins arched out of the water in a synchronized leap, landing with enough of a splash to drench Nola and Alston.

Nola jerked back, laughing hard, then pulled her legs up to a half stand so she could see better.

I heard Jack behind me. "Don't stand in the . . ."

Again, the two dolphins jumped from the water, a little farther away this time, but surprising Nola enough that she stumbled backward, grasping air, and then tumbled neatly into the water headfirst.

Jack was in the water at nearly the same moment and swimming toward her. Nola stayed on the surface, thanks to her life vest, but she must have inhaled a good deal of water, because she started coughing violently, gasping for breath in between her coughs.

With practiced and controlled movements, Jack came up from behind her and held her head back and out of the water until her coughing had mostly subsided. Then Nola started making an odd sound, and I wondered whether she was trying to cry or shout or scream at Jack. Instead, I saw that she was grinning broadly in a grin that wildly resembled her father's.

"That was a freaking dolphin!" Oblivious to the fact that she and her father were treading water in the open sea, she craned her head back to see her friend. "Did you see that, Alston? Two dolphins!"

After several attempts to hoist Nola back onto the kayak without rolling it and Alston into the water, Jack finally managed to hold the boat steady long enough for Nola to seat herself inside. He then swam back to our kayak and, after a few harrowing near rolls—which I thought he was doing on purpose to torment me—managed to reseat himself behind me.

Alston wiped the wet hair out of her face. "The dolphins were pretty cool. How did you do that, Mr. Trenholm?"

Nola regarded her father without the usual scowl. "Yeah, Jack, how did you do that?"

He picked up his oar and stuck it up in the air as a signal to Lew that we were fine and ready to move on. "I told you that I can't go out on the water without seeing a dolphin." He dipped the oar into the water and pushed. "Like I said, I always mean what I say."

I stabbed my oar into the water, feeling my cheeks warm as I realized he wasn't talking about the dolphins anymore.

CHAPTER 10

I sat in one of the low black leather chairs at Fabulous Frocks on Church Street, an upscale consignment bridal salon, watching as Sophie twirled in front of me wearing a white silk-and-chiffon concoction with delicate beading on the bodice and a train that would have made Princess Diana proud. Maybe it was the worn brown Birkenstocks peeping out from beneath the hem or Sophie's wild array of braids sprouting from her head, but despite the beauty of the dress it just looked . . . wrong.

I looked over at Nola, expecting her to be picking at her nail polish or texting on her new cell phone, but instead found her sitting on the edge of her seat, studying Sophie and the consultant, Gigi, with close interest.

"OMG. This is just like *Say Yes to the Dress!* You know, like when the bride walks out in the dress and everybody's watching her? Alston is just going to *die* when I tell her. Except in this case, Dr. Wallen, you should definitely be saying no. You look like a poodle at one of those dog shows."

Gigi and I both blinked silently at Nola, maybe because we were grateful to her for voicing our thoughts out loud, but unsure whether we should saying anything about comparing the prospective bride to a toy dog breed.

Gigi smiled helpfully. "I once had a bride try on eighty-six gowns before she found the One. You'll know it when you see it, sugar. You will."

Eighty-six? We'd suffered through ten try-ons already, and I was starting to think that it was time to ask to be taken outside and beaten senseless rather than face another one. It wasn't that sitting in the beautiful showroom with its ice blue walls and tall ceilings while surrounded by exquisite gowns was so awful. It was seeing the hopeful look on Sophie's face change to disappointment each time that was so hard to watch. Sophie was beautiful and . . . unique, and despite Gigi's best efforts at matching what Sophie *thought* she wanted in a wedding gown, nothing was working.

Tears began to well in Sophie's eyes. "I know. And I appreciate your help. I know this is the place to find my dress—this is the place all my friends have told me has the best wedding dresses—but I just don't think I can try on any more right now."

Gigi raised her hand. "Wait—how about one more? I'd almost forgotten about this one, because it just came in and is still in the office waiting to be steamed and tagged. It's an antique—nineteen twenties, I think—but it's satin and very simple and elegant. It was found in the attic in a house over on Queen Street, and the new owners have no use for it. Thought that selling it might help with some of the renovation costs."

"Unless it's lined with gold bars, I don't think a dress will help much."

Sophie shot me a hard look before turning back to Gigi. "All right, I'll look at it. But it's the last one today—really."

I stood and faced the consultant. "Let me see it before you bring it out. I'll know whether it's something Sophie will like or not."

Sophie looked at me gratefully as I followed Gigi out of the room and through a door into what appeared to be an office with a computer sitting on a large desk and surrounded by tulle, satin flowers, beads, veils, netting, and just about every other form of bridal paraphernalia. Gigi motioned me forward and then closed the door behind me. Hanging on a hook behind the door was a garment bag made out of an old sheet, the formerly red roses now faded into a graying pink. As soon as I saw it I smelled the heavy scent of gardenias, almost as if somebody had just wafted a bouquet underneath my nose.

"Do you smell that?" I asked.

"What?"

"Gardenias. I smell them really strongly right now."

Gigi raised her eyebrows. "The only thing I'm smelling right now is mothballs. This dress must have been buried in them inside a trunk in that attic. I've been trying to air it out, but I'm going to have to have it professionally fumigated, I think."

I took a deep sniff, smelling only the flowers, and for a brief moment I almost felt as if I were walking on a garden path filled with them.

"Are you sure . . . ?" I began when the phone rang.

"Can you excuse me for a moment? I need to get that, but I promise I'll be right back with you. If you like, you can go ahead and bring the dress to the dressing room across the hall to get a better look at it in the right light."

I nodded my thanks as she moved to the phone. The smell of flowers was now nearly gagging me as I reached up and took the hanger from the hook. Holding the gown as far away from my nose as I could possibly get it, I carried it to the dressing room, where Sophie's clothes lay in an inside-out heap, her ancient fringed leather purse on top guarding the pile.

Carefully, I placed the hanger on a hook over the large wall-to-wall mirror, then bent to raise the sheet that covered what I could see was off-white satin beneath. With my fingers gripping the hem I began lifting, then froze, my eyes focused on the mirror in front of me where the distinct apparition of a young woman appeared standing behind me.

I looked away, hoping she'd disappear before I looked back, but when I raised my eyes back to the mirror she was still there. I stared at her for a long moment, willing her to vanish, but her image instead grew stronger, more solid, almost as if she were drawing strength from my attention. Her hair was dark and short, curling softly around her face. Two curls folded over each cheek, in the style of the roaring twenties, her rosebud lips darkened heavily with lipstick. Around her neck she wore ropes of pearls, her slinky dress falling to midcalf, showing off shapely legs and white leather shoes with ankle straps. She was solid and real, and if her feet weren't hovering about six inches from the ground, I would have sworn she was a living and breathing person.

You can see me? she asked, her words carrying surprise.

I glanced away and started to sing to myself as I continued to raise the sheet, uncovering more and more of the dress. From years of practice, I'd learned that by my ignoring the ghosts, with a few notable exceptions, they usually gave up and went away.

You can see me, she said, an icy hand brushing my shoulder.

My voice rose as I sang the words to ABBA's "Take a Chance on Me," trying to block out the voice of the woman who shouldn't be there. The sheet reached the top of the gown. I tucked it behind the dress to examine it better and found myself holding my breath. As Gigi had said, it was simply cut, but elegant in its loose satin folds with a delicate lace overlayer. The sweetheart neckline draped demurely without being too revealing, the train in back short but pleated, as if made for the perfect wedding photo. It had been created for a petite figure like Sophie's, each embellishment perfectly placed and not too overwhelming. The satin, the color of candlelight, would be the perfect complement to Sophie's complexion.

Why are you pretending that you can't see me?

I focused again on the dress, the woman's words making me remember something my mother had said: something about how our gifts were for helping others instead of a source of embarrassment. I wasn't sure I'd ever see the day when I'd agree with her, but as I looked back at the spectral woman, I couldn't help but wonder about her story, or why she was still here.

I faced her in the mirror. Slowly, and very quietly, I said, "Yes, I can see you."

A heavy sigh filled the room, accompanied by a fresh scent of more gardenias. She smiled. *That's my dress.*

I guess I'd known that from the moment she'd first appeared. "It's very beautiful."

I know. She frowned, her delicate brow wrinkling. *I never got to wear it.*

Sadness flooded me, filling my chest and making my arms feel heavy. "What happened?"

I got sick. It was just a cold at first, but then . . . Her ghost eyes met mine. *I died.*

"I'm sorry," I said, forcing my heavy hands to flex. I looked at her carefully. "Why are you still here?"

My dress deserves to be worn. It's too beautiful to rot inside of a trunk, not when it was made to symbolize true love.

I looked from the dress and then back to her reflection. "I think this dress would be perfect for my friend. She loves antique things, which will make this dress especially dear to her. And she'll look beautiful in it, I know."

She smiled again, and the sadness lifted like a boat on a wave, leaving only the lightness of relief. *Finally,* she said.

"What is your name?"

Mary Gibson. I lived with my parents and younger brother on Queen Street. It was my mother who packed away my dress.

I turned around to face her and saw that she'd already begun to fade. "Is that all?" I asked, wondering at the same time if there was some instruction manual my mother needed to give me to tell me how this was supposed to be done.

Mary smiled, but shook her head. *Bonnie . . .* She stopped, her head tilted to the side as if she were listening to somebody I couldn't see.

"You know Bonnie?" I watched as her image began to blur, as if somebody had begun to erase her edges.

Her voice had become so faint I had to strain to hear it. *Tell Nola that Bonnie loves her and didn't mean to hurt her. She says you need to find my daughter's eyes.*

"What?" I reached out, trying to keep Mary with me just a little longer. "Why won't she talk to me?" I shouted to a thin strip of fading light.

Jack was all she said, and then she was gone.

"Mary! What about Jack?"

"Mellie? Who are you talking to?"

I swung around toward the open door and found Nola watching me the way people watch circus entertainers. I thought for a moment of just telling her the truth, but there was no easy way to tell her that her dead mother was communicating through another dead person to tell her that she loved her and hadn't wanted to hurt her. And that for reasons unknown to me she wouldn't talk to me directly because of Jack. Nola would probably look at me with an even stranger expression than she already was.

"Nobody. Just working out scenarios to convince Sophie that I think we found her dress." I stepped away so Nola could see better, glad for the distraction.

Her eyes widened. "That's freakin' perfect! It even looks like it would fit."

"Oh, I know it will. She's practically the same size as the woman it was made for."

Nola regarded me again with those piercing blue eyes. "How would you know that?"

"Um, just a guess. I mean, obviously if the dress fits Sophie, she would have to be the same size as the original owner, right?"

"Right," Nola said slowly. Giving me an odd look, she continued. "Let's go show this to Dr. Wallen. She's started talking about making her own dress from old sheets. I'm all for recycling, but even I think that's a bad idea."

I followed Nola out of the fitting room, giving one last glance behind me, realizing as I did so that the smell of gardenias had disappeared, too. "Rest in peace, Mary," I said quietly, then went to show Sophie the dress of her dreams.

Sophie and I sat in the front of my four-door sedan with Nola in the backseat. I'd insisted on driving, not because I thought Sophie's car was more like a tiny tin can—I did—but because I lost about a year off of my life every time I got in the car with her. She was easily distracted by historic architecture, which was as prevalent in Charleston as palmetto bugs, and had driven up onto a sidewalk more than once. I figured that I didn't need her prematurely pushing me onto the other side of forty.

Sophie was on her way to meet Chad at the home of a spiritual healer to have their chakras and auras read, and I was navigating my way in that direction when I caught sight of Nola in the backseat. The radio was very low, but her lips were moving silently as she sang along to the music.

Remembering her singing in the shower, I said, "You have a beautiful voice, Nola."

She clamped her lips shut. "How would you know?"

I almost told her that it was because I'd heard her in the shower, but I knew that would probably be the last time I would hear it. Instead, I said, "Just now. You were singing to the radio."

She narrowed her eyes at me. "Right."

Sophie sent me a warning glance. As a college professor she had a lot more experience with teens and young adults, but it wasn't my nature not to press a point.

"Your voice is really outstanding. Did you have any formal training?"

Nola stared out her side window, her jaw working.

"My mother is a well-known opera singer; did you know that?"

She spared me a glance in the rearview mirror, and I recognized a flash of interest. Satisfied, I said, "I'd like for you to sing for her. If you're as good as I think you are, she might suggest lessons or something."

Her eyes hardened. "I. Don't. Like. Singing. It's stupid, and pointless, and nothing I want to be wasting my time with, okay? So drop it."

I had opened my mouth to tell her I thought she needed to work on her manners and that she was just plain wrong when Sophie poked me in the side, making me shut up to catch my breath. Glancing back in the rearview mirror to see if Nola had noticed, I saw a halo of light next to her on the seat. It stretched and moved like a cat inside a bag, restless and determined to escape. It began to take the form of a woman with long blond hair parted in the middle, and pale eyes staring at me in accusation.

"Watch it!" Sophie screamed.

I jerked my gaze back to the road in front of me and narrowly missed a woman on a bicycle, and a parked car.

"Sorry," I said, stealing a glance in the backseat and fortunately finding only Nola. "I got distracted."

Sophie snorted. "Maybe I should drive next time."

I opened my mouth to give her my opinion on that thought when Nola's cell rang.

"Hey, Alston. What's up?" There was a brief pause. "Really? Whatever. Hang on while I give her the phone." Leaning forward, she tapped the cell phone on my shoulder. "Mellie? Alston needs to talk to you."

I raised my eyebrows but took the phone. "Hi, Alston. This is Melanie."

"Hi, Ms. Middleton. I'm sorry to bother you, but I thought you'd want to know that I think I figured out which house Nola's dollhouse is a copy of. You seemed real interested yesterday when I said it reminded me of something."

I glanced over at Sophie, who was watching me closely. "Yes, I'd love to know."

"Well, when I was little I used to take piano lessons at a house on Montagu Street. It's one of those old spooky Victorians behind Colonial Lake. Miss Manigault was my teacher, and she was as old as the dinosaurs back then, so she must be really ancient now. Anyway, she used to be the music teacher at Ashley Hall—which is how my mother knew her—and taught private lessons in her house after she retired. But I'm pretty sure it's her house. I think some of it's been changed, which is why I didn't recognize it right away, but the turret with that fancy woodwork on it is definitely her house."

"Do you remember the house number?" I wanted to be more excited, but couldn't. Despite my success at the bridal store, I wasn't all that enthusiastic about purposefully encountering more ghosts. Especially ones that threw boy and dog dolls out of windows and broke their necks.

"No, ma'am. But I think if you drive down the street looking at turrets, you can't miss it."

"Thanks, Alston."

We said good-bye; then I handed the phone back to Nola.

"What was that about?" she asked, looking more annoyed than interested.

I focused on keeping my tone neutral. "Your grandmother, father, and I have been trying to trace the house your dollhouse was most likely copied from. We were pretty sure it was from Charleston, but none of our leads turned up anything. Until yesterday, when Alston was in your room looking at your dollhouse and thought it looked familiar but couldn't figure out why. It finally came to her that it strongly resembles the house where she used to take piano lessons."

"So? Why would she be calling you about it?"

Sophie and I exchanged a glance. I'd already explained to her everything that had happened so far in the dollhouse, and she was in complete agreement that it was too soon to tell Nola about its ghosts or my ability to see them.

Trying to meet Nola's eyes in the rearview mirror, I said, "Because I'm curious. Don't you want to know anything about who owned your dollhouse and about the house it was fashioned after?"

"Whatever," she said, then returned to her perusal of the world outside her window.

Turning my attention back to the road, I nearly sideswiped a horse-drawn carriage carrying tourists. Sophie glared at me. "I'd like to live to wear that wedding dress, if you don't mind. Do that again and I will bodily remove you from the driver's seat, okay?"

I scowled at her. "Do you need me to drop you with Chad first or do you want to find the house?"

She looked at me over the top of her round sunglasses without comment.

"Fine. Then let me drive while you two look. Nola, you get the left-hand side; Sophie, you get the right."

I headed down Rutledge Avenue so we could start near the top of Montagu and work our way down. Many of the older homes in the Harleston Village area of Charleston had been subdivided into apartments, but there were a few intact grand dames of the nineteenth and twentieth centuries remaining. I hoped that Nola's house had been left whole. Not that I would admit this to anybody, but subdividing a historic single-family home had begun to feel like sacrilege to me, an odd sentiment, considering I'd once thought that large portions of the historic district would be better served by demolition balls. Of course, after receiving bills for the never-ending reconstruction of my Tradd Street house, I sometimes couldn't find too much fault with my previous thinking.

I drove slowly, pulling into driveways or against the curb when cars drove up behind me. A couple of times Nola informed us that she was bored, but Sophie and I ignored her, intent on our mission. We passed midcentury modest brick homes and Charleston singles, a few older Victorians and Greek Revivals, the houses a silent documentary of an older neighborhood.

"Stop!" Nola shouted from the backseat, and I stopped immediately, warranting an angry fist wave from a guy on a bike who had been behind me.

Without saying another word, Nola got out of the car and stood in front of a large house with peeling gray paint, a rusted iron gate hanging from a single remaining hinge, and weeds as high as my knees. But it was more than neglect the house wore; it sat on the side of the street like an empty shell, as if the life inside it had been suddenly and irrevocably extinguished.

I pulled the car over to the side of the road and Sophie and I got out to stand next to Nola.

"Wow," said Sophie. "Now, this is a specimen—I must bring my class to come see it." She pointed to the right corner of the house, where a tall circular tower was capped with a pointed roof and weather vane. "The turret with the stained-glass windows and all that fretwork is typical Queen Anne. But you can see from the centered pediment with its deep dentil moldings and even the fact that those columns are Doric that somewhere along the way somebody tried to disguise it and make it into a Greek Revival. Kind of hard to hide a turret, though."

I looked up at the house's facade, seeing the different architectural styles stuck onto the same house, and it made me think of a little girl dressing up in her mother's clothes: Despite the outside changes, she was still a little girl.

"It's my dollhouse, isn't it?" Nola asked. "At least, it used to be."

Sophie nodded. "Yep. I'm pretty sure it is."

"So what do we do now? Go and ring the doorbell?" Nola asked.

"Let me do some research first," Sophie said. "Find out whether the people living here are connected to the original family. From the looks of it either nobody lives here or whoever does doesn't want visitors."

Nola turned to look at both of us. "Why do we care? It's just a dumb dollhouse."

Sophie, adept at lecturing, started on her spiel of the importance of knowledge when it comes to architecture and its relevance to history. I was only half listening, as I was paying more attention to the skin rising on the back of my neck. I looked back at the house, my attention returning to the turret and up to the window facing the street, and froze. Staring at me from the previously empty glass was the face of an older man with pale hair, his expression radiating hate, his eyes empty black holes.

I blinked hard, hoping it was my imagination seeing something in the curvy waves of old glass. When I opened my eyes, the image was gone but not the thought that whoever it was I'd seen in the window wanted us to go away and never come back.

CHAPTER 11

I stood with my mother in the back garden of my Tradd Street home, trying to ignore the thumping sound of the hydraulic lift in its attempts to assist in lifting the house from its foundation to repair it, the architectural equivalent of putting an accident victim on life support. Once, I would have questioned whether all of the lifesaving heroics I'd pulled in the recent past had been worth it. But every time my mind wandered in that direction I couldn't help but remember what my benefactor, Mr. Vanderhorst, had once written about owning a historical house: *It's a piece of history you can hold in your hands*. His words always softened my heart a bit, at least until I got the next bill.

"Miz Middleton?" I turned to see the contractor, Rich Kobylt, approach while unwrapping what looked like a coleslaw sandwich. Rich and I had been working on my house for nearly two years, and I'd seen him eating coleslaw in one form or another at least one hundred times. I'd always wanted to ask him why not peanut butter or ham or really anything else, but I was afraid a conversation with him would steer toward the paranormal and the things I knew he saw in my house.

"Is there something wrong?" I asked, my standard greeting where Rich was concerned.

"No, ma'am. Just wanted to let you know that we're stopping for lunch now, so you ladies will have a bit of quiet to talk."

"Thank you. We appreciate it."

He tipped his Phillies baseball hat in our direction and turned to go back to his crew. My mother and I instinctively turned away, having already experienced more than once the unexpected sight of Rich's hindquarters displayed above his sagging pants. Rich and I didn't know each other outside of our client-contractor relationship, but I thought maybe a Christmas present of a belt would be a nice gesture on my part. I'd probably be able to get a lot of people to chip in.

My mother continued our conversation. "I thought we could set up the tent for the food here." She indicated the flat expanse of lawn by the old oak tree where a board swing still hung. "I've already contacted Callie White, because she's such a fabulous caterer and I wanted to make sure we had the date booked with her. And I thought over here"— her hands swept in a round motion, indicating the space in front of the ancient rose garden—"we could have a dance floor. We'll have a string quartet for dinner, of course—the tables will be set up inside the house and piazza—but I thought a live band and dancing after dinner would be perfect."

I nodded absently, trying to find even the tiniest bit of excitement. "Where are you going to put the billboard with my measurements and mentioning my good teeth?"

Moving forward to pluck a few dead leaves off of a red Louisa rose, she said, "I wouldn't do anything as tacky as a billboard, dear. I was just going to buy a full-page add in *Charleston* magazine."

I frowned. "Thanks for your tact."

"So what's bothering you, Mellie? Besides this party, that is."

I looked at her closely, wondering yet again why she was so good at reading my mind, and knowing, too, that it made no sense to lie, because she'd know that, too. "I sent another ghost into the light yesterday."

She raised her elegant brows but didn't say anything.

"Her name was Mary Gibson, and it's her wedding dress that Sophie will be wearing. That's all Mary wanted—for somebody to wear the dress that she never had a chance to." I shook my head. "I can't believe somebody would wait that long for something so . . . inconsequential. I always thought that spirits who were stuck here were here for something monumental. But a wedding dress?"

My mother bent again to pull a stray weed, straightening slowly as she studied it while twisting the stem between her fingers. "What is inconsequential to one person could mean the world to another. Even among the living you'll find people holding on to things much longer than you think they should. Grudges, grievances, old hurts. Things that a simple 'I'm sorry' or 'I love you' or 'I forgive you' are really all that's needed for healing and moving on."

She crumpled the weed in her hand and faced me. "When people die without having said those things, their spirits can be left earthbound, still waiting for the chance to say them. In my experience, it's those little words that hold spirits back much more often than unfinished business or from a sudden death where the spirit doesn't know they're dead. Hard to imagine, isn't it?"

My mother's eyes met mine and I felt the flash of old anger, the anger I'd held on to for more than thirty-three years. Regardless of her justification for leaving me when I was only six years old, I had still been abandoned by my mother and had lived my life defined by it. So what was she trying to tell me now? That I should forget about it?

As if she could read my mind, she said, "Forgetting is not the same as forgiving." She took a deep breath. "I'm sorry for all the pain I caused you in the past, Mellie. None of it was meant to hurt you, and I truly believed that I was acting in your best interests. I can't even say that I would have done any of it differently. Because when you get right down to it, is your life so bad now?"

I wanted to tell her that the jury was still out on my life, the admission of which I was sure would send me on a downward spiral of self-pity. Yes, there was a lot of good in my life. But there still seemed to be something unnameable—and unreachable—missing. However, I was *not* having this conversation with her. Too many conflicting emotions battled in my head. I'd never been asked, at least before I'd met Jack, to examine my conscience or my actions, and I wasn't about to start now in the garden of the house I still wasn't sure I wanted and within earshot of an entire construction crew.

I stared at the Louisa roses, their garish red petals like a smear on the abundance of shiny green leaves, so deceptive in their beauty, as they hid their thorns beneath the blooms. *Like a mother's love,* I thought, remembering again the encounter I'd had with the ghost of Mary Gibson.

Instead of answering, I said, "There was something else, too, that Mary said. She had a message from Bonnie for me to give to Nola."

"And?" my mother asked softly.

My voice sounded accusing. "Bonnie wanted Nola to know that she loves her and didn't mean to hurt her." I paused, letting the words sink in. "And to look for 'my daughter's eyes.' I have no idea what that means, or how to tell Nola, or even why Bonnie won't speak directly to me. I did ask Mary about that last part, and all she said was 'Jack.'"

My mother nodded slowly, her green eyes registering that she hadn't forgotten her question. "You need to find a way to tell Nola. I agree that she's not ready—yet. But soon. That could be all Bonnie needs to move on."

"And if she doesn't?"

"Then there's something else, and you'll need to find out what it is so she and Nola can both find peace."

I shook my head. "I have a full-time job, remember? I don't have a lot of time to go chasing ghosts. Can't you try to speak with her?"

A small smile lifted my mother's lips. "It's you she keeps appearing to, which means she feels a connection. Maybe it's Nola, since you're spending so much time with her. Or Jack."

Ignoring the last part, I asked, "But why won't she talk to me? This could be a lot easier than she's making it."

"She killed herself. If she feels shame, she might have difficulty approaching you directly. Or she could be jealous, and sees you as a rival for Jack's affections."

Heat flamed my cheeks. "There are no affections there beyond the platonic. Surely she knows that from wherever she is?"

"Mellie." My mother's tone of voice made me think of what she might have sounded like if she'd been around to scold me when I was a child. The rest of what she was going to say was lost to the sound of an earsplitting scream from inside the house. It was the last day anybody would be allowed inside the house during the foundation work, and I'd left Nola with a book in the kitchen, where she'd promised to stay in the otherwise empty house. My mother and I both turned and ran down the garden path to the kitchen door.

I flung it open and paused in the threshold, waiting for my eyes to adjust to the light, my relief at finding Nola alone quickly replaced by the unease that she'd seen something I wasn't prepared to explain to her.

"What's wrong?" I asked, walking toward her where she was pressing herself against the refrigerator as if trying to make herself blend in with the stainless steel.

She shuddered, then pointed to a spot behind me. Bracing myself, I turned, expecting to see Bonnie or one of the harmless spirits that still walked the rooms of the house on Tradd Street, seemingly content to exist in their shadow world. Instead, my gaze immediately settled on her source of terror: A large palmetto bug—known to the rest of the world as a flying cockroach—rested on the lip of the granite counter by the farmhouse sink, its reddish brown shell reflecting the overhead light, its long antennae twitching. I would have preferred a ghost, or a snake, a mouse, or even a charging bull. As much as I loved the city of my birth, the ubiquitous insect was almost enough for me to relinquish all claims to the Holy City.

My mother stood frozen in the doorway, and I thought for a moment what a picture we must make: three able-bodied and intelligent women petrified at the sight of a six-legged bug. A three-inch six-legged bug with wings, but still.

"What *is* that?" Nola shrieked.

Standing with my back to Nola so I could keep my eye on the unwanted visitor, I said, "It's the South Carolina state bird." I kept my tone light so she wouldn't know that I was petrified of the little beasts.

"It *flies?*"

As if it understood what Nola was saying, it fluttered its wings in warning.

Nola screamed again and ran for the door into the hallway, starting a chain reaction as my mother and I followed.

Nola almost crashed into Jack, who was running from the front door to the kitchen. He grasped Nola by the shoulders. "What's wrong?"

The panic on his face reminded me of the look he had right before he dived from the kayak after Nola fell into the water. It made my heart squish a little in my chest before I remembered what had caused the crisis.

"It's a palmetto bug in the kitchen." I was a strongly independent woman who'd never relied on a man for anything, yet I would be a fool to bypass this opportunity. "Can you go get rid of it?"

His hands dropped as his gaze took in all three of us. "A bug? You're screaming and running through the house because of a bug."

"A big, flying bug," my mother added.

"And it's about five inches long," Nola added.

"Five inches?" Jack repeated.

Nola nodded.

"All right. I'm prepared to do battle. Where is it?"

"On the sink," I said, pushing him forward. "Just don't squish him—see if you can get him outside first and then kill him."

"Do you have to kill him?" Nola asked, chewing on her lower lip.

I gave her the look I usually saved for clients whose lowball offer for a house bordered on insulting. "It's a cockroach," I said.

"A palmetto bug," Jack and my mother said in unison, as if the more genteel name made it less of an insect.

Nola continued to look at her father, her eyes hopeful.

"Fine," he said. "I'll scoop it up in a cup and set it free outside, okay?"

Nola nodded, and her lips twitched into what might have been a smile.

"Don't use one of the good cups," I said to his departing back. "And throw the cup in the garbage when you're finished."

"Yes, Mellie," he said as he disappeared into the kitchen.

"That's one thing men are good for," I said to Nola, feeling it was my duty to instruct her in the ways of the world.

"I heard that," Jack shouted from the other side of the kitchen door.

When he returned a few minutes later, he looked like a knight returning from the Crusades. "Taken care of. He's off amid the blades of grass, ready to populate the world with baby palmetto bugs." He smiled at me. "Ready to go?"

"Where are you going?" my mother asked.

"We're going back to the house we saw earlier this week—the one that we think the dollhouse was modeled after. Jack and Sophie did some digging and found out that the woman who lives there, Julia Manigault, is the last remaining member of her family—the same family who's owned the house since the late eighteen hundreds. From what

Sophie found, it looks like Julia is in her nineties now, and the dollhouse might have been hers."

"Seriously, who cares?" Nola asked. "I don't give a rat's a—" My mother sent her a sharp look. Nola continued. ". . . rat's paw who it belonged to. Why should we care?"

My eyes met Jack's for a brief moment over Nola's head, long enough to acknowledge our shared secret and for me to feel a little flush of heat flood my body.

Nola continued. "I mean, really. Do I have to go and talk with some old lady? She's probably too senile to remember a stupid dollhouse any-way."

Jack turned to her. "I guess not, but if you don't I could make you spend the weekend with Rebecca and me at her parents' home in Sum-merville instead. Your choice."

Nola rolled her eyes. "I think I'd rather move in with the old lady," she mumbled as she stared at the floor like she'd never seen it before. She glared back at her father. "But why are you going?"

Jack shrugged. "Because I'm always on the lookout for the next book idea. And besides, Mellie asked me."

I hadn't, but I didn't bother to mention it. Jack and I had been in-vestigating past lives in old houses long enough that it didn't occur to me that he needed to be asked or that he wouldn't naturally assume he should accompany me.

"Julia Manigault," my mother repeated. She looked up, her eyes widening. "Do you know whether she ever taught at Ashley Hall?"

"Yes, she did," I said. "I didn't think to ask whether you knew her. Alston said she taught music at Ashley Hall until she retired, then taught piano lessons from her home—that's how Alston knew the house."

My mother smiled, a faraway look in her eyes. "She was my first vocal teacher. I went to her to take piano lessons, but when she heard me sing we focused on voice. I only stayed with her that first year, before my parents found a more specialized teacher, but I've always credited her with being the person who inspired me to pursue my singing. I had no idea she was still alive. She was pretty old when I knew her." She gave a little laugh. "Although she was probably younger than I am now."

"Come with us, then. I'm sure she'd be thrilled to see you. I called and spoke to her housekeeper and set up an appointment—I doubt bringing one more would be a problem."

"I'd love to, but I have another appointment that I can't change at the last minute." She gave me a sideways glance. "It's to see Mr. Mc-Ghee regarding his late wife." She glanced up at Jack and me so we would understand what sort of appointment she was referring to. "Please give her my best and tell her I will come by to see her soon."

Nola headed to the door. "Can we go now? The sooner we get there, the sooner we can leave."

My mother touched my arm. "May I have a word with you, Mellie?"

I had the sinking feeling she was hoping to continue our previous conversation. I looked to Jack for help, but he either missed or ignored my silent plea.

"Can we take your car?" he asked. "I don't want Nola in the back-seat of the Porsche—it's too cramped, and to be honest I don't know how safe it is."

I handed him my car key, then stared at his back for a moment as he headed to my car, remembering the times I'd been forced into his back-seat to allow Rebecca in the front. "I'll drive. Go wait by the car and I'll be right there."

He cocked an eyebrow, then said good-bye to my mother before sauntering toward my car with Nola.

"Yes?" I asked.

"I've been thinking about what you said—how Bonnie said Jack's name when you wanted to know why she won't speak to you directly."

I relaxed a bit. "Did you come up with something?"

"Maybe Bonnie wasn't answering your question at all. Maybe she was trying to tell you something else entirely."

"Like what?"

She looked over my shoulder to make sure we weren't within ear-shot of Jack or Nola. "I spoke to your grandmother last night."

I looked at her, surprised. My grandmother always communicated with me first. It had always been that way, even when she'd been alive. "I wonder why she didn't speak with me."

"She already has, but apparently you weren't listening."

I remembered the phone call the night I'd found Jack's wallet on my dresser, something about listening to my heart. "I don't understand."

"Jack's in trouble, Mellie. I don't know how or why, but maybe that's what Bonnie was trying to tell you."

"But why me? Why not Rebecca?"

My mother looked at me, her eyes hard. "Let it go, Mellie. Whatever it is you're holding on to that's preventing you from seeing what everybody else sees so clearly, let it go."

I thought of Jack, and the way he'd always made me feel as if I were standing at the edge of a cliff, and how unprepared I was for the free fall if I should take a step forward. And I had no idea what it was that made me cling so hard to solid ground.

"They're waiting for me. I've got to go."

I looked away quickly from the disappointment in her eyes, and walked to the car wondering how I was supposed to save Jack when I had no idea how to save myself.

CHAPTER 12

It was a short drive to Montagu Street, and I found parking in front of the house. As we stood on the opposite side of the street from the house, I took it as a good sign that a bird sang from the overgrown crape myrtle that obscured most of the front garden and walk. I didn't dare look up at the turret window.

Jack faced the house, studying it with a practiced eye. From his younger years, when he'd helped his parents find items for the store at estate sales, he'd developed a good sense for fine lines and quality workmanship in both furniture and houses. And probably women, too, but that was something I tried not to dwell on.

"Sophie must have jumped out of her Birkenstocks when she saw this," he said, leaning back to see the weather vane on top of the turret roof. I followed his gaze, stopping at the bottom of the window.

"Pretty much. And neither one of us has any doubts this is the house."

"Me, neither. I'm thinking the paint used to be blue instead of gray, although I'm guessing the original color was yellow, like the dollhouse," he said, stepping back to allow Nola and me to proceed ahead of him.

We had to duck down to pass beneath the crape myrtle's branches while simultaneously watching our step to make sure we didn't get stuck in any of the holes in the path from broken or missing bricks. The front steps seemed solid enough as we climbed them to the front porch that wrapped around the front and sides of the house. The paint covering the Doric columns that supported the porch roof was peeling and chipped, as was the haint blue ceiling. The color was supposed to ward off evil spirits and nesting birds—something it had failed to do on both counts, judging from the large amount of bird droppings liberally deposited at the base of two of the columns, and my previous experience with the man in the turret window.

The double front doors, heavy wood with a leaded-glass transom, badly needed refinishing, as did the splintered wooden floorboards of the porch. I stopped myself from examining anything else, embarrassed by how naturally my train of thought now went to restoration details.

A tarnished brass button next to the door drew our attention. With a backward glance at Nola and me, Jack pressed it. A distant tinkling bell sounded from inside of the house, and for the first time Nola looked nervous.

"I wonder if the house is haunted," she said. "If you believe in that kind of thing," she added quickly. "No way would I come trick-or-treating here if I was a little kid."

I kept my gaze trained on the front door, afraid to look at either Nola or Jack lest my expression give me away.

After a few moments the sound of heavy footsteps approached the doors before one of them was opened by a middle-aged heavyset woman with sandy blond hair held back in a ponytail, curly wisps straggling down the sides of her cheeks. She wore a loose white T-shirt, black capris, and flip-flops, all three speckled liberally with what looked like paint.

The woman smiled brightly, her blue eyes examining us closely, her gaze settling on Jack. Her smile widened. "Can I help you?"

Attempting to redirect her attention, I stepped forward. "I'm Melanie Middleton. I believe we spoke on the phone yesterday about coming to see Miss Manigault?"

Her eyes didn't leave Jack's face. "Oh, right. I forgot—must be the paint fumes. I'm Deanna Davenport, Miss Manigault's house manager or whatever you want to call me. I'm sort of her hands and feet, so to speak, since she can't do for herself anymore." She straightened, her ample bosom pressing against her T-shirt. Still looking at Jack, she said, "I'd shake your hand, but I've got glue all over my fingers. And you can call me Dee for short."

Nola and I exchanged a look as Jack smiled back. "May we come in?"

Distracted, Dee finally stepped back. "Oh, of course. Where are my manners? Come in, come in. She's in the library. Let me show you in and I'll go fix some tea."

We followed her into a large alcove and waited while Dee closed the door behind us. The first thing I noticed was the ornate furniture and heavy dark wood everywhere. And where there wasn't dark wood on the cantilevered ceilings, stair balustrades, furniture, or walls, the fabrics and paints were all in matching somber hues. We passed through the alcove into a huge foyer dominated by a wide staircase that wound its way up to the upper levels in a box design. The maroon-colored runner and thick, nearly black banisters and spindles did nothing to lighten the space; nor did the small lamp burning on a hall table. A stained-glass window, nearly covering the wall at the first landing, let in little light through the intricate pattern that was almost completely obscured by dirt on the outside.

We passed by what looked like a drawing room, the forest green velvet drapes closed against any encroachment of light, and a music room with a grand piano featured prominently in the center. I remembered what Alston had said and wondered whether this was the piano where she'd once taken lessons.

"OMG." Nola had stopped in front of the music room. "It's like I'm inside my dollhouse, and it's freaking me out. I mean, everything's the exact same—even the wallpaper. Except it's not peeling off the walls like it is here."

She was right. It appeared that the house had been built and decorated around the turn of the last century and not touched since. Except for the addition of electricity and, I hoped, modern plumbing, the house was perfectly preserved to show life as it was over one hundred years ago. On closer inspection, I saw that the rugs sported bare patches, the wood floors missing pieces of the inlaid patterns, the paint flaking, the wallpaper drooping or missing in spots. The last time I'd walked into a house in such dire need of restoration I'd ended up owning it. That thought alone almost made me run screaming into the street. Instead I followed Jack and Dee, assuming Nola was close behind.

At the end of a short corridor, Dee slid open a pair of pocket doors and stepped back, waiting for us to enter. We blinked at the sudden brightness after such solemn darkness in the rest of the house. Three large windows, each arched at the top like frowns, went from the floor to the ceiling. Part of the wraparound porch was visible through them, and I wondered whether the windows slid open to act as doorways. From the stale smell of dust and something else I couldn't identify, it was apparent the windows hadn't been opened in a very long time.

When my eyes adjusted I tried to take in the rest of the room, and had to blink a few times to make sure I wasn't hallucinating. The room was large and round in a rear turret not visible from the street. Shelves lined the curved walls, apparently intended for books but now filled with . . . Santa Clauses? I took a step closer to one of the shelves, where a jolly Saint Nick wearing a red velvet suit and matching hat stared jovially back at me. There were hundreds of Santas—sitting, standing, riding various animals and sleighs. All had the same face, with rosy cheeks, bright blue eyes, and noses with pink tips. I remembered Dee's paint-splattered clothing and wondered whether she might be responsible for some of the ceramic craftwork.

"Miss Julia loves Christmas," Dee explained. "It's sort of become my hobby."

I nodded, taking in the miniature decorated trees that sat on every available surface, the paper cutout snowflakes strung from the ceiling, the snowmen figurines clumped together in family groups.

"Miss Julia?" Dee said, and I turned my attention to the far side of the room. The woman was very old, and very small, which was probably why I hadn't seen her or her wheelchair when I first walked in. She was dressed all in charcoal gray, her white hair and very pale face in stark contrast. Her dark eyes, almost black, looked back with surprising alertness. She was bent over nearly in half, her chin bobbing as she tried to look up at her visitors.

Jack stepped forward first, then knelt with one knee in front of her wheelchair so she wouldn't have to strain her neck. "Miss Manigault, I'm Jack Trenholm. It's a pleasure to meet you."

He held out his hand and she placed a small, knobby hand into it. "Are you the writer?" she asked, her voice strong and clear, a smile forming on her wrinkled lips.

"Yes, actually, I am. Have you read my books?"

She smiled up at him and fluttered her eyelids, and I wondered whether she might actually be *flirting* with him. "Every last one of them. Dee here goes to your signings to get me autographed copies. I've been waiting for quite a while for your next book. It had better be soon, as I don't think I can wait too much longer."

Jack's own grin dimmed somewhat. "It's in the works right now. I'll bring an autographed copy personally, if you'd like."

She practically beamed at him, and I resisted the urge to roll my eyes.

I stepped forward and leaned down over the wheelchair. "I'm Melanie Middleton. I believe you knew my mother, Ginnette Prioleau."

Her eyes widened. "Oh, my dear Ginnette. What a voice! Has she come with you today?"

"She couldn't make it, but promised to come by another time."

"Did you inherit any of her singing talent?"

"No," Jack answered before I could, eliciting a frown from me.

"And this is . . ." I turned around for Nola, but saw she wasn't there.

"Why don't you two take a seat and I'll go get tea and find out what's keeping the young lady," Dee said before leaving the room.

We eyed two gothic-style armed chairs, one with splotchy red velvet, the other a dark brown horsehair with a healthy collection of dust. A small sofa in the room, covered in heavy brocade and draped in lace doilies, sat against a wall. We were considering our seating options when the sound of piano music glided into the room.

Jack and I looked at each other. "Nola?" we said in unison.

Dee reappeared. "I think I found her."

The music grew in volume and insistency, and for a long moment we stayed where we were, listening. It wasn't the grunge or heavy-metal music I heard from her bedroom or from the radio when she got in the car before me and changed the station. This was . . . beautiful, haunting. It reminded me of the melody of the song I'd heard Nola singing in the shower, and I wanted to simply stay where I was and listen for as long as she would play.

"Dee," Miss Julia commanded, the strength of her voice once again surprising me. "I want to see who's playing."

Dee moved behind the wheelchair and pushed Miss Julia out of the room, Jack and I following close behind. We paused in the doorway to the music room, taking in the scene of the young girl seated at the grand piano, her fuchsia sneakers the only bright spot in the room with burgundy walls, thick brocade drapes, and closed venetian blinds. Her face was devoid of the usual cynical grimace or blank stare, both replaced by an almost single-minded attention to her fingers as they glided over the ivory keys of the old piano. To my amazement, her cheek lifted into what I was pretty sure was a small smile.

Something brushed my leg, and I looked down to find a shaggy dog sitting on its haunches staring up at me, his ears cocked as if listening to the music. I bent to scratch him behind the ears, just like General Lee liked me to do, and it was as if by moving I broke the spell. Nola's fingers crashed down on the keys, the notes colliding together in a cacophony of sound.

She looked at us with the eyes of a person just awakened from a dream. She blinked slowly, taking in Dee and the woman in the wheelchair, and then Jack and me. "That was totally weird," she said. "I just saw the piano and it was like it wanted me to play it." She thought for a moment. "The one in the dollhouse plays, too, but it only has twenty keys."

I didn't know what surprised me more: the fact that the dog seemed to have vanished under my hand or that Nola had counted the keys on the miniature piano.

Jack stepped forward, his eyes uncertain. "Nola, that was incredible. I had no idea you could play or sing, and the music itself . . ." He stopped next to his daughter and seemed to consider something before speaking. Softly, he asked, "Did your mother write it?"

Her expression changed as if she'd been struck. She looked at him as if she were seeing him for the first time, realizing that this was the father who she believed had abandoned her and her mother without a second thought. She stood abruptly, the bench teetering behind her.

"No," she said quietly, her gaze frantically moving from one face to another. "No!" she said again, louder this time.

"Sweetheart." Jack took a step toward her, his arms outstretched.

She sidestepped him, her eyes wide with panic and something that looked a lot like fear. "No," she whispered as she raced past us and out the front door.

"I'll get her," Jack said as he walked quickly past our little group huddled in the doorway. He followed Nola through the front door as I turned to Dee and Miss Julia.

"I'm so sorry about that, Miss Manigault. I have no idea what that was all about—"

Miss Julia cut me off. "What dollhouse?" she asked, her words low and deep.

"It's a dollhouse that looks just like this house. It was a gift to Nola from her grandparents. We think it might have belonged to somebody who once lived in this house. . . ."

"Get out," she said.

"Excuse me?" I was sure I'd misheard.

"Get out," the old woman said again, louder this time.

"I don't under—"

"I'm sorry, Miss Middleton," Dee said, her face serious. "I'm afraid you're going to have to leave."

"I just wanted to ask about the dollhouse," I persisted. "Do you know whether—"

"Get out!" the old woman screamed at me.

Her face wore two dots of pink on her cheeks, reminding me of the Santa Clauses in the library.

"All right," I said, backing toward the door. "I'm sorry to have upset you. I really am." I opened the door and stepped out onto the porch, the sunshine from outside illuminating the shaggy dog sitting next to the wheelchair again. "Good-bye," I said, closing the door behind me.

I ran down the steps, feeling the nape of my neck prickle. Standing on the sidewalk in front of the house, I turned around and looked up at the turret window. The same man I'd seen before stood there, with the same empty sockets for eyes, the same pale face. Except this time his thin lips were pulled away from his teeth in an awful smile, grinning down at us as if he were glad to see us go.

CHAPTER 13

I worked silently in my bedroom at my mother's house, using my labeling gun to sticker the new bins I'd stacked in my temporary closet, absently wondering whether I should organize my shoes alphabetically by designer, by season, or by type. I paused every once in a while to see whether I could hear anything from Nola's room, each time being met with silence. It had been that way since we'd returned home and she'd escaped to her bedroom, not even being tempted out of it by a soy burger or glazed doughnut.

Jack had stayed outside her door, pleading, cajoling, apologizing, threatening, and apologizing again until he'd also reverted to silence. At my insistence, he'd left, but only if I promised to call him if she came out of her room.

The clock showed it was midnight. My parents were out again—doing what, I had no idea—and although I had an early-morning showing the next day, I couldn't go to bed knowing that Nola was still awake and miserable.

When I was a young girl, my grandmother would bring me hot cocoa before bed and talk about my day with me. Despite the haphazard relationship between Nola and me, I realized I had no other source of inspiration or ideas, and that it couldn't hurt to try to open up some sort of communication avenue. Or just make her feel good. I didn't know whether there was such a thing as vegan cocoa, but we'd just have to make do.

Placing my labeling gun on my nightstand, I headed for the door. As my hand touched the doorknob, a small knock sounded from the other side. Relieved that Nola must be feeling better, I threw the door open and started in surprise when I saw Jack standing in the hallway.

Throwing one hand over my mouth, I used the other to grab his arm and pull him inside.

"Wow, Mellie," he said as a dimple deepened in his cheek. "Your eagerness to get me into your bedroom is flattering." His eyes slowly swept over me, returning to my face with a satisfied look of appreciation. Belatedly, I realized I wore a nearly sheer summer nightgown that my mother had given me after the air-conditioning on the top floor had lost its cooling power and we'd been left to suffer for a few days until the repairman could come and fix it. It was almost like sleeping naked— something I'd never done—but gave the illusion of wearing a nightgown.

Quickly crossing my arms over my chest, I backed across the room until I reached my bathroom, where I pulled my thick bathrobe off a hook and threw it on.

Jack looked disappointed when I reappeared. "I liked the other out-fit better."

I belted the tie around my waist. "What are you doing here, and how did you get in?"

He dangled a key in front of me. "Your mother gave it to me."

I opened my mouth to speculate on why she'd done so, hoping it had something to do with Nola, but quickly shut it when I realized it might have nothing to do with his daughter at all. I made a mental note to talk to my mother about it later.

I glanced back at my bed, where General Lee, happily ensconced on the pillow, lay with his eyes half-open. "You're a great watchdog, pal. Thanks for the warning that a stranger was in the house."

The dog's eyes slowly closed in response, followed by a soft snore.

Jack continued. "I've been trying to call your cell."

I looked at my nightstand, where I normally kept it. "I guess I left it in my purse in the kitchen." I frowned at him. "What was so impor-tant that it couldn't wait until morning?"

It was his turn to frown. "My daughter was so distraught and un-communicative when I left that I needed to know whether she was okay. She's not answering her cell, either."

My heart did that little squishing thing it did every time Jack allowed me to see this softer side of him. My shoulders relaxed. "I told you I would call you. Anyway, nothing's changed. I still can't get her to talk. I was just about to go downstairs and make hot cocoa and bring it in to her to see if that might help."

He wiped the side of his neck. "It's a hundred degrees up here—do you think hot chocolate is the right way to go?"

"It worked for me when my grandmother gave it to me when I was little." I sounded a little defensive.

The side of his mouth curled up. "Besides, I don't think she likes sweets."

I remembered Nola's and my secret rendezvous over doughnuts in the kitchen and my promise to keep it secret. "I thought I could at least try. I don't know what else I can do."

He took a step toward me and my nerves began to press against my skin, making me hypersensitive to the air that moved over me. He reached up to touch my hair, moving it behind my shoulder, his expression indecipherable. "Thank you."

"For what?" I hoped he hadn't heard my voice crack. His standing so near made my body respond in ways it wasn't supposed to.

His eyebrow lifted slowly and I knew he'd heard. "For helping me with Nola. You've been good for her."

I shrugged. "I've had a lot of help—from both our mothers. And you, too."

"How? She still doesn't want me around."

"Not yet. But she sees that you care, and that you keep trying. She tries to hide it, but she notices. She just needs time, I think." I found myself staring at the buttons of his pale blue oxford-cloth shirt, not wanting to stand this close to him face-to-face.

"Mellie?"

"Hm?" I saw that one of the threads in his button was loose, and found myself wondering who did his mending.

His fingers touched my chin and tilted my face upward so that I was forced to look into the deep blue of his eyes. His lips were close enough to mine that I could almost feel them, could remember clearly how they'd tasted even though it had been months since our first—and last—kiss.

Looking intently into my eyes, he said, "You'd make a great mother, you know."

Whatever it was I'd expected him to say, it wasn't that. I twisted my chin out of his grasp. "I have no idea how that's supposed to happen."

His face widened with a grin, although his eyes lost none of their intensity. "I thought you knew. But I'd be happy to show you." He moved even closer, then stopped, cocking his head to the side. "Did you hear that?"

I shook my head, then walked to my door and pulled it open. The sound of muffled sobs carried across the dim hallway.

Jack flipped on the hall light, then walked past me, and before I could stop him he had tapped gently on Nola's door. "Nola, sweetie? It's . . ." I watched as he struggled with what to call himself. "It's Jack. Can I come in?"

"No! Go away! It's all your fault." The words seemed to pass through the door like a physical blow, forcing Jack to recoil.

I put my hand on his arm. Quietly, I said, "Let me try. She's more comfortable with me. Maybe I can find out what's wrong."

His eyes were so stricken that I found myself leaning up to kiss him softly on the cheek. "It's going to be all right. It will." I wasn't sure I was telling the truth, or how everything would be all right, but I needed to tell Jack something to wipe that look off of his face.

His hand was touching his cheek where my lips had been when I tapped on the door and went inside.

The first thing I noticed were the pages of music scattered around the room like a dusting of black-dotted snow. The second thing I noticed was that the dollhouse had been moved to the foot of her bed, but with so much force that it leaned backward where its forward movement had been stopped by the bottom bed rail.

I stood next to the four-poster, where Nola lay curled in a fetal position on top of her bedspread, still fully dressed. Through the triangle of light from the hallway I watched my breath vaporize in front of me. I shivered in the icy air, glad I had on my thick robe.

"Nola? Are you okay?" I put my hand on her arm and felt goose bumps. "You're freezing," I said as I pulled up the quilt that had been draped at the foot of the bed and placed it over her. Gingerly, I sat down on the bed next to her; then, not knowing what else to do, I put my hand on her shoulder. We were both silent, waiting for the other to speak.

I tried to remember back when I was her age, when I lived with my father without a mother to confide in or many friends. I'd had a doll who'd witnessed all of my tearstained confessions and insecurities, unappreciated, because I'd never stopped wishing my mother would suddenly reappear to make everything all right.

Reaching over, I snagged the teddy bear from the corner, tucking it under the quilt with Nola. Without a word, Nola reached over and hugged it to her, and I resisted the impulse to smile. Instead, I said, "I know I'm not your mother, but I am a girl, and I even used to be thirteen."

"A million years ago," came the muffled response.

I was so relieved to see some of the old Nola return that I wasn't too offended.

"Yes. A million or so years ago. But what I'm trying to say is that even though I don't know exactly what you're going through, if you need somebody to listen, I'm here." I took a deep breath, trying to see in the darkened shadows of the room, my breath gathering like storm clouds over the bed. I remembered huddling in my own bed as a child, feeling the presence of others around me but knowing I was still horribly and irrevocably alone. I looked down at the child huddled in the quilt, and wondered how much I could tell her.

"When I was about your age, I didn't have any friends. I was . . . different from the other kids." *That's one way of putting it.* "That's when I started making lists. I'd keep paper and pencil by my bed, and whenever I felt alone or scared, I'd jot down things I needed to do or wanted to do. It helped me get my life in control when so much of it seemed as if I couldn't. It's sort of taken over my life now, but it really saved me back then. I'm thinking you don't need to do that because you have me to talk to, but if you want me to get you a pad and pencil instead, I will."

She lay there quietly, but I knew she hadn't gone to sleep. By her silence, I assumed I had her answer and began to stand so I could go find her something to write on. Her hand clasped my wrist, stopping me, and I sat back down on the edge of the bed.

"I'm scared," she whispered.

"Of what?"

There was a short pause. "That I'm going crazy."

My heart tightened in my chest. "Why do you think that?"

"Because I'm too much like my mom." She began sobbing, deep, choking sobs that left her gasping for breath. I grabbed a handful of tissues from a box on her nightstand and tucked them into her hand. Unsure what to do next, I patted her shoulder, remembering the events of the afternoon, trying to come up with a reason that would have led Nola to the conclusion that she was losing her mind.

"That song you were playing today on Miss Manigault's piano—did your mother write it?"

She shook her head, her hair rasping against the pillowcase. "We wrote it together. But we never finished it."

"It was beautiful, Nola. We all thought so. But why would that make you think you're going crazy?"

Her body shivered with a silent sob. Very quietly, she said, "Because I keep doing crazy things and I don't remember doing them. At first I thought it was the dog, but I figured out that he couldn't be doing some of the stuff."

I sat very still. "Like what kind of stuff?"

Without looking up, she waved her hand in the direction of the dollhouse. "I find it in different spots all over the room, and I don't remember moving it. I don't even think that I could if I tried." She sniffed again, then pointed to the corner where Bonnie's guitar case rested against the wall. "And my mom's guitar, and all that sheet music—they're never where I left them." She began to sob again, and I knew I was hearing the sound of a heart breaking.

I wasn't even sure how to begin this conversation, but I had to try. "You're not crazy, Nola. There's a logical explanation for all of it." Well, maybe not *logical,* but at least it was an explanation. "But your mother wasn't crazy. I didn't know her, but from what I've heard about her from Jack and from you, I'm guessing she might have been sad that her career wasn't where she wanted it to be, and she tried to hide from her sadness with drugs and alcohol. Unfortunately, that happens to a lot of people. But that doesn't make her crazy."

Nola shook her head vigorously. I had to struggle to make out her words between sobs. "I was such a good kid. I took really good care of her. I didn't do drugs or drink, or hang out with the bad kids, and I made sure she ate good when I could get food in her. But she killed herself anyway, like I didn't matter. Like she didn't love me. Why would she do that unless she was out of her mind?"

I was crying now, too, and knew I had no choice but to tell her the truth regardless of the consequences. "Oh, no, Nola. Your mother loved you very, very much. Please believe me, because I know it's true."

Her fists hammered the mattress. "You're lying," she screeched, and I shrank back. "How would you know? She's dead!"

I said the words before I could talk myself out of it. "Because she told me."

She went absolutely still, her tearstained eyes glaring up at me. "What do you mean?"

Closing my eyes, I tried to think of the best way to make her understand, and blurted out the first thing that came to mind. "I can communicate with people who have passed on."

Her eyes blinked slowly up at me as I waited for my words to register. Finally, she said, "You can talk to dead people? Like in that movie with the little boy and Bruce Willis?"

I sighed. "Yeah. Pretty much." I'd never seen *The Sixth Sense* until recently, when Sophie and Chad had invited me over for movie night and organic popcorn. I wouldn't have gone if I'd known which movie Chad had chosen.

Nola hiccuped. "And you saw my mom?"

Nodding, I said, "She wanted me to tell you that she loves you, and never meant to hurt you." I paused, trying to make up my mind as to how much I should tell her. "I see her around you a lot, like she wants to make sure you're okay."

Her shoulder relaxed under my hand, as if all the tension inside of her had somehow seeped from her body. In a very small voice, she said, "Did you ask her why she did it? Why she left me all alone?"

"I don't know why, but she won't speak directly to me. You remember when we were at the bridal salon and you heard me talking to someone? I was speaking with the bride who was the gown's original owner. Your mother sent her message through her." I placed the backs of my fingers against her cheek. "And you're not alone. You've got Jack and me, your grandparents, my parents, and Alston. Even General Lee is a fan. I think your mother might have known that she wouldn't be leaving you alone. That's why she led you to Trenholm's Antiques."

Nola was silent for a moment. "Why won't she speak to you directly?"

I shook my head. "I'm not sure. My mother thinks it has something to do with Jack, because your mother said his name, but that could mean a lot of things."

"But why would she be moving the dollhouse?"

I realized that she'd probably had all the information she could digest in one sitting and that I needed to save the rest for another time. Still, I tried to be as honest as I could. "There's a lot going on here that I don't understand. I was hoping that if I just ignored it, it would go away, but I don't think that's going to happen."

"But isn't the whole point of you being able to talk to dead people so that you can help them?"

Out of the mouths of babes. "I've been trying to figure that out my whole life. I used to think it was something I was supposed to tolerate—like being too tall, or having straight hair that wouldn't curl. It's only recently—thanks to my mother—that I've begun to look at it a little differently. Sort of like more of a gift than a curse."

She wiped the back of her hand across her face, then stared up at me. I was surprised and happy to see that she wasn't looking at me like a two-headed sideshow freak. "Your mom knows about you?"

I nodded. "She's actually psychic, too. And Jack and Sophie know, but that's about it. It's not the sort of thing I'm comfortable telling everybody."

"I think it's cool. In a creepy-weird way, but cool. I mean, you get to help people who get stuck here, you know? There're probably not that many people who can do that." She shifted out of the quilt covering her, and I realized the temperature in the room had returned to stifling. "Mellie?"

"Mm?" I wiped her damp hair off of her forehead.

"Can you stay here until I go to sleep?"

I smiled. "Of course," I said, knowing it wouldn't be too much longer. Her eyes were already drooping.

Her words slurred when she spoke again. "I still love my dollhouse, but it's creeping me out now. Do you think we can move it to another room tomorrow?"

"Definitely." I continued to sit on the bed and watch as her eyes finally slid closed and her breathing became slow and even. Gently, I stood, waiting a moment to make sure I hadn't awakened her before walking silently to the door, a shaft of light from the hall illuminating the bed in a yellow triangle.

"Mellie?"

I stopped and turned at the sound of Nola's voice, heavy with sleep. "Yes?"

"I think you and Jack have the hots for each other. It wouldn't make me hurl if the two of you hooked up."

I crossed my arms over my chest. "Are you really that interested in seeing us together or are you just trying to get Rebecca out of the picture?"

A soft snort came from the pillow, and then silence. I waited for a moment but heard only soft, gentle breathing.

I closed the door silently, then turned to find the hallway empty. I pushed back my disappointment, telling myself I had just been eager to tell Jack that I'd told Nola my secret and that she seemed to be okay with it.

I walked across the hall to my room, untying my robe as I did so, my eyes heavy with exhaustion. My hand was on the light switch when I stopped abruptly. General Lee had been replaced by Jack, who lay fully clothed—fortunately—on the top of my bed, his fingers laced behind his head. A spark of electricity zinged through my blood as I looked at him on my bed, the realization hitting me that all I had to do was take a few steps forward and then I wouldn't have to think about anything at all.

"That was sweet," he said.

Instead I leaned back against the door and closed my eyes so I wouldn't have to see him. "How much did you hear?"

The bedsprings creaked, and when I opened my eyes again Jack was standing in front of me, his arms pressed against the door, effectively trapping me between them.

"All of it," he said softly.

"She seemed to handle all of what I told her pretty well."

"Mm-hm," he murmured, lowering his face so that our noses nearly touched. "Is that really how all your list making started? Because you needed to find some sort of control in your life?"

"Pretty much."

He let out a small breath. "That explains a lot. But you still managed to become a nurturer to those around you who need nurturing."

I shook my head. "If you're referring to Nola, I think I did what anybody would have done. It's so obvious how much she needs some-body to talk to."

"Rebecca doesn't see that at all. She thinks what Nola really needs is a boarding school. In another state. Preferably another country."

Half of my mouth turned up. "Yeah, I can see her point. Until you really spend time with Nola and get to know her better. Because under the makeup and neon clothing, she's a pretty neat kid."

"Of course she is. She's half mine." His nose nuzzled mine and my lips parted involuntarily. I'd meant to use the next opportunity when we were alone to discuss what my mother had said about his being in trouble, but found now that I couldn't form a single coherent thought. "And she thinks we have the hots for each other."

I stumbled over words in my head, trying to come up with a re-sponse, and failed miserably.

He was standing so close I could feel his chest rumble when he spoke. "Remember when we were on the kayak and I told you that you and I weren't over yet? This is what I was talking about."

My chin tilted up as his lips angled toward mine. I closed my eyes in anticipation, just in time to hear the front door open downstairs and my parents' voices as they climbed the steps toward my mother's room next to mine.

My eyes flicked open, meeting Jack's amused ones. I put my finger to my lips as we listened to my father say good-night to my mother, then retreat—luckily—back down the steps and out the front door again.

I glanced meaningfully at the connecting door to my mother's suite of rooms and made a flicking gesture at Jack so that he'd know he needed to leave.

Leaning very close to my ear, he whispered, "And that was almost-kiss number six." He straightened and I pulled away from the door, trying to recall my former equilibrium.

He turned the knob very slowly and stepped out into the hallway, the light from under my mother's door guiding his way to the steps. As if in afterthought, he turned and said, "I'll be back tomorrow."

My heart skidded and thumped in my chest. Without thinking, I blurted, "To finish the kiss?"

He raised an eyebrow, his face creased in a smile. "To move the dollhouse."

I stepped back, straightened. "Good. Because I was going to tell you not to bother if it was about the kiss. You're dating my cousin, remember?"

"Good night, Mellie," he whispered, then headed toward the stairs. I could hear his soft laughter and retreating footsteps as I closed my door, wondering how Nola could see so clearly the one thing I couldn't bring myself to acknowledge.

CHAPTER 14

I struggled home the following afternoon after a horrendous day at work. It had started with Charlene, the new receptionist, swapping out my latte for green tea, leaving me with a caffeine deficit that nobody appreciated. Then I'd spent the entire day showing historic homes in the Radcliffeborough neighborhood to a couple from Mount Pleasant, only to be told after touring house number seven that they weren't ready to move just yet. But the icing on the cake of my day had been my trip to the home of Sophie's friend Carmen, from her yoga class, who was making the bridesmaids' dresses. My dress was little more than a toga with a leotard underneath. Even a Wonderbra couldn't help me look like anything but a male nymph stuck in time. My headpiece would be a crown of flowers, and the length of my dress wouldn't matter because I would, indeed, be barefoot.

I paused on the front walk of my mother's house, studying the two cars parked at the curb. The first was Jack's Porsche. I'd planned to not be at home when he came to move the dollhouse, although now I realized that he couldn't move it alone and most likely would have had to wait until Chad was finished teaching for the day. My gaze strayed to the porch, where I recognized Chad's bike, the identifying peace sign on the back fender faded from the sun.

I considered retreating to my car for a much-needed nap, but the car parked behind the Porsche captured my attention. It was a bright red Beetle with curb feelers protruding from the wheel wells, a red-and-green fuzzy cover over the steering wheel. A small Christmas wreath was affixed to the front grille, and a handicap tag dangled from the rearview mirror.

Curious, I walked a little faster, almost jogging up the front steps and into the house. Dropping my briefcase and purse in the foyer, I followed the sound of voices into the front parlor with the large stained-glass window. Normally, the window was the topic of conversation for new visitors to the house, but I could tell from the tone of the conversation that they weren't talking about a window.

My mother met me in the doorway. "Mellie, I'm glad you're here. We have company."

With a worried frown, she led me into the room. A square block of glass, something I recognized as a remnant from the garden that had been left behind by the former occupants, sat in the middle of the room in the same spot my grandmother's Chippendale table had sat as of earlier that day. Julia Manigault sat in her wheelchair in front of it with her house manager, Dee Davenport, next to her and Nola on the other side. But the oddest part of the entire tableau was General Lee casually sniffing the rear end of the shaggy dog I'd seen before, who insisted on vanishing as soon as he caught me watching him.

I stepped forward to greet Julia. "This is a surprise, Miss Manigault. I didn't expect to see you again."

Her gaze held nothing of the venom I'd seen the previous day. "I wanted to tell you how sorry I was for my behavior. I don't handle surprises very well, and your mention of the dollhouse . . ." She paused. "And I needed to see the dollhouse. To make sure it's the same one."

I glanced at Nola, who just shrugged. "The same one as what?"

"The same dollhouse that was given to me by my father in 1931, when I was ten years old." I waited for her to say more that might unlock part of the mystery surrounding the dollhouse, but she pursed her lips tightly, as if afraid something she didn't want revealed would escape.

Dee stood and took my hand. "I'm sorry to come unannounced, but Miss Julia insisted on coming right over. She wanted to apologize in person for the . . . misunderstanding yesterday."

I raised my brow. *Misunderstanding?* The woman had screamed at me to leave. "I see," I said, my Charleston upbringing not allowing me to demand that she define *misunderstanding* in a language I could understand. "How did you know how to find me?"

Dee grinned. "Your real estate ads are in the papers all the time. Not the best picture of you, Miss Julia pointed out, but we recognized you. We called your office, and when Charlene Rose answered the phone—she used to live two doors down from Miss Julia—I asked her for your home address."

I made a mental note to confront Charlene about how it wasn't a good idea to be handing out my home address to anybody who asked—neighbor or not.

She continued. "We went to your house on Tradd Street and the most peculiar man with pants that didn't fit him very well told us we could find you here at your mother's house. Which was a bonus, seeing how Miss Julia wanted to see Mrs. Middleton again anyway."

I sat down on the sofa opposite them and nodded to Mrs. Houlihan, who'd just brought in a tray of sweet tea and cookies and began passing glasses and plates around to the small group.

Miss Julia's eyes bored into mine. "I knew I'd seen you before, though, when you showed up on my doorstep. You were involved in that business with Nevin Vanderhorst's house and the dead bodies buried in the garden. The papers didn't mention anything besides what the police told them, but people in this town talk, and a lot of them were saying how you could see ghosts and that's how you found out about what happened to poor Louisa Vanderhorst."

I felt my tongue stick to the roof of my mouth, suddenly glad that I'd already had the conversation with Nola about my "gift." "Yes, well, you can never believe what you hear, can you?" My voice trailed off as everyone's attention was directed toward the foyer, where the sounds of heavy footsteps and men's voices became louder and louder.

I stood and turned to see Jack and Chad with the dollhouse between them, their faces strained from exertion as they carried the large structure to the glass block and set it down in front of us.

My mother stood to get out of the way. "Since Nola didn't want it in her room anymore, we figured it would be easier moving it down here than bringing Miss Manigault upstairs to see it."

Chad gave us a quick good-bye and left, Dee's gaze following his backside as he walked toward the door. Nobody else noticed, as all attention was focused on Julia Manigault as she examined the dollhouse. She pressed her hand against her heart, and her eyes widened in what I could only describe as fear. Whether she would admit it or not, she knew this dollhouse well.

"I want to see it close up," she barked, and Dee stood immediately before wheeling her charge toward the rear of the dollhouse. Julia's head jerked back and forth as she studied each room in detail, each cushion, each window treatment. She even stuck her finger inside and hit the small piano, an odd tinny sound adding to the strangeness of the moment.

"Where are the people? The family that goes inside?"

Nola sat up straight. "I put them all inside their beds last night. They should still be there."

"They're not," Julia said, her voice low as she turned her attention on me.

Feeling chastised, I stood. "Maybe you took them out and forgot," I said, hoping Nola knew I wasn't doubting her. "I'll go look."

"I'll help," Nola said, shooting out of her chair.

We excused ourselves and climbed the steps to Nola's room. As we stood outside her door, she grabbed my arm. "Do you think my mom moved them? Because they were still in their beds this morning when I left for Alston's house."

"I'm not sure," I said carefully. Knowing the dollhouse was out of her room encouraged me to tell her more. "I don't think your mother is responsible. There's something else here, something that's not a gentle spirit like Bonnie."

"What do you mean?" Her face paled.

"The way the figures were thrown, and the two broken, for instance. And I saw a man at Miss Manigault's house who definitely didn't want us around. I'm thinking they could be connected."

Nola squeezed my arm tighter. "And you let me put it in my room?"

"We tried to talk you out of it, remember? But you insisted. And if I really thought you were in danger, I would have done something sooner. I also knew that your mother was there protecting you."

Her face softened and her eyes began to fill. She looked away quickly, then jutted her chin toward the door. "You open it."

I turned the handle and pushed. The door gave way a little, then slammed hard in my face.

"Is it stuck?" Nola asked, taking a step away from the door.

I shook my head. "No." Taking a deep breath, I began to repeat out loud the mantra my mother had taught me. "I am stronger than you; I am stronger than you," I said quietly. I turned the handle again, but before pushing, I faced Nola. "You don't have to come in. In fact, it might be better if you stayed in the hallway."

"As if. You think I want to miss this?"

"You are *so* Jack's daughter," I said, shaking my head. "Come on and help me push, then."

She joined me and pressed her shoulder against the door. "Ready." I wasn't surprised to see no fear in her eyes at all.

I began repeating my mantra again, and Nola joined me as I turned the handle and both of us pressed hard on the door. It gave way easily, making us stumble into the room. The sheet music that Nola had picked up that morning and stored in the guitar case was scattered around the room again, flopping like unsettled moths in the breeze from the open windows. Heat from outside mixed with the icy cold of the room, creating an odd fog that hovered near the ceiling.

I felt, rather than saw, Bonnie in the corner, and knew that if I turned to look at her, she'd disappear.

"Why do they have to do that to the music?" Nola groaned, stooping down to begin picking it up.

"It's your mother. To let you know she's near."

Slowly, Nola stood, the music slipping from her hands. "Mom?"

The corner where the guitar case rested against the wall shimmered with light. I turned toward it. "Bonnie?"

As if a light switch had been hit, the shimmering stopped. "Is she gone?" Nola whispered.

I nodded. "I won't give up, okay? I'll figure out a way to find out why she's still here."

"But why would she open the windows, too? It just makes more of a mess."

"Maybe she didn't," I said, my attention drawn to the wall behind the headboard. Scratched into the paint and plaster in bold lettering were the words "Stop her." My gaze slid down to the nightstand by the bed where the figure of the boy lay on its side, the head covered with plaster dust.

"What the . . . ?" Nola started.

I sent her a hard stare.

"Heck," she finished.

I glanced around the room. "Where are the rest of the figures?"

Nola began walking around, opening drawers, pulling aside the drapes. Finally, she knelt on the floor next to the bed and peered underneath. "I found them."

Something in her voice made me kneel down next to her. The remaining family members lay side by side, the father separated from the other two. A shiver coursed through me; all three figures were lying facedown, their eyes hidden. I reached under the bed and grabbed them before standing again. "Do you see the dog?"

Nola shook her head. "He's missing."

"Not really," I said under my breath, remembering General Lee's playmate downstairs. "We'll look for him later. Right now, let's get these out of your room and bring them down to Miss Manigault. But close your windows first. Unless you want palmetto bugs inside."

I'd never seen her move so fast as she hurried to latch the windows shut, being very conscious of where she put her hands and checking the wall for what might be crawling beside her. I would have laughed but then I would be a hypocrite.

General Lee was running circles around the foyer as we descended the steps, only the disembodied tail of the other dog visible to me. I remembered the broken dog figurine and wondered where it might be. And wondered how the real dog might have died.

I walked over to where Julia sat in her wheelchair in front of the dollhouse and handed her the dolls. The skin on her hands was as transparent as tissue paper, the blue veins like road maps. But they showed no sign of arthritis as she clutched the figures tightly before laying them out in her lap. She pointed to the chalky blond head of the boy with a shaking finger. "This is my brother, William. Always making a mess, isn't he? Always trying to tell you something." She looked up at me, her dark eyes fathomless.

She knows, I thought. *She's seen the writing before.*

"Who are the others?" I asked.

She pointed to the man and woman. "This is Mama and Papa— Anne and Harold Manigault. And this," she said, pointing to the young girl with the dark hair, "is me." Her brows formed a "V" over her nose. "Where is Buddy?"

"The dog?" Nola leaned forward. "He was in the house earlier, but now I can't find him. I'm sure he's around somewhere."

I caught my mother's gaze and knew she'd figured out what General Lee was chasing, too.

"Buddy was a gift from my papa, too. But he ran away the same night William did. I never knew what happened to him."

I had a strong feeling it hadn't been a natural death, but I didn't think now was the time to tell her. Instead, I said, "The dollhouse was a gift to you from your father. I would think you'd want to save it to give it to your daughter or granddaughter."

Her face grew hard. "I never married."

This time, I shared a glance with Jack, who'd moved to stand behind his daughter, remembering what he'd told me of what he knew about the dollhouse, and how the sales records discovered for the dollhouse dated back to the late nineteen thirties, when Julia would have been young enough to still be contemplating marriage and children.

I tried to lighten the tension that seemed to have thrown a thick cloud over the room. "Nola has really been enjoying the dollhouse. All the tiniest details are really astounding. It's impossible to find that kind of craftsmanship today."

Julia looked past me as if I hadn't spoken. "Nola. That's such an unusual name."

I shot a warning look at Nola as she opened her mouth to respond. She frowned at me, but paused, finally saying, "It's a nickname." Very quietly she added, "My real name is Emmaline."

"Much more suitable," Julia said. "Emmaline, what sort of musical training have you had?"

I watched as Jack placed his hand on Nola's shoulder and she didn't flinch. Her eyes darted around to each of the room's occupants, as if waiting for somebody else to answer. Finally, she said, "I haven't."

Upstairs, a radio burst into life, the song "I'm Just Getting Started" blaring at high volume. Nola blanched as I looked at Jack and smiled thinly. "I think there's a short in Nola's radio—it keeps going on all by itself. Could you please unplug it from the wall?"

He sent me an odd look as he left the room. I turned back to Julia, who continued to scrutinize Nola. "No formal training at all? I heard you on the piano yesterday, and that was no amateur playing. You play by ear then? But surely you've been exposed to music before."

Nola's chipped and black-painted nails dug into the thighs of her torn jeans. She angled her face down, but I could see the bright red of her skin. Very quietly, she said, "My mother taught me how to play the guitar. I taught myself how to play the small keyboard we had until she sold it for drugs." She looked up defiantly, not averting her gaze from the old woman.

Jack had returned to the room in time to hear the last part, and I watched his face transform from the jovial Jack I knew into Papa Bear. He marched into the room and stood behind Nola again, both hands on her shoulders. He fixed a smile on his face as he addressed the woman in the wheelchair. "Is there a reason for this interrogation? You came to see the dollhouse and verify that it was yours. I hope you're not wanting it back, because I doubt my daughter would sell it to you at any price. So, if that's all, Nola and I have dinner plans."

Nola nodded vigorously. "Yes, we do."

Dee stood, smiling apologetically. "We're so sorry to have taken up so much of your time. Miss Manigault did so want to see Mrs. Middleton again as well as the dollhouse, and since we've already seen both . . ."

Julia glared at Dee, halting her progress. Turning back to Nola, she said, "Would you be interested in a formal musical education? Whether you like it or not, you have a lot of musical talent. It would be a shame for it to go to waste."

Nola had begun shaking her head before the old woman finished speaking. "No. I don't like music."

Having listened to the stuff she normally played on her radio, I'd have to agree with that one. But I'd also heard her singing and playing the piano, and as much as I hated to, I had to agree with Julia Manigault's assessment of Nola's potential.

"She writes music, too," I said, avoiding Nola's glance. Whatever was holding her back from acknowledging her gift had nothing to do with music; of that I was sure. I'd trodden that same path before and recognized it. It had everything to do with Bonnie and their mother-daughter relationship, and that was something I knew I could work with. The music part, not so much.

"And she definitely knows how to sing," my mother added. She turned to Nola. "You always sing in the shower and it's hard not to notice. You have an extraordinary voice."

I sent my mother a grateful look, glad I wasn't standing alone and feeling like a bully.

Nola's flush deepened. "I don't like music," she repeated, but she sounded less adamant.

"Why are you asking?" Jack leaned forward, his shoulders creating a barrier behind Nola.

Julia tilted her chin as high as her hunched back would allow. "Because I would like to teach her. She shows great promise despite her reluctance to pursue her talents. That's the problem with youngsters nowadays. Too lazy. They don't want to work at anything. They want to play with their phones and chat on Bookface all day long."

"Facebook," Nola and I said in unison.

Nola stood. "I am *not* lazy. I've always made straight As, and I helped my mom clean apartments when I wasn't in school. I know how to work hard." She was breathing heavily, her face flushed.

A look of triumph passed over Julia's face. "Then prove it. Mrs. Middleton was telling me that you're applying to Ashley Hall. It couldn't hurt your résumé to list my name as a private music tutor."

"Who cares if I get in? There are lots of schools I could go to." Her jaw jutted out in an excellent impersonation of her father, who was doing the same thing.

"Ah," said Julia, tapping her thin fingers on the arms of her wheel-chair. "It's that hard-work thing again, isn't it? Ashley Hall girls aren't known for being slackers. I'm sure there are plenty of other schools in Charleston. I just never saw the need to know about them."

"Now, wait just a minute," Jack said, coming around the sofa to stand in front of Julia. Dee stood as if the old lady might need a body-guard. "You don't know my daughter well enough to be making any sort of judgment about her. You have no idea what she's gone through, especially this last year. Stuff that would send most kids—and a lot of adults—into a wall. She could run rings around those Ashley Hall girls. And of course she's musically gifted. Her mother was a damned fine musician, bordering on genius. You'd be lucky to have her as your student."

"So it's settled then." Julia glanced up at Dee, who settled a shawl on her shoulders and unlocked the brake on the back wheels. "I'll have Dee call with details."

"What are you . . . ?" Jack began.

I stopped him with a hand on his arm. "We'll discuss it and let you know."

"Wait!" Nola shouted.

We all stopped and stared at her.

"You still have the dolls from the dollhouse."

"So I do," said Julia, as she scooped them from her lap and held them out to Nola. "Be careful with them. And never put William and Papa in the same room together. They don't like that very much."

Nola's eyes widened as she accepted the dolls, then watched as Dee wheeled the old woman out of the room to the front door. I let them out, carrying the folded wheelchair while Dee helped Julia down the steps.

As Dee settled Julia in the chair again to wheel her down the walk to the car, the old lady grasped my arm. "You be sure to be the one to bring Emmaline. Do you understand?"

I straightened and gently pulled my arm away, understanding exactly what she meant. "I need to discuss it with Nola and her father. I'll be in touch."

"You do that," she said, turning her back on me as Dee wheeled her away. I didn't wait to see how they managed to fit the old lady and her wheelchair in the Beetle, and hurriedly ran up the steps and closed the door behind me.

I was halfway across the foyer when the radio upstairs blasted on again, "I'm Just Getting Started" playing as loudly as before. Without a word, I detoured to the stairs, knowing that I would find the radio unplugged when I went to Nola's room to turn it off, and knowing, too, that Julia Manigault's visit today had nothing at all to do with teaching music.

CHAPTER 15

I had just slipped on my nightgown when my mother tapped on my bedroom door. After I told her to come in, she stuck her head around the edge of the door and said, "I have a surprise for you."

She walked in, a dress bag from Berlins draped over one arm. "I think I found your dress for the party."

"Mother! You went shopping without me?"

"We figured it would be better that way."

"'We'?"

"Sophie, Nola, and me."

There was a heavy pause as her words sank in. Slowly, I said, "You took Sophie and Nola to help pick out a dress for me?" I looked at the bag in horror.

"Technically, no. I took Nola shopping—the poor girl needs clothes that fit in a desperate way—and brought Sophie along to help with that. Sophie knows all the young, hip stores and I don't."

I was having trouble trying to sort through what my mother was telling me. "So you let Sophie pick out clothes for Nola?" I looked around the room. "There's a hidden camera in here somewhere, isn't there?"

My mother turned to the tall armoire behind her and hooked the hanger on one of the doors before unrolling the plastic bag from the bottom. Gradually, something silky and deep, dark red began to appear. "Don't be ridiculous, Mellie. I said Sophie knows where to shop, not *how* to shop. Nola has a good sense of style. It might not be our style, but she makes it work for her. She knows how to put things together that give her that edgy California-artist look that suits her. Sophie just puts anything together so that she looks like a train wreck, but that somehow suits her, too."

She finished unwrapping the dress, blocking it from my view as if she wasn't ready to reveal it yet. "When I told the saleslady at Berlins what I was looking for, she brought me this dress and I knew this was the one." She stepped aside with a flourish of both arms. "What do you think?"

I stared at the red silk confection, thinking that it belonged more on a starlet on the red carpet than hanging in my bedroom. It was off-the-shoulder, with a plunging sweetheart neckline. The midsection was gathered in to accentuate the waist, then flared in a tango-style hem past the hips. It was . . . exquisite.

"I can't wear that," I said, my voice harsher than I'd intended.

"Why not?" She sounded hurt.

More gently, I said, "It's a very beautiful dress." My mouth opened and closed a few times as I searched for a reason, not completely sure I knew what it was. I continued. "But I can't wear it because for one I'd need a turtleneck to wear under it so nobody could see my navel. And for two because it's, well, it's . . . it's not me."

She crossed her arms and lowered her chin. "This dress *is* you. Or the you that you never allow anybody else to see. You're not all businesswoman, Mellie. You're also a very attractive woman who could use a dress like this to build up her confidence."

"I am confident! I couldn't be successful if I weren't."

"Yes, confident at work. But what about with men? You hide behind your power suits and pearls when you're working. But when you put on a dress like this, you have to rely on your other . . . assets."

I stared pointedly at the neckline. "I don't have any other . . . assets."

My mother threw back her head and laughed. "That's not what I was talking about, but not to worry. See the ruching here?" She pointed to the gathered silk that wrapped across the breasts. "It gives extra volume just where you need it."

I shook my head, trying to clear the image of me wearing that dress. And Jack walking toward me . . .

As if reading my mind, my mother said, "I think Jack will like it."

I stepped closer to the dress, pretending to study it more closely to hide my face. "Why do you care what Jack thinks?"

"Because you obviously do. I'm assuming it was his voice I heard in here last night."

My cheeks heated. "It's not what you're thinking. He came by last night to check on Nola, since she was so upset when we left Julia Manigault's house. I wouldn't have let him in, but apparently he has a key." I looked pointedly at my mother. "What were you thinking, giving him a key?"

My mother feigned innocence. "His daughter is living here with me. I thought it made sense so he could come and go as he wanted." Fluffing out the bottom of the dress, she said, "There were some delectable shoes in the window at Bob Ellis, but you can do that on your own. They're carrying Ann Roth shoes there now—remember the tapestry ones I bought that you love so much? Anyway, Sophie and Nola had joined me by then, and I don't think that store has ever seen Birkenstocks cross their threshold. I didn't want anybody to get upset."

Facing the armoire, she slipped the plastic back over the dress. "Go ahead and try it on. It's your size and I know it will look fabulous on you, but I kept the receipt just in case you want to chicken out and buy something bland that a debutante would wear to the St. Cecilia ball."

I frowned as she kissed me good night on the cheek, wondering why I couldn't shake the image of Jack seeing me in that red dress, and why the thought didn't horrify me as much as it should.

☙

I was in the kitchen making myself a cup of cocoa and finishing off a box of doughnut holes before I went to bed when Jack brought Nola home. When Jack had said earlier that he was taking Nola out to dinner to get Julia Manigault to leave, I'd never expected it to really happen. I suppose that Jack's valiant defense of Nola in front of a roomful of people made her decide to lighten up a bit where he was concerned and actually agree to spend time alone with him.

I peered out of the kitchen in time to see Nola, with a deep scowl on her face, stomping up the stairs while Jack stood at the bottom frowning as he stared up at her.

"Good night, Nola," he called up to her.

She slammed the door in response.

"So dinner went well," I said, leaning against the doorjamb and taking a sip from my mug.

He saw me for the first time. "Better than a sharp stick in the eye, anyway." He spotted my mug. "What are you drinking?"

"Hot cocoa." I jerked my head in the direction of the kitchen. "Come on; I'll make you some."

"You do know it's summer, right?" he asked, following me into the kitchen.

"Yeah, but there's never a wrong time for hot cocoa."

"I was actually talking about what you're wearing."

I filled the kettle and set it on the stove. "We got the air conditioner fixed, so my mother feels like she needs to make up for lost time by cranking it down to subzero temperatures."

"It actually feels pretty good in here to me."

I dumped four teaspoons of cocoa into a large mug, then remembered it wasn't for me and returned two teaspoons back to the container. "I'm pretty cold-natured," I said, licking the spoon before remembering I needed it to stir in the water.

"I've heard that before," he said, smiling innocently at me as I dumped the spoon in the sink and took a clean one out of the drawer.

I waited for the kettle to whistle, then poured the hot water into the mug before handing it to Jack with the spoon. "Don't burn yourself."

"I've heard that before, too," he said quietly as he blew on his mug.

I took a long sip of cocoa, needing something to open my throat again. "So, where did you go to dinner?"

"Cru Café. I hadn't been there in a while but thought Nola might like it. They've got a great menu and a cool atmosphere."

"Yeah, but do they have vegan choices?"

He leaned back in his chair, tapping his fingertips on his mug. "Not exactly. They were very accommodating, however, and came up with a pasta-and-risotto dish that Nola seemed to like. She even ordered dessert, which surprised me."

"Good. So the dinner itself wasn't a disaster."

"It wasn't. The food was great, and I actually thought that we were getting along. We stayed away from sore subjects—like her mom, and why I wasn't there while she was growing up. We talked about things like her favorite bands, the differences between California and South Carolina, palmetto bugs." He flashed his award-winning grin at me. "Important things like that."

"So why was she so angry just now?"

"Because I made the mistake when I was standing out on the porch with her of telling her that I thought her mother would want her to pursue her musical talents." He shrugged. "She's obviously gifted—we all heard her, so it's not like I'm the only one who thinks so. And she told me something tonight that explained a lot about why she runs away every time somebody wants to tell her how musically gifted she is."

I leaned forward, my hands cupping the cooling mug. "She says it's because she hates music, but she's never without it—either singing it or listening to it. When she thinks I'm not around, she'll listen to the classical music station. The one thing she won't do is pick up her mother's guitar. I've yet to hear her strum a note."

"That doesn't surprise me. That's sort of what I figured out tonight. Nola told me that music made her feel like the ugly stepsister. That's all she'd say on the subject, but it spoke volumes. I think Nola considered music to be her mother's favorite child. It was the one thing Bonnie sacrificed everything for—including her flesh-and-blood daughter. Nola didn't fail her; her music did. Bonnie always had dreams of driving along and hearing one of her songs on the radio. I guess after so many years of trying, she finally gave up, feeling the music had failed her. And that's when she killed herself. Nola must believe that she wasn't enough of a reason for her mother to stick around. That without the music, Bonnie didn't see anything else worth living for."

I regarded Jack silently for a long moment, watching as he drained his mug, then slid it away from him. "I didn't expect that from you."

He looked at me warily. "Expect what?"

"For you to be so astute. For a guy, that was pretty insightful"

His eyes met mine, making me nervous. "I've said this before, Mellie, but I think it bears repeating. There's a lot you don't know about me."

My leg started jiggling, a nervous habit I'd had since childhood, and I stood quickly so he wouldn't notice, then picked up both mugs. "For what it's worth, I think you might be right. Obviously, there were the drugs and alcohol that heavily influenced Bonnie's decision, but Nola's only thirteen. It would make sense that somebody that young who'd lived the life she did would reach that conclusion." I placed the mugs in the sink. "So what do we do now?"

"We?"

I paused, wondering why I'd said that inclusive word as well. And why it had come so naturally. I told myself it was because I liked Nola and I wasn't ready to let her start navigating her life without me, but even I wasn't so adept at lying to myself that I actually thought that was the only reason. Plastering a smile on my face, I turned and leaned against the counter, my arms crossed in front of me. "Jack, you have a teenage daughter. In the not-so-distant future she'll be dating boys. Boys like the boy you used to be. Do you really want to handle it alone?"

His face sobered. "I'm sure there are convents in Ireland where I can send her until she's ready to date. Around the age of thirty or so."

My own smile faltered as I considered something else. "Unless, of course, Rebecca wants to step in.".

Jack slid back his chair and snorted. "Who do you think gave me the convent idea?"

I nodded, understanding completely. "So," I repeated, "what do we do now?"

He stood, his expression thoughtful. "I'll arrange a schedule with Miss Manigault. But for the first few times, at least until Nola's comfortable, I'd love it if you and your mother wouldn't mind taking her over. She's much happier when you two are around, and I thought that might help acclimate her."

"So Nola agreed to go?" I knew his powers of persuasion were legendary, but he'd seemed to hit a brick wall where his daughter was concerned.

"Not exactly. But she agreed to go at least once, if only to prove to Miss Manigault that she's not lazy. I'll figure out a way to convince her to keep going."

He began to walk toward me, and I kept my arms folded across my chest. "I'd like to go back, and Julia requested that I accompany Nola.

She knew who I was—about me seeing ghosts. I think she wants me to help her with the spirits that are haunting the dollhouse—and her house, apparently. I saw one both times I was there, and he wasn't the warm, fuzzy sort."

Jack stopped in front of me, his gaze resting on my folded arms. "Yeah, I thought there was something besides the desire to teach music to Nola that brought her over here. And the way she talked about that doll that looked like her brother, William, I knew there was something she wasn't telling us. So of course I went to see Yvonne and did a little research."

Yvonne Craig worked at the library of the South Carolina Historical Society and had been a huge resource for both Jack and me in searching through historical archives relating to both my house on Tradd Street and my mother's house. She was at least eighty years old but looked two decades younger. And had a huge crush on Jack, of course.

It was my turn to raise a brow. "And what did you find?"

"That her brother, William Manigault, disappeared from the public record in 1938, which, coincidentally or not, is the same year the Manigaults sold the dollhouse. The same year Julia's mother, Anne Manigault, was committed to a home for the mentally weak. She died a year later."

"But as you've said more than once, there's no such thing as coincidence," I said.

"Exactly." He reached a hand toward me.

I held my breath and waited, then felt his fingers brush something off my chin. "Powdered sugar," he said, bringing his hand back down to his side.

Embarrassed, I tried to think of something witty to say but was cut short by the sound of a radio blaring at high volume. We both followed the sound out of the kitchen, then stopped, trying to make sense of what we were seeing. Floating from seemingly thin air, pages and pages of loose sheet music drifted like snow into the foyer, carpeting the floor like rose petals.

"What the . . . ?" Jack began before we heard a door being flung open with enough force to crash into the wall, the song from the radio, "I'm Just Getting Started," even louder now.

"Mellie!" Nola shrieked as she skidded to a halt at the top of the stairs. In her hands she held Bonnie's guitar, each and every string snapped in half and curling over the brown varnished wood of the guitar's body.

Something flew through the air and whizzed by my face, striking Jack in the arm.

"Ouch," he said, before leaning down to pick up whatever had hit him. Our eyes met over the dollhouse figure of William Manigault.

"Nope," he said. "There're no such thing as coincidence."

I looked up the stairs at a white-faced Nola watching another sheet of music floating past her face.

I put my foot on the first step and looked down, the acrid scent of smoldering carpet heavy in my nostrils. The words "Stop her" had been burned into the runner, the edges still smoldering.

My worried gaze met Jack's. "This is probably the only time you'll ever hear me say this, but I think you might be right."

CHAPTER 16

I parked my car on Queen Street, then studied my face in the rearview mirror. I was meeting Marc for dinner at Husk, and I wanted to make sure I conveyed the right message: not too sexy, not too interested. Just dinner between old friends, if you could even call us that. He'd left a message with Charlene earlier, saying that he had reservations at seven and that he had something important to tell me. I'd tried to call him back to find out more, but his secretary had said he was in meetings all day and couldn't be reached. I'd left a message with her, saying I'd be there, then proceeded to spend two hours in my closet trying to find the right outfit that would make me appear as neutral as Switzerland.

I locked the car door, then tried to wipe a finger smudge off the back window left by a client's child. I made a mental note to get my car detailed later to not only remove all finger and nose smudges, but also the french fries embedded in my carpets and sticky drips from leaking juice boxes off the leather upholstery. It was part of doing business, and since the clients had purchased a nice single home on Rutledge, it took the edge off of the sugar-coated seats and smudgy doors.

I recognized Marc walking toward me on the sidewalk, both of us habitually early for any appointment. We hugged and gave double cheek kisses and then I waited as he held me at arm's length.

"Always beautiful, Melanie, but tonight especially."

I blushed, wondering whether the Diane von Furstenberg wrap dress leaned too far on the sexy side and whether I should have worn a camisole underneath so the V-neck wouldn't have seemed so, well,

"V"-shaped. "Thank you, Marc. And you look handsome and suave, as usual."

We stood smiling at each other for a moment in mutual admiration until Marc looked behind me to frown at my car. "I wish you'd have allowed me to come pick you up."

"I know, but I had a late appointment and didn't know whether I'd have time to go home first," I lied. I'm not sure why I wanted to have my own transportation other than the certainty that being desperate and lonely wasn't a good combination when having dinner with a man I wasn't sure I even liked.

Marc offered his arm and I took it as he led me toward the restaurant. The building was a restored double house with a sweet-smelling fountain filled with flowers dominating the small garden. As we walked up the steps to the front porch, I spotted a woman in period costume from the 1860s holding a baby. She was staring at me like she needed to ask me something. Turning to Marc, I said, "I love the costumed actors."

He gave me a confused glance, causing me to look back at the woman, who was now walking toward me, close enough that I could see the courtyard fountain through her. Out of habit, I quickly turned away and walked through the front door, humming ABBA's "Take a Chance on Me" and causing Marc to send me another look.

The maître d' greeted Marc by name and escorted us to a cozy table for two by a window overlooking Queen Street. Despite the antique exterior of the home, the interior was done in a soothing contemporary style, with cool blue walls and floor-to-ceiling curtains done in a fabric of bright splotches of color that resembled flowers. The restaurant was crowded, the low hubbub of voices a soothing backdrop to the sounds of silverware on black skillet plates and the clinking of wineglasses.

I paused in front of our table, where a bottle of champagne sat chilling in an ice bucket, two flutes sitting next to it. A pang of panic hit me as my eyes darted around for a ring box. As far-flung as that conclusion seemed to be, I couldn't think of any other reason why he'd have brought me here for a celebratory dinner. Besides, I'd never been proposed to before, so I had no frame of reference.

"Mellie? Matt? Is that you?"

We both whipped around to a neighboring table for two by the side window, where Jack was in the process of standing. Rebecca looked pretty in a bland Barbie-doll way, in a pink sundress with a bow on one of the straps, and looking less than thrilled to see us. I remembered what Sophie had said about my own expression when I saw Jack with Rebecca and forced my face to remain neutral.

Jack approached with his hand held out to Marc. "What a thrill to see you both here; isn't it, Rebecca?"

Rebecca nodded, her enthusiasm tepid. She stood, too, and I wasn't sure whether it was to embrace me—which she did, including a kiss on each cheek, or to show off her adorable pink linen peep-toe platform pumps. "Hello, cousin," she said, following my gaze. "Aren't they great? They're from the Ann Roth summer collection. I got them at Bob Ellis."

"My mother mentioned I needed to stop by the store—I guess I'll have to."

She sent me an odd look, as if just remembering something.

"What is it?" I asked.

"Nothing, really. Just when you mentioned your mother it reminded me of a dream I had the other night."

I raised both eyebrows. Rebecca's psychic inheritance had been the gift of prophetic dreams. But, as with communicating with ghosts, her visions usually lacked clarity but were more like puzzle pieces given upside down and out of order. "About my mother?"

"Yes." She gave a little laugh. "She was holding a baby. Of course, the baby could be symbolic—like the start of something new for her. Or even about her relationship with you, her only child. Obviously, your mother is past menopause, so it's doubtful the dream has a literal interpretation, although there are certain scientific breakthroughs that would allow . . ."

I held up my hand. "That's enough, thank you. I'll let her know. Maybe she'll have an idea what it's about."

We turned back to the men, who were waiting with restrained impatience. I noticed that both Jack and Rebecca were surreptitiously eyeing the champagne and flutes. Marc noticed and stepped back to give them a better view. "Yes, Melanie and I are about to celebrate some very exciting news."

When he offered nothing more, Rebecca and Jack turned to me. I shrugged my shoulders. "I'm in the dark, too, I'm afraid."

Marc continued. "And I'd invite you both to share in the celebration, but we only have room for two, and it's a full house tonight."

Jack had already turned and begun to drag his table next to ours, ignoring the glowers of the maître d', the other diners, and Marc. "Problem solved," he said, straightening the silverware before retrieving their chairs.

Our waiter appeared, his smile trying to hide his annoyance at having to weave through the crowded aisle to reach us. "Two more champagne flutes?" he asked.

"Absolutely," Marc said, his tone and his expression holding a hint of restraint and something else, something that reminded me of a smoldering fire that was about to have a revitalizing puff of air bring it to life.

"And a bottle of sparkling apple cider for me, please," Jack said to the waiter.

Marc held out a chair for Rebecca to sit, then took the chair next to hers, leaving Jack and me on the opposite side, with me facing Marc. We proceeded to engage in innocuous small talk that said nothing while the glances shooting among the four of us spoke volumes. Rebecca's attention was divided almost equally between Marc and Jack, while I preferred to concentrate more on the excellent menu. I was starving and I saw no reason to embroil myself in the undercurrent of whatever was flowing between Jack and Marc. And Rebecca and Jack. And Marc and Rebecca. It was exhausting, and I really, really needed to eat before I drank a glass of champagne.

We ordered a first course of salads and locally harvested oysters while the sommelier appeared with two more glasses and Jack's sparkling cider.

"So, what are we celebrating tonight?" Jack asked, his jovial question edged with something hard and sharp. I watched as his gaze slid to my empty left ring finger before his eyes met mine with a look of . . . relief?

"Yes," Rebecca said, turning to Marc. "I've been dying to know since I saw the champagne bottle." Long lashes swept over her crystal-blue eyes, and I wanted to tell her she looked more like a talking baby doll than the sexy woman I was sure she was trying to be. I almost expected her to say, "Change me," next.

We sat with our glasses in our hands, each of us with an unreadable expression. Raising his glass, Marc said, "To my book. It's been scheduled for a December first release, and the publisher is going to be pushing it big-time in all the stores for a huge Christmas sellout. My print run is already through the roof, and the preorders are beyond even my expectations. They're not promising anything, but my publisher's saying he's expecting it to be top ten on all the major lists. And . . ." He paused for emphasis. "Sony Pictures has just purchased the film rights, and they're already talking to Ben Affleck about playing the lead."

Rebecca, Marc, and I took long sips, while I noticed Jack just pretended to hold the glass to his lips. Rebecca put her glass down and clapped her hands. "Tell us more! I'm sure I'll be able to get you some front-page coverage in the paper, since you're local. And I'm still doing some freelance work for *Charleston* magazine, too, so maybe we can set up an interview and see what happens."

"Yes," Jack said slowly. "Tell us more. We're all dying to hear." His eyebrows knitted. "I thought you were self-publishing your book for a few friends and family."

Marc sent him a withering look. "Actually, it's being published by Bigglesmann House in New York. It's one of the largest publishers."

I turned to Jack, surprised. "That's your publisher, isn't it?"

"Yes," he said before slugging back his flute of cider. I watched as he eyed the champagne bottle only an arm's length away. "It is."

"What a coincidence," Marc said, his smile showing that he'd been waiting a long time to drop that bomb on Jack. "I've found them to be so receptive and enthusiastic so far. They're even talking about more books already, and this one hasn't even hit the shelves."

"How exciting," said Jack. "I didn't know there was such a market for picture books."

"Actually," Marc said very slowly, as if speaking to a small child, "it's adult nonfiction. But my publisher has asked me not to discuss anything more, so I'm afraid I'm going to have to leave it at that."

Without waiting for the wine steward, Jack refilled his cider and threw it back like a shot of whiskey. "What a disappointment," he said. "I was so looking forward to hearing every detail for the rest of my dinner."

Both Rebecca and I turned to stare at Jack. That was low, even for Jack. And I didn't think to remind him that it had been he who'd moved the tables so he could join us.

Marc seemed unfazed. "When's your next book out, Jack? Maybe you and I can do a double event or something if it's released around the same time as mine."

As the waiter approached, Jack looked at the man like a drowning person looks at a sandbar. "Great. I'm starved. Is everybody ready to order?" He gave a cursory glance around the table. "All right then. Let's have another bottle of the best bubbly you have and another of the sparkling cider for me. And please put this on Mr. Longo's tab, since he's a big-deal author now."

Marc's eyes widened slightly before he cleared his throat. "I was about to suggest that myself. It's my celebration, after all." He lifted his glass again and saluted Jack before sipping, his eyes like those of a cat that had eaten the cream, and the whole bowl, too.

I was mentally exhausted by the time I returned to my mother's house. The front lights had been left burning, giving me a warm sense of belonging, as if the lights signified that somebody had thought of me. It would be one of the things I'd miss when I returned alone to my house on Tradd Street.

After quietly sliding the dead bolt on the front door and setting the alarm, I turned toward the stairs.

"Melanie?"

I started at the sound of my father's voice from the front parlor. I walked toward it, the room illuminated by moonlight streaming in through the stained-glass window, painting patches of color along the floors and walls. I felt rather than saw the hulking shadow of the dollhouse on the far side of the room where the light couldn't reach it. "Daddy? Why are you sitting here in the dark?"

"I didn't want your mother to know that I was still here. She'd want to keep me company and feed me. Not that I don't love that, but I just really needed to talk with you."

I tried not to focus on what he meant by "still here" and moved on to the next subject. "What about?" I asked as I slid onto the sofa next to him.

"There's something not right about that dollhouse."

I resisted the impulse to snort and instead waited for him to continue. Until he'd witnessed the ghost of my Hessian soldier, my father had been dismissive at best about my and my mother's psychic abilities. Even though he was no longer dismissive or derisive, he still wasn't comfortable with acknowledging that there was something out there that we could see and he couldn't. When he didn't say anything else, I said, "What do you mean?"

He paused before answering. "While I was sitting here waiting for you, I could swear I heard it . . . breathe. I actually thought somebody might be in the room, so I switched on a lamp to go look and this is what I found." Leaning over, he turned on the lamp by the sofa, illuminating the coffee table in front of us. The figures of the boy and the dog lay faceup, their cold eyes staring at the ceiling, the boy's head at an odd angle and the dog's skull cracked in half.

"Where were the other figures?" I asked quietly.

His eyes regarded me steadily. "Crowded in front of the turret window."

I swallowed, the sound loud enough that I'm sure my father heard. He reached over and turned off the light. "Do you know what that's about?" he asked.

"No. Not yet, anyway. Jack and I are trying to find out what's going on."

He was silent again for a moment. "I don't like this business with the burned stair runner and the scratched walls—and not just because I'm the go-to guy for getting it all fixed. It's just . . . well, be careful, all right?" His voice was gruff. "I don't like thinking of the two of you fighting something I can't. It's just . . . not right."

I reached for his hand. "Daddy, Mother and I can handle this. We actually make a pretty good team."

"And what were you thinking, putting that thing in Nola's room? She's young and helpless and can't be expected to defend herself. . . ."

"She's hardly helpless," I said, my warm and fuzzy feelings toward him beginning to cool slightly. "You know we'll take care of her."

"I know," he said, patting my arm with his other hand. "It's only that with her not having a mother and then Jack . . ." He stopped.

I recalled how he said he was waiting for me when he heard a sound from the dollhouse. "You weren't waiting for me to talk about the dollhouse, were you?"

He shook his head. "No. I wanted to talk to you about something more . . . personal."

"Oh." His words took me by surprise. Our relationship had made leaps and bounds in the last two years, but not to the level where we shared confidences late at night. I just hoped it wasn't about my mother. Or that I was going to have a little brother or sister. "About what?"

"Jack."

"Oh," I said again, surprised. "What about Jack?"

"He called me about an hour ago—he was still at the restaurant with you. Said he wanted to take a drink."

I went very still. Jack had been my father's sponsor in AA, and I wasn't prepared for this role reversal. I remembered Jack excusing himself from the table to make a phone call, but I'd never expected this. "What did you tell him?"

"That I would come get him, but he didn't want that. He just wanted to talk, so we did. He seemed better after that, and promised that if he felt the urge again he'd call no matter what time it was. But I think . . ." He stopped.

"You think what?" I prompted.

"That you should talk to him. I don't know whatever this thing between you is, but the two of you drag it behind you like a ball and chain. There're other things going on in his career, but I think he can handle it if the two of you could just . . ." Again he stopped.

I was afraid he would say, "sleep together," so I quickly said, "I'll talk to him. I've been meaning to for a while now; I just haven't had a chance. But I will."

My father sat up. "Will you do it soon?"

I nodded. "Sure. I promise."

"Great." His voice sounded relieved. Patting my knee, he said, "It's late. Why don't you go on ahead and get some sleep. I think I'll stay here for a little while and keep an eye on that . . . dollhouse. I'll go glue those dolls back together, too, before Nola finds them broken."   .

"You don't have to, Daddy. I can do that."

"I know. Just let an old man feel useful."

I snorted. "You're hardly old, and you've re-created a beautiful garden at my house. I think that qualifies as being useful."

He was silent for a moment, and I knew we were both thinking of all the lost years of my childhood. Finally, he said, "What do you want for your birthday?"

Jack. It was the first word that came to mind, but I didn't say it aloud. Instead, I said, "I have everything I need."

I felt his eyes on me in the dark. "Well, I hope you get everything you want."

Leaning over, I kissed him on the cheek. "Good night, Daddy."

"Good night, Melanie."

I left him on the sofa and made my way toward the stairs, wishing I knew what I was going to say to Jack and feeling more than one set of eyes on my back as I went up the steps.

CHAPTER 17

I hopped on one foot and then the other as I slipped on my flats, hurrying out of my bedroom door to collect Nola and my mother before heading to Julia Manigault's house for the first music lesson, currently being referred to as a piano/voice lesson until either Julia or Nola decided which to focus on. I paused outside Nola's opened door with my arm raised, prepared to knock on the doorframe, as the sound of quiet conversation came from inside. I stuck my head around the corner to get her attention so I could point at my watch to let her know that we were perilously close to being on time instead of early.

Nola sat on the floor with her back to me, her opened backpack in front of her with all of its contents, including her mother's music, scattered around her. Her new iPhone—upgraded from a generic flipphone and part of the deal she'd made with Jack in exchange for agreeing to try the music lessons—was held to her ear, and she was speaking very quietly. Assuming it was Alston and not wanting to eavesdrop, I began to back away from the door, but stopped when I heard Nola sniff.

"I told you, she wasn't working on anything. I would have known." She shook her head. "Yeah, I guess maybe when I was in school during the day, but she wouldn't have hidden it from me. She always shared what she was working on, because"—Nola sniffed—"because she said I always had a really good ear."

She was silent for a moment, listening to the person on the other end. "I told you—I've looked through everything and I didn't find anything. I promise to call you if I do. And would you . . ." She rubbed the heel of her hand into her eye. "Would you please let me know what you find out about Jimmy Gordon? Somebody needs to tell the world what a fake he is." There was another brief pause and then she said good-bye.

I'd almost made it out of her range of vision when the teddy bear that had been nestled in the sheets of the unmade bed hurled itself across the room, coming to rest at my feet and turning Nola's head so that she spotted me in the doorway. I bent to pick it up, avoiding Nola's eyes for a moment while I tried to justify eavesdropping versus my need to know as a parental figure.

I examined the worn teddy bear and his football jersey with what looked like hand-stitched numbers, trying to see with my peripheral vision whether Bonnie was still there, and wondering why she'd thrown the bear at me. I thought I could hear a sweet melody being hummed, but when I turned my head it stopped.

Nola stood and wiped her arms across her face, then glowered at me. "It's rude to listen to other people's conversations," she said.

"You're right, and I'm sorry. It's just that I heard you crying and I got concerned. Who was that?"

I thought for a moment that she wasn't going to tell me. She chewed on her lower lip, then said, "That was Rick Chase. My mom's last boy-friend. He wanted to know where I was and how I was doing."

Cautiously, I asked, "How did he get your cell number?"

Nola made a big production of fishing her boots out from under her bed and spent a lot of time focusing on the laces. "Actually, I called him. He found me on Facebook and sent me a message."

I raised my eyebrows. As of yet, Nola didn't have a computer and Facebook wasn't one of the apps allowed on her phone by her father. And he checked regularly.

"Alston let me use her laptop to set up an account."

"Without the proper security settings, obviously, if he was able to find you and message you."

She glared at me under lowered eyebrows. "I'm not a moron. I wouldn't have messaged back if he was a stranger. But I know him— and he left his phone number so I could call him."

I felt a little better. Still, I'd have to tell Jack so he could set parameters for Nola and her use of social media. If I knew how, I'd probably find out whether she had a Twitter account, too. All stuff we'd deal with later. Softly, I said, "What was that about Jimmy Gordon?"

She stood, her face thunderous. "MYOB. Can we go now and get this stupid music lesson over with?" She stomped past me and I listened to her boots clomp down the stairs while I tried to figure out what MYOB meant.

Nola was waiting by my car when my mother and I exited the house. I looked at her feet. "It's less than a mile, so we're going to walk, since the weather is still so mild. We'll wait if you want to change shoes."

She looked at me as if I'd lost my mind. "Walk?"

"Yes. You know, put one foot in front of the other. Walk. Something I assume you've been doing since you were a toddler." I wanted to clap myself on the back. My sarcastic response wasn't as good as one of hers but it was a fine showing.

"Nobody walks in LA. It's just . . . lame."

I began to head down the sidewalk. "Well, we're not in LA, so we're walking. It should take less than fifteen minutes, but if you keep stalling you'll have to jog."

My mother held out her hand toward Nola. "Come on. You can appreciate the houses and gardens better when you're on foot."

"Wow. Can't wait." Reluctantly, Nola let my mother pull her up from where she'd been leaning on my car. With a heavy sigh and requisite roll of her eyes, she began walking next to my mother. "For the record, I've been walking since I was nine months old. Not that I remember, but that's what Mom told me."

I looked at Nola from the corner of my eye, trying to determine whether she realized she'd just spoken about her mother and their shared past without a hint of animosity or resentment. Maybe Nola had been in Charleston long enough that she could see her previous life through the forgiving filter of time. Or maybe there had once been a period in her life with Bonnie when things hadn't been so desperate.

"You must have been a very precocious child," my mother said, lifting her delicate shoe over a crack in the sidewalk.

"I'm guessing she got that from her father," I said under my breath, causing my mother to poke me in the back.

She continued. "Mellie was, too. She was speaking in full, coherent sentences by the time she was two. Her father said it was because she had the undivided attention of both parents, who didn't speak to her as if she were a baby. I think it was because even back then she knew what she wanted, and wanted everybody else to know it, too."

I looked at my mother, too surprised to be offended. I didn't know a lot about my early childhood. After my mother left, my father wasn't prone to sentimental reminiscences, so my earliest memories were of me as a motherless child whose entry and earliest ramblings in this world were parts of an invisible past.

I stared hard at the sidewalk in front of me, concentrating on placing each foot in front of the other. I would make sure to tell Jack about how Nola walked at nine months, because he should know. Because when she grew older, she'd want to know that somebody remembered it enough to tell others.

"What's that sound?" Nola asked.

I paused, trying to hear whatever Nola was. "What sound?"

"It's like bells ringing or something."

I'd lived in Charleston long enough that I rarely heard the bells of the numerous churches that rang throughout the city in fifteen-minute intervals. "It's bells—church bells. We have so many churches here in Charleston that it's known as the Holy City."

Her boots clomped heavily on the sidewalk. "Sort of like Las Vegas being called Sin City, huh?"

I watched my mother try to hide a smile as she brushed away yellow lantana escaping through a wrought-iron fence on Rutledge Avenue. I peeked inside the gate as I passed, noticing the creeping heliotrope and yellow bells displayed in riotous confusion alongside immaculate brick paths. I remembered a time when the only flower I could name was a rose, yet I'd somehow become a person who demanded to have wisteria and tea olives in her garden because of their spring scents and the way the purple blooms of the wisteria draped the old walls of my beloved city as early as March. When I'd lived all over the world with my father,

I always remembered the wisteria, even though I couldn't name it. I think Charleston in the spring is what eventually brought me home.

Nola continued. "What do they call LA?"

I caught my mother's eye as we both recalled how my father referred to it as the land of fruits and nuts. To distract Nola, I said, "Do you smell the Confederate jasmine?"

She gave an exaggerated sniff. "I smell perfume."

"Exactly." I lifted a cluster of the star-shaped white flowers that clung to a low brick wall. "Is this what you're smelling?"

Leaning down with her hands on her torn and ratty stockings and her thin legs shoved into combat boots, her shiny black hair tucked carefully behind her ears, she cut a dramatic picture as she smelled the flowers. I wished I had a camera so that I could show Jack. She sniffed deeply, then surprised me by smiling broadly.

"Wow. It's like a perfume bottle." She scrunched her eyebrows together. "I don't think we have flowers in LA."

I noted her use of present tense, but didn't comment on it. We were almost at Julia Manigault's house and she was going willingly. I didn't want to give her a reason to balk now, since I didn't know whether my mother and I could physically drag her kicking and screaming up the stairs. Not that I was overly eager to go inside the house again and mingle with the living or nonliving residents. But when I remembered the burned rug and chiseled wall in my mother's house, I knew this was yet another spirit I couldn't ignore. Maybe it would be easier this time, since I wasn't related to these spirits; nor did I have a vested interest in anything the ghosts might be clinging to. Bonnie was another matter entirely, but I'd deal with her later.

We climbed the porch steps, but before I could ring the doorbell my mother grabbed my arm. "Do you feel it?"

I nodded. Icy pinpricks had been racing down my spine since we'd turned the corner onto Montagu Street.

"It reminds me of Rose," she said, recalling the last ghost we'd put to rest, who hadn't been all that happy to go. "Remember, Mellie. We're stronger than them."

I nodded again, then rang the bell. While waiting for Dee to answer the door, I stole a glance at Nola. She stood with both combat boots planted firmly on the floor, her jaw jutting forward as if heading out to battle. But the slight lift at the corner of her mouth that looked suspiciously like a half smile surprised me. I thought about what Jack had told me about how Nola considered music her mother's favorite child, and how she'd always felt like the ugly stepsister in comparison. Maybe she'd reconciled her presence here by thinking that this could be her chance to master this sibling rivalry and finally lay it to rest.

The sound of approaching footsteps inside focused our attention back to the door, but as I heard the dead bolts being slid open, I looked back at Nola and saw Bonnie standing behind her, a similar smile on her lips. Her eyes met mine for a brief moment before she disappeared, and for the first time in my life I understood what a ghost was trying to tell me without having to speak a word. In that brief second I'd felt the power of a mother's love, a certainty that it could transcend death, and I knew that Nola had felt it, too. Felt it enough, perhaps, to make her walk into Julia Manigault's house when Dee Davenport opened the door.

"You're early! Miss Julia will appreciate that. Can't stand for anybody to be late. Come in, come in," she said, ushering us into the musty foyer. "I've got refreshments in the rear parlor, where you ladies are welcome to stay when Miss Julia and Nola retire to the music room."

Nola sent a panicked look at us, prompting my mother to speak up. "Actually, I was hoping to sit in on her first lesson. Perhaps by understanding how Miss Julia will be instructing Nola, I can help her with her practicing at home."

Dee tucked her chin into her ample neck. "You'll have to speak with Miss Julia about that. She normally doesn't like—"

My mother interrupted her. "She'll allow me." Her words were soft, but her meaning was clear. Dee's jowls warbled with disapproval as she led us back through the long hallway toward the creepy Christmas room.

I watched as my mother took in the dark paneling and somber tones of the house, the heavy furniture and closed drapes, the cobwebs and dust. There were no zebra rugs or neon upholstery, like she'd found in her house when she'd purchased it, but when she glanced back at me I could almost see her mind working as she redecorated each room as we

passed. I shook my head quickly just to let her know that I had no interest in traveling down that path once again.

As before, Miss Julia sat in her wheelchair, a gray blanket thrown
over her legs despite the warm temperature. "Emmaline. I'm glad you
saw reason and chose to come." She nodded at my mother and me as we
greeted her. "Ladies," she said, indicating a sofa and a horsehair-covered
chair with a refreshment tray set up on a low coffee table.

My mother perused the room, taking in the Santas and snowmen
and all the red and green glittery things that decorated the room like
confetti. "I remember how much you loved Christmas. I used to love
to go to your room for my lessons because it was always Christmas
there."

With slightly trembling hands, Julia lifted a bone teacup with a holly
pattern around the lip. "My father didn't believe in celebrating Christmas. Called it pagan. I suppose that was my one rebellion, although I
didn't start until after he'd been dead for several years, so I don't know
whether it could even be called that."

Nola eyed the plate of cookies. "Are these made with sugar?"

"Of course, Emmaline," Julia snapped. "Why? Are you diabetic?"

"No. Ma'am." She added this last after my mother sent her "the
look." I waited for Nola to explain her dietary requirements to the old
woman and was relieved when she remained silent.

"So," I said. "How would you like to do this? My mother would like
to sit in on the lesson and can walk Nola home. I have an appointment
in an hour, so I'll be leaving early."

Miss Julia pursed her lips, and if I'd been younger, I might have been
afraid waiting for her next words. With apparent effort, she forced a
smile that looked more like a grimace. "Ginnette, I have a stack of
music on the small table by the door. Please take them with you now
and show them to Nola in the music room. I'd like to speak with Miss
Middleton for a moment."

I watched as my mother stood, then hesitated only for a moment
before picking up the short stack of worn music books. She wasn't wearing her gloves, and I knew the moment she touched them that they
were trying to tell her something. She stood very still for a long moment as she squeezed her eyes shut, her knuckles white where she

clutched the stack, her lips moving silently. She seemed to mentally shake herself, forcing her eyes open again. Turning toward Nola, she quickly handed the books to her. "Take these."

Nola took them without complaint while regarding my mother curiously. I hadn't yet had a chance to explain my mother's abilities but figured I might not have to now. They began walking toward the open doorway before my mother stopped and turned back to Miss Julia.

"Your brother, William. Did he play the piano?"

The old woman's face stilled, her skin the color of parchment. "Yes. He was very good—much better than I. Those were his books, actually. Not that he needed them. He needed to hear a song only once and he could play it perfectly note for note. I always needed the music." She paused briefly. "Why do you ask?"

My mother met her gaze. "Just curious." Clearing her throat, she said, "Nola and I will go through the books, looking for good vocal selections and scales to get started. We'll wait for you there."

She ushered Nola from the room, Dee following and closing the door behind them.

I stared into my teacup, recalling the image of the man in the upstairs window and the impressions I'd received from the dollhouse. I wondered if it was William, and waited for Julia to tell me about him, and what my mother might have seen when she touched his music books. When Julia didn't say anything, I prompted, "What did you want to tell me?"

She didn't answer right away. "Emmaline is very gifted. She needs instruction, especially if she hopes to enter Ashley Hall in the fall."

I popped a key lime cookie into my mouth and chewed thoughtfully. "I guess that might be part of it. But I'm thinking the other part has to do with the dollhouse." I paused for emphasis, waiting for her expression to tell me something. It didn't. "Why did you give it away?" A rush of cold air brushed the back of my neck, but I didn't take my gaze away from Julia.

Her lips moved as if she were chewing her words before actually speaking. "There was something . . . not quite right with it."

"Haunted, do you mean?"

Her dark eyes widened. "Yes. I suppose you could say that. Things being moved around, figures posed in improbable positions. I told my father to get rid of it."

I wondered how much further I could go, and decided to press on. "That was 1938, the same year your brother disappeared, right?"

Two spots of color formed on her cheeks. "Yes, but they're not related. My brother finally got tired of not quite meeting our father's expectations, so he left."

"He just left?"

Julia nodded. "Yes. I heard them arguing that last night he was home, and then . . . he was just gone."

"Did you ever hear from him again?"

I had to lean forward to hear her answer.

"No."

I sat back in my chair. I could leave now, and continue with the ruse that Nola was here simply to explore her musical abilities. Or I could try to bring peace to the restless spirits that hovered around Julia Manigault, whether or not she wanted to acknowledge them. I recalled Nola telling me that she thought helping spirits move on was a cool thing. I still wasn't completely convinced, but I couldn't deny the satisfaction that I'd gotten from sending Mary Gibson and my Hessian soldier into the light, and couldn't help but wonder whether that dollhouse had been put in my path for a reason. After all, there were lots of things in my life that defied explanation: my ability to see ghosts and to resist Jack Trenholm's charms being just two of them.

But if Julia wanted me there for a reason, I needed her to ask me. I wasn't so gung ho about ghostbusting that I'd volunteer my services. Maybe, if I was lucky, I'd misunderstood her intentions. I placed my teacup and saucer on the coffee table. "What do you need from me, Miss Manigault?"

She seemed to shrink even smaller into her wheelchair, as if asking for help had somehow diminished her. "It is my understanding that you . . . communicate with the dead. I want to speak with my brother, William."

Ah. I nodded. "All right. But you need to understand that it's a two-way street when it comes to spirits. Is there a reason he might be reluctant to speak with you?"

Her eyes darkened and for a moment I thought she might start crying. I half rose from my chair, ready to find Dee. Julia raised her hand, palm out, and I lowered myself back into the chair. "No. Of course not." Her gaze skittered away as I continued to regard her closely.

I cleared my throat. "I don't think William's alone. There's another spirit—I've seen him here, in your house. Looking out the turret window."

Her eyes were clouded with alarm, her fingers like brittle twigs as she tightly gripped the arm of her chair. "Jonathan?" she asked, her voice barely over a whisper.

"Who's Jonathan?"

"My fiancé. He died . . . he died that same year William went away."

I shook my head. "The man I've seen in the window is much older. I was thinking it might be your father."

A frown pulled at her skin, making her face seem as if it were melting. "I don't go in that part of the house. It was my parents' wing. He'd never come in here, though. Too much Christmas." She opened her mouth and laughed, the sound more like a cackle, then sobered quickly. "I'm not interested in speaking with him." She tapped her fingers on the arms of her chair. "If you can help me speak with William, I will make it worth your while."

I sat up, stricken, envisioning me inheriting yet another dilapidated house in Charleston. "I don't need anything, Miss Julia," I said quickly. "I'm just looking for an opportunity to hopefully put a spirit to rest."

"And if you find out certain . . . things about a family along the way, what do you do with that information?"

I looked at her with surprise. "To be honest, my experiences so far have only been personal. But anything I discovered would be completely confidential, of course. Although it might help if you told me everything up front. I don't want to give the ghosts the advantage."

"There's nothing you need to know, Miss Middleton. All I want is to speak with William."

I looked at her dubiously. A mantel clock in the form of Santa's sleigh chimed from the bookshelf behind Julia, reminding me of the time. "I have to leave now. If you think of anything, please let me know. In the meantime, I'll do what I can to speak with William." I stood. "Would you like me to take you to the music room on my way out?"

She nodded, and I opened the door before positioning myself behind the wheelchair. I paused in the doorway to the music room, admiring the picture of my mother and Nola on the piano bench with their heads together as they harmonized to a piece of music I didn't recognize.

"I'm leaving now," I announced as I pushed Miss Julia up to the piano. I turned to Nola. "Your grandmother is coming to get you around four o'clock to spend the rest of the weekend with them—she bought a futon you can sleep on in the living room, so you'll have your own space. Don't forget you're doing the admission testing for Ashley Hall tomorrow morning, so make sure you get plenty of sleep."

"Whatever," Nola said, rolling her eyes.

"Where are you going?" my mother asked.

I made a show of placing the wheelchair in the right position. "I'm having lunch with Jack. We have things to discuss."

My mother's eyebrows went up, but I studiously ignored them. "I won't be long."

"Take your time, Mellie. Nola and I will be just fine without you." She smiled.

I said good-bye, then turned to leave. I'd reached the front door before stopping and retracing my steps. "Miss Julia, if your brother wanted to say something to you, would it be 'Stop her'?"

Her lips thinned so that they almost disappeared into her face. "I'm quite sure I don't know what that means."

I nodded, then left, knowing two things about Julia Manigault: She was a terrible liar, and she was almost as afraid of William as I was.

CHAPTER 18

I spotted Jack's black Porsche at the curb on the opposite side of the street as soon as I stepped out onto the front porch of the Manigault house. He hopped out and opened the passenger side as I approached. I felt the telltale pricking of the skin at the back of my neck as I slid into the car, deliberately keeping my head turned away from the turret window.

As I buckled my seat belt, the scent of Rebecca's perfume assaulted me, followed quickly by the thick aroma of food. I looked at the small ledge that passed for a backseat and spotted the bags from Brent's on Broad. Trying to keep the disappointment from my voice, I said, "I thought we were going out for lunch."

"We are," Jack said as he pulled away from the curb. "Thought we'd dine al fresco at White Point Gardens. The weather is still mild so I figured we should take advantage of it while we can." He slid his sunglasses on, but not before I noticed the dark circles under his eyes. "How did it go in there with Nola?"

"She handled it surprisingly well, thanks to my mother. You owe her for that, by the way. Personally, I don't think you needed to bribe Nola with an iPhone. I sincerely believe that she would have gone anyway."

"How do you figure?" He cut a sharp right on Meeting Street from Broad, nearly hitting a large man standing in the middle of the road snapping a picture of St. Michael's. Jack swerved around him, the man oblivious as he pointed the lens up toward the most recognized steeple in the Holy City.

"I think Nola sees this as an opportunity to not only become serious about her talent, but also to prove her mother wrong, to show Bonnie what she's missing."

"You think? That sounds so . . . wrong. They're mother and daughter, after all."

"Trust me. The mother-daughter relationship is something you will never be able to understand, Jack, so don't even try. Makes finding the cure for cancer seem easy."

"And you would know."

"Absolutely." I pointed to a Volvo station wagon with a Porter-Gaud window sticker pulling away from the curb on East Battery.

As Jack sped toward the available parking spot, he said, "Do you happen to know Nola's shoe size?"

"She's a six and a half narrow. Why?"

He parallel parked, the car sliding perfectly into the spot the first time. I wouldn't have expected anything less. "I'm just preparing myself for the part where we tell Nola she'll have to wear a uniform at Ashley Hall. For their dress days when they have to wear the school blazer, they can wear black or purple closed-toe shoes. I was thinking a pair of purple Converses might work."

I wasn't sure the administrators at the school would approve, but the gesture wouldn't be lost on Nola—or me, judging by the way my blood was going all slushy in my head. I reached behind me and grabbed the to-go bags as Jack walked around the car to open my door. "You've already studied the uniform list? She hasn't even taken the independent school entrance exam yet."

He locked the door and grinned. "I've already purchased everything she'll need, except for the leggings, because they're not sold at the uniform store and I'm not really sure what they are."

I experienced that squishy feeling again. "You're that confident she'll get in, huh?"

"I saw her transcript from her school in Los Angeles, as well as her standardized test scores. They'd be stupid not to let her in, regardless that she's a legacy." He stopped walking and faced me. "If you think about what she's been through and what an amazingly independent and strong-minded girl she is despite everything, and throw in her music talent and her . . . well, her Nola-ness, she's a shoo-in."

I nodded, but didn't say anything, not because I didn't agree with everything he said—I did—but because I was afraid I'd do something stupid like kiss him.

As we approached the pineapple fountain at the center of White Point Gardens, a tour group that had been sitting on an adjacent wrought-iron bench and listening to their guide stood up and moved on, leaving the spot completely open. When I was with Jack, things like that always seemed to happen. I glanced out at the water in the harbor, wondering whether I'd see dolphins, too, but was rewarded with only the picture-postcard view of a sailboat.

We began taking our lunch out of the bags, a turkey Reuben wrap for me and a veggie wrap for Jack. I narrowed my eyes at him. "*Et tu, Brute?*"

He shrugged. "I can't see myself going vegan, but I like vegetables, so I figured, why not?" He eyed my Reuben. "But if that's too much meat for you, I'd be happy to stick some on mine."

I snorted, indicating he had as much chance of getting hold of any of my wrap as of Nola looking forward to wearing a blazer to school. Peering into the bottom of the bag, I tried to quell my disappointment.

"Don't worry—they're in the other one."

I glanced into the second bag, relieved to see two brownies. Jack didn't eat sweets, so I knew they were both for me. We were almost like an old married couple, except for the fact that we hadn't ever dated or slept in the same room. The thought made me blush, so I turned away to face the harbor.

The Battery was crowded with tourists and residents alike, enjoying what was surely one of the last days before the unbearable heat and humidity descended on the city like a sodden blanket. I'd be back to wearing my hair up in a usually vain attempt to quell its desire to frizz up into a Brillo pad look-alike.

Picnickers lounged in the grass, while others posed for pictures, precariously perched on the displays of antique weaponry pointed out into the harbor and the distant Fort Sumter. Whereas pirates and Yankees had once been the enemy to aim for, the armory was pretty much harmless now, unless you considered the alarmingly large number of tourists maimed by tumbles from cannons and cannonball pyramids.

"I found out a little bit about Jimmy Gordon."

I focused my attention back to Jack as I took another bite of my sandwich, a long string of sauerkraut refusing to make it completely into my mouth. Since it was only Jack, who'd seen me more than once in granny sleepwear, I wasn't too self-conscious about shoveling it into my mouth with a finger.

He watched me with an amused grin. "From all accounts he's a pretty nice guy. Either he's still too new to the music business for any of the hoopla to have affected him, or he's actually the real deal. Couldn't find any connection between him and Bonnie. But Nola said she'd met him, right?"

I nodded, taking a long sip of my sweet tea through a straw. "Yeah, and she called him a jerk, but that's all she'd say about him. I'll try to ask again. I actually heard her talking about him on the phone this morning—called him a fake, I think was her word."

"Who was she talking with?"

"Some guy named Rick—she said it was her mother's old boyfriend who'd found her on Facebook and wanted to find out how she was doing."

Jack put his half-eaten wrap down into the wrapper. "Since when does she have a Facebook account? Do you know how many perverts are out there looking for somebody like Nola?"

I held up my hand. "Technically, you told her you didn't want her to have a Facebook app—and she doesn't. She borrowed Alston's laptop and set up an account there. Regardless, you do need to sit down with her and come up with some rules about using social media, but I think she's pretty savvy about it. He found her and posted his phone number so she could call him, since she knows him. She assured me she wouldn't have done that if she didn't know who the guy was. . . ."

Jack shook his head. "I don't care. I think thirteen is way too young for a Facebook page—whether it's accessed through an iPhone app or a computer."

I kept the smile off my face as I considered the source of the parental concern and wondered how many parents during Jack's formative years quaked in fear that somebody like Jack Trenholm would want to date their daughter. "Granted, she knows a lot more about the world than most kids her age—and older—but still, I think you're right."

Jack picked up his wrap again. "Did she mention the last name? Rick sounds pretty familiar—like I might have come across it while researching Bonnie."

"Yeah, it's Chase. Do you want me to ask her more about him?"

"No. I don't want Nola to think that I'm prying, especially if he's only who he says he is. I just want to make sure."

I nodded again, my attention now focused on two guys wearing College of Charleston T-shirts and throwing a yellow Frisbee. "Does 'my daughter's eyes' mean anything to you?"

"No. Should it?"

I shrugged, then dug into the bag for the first brownie. "I sort of spoke with Bonnie—while I was with Sophie at the bridal shop. It's a long story, and the words weren't directly from her, but basically she told me to look for 'my daughter's eyes.' I have no idea what she meant."

Jack chewed thoughtfully for a long moment while slowly rolling one of the paper bags into a ball. "I don't have a clue. Did you ask Nola?"

"Not yet. She's still so prickly about her mother that I really have to search hard for the right time to spring something like that on her. Stop by Ruth's Bakery on your way home to drop me off and I'll bring home her favorite doughnuts. Bribery couldn't hurt."

"Doughnuts? Nola?"

"Yep. Don't ask me how I know, but I have my ways."

Jack leered at me. "I know."

My cheeks warmed, and I concentrated on digging into the bag for my second brownie. "We need to find out more about the Manigault family. I was right about Julia having ulterior motives. When I asked her what she really wanted she said she just wants to speak with William, but there's something more there. She claims that 'stop her' doesn't mean anything to her, but she's afraid of something—of William, I think." I took a bite of brownie. "And we need to find out more about her fiancé, too. She said his first name was Jonathan. Do you think we need the last name, too?"

"'We'? I like the way you assume we're a package deal in all this."
He smirked. "As for getting the information we need, with Yvonne, all
things are possible."

I took a sip of my drink so I didn't have to say anything. He gave me
his Jack smile and I forced myself not to look away.

"You should wear that color more often, Mellie."

I looked down at my Anne Fontaine blouse. "White?"

"No. Pink. Like the color of your cheeks."

I made a concentrated effort to focus on my brownie. "It's because
I'm hot," I said finally. "I walked a lot today."

"Uh-huh." He slipped his sunglasses in his shirt pocket. "So, what
did you want to talk with me about—besides Bonnie and Miss Julia?"

I met his eyes and steeled myself so that I wouldn't notice how very
blue they were. "We're friends, right?"

He raised an eyebrow.

I took a deep breath. "I just . . . well, I . . ." I stopped and took another breath, totally unprepared for this kind of conversation. I'd had
them before, but I was always the bug under the magnifying glass, and
Sophie was the one holding it. "Look, are you all right?"

His eyes narrowed. "What do you mean? Do you think I'm sick or
something?"

I let the words fall out of my mouth before I could pull them back.
"Are you drinking again?"

He wore the expression of a man who'd just been punched in the
gut. Hard. With measured precision, he said, "Why are you asking?"

"You're just . . . you're not yourself. I know you're having problems
with your publisher right now, and I know that can't be easy. Your
career is important to you—like mine is to me—and it must be frustrat-
ing not knowing what's going on."

"Did your dad put you up to this?"

I shook my head. "Not exactly. My mom and Nola, too. We've all
noticed it. They thought that since you and I, well . . ." I couldn't think
of what to call us, so I just kept going, hoping he didn't notice I wasn't
filling in the blanks. "And you look so tired and preoccupied every time
I see you. I just wanted to know whether you were all right. If things
were getting to be too much for you so that you were tempted . . ." I

stopped, his expression scaring me. Not that I would ever think he'd physically hurt me, but I knew his words could create permanent wounds.

He leaned toward me so that I could see my reflection in the dark blue of his eyes. "And what would you do if I said I wasn't all right? Would you sleep with me if I said it would make me feel better?"

It was like I'd been plunged into a deep pool of warm, warm water, dunked so suddenly that my lungs filled, making it impossible for me to speak.

With jerky movements, he began to throw all of our garbage into the remaining bag, ripping off the handle. He tossed the half-eaten brownie into the bag, but I couldn't bring myself to protest.

I stood and brought my shoulders back. I barely recognized my voice when I found the air to push out the words. "You didn't answer my question, Jack. Are you drinking again?"

He walked to a nearby garbage can and stuffed the bags inside before turning back to me. I'd never seen him this angry before, but the subject was too important to let it drop. Or to think about the consequences.

I had to force myself not to take a step backward. He stood directly in front of me, close enough that I could smell the soft scent of his cologne. "And you didn't answer my question, either."

I felt the blood rush to my face, but I didn't look away. "You first."

His eyes smoldered with anger. Very slowly and deliberately, he said, "As I believe I've mentioned more than once, there's a lot you don't know about me." He spun around and began stalking away.

"Where are you going?"

"Not to a bar, if that's what you're thinking."

"That's not what I was thinking," I said, jogging after him, feeling like I'd just made a permanent mistake, but not quite understanding what it was. "I'm sorry, Jack, if I said the wrong thing. I'm worried about you."

He kept walking.

"Jack, please!" I was embarrassed to find that I was close to tears and I still had no idea why.

Without looking back at me he said, "What?"

I was winded, and emotionally exhausted, and all my explanations of why I was worried about him and how I only wanted to help shriveled in the heat and humidity. Regardless of what I said, he'd made up his mind. *There's a lot you don't know about me.*

With resignation, I said, "I was wondering if you could drive me back to my office."

He stopped so suddenly that I almost ran into him. "Always so practical, Mellie. Here." He dug into the pocket of his khakis. "I'll pick the car up at your house later. Leave it on the curb and lock the doors. I have another set of keys."

It took me a moment to register that he'd placed his car keys in my hand. "But I don't know how to drive a stick shift. . . ."

"Try something new for a change. Maybe you'll learn something."

I held up the keys again to protest, feeling like I'd lost something I hadn't known I'd had in the first place, but he'd already walked away.

I parked four blocks away from my mother's house, because I needed two spots together to be able to maneuver Jack's car into a parallel parking space. After much trial and error and an emergency phone call to my father to talk me through the rudiments of a manual transmission, I'd managed to get the car into second gear and left it there, coasting through stop signs and lights so I wouldn't have to stop and start again. The engine was making a funny grinding noise by the time I thankfully pulled up the emergency brake, but I didn't care.

Mrs. Houlihan and General Lee were in the kitchen, the smell of barbecued meat loaf wafting to my nostrils. I was about to remind her about Nola's dietary restrictions before remembering that Nola was with her grandparents all weekend, and did a little fist pump in the air at the thought of three whole days of meat and preservative-rich delicacies. The housekeeper slapped my hand as I pinched off a corner of her buttery sweet corn bread. "Save something for your daddy and mama—they'll both be here for supper."

I looked at the clock on the microwave. "What time will the food be ready?"

"About six—but it'll be later if I can't get some peace and quiet in this kitchen."

General Lee tugged at his leash, which hung on a peg by the back door, his eyes pleading. Even without psychic powers, I knew what he was saying. "I'm going to take the dog for a walk so we'll both be out of your way."

I clipped the leash on General Lee's collar and allowed him to pull me through the back door. I knew better than to force him to go where I wanted to; he was adept at locking all four legs if his desire to lead was questioned. I'd tried dragging him down the sidewalk with locked legs before, but apparently Charleston had a lot of dog-loving residents, and judging by the looks I'd received I realized it was just a lot less stressful to let General Lee take charge.

Today he led me north on Legare toward Broad Street, took a right on Queen and then a left on Meeting. I should have been paying more attention, but I was too busy rewinding my conversation with Jack, and going over in my head the unspoken answers to both questions. When General Lee finally stopped, I almost tripped over him, then let out a groan when I saw where his ramblings had led us.

We were in front of the ancient cemetery adjacent to the Circular Congressional Church on Meeting Street. He stared up at the sign on the gate as if he could read it. ESTABLISHED 1681. ALL VISITORS ARE WELCOME WHEN GATES ARE UNLOCKED. Then he looked at me.

"No, sir," I said. "I don't do cemeteries. Especially not this one." The church had been burned and rebuilt at least once, and tombstones and bodies moved as part of the new construction, not necessarily together—which was never a good idea. Apparently the displaced residents sometimes let their displeasure be known during Sunday services inside the church. Imagine the spirits' excitement if they knew I was there. I looked down at my dog, whose pink tongue was hanging out in a display of canine cuteness. "And I'm sure they don't welcome dogs, even if it doesn't say so on the sign."

As if he hadn't understood a word—or had and didn't care—General

Lee bolted inside the gate, nearly taking my arm out of the socket, yanking the leash from my hand. In all of my years of seeing dead people, there was one sure thing I'd learned: They expected respect when someone was visiting them in their place of rest and got very agitated when visitors traipsed over graves like they were at a playground. That's why if I did venture into a cemetery I never stepped on the ground between a headstone and footstone, spoke quietly, and I most definitely did not allow my dog to run amok over the antiquated graves of the dearly departed.

"General Lee!" I shouted, startling a middle-aged woman and her teenage daughter who were taking pictures of tombstones with an old-fashioned Polaroid camera and reading inscriptions. I'd heard that some amateur ghost hunters thought that Polaroids captured ghostly images better than digital cameras. I had no idea, as I'd never needed any camera to see what wasn't there. I turned back to where General Lee had run, already hearing the murmur of conversation as those seeking a voice into the world of the living became aware of my presence.

I started humming "Mamma Mia" to ignore the sound as the little fur ball bolted past the mother and daughter and into the back corner of the cemetery, an older section where it was hard to distinguish what was grave and what was a stepping path in the jumble of cracked marble and missing headstones. Circling a large brick mausoleum with a gray granite plaque on the side, he let out a bark. I started to shush him, but stopped as he took off again to the other side of the mausoleum, following the transparent tail of a bushy dog as it disappeared around the corner.

I was about to start chasing him again when my gaze was caught by the skull-and-wings engraving on the plaque on the mausoleum, right above the name chiseled in large block lettering: MANIGAULT.

I stopped to scan the list of names dating back several generations to before the American Revolution. Inscribed near the top were the names Harold Wentworth Manigault and his wife, Anne. She'd died in 1939, and her husband the same year. Julia's name and date of birth were there below theirs, along with a hyphen preceding a blank space, presumably for her date of death. But, even though there was room, Julia's brother, William, wasn't listed below or above Julia's name, or anywhere else on the plaque. It was as if he'd been forgotten entirely.

General Lee raced around the corner, his friend in hot pursuit, before making an abrupt turn and pouncing on the spectral dog, tumbling with him in a large ball of fur.

The teenage daughter I'd spotted before looked over with interest. I just smiled, trying to figure out what she thought she was seeing.

Small tremors erupted in the earth beneath my feet, the soil crumbling as it was sucked downward. I looked around, suddenly remembering the devastating earthquake of 1886. But nothing else seemed to be moving. I glanced down at my shoes and saw them sinking, the shifting earth already covering the toes.

I cried out, trying to lift my feet, but they seemed glued to the dark, crumbling earth, as if something from beneath the soil held on tightly. Emanating as a small stain at the base of the mausoleum, a dark shadow stretched and grew, spreading like black ink up the brick wall, undulating like a cobra under a flute's spell. My feet remained immobile as my skin chilled, the sun suddenly disappearing behind a thick cloud.

Go away! The voice boomed in my ear, and I turned to the mother and daughter to see whether they'd heard it, too. But they remained focused on the grave in front of them, the daughter snapping photos as the mother jotted down something in a notebook, both seemingly unaware that the earth had begun to open and something vile and dark had found me.

"I am stronger than you," I tried to shout, but the words were barely louder than a whisper. "I am stronger than you," I said, loud enough this time that the mother and daughter turned in my direction. The flash of the camera had the dual effect of creating moving balls of light inside my field of vision as well as releasing my feet from the hold of whatever had imprisoned them.

"Are you all right?" the mother asked, pulling me up from where I'd apparently been kneeling in the dirt.

"Yes. Yes, I'm fine," I said, brushing off my knees. I looked down at the carved groove in the grassy dirt. "I guess I didn't see the little dip here."

They both looked at me as if waiting for me to explain whom I'd been speaking to. I was saved by the appearance of General Lee, who bounded from around the corner and ran straight toward me. I grabbed his leash even though he showed no further inclination to bolt.

The girl was staring at the photo she'd taken, waiting for the image to form.

"Thank you," I said, more than ready to leave. General Lee had other ideas as he sat and stared up at my would-be rescuers.

"What a cute dog," the mother said, bending down to scratch him behind the ears. "What kind is he?"

Resigned to stay for a few more minutes, I said, "I sort of inherited him, so I'm not positive, but other people have said he's at least half Havanese—one of those nonshedding dogs. Not sure what the other half is."

"He's just adorable. And so sweet, too."

"Mom! I think I see a shadow. And a face!" the girl said, her voice rising with excitement.

I tugged on the leash. "Come on, General Lee. Let's go."

The girl thrust the photo at me. "Look! Do you see the eyes and the mouth? It's definitely a face. And it looks like he's leaning down to you to say something in your ear."

Reluctantly, I looked at the photograph. It was, indeed, a face, and one I recognized as the man I'd seen in the turret in the house on Montagu Street. I forced my voice to sound normal. "It's more like a blob to me, but I guess with a little imagination I suppose it could be made out to be a face."

They both looked at me with identical puckered frowns, as if not sure whether I was dim-witted or just blind. "I've got to go now. Thanks again." Not wanting to get into a power struggle with my dog, I reached down and picked him up, tucking him under my arm like a furry football, and walked quickly out of the cemetery gates.

I looked back once, wondering whether they'd also seen the clear form of a woman with long light-colored hair whose hazy figure could be seen standing between me and the dark shadow. I'd felt her presence,

I recalled now, before the girl and her mother had appeared, and had felt the calming presence as if my own mother had stood beside me waiting to do battle for me.

I set down the dog and sped up my pace, eager to put as much distance as I could between me and the cemetery, and wondering the whole time why Bonnie had been there, and why the haunting melody of a song I'd never heard before reverberated in the air around me.

CHAPTER 19

I hurried up the stairs of the Fireproof Building on Meeting Street, where the library for the South Carolina Historical Society was located. Nola clomped up the stairs behind me, her slow pace indicative of her lack of enthusiasm about our errand. But it had been nearly two weeks since I'd seen or spoken to Jack, so out of desperation I'd finally taken matters into my own hands and volunteered to drive Nola to Jack's loft for their twice-weekly visit instead of letting her walk. I had an appointment with Yvonne Craig first to find out whether she'd been able to discover anything about the Manigault family, and hopefully to glean information on Jack.

We ascended the circular stone staircase and found Yvonne in one of the book-filled rooms, seated at an oval dark wood table with several stacks of books and notepads on the table beside her. She glanced at her watch as we approached, a broad smile on her face. "Five minutes early to the second. I beat Jack by two minutes."

I stopped in front of the table. "What do you mean, you 'beat Jack'?"

"We've a running bet to see how early you're going to be for each appointment. If I win, I get a red velvet cupcake from Cupcake on King. If Jack wins, I have to buy him a handmade cigar from Lianos Dos Palmas."

I frowned for a moment before remembering my manners. "Yvonne, I'd like you to meet Jack's daughter, Nola. Nola, this is Mrs. Craig, a good friend of your father's."

Yvonne's smile brightened as she stood, her cheeks matching her pale pink twinset, a strand of pearls mixing with the beaded chain that held her reading glasses around her neck. She wore a round button pinned to her sweater that read, LIBRARIANS: THE ORIGINAL SEARCH ENGINE. "Oh, yes. Jack has told me all about you. From the way he talks, I expected you to be floating ten inches off the ground and glowing with light." She beamed as she held out her hands to Nola. "My goodness, but aren't you the spitting image of your father! Won't he have a time of it, turning all of those boys away when you're a little older." She winked at me before turning back to Nola. "Lovely name, by the way. Very unusual. My parents used to call me Nola when I was a little girl as a kind of nickname. Could never figure out where they got 'Nola' from 'Yvonne.'"

I watched Nola's face register surprise, and then turn bright pink as she tried to suppress a laugh. "It's nice to meet you, Mrs. Craig," she finally managed.

"I like your pin, Yvonne."

Sitting down again, she touched the pin reverently and looked up at us, smiling. "Jack gave it to me."

I raised my eyebrows expectantly. "He's been here?"

Her face fell. "Not recently, no. He did stop by several weeks ago to ask a few questions about the Manigaults, but it wasn't for his next book. I've been waiting for him to come in again with his long list of questions and theories—as soon as he's through with one book he's usually ready to start researching the next."

I sat down next to Yvonne as Nola took a seat across the table and immediately took out her phone and began texting. I was glad that Alston had introduced her to some of her friends and Ashley Hall schoolmates, but the incessant texting was nothing short of irritating. I sent her "the look" and she immediately muted the sound of the clacking keys. I was surprised that nobody had yet to be killed by somebody annoyed enough by that clicky little sound that reminded me too much of Chinese water torture.

Turning to Yvonne, I said, "He's taking a little break right now between projects. I'm sure he'll be back in the saddle in no time." I sent her a reassuring smile.

Lowering her voice to a conspiratorial whisper, she said, "I know he wanted to write that book about your family being wreckers and all of that business with the sunken ship and skeleton they found out in the harbor. Maybe he's working on that, since he already has everything he needs to write it."

I felt the blood drain from my face. "He, um, he told you that?"

She shook her head. "Not exactly. But when he was here a while back with that Rebecca person, she kept telling him what a good book it would make. As much as I hate to agree with her, she's right. Of course, it's your family and your personal history. Don't know how much you want the rest of the world to know about it." She raised her eyebrows meaningfully.

I wasn't sure whether Yvonne knew the entire story of how my ancestor had swapped places with Rose Prioleau and assumed her identity, a secret that was still unknown to everyone except for my parents, Jack, and me. And Rebecca. A book detailing all the sordid particulars of how the real Rose Prioleau's body found itself at the bottom of Charleston Harbor would be devastating at best, and humiliating at worst, to not just me, but to my entire family.

I placed my hands flat on the scarred wood surface of the table and forced a smile. "Yes, well, he hasn't mentioned anything to me. So," I said, eager to change the subject, "what have you been able to discover about Julia Manigault's family?"

Yvonne began taking folders out of a box on the table, each one labeled with brightly colored Post-it notes. "Quite a bit, actually. A very prominent family, as you probably know, but not closely related to the Manigaults in your own family tree."

"That's a relief."

She looked up and paused, as if waiting for me to elaborate, before turning back to sorting the folders when I didn't. "At your request, I didn't delve any farther back than Harold and Anne, although there is a lot of information dating back to much earlier, of course. The first Manigaults were Huguenots, but you're not interested in all that." I sensed a note of disappointment in her voice.

She opened a folder and slid it over to me. "I took the liberty of photocopying several newspaper clippings and articles referencing the family."

Yvonne had already organized everything in chronological order, with pertinent facts highlighted in pale blue. I made a mental note to send her a box of red velvet cupcakes with cream cheese frosting from Cupcake, and/or my firstborn. The woman was amazing, and so much like me, at least in the organizational category, it was almost scary.

A pink-tipped finger pointed at one of the pages. "Harold was born by the coast in Georgetown County on the family's old rice plantation on the Santee River—Belle Meade—but was the youngest of three sons. Went to USC in Columbia, then to Charleston for medical school. Inherited a great deal of money when his father died, invested it in railroads and property, and was a wealthy man by the time he married Anne Ward of Florence, South Carolina. Built her that house on Montagu Street as a wedding present."

Nola paused in her texting. "She got a *house* for a wedding present?"

Yvonne nodded. "Yes, dear. That was something wealthy people did back then. Sometimes it was a way to keep property in a family, and sometimes it was just to sweeten the deal, as they would say nowadays."

Nola raised her eyebrows, then went back to her texting.

"What about William? Did you find out anything about him?"

With a patient smile, Yvonne slid a photocopied clipping from the stack inside the folder. A grainy and yellowed photograph of a young man with blond hair and a slender build circa the mid-thirties stared out of the photograph. I felt Nola lean across the table. "That's him, Mellie. That's the boy doll."

I nodded, half with acknowledgment and half with relief that it wasn't the face I'd seen in the window. I turned to Yvonne to explain. "Amelia Trenholm, Jack's mother, gave Nola a dollhouse and it appears to have been made for and given to Julia Manigault for her birthday when she was ten. It's an exact replica of the house on Montagu Street, and came with dolls resembling family members, including the family dog."

Her brow puckered. "A dollhouse? That doesn't sound right." She pulled the folder closer to her and began paging through it, finally pulling several pages out and sliding them in front of me. "Julia Manigault was an avid equestrian. She competed against boys her age in boys-only events and usually won. She was also an expert marksman and accompanied her uncle and cousins on hunts, even at an early age."

I visually scanned the pages, examining the numerous pictures of a younger Julia astride a horse or holding a shotgun or a dead bird, and some of all three. I looked up and met Yvonne's eyes. "She was a tomboy."

"Exactly. There's even an article in there about how she wasn't allowed to make her debut at St. Cecilia's because she'd been seen wearing trousers in public. Apparently, young Julia was raised at her uncle's plantation with his five sons. Her mother was what they used to term 'delicate,' which now probably would just mean she needed a little Valium to cope with life. Julia wasn't brought back to Charleston until she was about ten."

"So why would her father have given her a dollhouse if that's obviously not where her interests lie?"

Nola interrupted with a heavy sigh meant to convey, I was sure, our apparent lack of mental acuity. "To help her be more like a girl. Duh. I mean, he already had a son, right? So he wanted his daughter to be a real girl and do girl things." Nola raised her eyes briefly, then returned to flying her fingers across the screen of her iPhone. She shook her head. "Jack says he's glad I'm not too girly-girly, like that Rebecca chick. Says that if he had to go to a store and pick out a girl to be his daughter, he'd still pick me." She snorted. "As if."

I regarded Nola for a moment, wondering whether she realized what she'd just said, realized that Jack was glad she was his no matter what. That even if she'd yet to come to terms with the fact that she had a father and that he wanted her in his life, he'd reached that conclusion long ago.

I focused again on the papers in front of me and swallowed a lump in my throat. "What did you find out about William? I accidentally came across the Manigault mausoleum at the Circular Church cemetery and he's not listed on the plaque—just his parents, and there's a spot for Julia. Jack said the paper trail for William vanishes completely in 1938."

Yvonne nodded. "There's actually quite a bit prior to 1938. He studied engineering at Clemson, but there's no record of him graduating. He apparently dropped out of school in his fourth year, but there's simply nothing else to tell us what he did afterward."

"Julia said that he and her father argued and William left. She never heard from him again."

"Not a word? Ever?"

I shook my head. "I suppose it's possible to completely cut off your own family, but the fact that he was never seen again or never left any clues as to where he might have gone makes it highly suspicious."

Without bothering to look up from her phone, Nola said, "My mother moved to California and her family never heard from her again."

"Yes," said Yvonne. "Things like that happen all the time. But to have no bank accounts or mortgage or will or a grave site just makes it all so suspicious. Your mother at least had you as her connection with her past."

Nola just sighed and continued texting.

"I don't think Harold Manigault was a nice man," I said. "I wouldn't be surprised to hear that he had something to do with William's vanishing act."

Yvonne regarded me with raised eyebrows, as if expecting me to explain how I might have known that about Harold. Clearing my throat, I said, "Julia must have told me something to give me that impression."

"Mm-hm" was all she said as she pulled out another folder and began rifling through the pages. "There was one other thing that I thought you might find interesting. Remember I mentioned that Harold Manigault made some of his money from investing in property? At one point he owned almost one thousand acres in Georgetown County, including his family's old home and what was left of the plantation—he apparently got it from his brother in exchange for settling some pretty hefty debts his brother had accumulated. As you can imagine, the land is quite valuable now, and developers have been chomping at the bit for years to build on it. And very recently, it appears they're going to get their chance."

"And the land has been in the family that whole time?" I asked.

"Yes. Prime real estate on the river just sitting there. Seems Miss Julia liked the offer a developer made to her, and they're scheduled to start clearing the land as soon as all the permits go through. Lots of ruckus in the papers lately from the preservationists and green people. I'm sure you've read all about it in the paper."

I smiled, too embarrassed to admit that the only newspaper reading I ever did was the real estate ads. "I, uh, must have missed that."

"Yes, well, Cobb Homebuilders is planning a multiuse development of the land. One of those all-inclusive neighborhoods with shops and entertainment as well as residential areas. The whole purpose is for people to walk everywhere instead of drive. Sort of how all American towns started out, if you ask me." She fluttered her hands in front of her face as if to clear the air. "Anyway, the sale is pending, as there has been a slew of lawsuits filed on behalf of the various environmental groups. The National Trust is involved, too, because of an overseer's cottage still on the property. The main house was destroyed by fire back in the thirties, but the preservation people seem to think there's some historical significance in the cottage. Regardless, the Cobb people seem very confident that they'll win, considering they're already working on the permitting process."

"I wonder why Julia would sell now, after all this time?"

Yvonne folded her hands neatly on top of the table. "To put it bluntly, I suspect she needs the money. I don't know her all that well, just through mutual acquaintances, really, but she's been retired for a long time. She'd have her retirement pension and all of that, but I've passed by her house enough times to know that it's falling apart. Keeping that old house in one piece must be sending her to the poorhouse."

I raised my eyebrows. "Welcome to my world. And if her inheritance money has run out or she made a few bad investments, and she's existing solely on her pension, I could see why she'd need the money."

"And, unfortunately, she's the last of her line. Of her five boy cousins, only one married and they had no children, so there are no relatives to ask for help. No children to support her in her old age. It must be a very lonely and sad existence. I'm so thankful for my children and grandchildren, you have no idea."

I had a sudden vision of an older and crinkled me sitting in my crumbling house on Tradd Street with no children to comfort me in my dotage. I'd have cats, lots of them, and I'd scare any child brave enough to ring my doorbell on Halloween. I'd hire somebody like Dee Davenport to feed me soft food and change my diapers. I shuddered.

"What did you find out about her fiancé? Jonathan was his first name, but I don't know his last."

She smiled a smile that could be called patronizing on anybody else, but on Yvonne it was just simply her all-knowing, confident smile that I'd come to rely on. She stood and moved back to the box and pulled out another folder. "I wasn't sure whether you'd want any of this, so I put it all in a separate folder just in case. It's birth, wedding, and death announcements regarding the family. There's an engagement notice you might be interested in."

She opened the folder and plucked something out of it before sliding it toward me. It was a photocopy of a sepia-toned photograph of a man and a woman. The woman, with gleaming dark hair piled high on her head, sat in a large leather-covered armchair, a tall and willowy dark-haired man standing behind her with his hand on her shoulder. The young woman wore a loose-fitting dress indicative of the nineteen thirties. Her left hand, folded demurely on top of the other and resting on her knee, held a large ring with a dark stone that could have been a sapphire. I wouldn't have called her beautiful, but she was pretty, with pale skin and bright, clear eyes. Her smile, however, transformed her face in such a way that it was hard to look away, or even to understand that this was the same dour Julia Manigault that I knew.

The man, however, was handsome—some might call him beautiful—by anybody's definition. With strong, chiseled features and dark eyes, he could easily be featured today in an Abercrombie ad. Or maybe Brooks Brothers. He was almost too refined for the beefy Abercrombie models. He was smiling softly, showing no teeth and reminding me a little of the Mona Lisa's mysterious smile. I held the photo closer, wondering why it looked like he was holding on to a secret.

The caption below the photo read:

Miss Julia Drayton Manigault, daughter of Mr. and Mrs. Harold Manigault of Montagu Street, Charleston, is engaged to be united in holy matrimony to Mr. Jonathan Crisler Watts of Georgetown. Nuptials will be held Saturday, August twelfth, at St. Mary's Catholic Church.

I looked up. "What happened to Jonathan?"

As if she'd already anticipated my question, she handed me another photocopied page. Glancing down, I saw it was a death announcement. I squinted, yet again chastising myself for not bringing my glasses that would have made reading the tiny print of the small clipping possible.

"Should I?" Yvonne asked, holding out her hand.

Settling the glasses that hung around her neck on her nose, she cleared her throat, then read: "'Jonathan C. Watts, aged twenty-two years and three months, succumbed to influenza after a short illness at his parents' home in Georgetown on Thursday evening. Survivors include his father and mother, Mr. and Mrs. Arthur Crisler Watts, and a brother, Henry A. Watts of Murrells Inlet. A viewing will take place . . .'"

She stopped. "You probably don't need me to read any of the details of the funeral, but you might find the date of his death interesting." After pausing for dramatic effect, she said, "July twenty-ninth, 1938."

I raised both eyebrows. "Poor Julia. The same year that William disappeared, and both parents died the following year. To lose all four in such quick succession must have been devastating." *There's no such thing as coincidence.* I thought of Jack's words, wondering whether in this case it was simply a horrible and unfortunate coincidence.

"Mellie?" Nola interrupted my musings.

I speared her with a look that would have made my mother proud.

"I mean, excuse me, Mellie?"

"Yes, Nola?"

"Jack just texted me and wanted to know where I was."

I looked at my watch, surprised to see that we were running late. I quickly stuck the papers back into the folders and slid them into my large handbag. "Thank you so much, Yvonne. As always, you've been amazing. I'll let you know if we need anything else."

"You're more than welcome. You know I love working on these little mysteries for you and Jack. Keep me posted if you find out anything more, and I'll do the same."

Nola stood, too, and without prompting said, "It was a pleasure to meet you, Mrs. Craig."

"And you, too, Nola." She studied Nola's iPhone for a moment. "Can I text something to your father really quick?"

With a confused glance in my direction, Nola handed Yvonne her phone. "Sure."

We watched as Yvonne slowly and deliberately pressed each key as she typed her text.

"It would be faster if you'd tell me what you wanted to say and let me do the texting," Nola offered hopefully.

"No need," Yvonne said, before typing a few last characters and handing the phone back to Nola. "I don't know how to send on your phone, so I'll let you do it. We have pretty bad reception in here, so you might want to wait until you get outside to send it."

We said our good-byes, then made our exit. Nola paused on the sidewalk outside the building and stared at the screen on her phone, her eyes wide. Without a word, she turned it so I could read the screen. Squinting, I scanned the words before meeting Nola's eyes.

C u later, hottie. Come up and c me sometime.

"Should I send it?"

"Absolutely. It might make his day. Just make sure he knows it's from Yvonne."

She typed something, then hit the "send" button before bursting out laughing. I joined her, hoping that at the very least it would put Jack in a better mood than when I'd last seen him.

∞

When the elevator opened on Jack's floor, the door to his loft was open. I knocked firmly on the door. "Jack? Are you decent? It's Mellie and Nola."

"Come in." His voice came from somewhere in the back.

We pushed open the door and entered the apartment, the smell of bleach and Windex wafting heavily throughout. Beautiful antiques, from seventeenth-century French to art deco, blended seamlessly with the stainless steel and black granite of the kitchen, the contemporary light fixtures and redbrick walls of the interior adding a sedate backdrop. I knew Jack's impeccable sense of style had a lot to do with growing up in his parents' antique store, but his ability to pull it all together was definitely a talent. I might have even found him a little more attractive because of it, but all of his other annoying traits really helped to level the playing field.

"I'm back here," Jack called.

We followed the sound of his voice to the back bedroom, done in black and chrome, with an amazing chinoiserie armoire converted to an entertainment unit dominating the wall opposite the large king-size bed. I'd never been this far into Jack's apartment before, and was grateful that Nola was with me. Fortunately, the bed was made, and no dirty laundry littered the floor. And no bras, either. I'd experienced that once already and was in no mood for a replay.

Actually, I realized, there was very little clutter anywhere. In past visits, there'd always been newspapers and magazines, clothes and dishes scattered just about on every surface. The apartment now was spotless.

Jack appeared in the doorway to the connecting master bathroom wearing a white crewneck undershirt and torn jeans. My throat closed a little bit until I registered that he was wearing yellow rubber gloves and holding a spray bottle of foaming bathroom cleanser.

"Are we interrupting something?" I ventured.

He waited to smile until he faced Nola. "No, not at all. Just keeping busy until Nola got here."

I looked past him to the gleaming chrome and marble of the two-sink vanity, happily devoid of toiletries of both the male and female variety. "Don't you have a cleaning service?"

"Yes, but sometimes I just get the urge to clean a little more deeply than a weekly cleaning, you know?" His smile faded as he turned back to me. "Why are you here?"

I hid my face by digging into my purse, embarrassed at how hurt his tone of voice made me feel. I pulled out his car keys. "I wanted to give these back to you."

"You could have just given them to Nola."

"My mom used to do that, too," Nola said quietly.

We both turned to her. "Do what?" I asked.

"Clean everything. When she was trying to get better, she would go on this wild cleaning kick. Said it kept her mind off of things and kept her hands too busy to . . ." Her voice trailed off.

My eyes met Jack's as if we were both recalling my unanswered question. *Are you drinking again?* I was pretty sure now that he wasn't, although I'd asked my dad to keep tabs on Jack to be sure. Just to let Jack know that he wasn't alone in fighting his demons. A part of me wished I could be that person, but his own unanswered question opened up too many parameters for me to be able to fit into that role. *Would you sleep with me if I said it would make me feel better?* I blushed at the memory, but didn't look away.

"Nola and I have a full afternoon planned, so is there anything else you need?"

I'd thought that by my coming over we could work things out between us. That we could apologize—for what, I wasn't sure—and then get on with whatever we had going on before that little scene on the Battery. Like a child not ready to leave a candy store, I blurted out, "Actually, there is one more thing. My mother mentioned that you hadn't RSVP'd to my birthday party yet, and I just wanted to make sure that you'd received the invitation." I cringed, having had no idea that I was going to say that. Not only was asking somebody about an RSVP bad manners, but I really didn't want him to know that I'd noticed or cared.

I thought I saw his lip twitch, but other than that his face was immobile. "I got it."

"Great." I smiled, wishing he'd say something else, like, *Of course I'm coming,* but instead he remained silent—probably because he knew I was waiting for it.

Feeling like an idiot who didn't know when to come in from the rain, I pressed on. "Because Rebecca got one, too, and RSVP'd that two people were coming, but just in case I wanted you to know that you're invited, too, with or without Rebecca. Because she's my cousin, so of course she's invited, but you, well, we're old friends, so you should come, too. With or without Rebecca. So that's why I sent you your own invitation. Because we're friends. And there will be lots of really good food. Callie White is catering, and you know she's the best. My mother had to practically sell her soul to get her booked, because you know that everybody wants her to do their parties now."

Even Nola was looking at me strangely as I blathered on and on about the stupid invitation and party. I think I was probably more coherent when I was two and just learning how to speak.

When he still didn't say anything, I said, "Well, I guess I should be going. I've got another closing at three and an open house at six. Busy, busy."

"I bet," he said. "Well, don't let us keep you."

"Right." I turned on my heel and headed back toward the front door. "Have fun, Nola. I'll see you later tonight."

I turned the knob and was halfway out the door before Jack spoke. "Oh, before you go. I've had a couple of chances to chat with Miss Julia. Not only when I've brought Nola over for her lesson, but I've also volunteered to do a little carpentry work, repairing floorboards and spindles or whatever."

I tried to let the fact that he was handy with tools not affect me, but it was a losing battle. "Yes?" I prompted, trying not to show my surprise that he was still interested in the Manigaults and their ghosts.

"She keeps a note or a letter—something so old and read so many times that it's almost in shreds—in a Santa head–shaped box in her Christmas room. I think it's important, but since she doesn't know I've seen her taking it out and putting it back, and hasn't mentioned it, I can't really bring it up. But if you're wondering what to ask William when you speak with him, that would be a good place to start, I think. Because then she'll know that you really are talking with him when you ask her about the note."

It was an olive branch of sorts, and one I was happy to accept. "Thank you," I said. "I will." I didn't mention that I'd made only a few halfhearted attempts to contact William, and given in way too easily. My life was in a tenable holding pattern, almost like it had once been before I met Jack and before my mother had come back into my life. I wasn't sure I wanted to rock it enough to send it off course again.

I began to walk toward the elevator when his voice called me back again. "I read something the other day that made me think of you."

Pleased that he would think of me when I wasn't with him scooted pleasant electrical pulses through my veins. I turned back to him with a smile. "What was that?"

"'Life begins where your comfort zone ends.' It was embroidered on a pillow in a shop window."

I held my breath, waiting for the words to come to explain to him that I was happy the way that I was, that not everybody needed to jump out of airplanes, or jump into bed with someone, or irritate angry ghosts to make life worthwhile. There were plenty of things in my life that made it great. I just couldn't think of any of them at the moment.

Instead of responding, or standing silent in the hallway waiting for the elevator, I headed for the stairs, the clicking of my heels on the wooden steps a sad and pathetic response to his challenge.

CHAPTER 20

Dusk in Charleston settles on the city like an unexpected surprise, tinting the church steeples and stuccoed houses with shades of pink and purple, adorning the city with a shawl of ethereal light. I often wondered whether all this beauty was one of the reasons why so many past residents refused to leave the city, even after death.

I found my mother in the parterre garden of her house, the garden in which I remembered spending so much time with my grandmother. It must have been a special place for my mother, too, as her directions for my father's reconstruction of it made it an exact replica of my childhood garden.

An untouched cup of tea sat in front of her, the cream stagnant on top of the cooled liquid. General Lee lay at her feet, giving a lazy swipe of his tail in greeting before lowering his head and closing his eyes again.

My mother looked up at me, but in the dim light I didn't see that she wasn't smiling until I sat down next to her. Her hands were folded in her lap, a paper bag sitting on the wrought-iron table in front of her. Next to it were the gloves she normally wore to prevent herself from touching things that might have something to say to her.

"How was your day?" she asked as I felt the side of the carafe, the ceramic cold to the touch.

"The usual. Lots of out-of-towners looking for deals and leaving disappointed. My new receptionist, Charlene, canceled an appointment to preview a house—without my approval—so I'd have time to do yoga with her, and Sophie called about three hundred times to ask about flowers for the wedding. When Charlene volunteered that she used to be a wedding planner, I just handed the phone to her. Killed two birds with one stone."

A soft smile lifted my mother's mouth.

"But I did close on a warehouse loft today on East Bay Street and made a nice commission." My smile faltered only when I started to think about how much of that commission was going to go into the new foundation of the house on Tradd Street.

When she didn't say anything, I looked at her more closely, seeing how drawn she looked, how tired and pale she seemed. Wary, I leaned toward her. "What's wrong?" I asked, my attention focused on the bag.

She raised her eyebrows. "I think it's time you took this seriously."

"Oh, no, you didn't." I shook my head as I opened up the bag and stared inside. The four dollhouse family members lay inside, nestled together like cords of firewood. "Why would you touch them? Especially without me here?"

"I only held the mother without my gloves. She was the weakest, so I deemed her the safest. But they've been coming to me. In my dreams—or nightmares, I should say. Anne, the mother, keeps wanting to show me something, but William and Harold hold her back. There's something they're desperate to keep hidden."

"You should have told me about the dreams."

"I thought that you might be having your own, but you were keeping it to yourself. Until Nola told me this morning that she'd had a bad dream, and it was the same dream I'd been having, and I realized that they had chosen Nola and me for a reason."

"Nola? Why would they pick her?"

Her tired eyes met mine. "Because she's vulnerable." She leaned back in her chair, her eyes still on mine. "She told me that in her dream her mother came and made them go away."

"Like a guardian angel," I said softly. "I told Nola that was probably why Bonnie was still here. To watch over her. I think knowing that has helped Nola a lot." I remembered my experience in the Circular Church cemetery, and the photograph the teenage girl had shown me, and told my mother. "She was protecting me from Harold, but I don't why. Nola wasn't even with me."

My mother shifted in her seat, more alert. "And it was definitely Bonnie?"

I nodded. "Definitely. I've seen her enough around Nola to recognize her."

"She feels maternal around you for some reason, but I can't imagine why."

She continued to study me long enough to make me feel uncomfortable. "So why are they coming to you and Nola in dreams but not to me?"

"They're trying to scare us away."

"From what?" I asked, dropping the bag on the table, not wanting to touch it any longer than I had to.

"They know you're the strongest, that you have the ability to seek Anne out and isolate her, to find what they want to remain hidden. They must believe that Nola and I will make you stop."

Stop her. "Is that what the words burned into the stair runner and carved into Nola's wall meant, do you think?"

She shook her head. "I'm not sure, but I don't think so. After all, you haven't really done anything yet that would make them believe you're much of a threat. I think the incident in the cemetery was more from opportunity than anything else."

"I have to admit that they've convinced me to cease and desist. And if Nola didn't love that dollhouse so much, I'd suggest giving it back to Amelia to sell and just being done with it."

My mother let out a deep sigh. "There are some very unhappy spirits connected to that dollhouse, Mellie. And a very unhappy woman who's still living and who wants to speak with her brother. We can help them, Mellie. Doesn't that make you feel at least a little bit obligated?"

My immediate "no" lingered in my mouth, as if to speak it out loud would make me a liar. Another thought intruded. "Why didn't Nola tell me about her dreams?"

Smiling softly, she said, "Because if you send the Manigaults away, you'll most likely send her mother away, too. I think Nola likes having her here."

"Is that a problem? Hanging around to be close to a loved one?"

"I don't know the answer to that, Mellie. Remember, there's no handbook for what we do. But from my experience, only troubled spirits linger, and when their questions are answered, they suddenly see the light and follow it. Being earthbound is a temporary state, holding them back from what lies beyond death."

The sun dipped lower in the sky and I sighed with resignation. "Would you help me contact William? If we can keep Harold at bay, we might be able to get a message for Julia."

"That's what I was thinking, too, since trying to contact Anne didn't work."

I stood and picked up the bag holding the doll figures. "Put on your gloves. Your attempt to communicate with Anne has already weakened you. You're not ready for William. Let me try it myself—with you in the room, of course. I'm not *that* strong."

Without argument, my mother slipped on her gloves, then, using the table for support, pulled herself up to a stand. "Let's roll," she said, her voice a lot more confident than she looked.

We turned the hall light on, but left everything else in darkness. Of all the ghost movies I'd seen on TV, the one thing that Hollywood got right was that most ghosts really did prefer the dark. I suppose it made sense. They had once been living people, and most people I knew didn't like the harsh light of day to show all of their flaws and shortcomings. Dead people shouldn't be any different, and their most obvious shortcoming was their inability to die completely.

We walked slowly into the drawing room, General Lee prancing behind us, our steps muted on the Aubusson rug. The streetlights streaming through the stained-glass window splashed unintentional color onto the walls and furniture, but left the dollhouse, now moved back against the far wall, in its own black space devoid of light.

"Take William out of the bag," my mother directed. "Then fold up the top and leave the rest in the bag on the hall table."

I brought the bag back into the hall to see better. Glancing inside, I could have sworn Harold's face glowered at me. Quickly finding William, I plucked him out of the bag and with one hand folded the top of the bag and placed it on top of a Chippendale console.

My fingers seemed to hum and vibrate, the tips warming as if I were touching a living, breathing person. Eager to put him down, I walked quickly back to the drawing room and set the figure down on the coffee table. "What do I do now?"

I felt rather than saw my mother's reproving glance in my direction. "What did you do with the Hessian soldier and Mary Gibson?"

"I just spoke to them, like I'm speaking to you now."

"There you go. Speak to William, and tell him what you want."

I sat down on the sofa opposite my mother, the William doll on the table between us, and took a deep breath. Placing both hands flat on my knees, I cleared my throat. "William Manigault? Are you here?"

Nothing happened, the only noise that of the mantel clock and the sound of General Lee licking himself. I glared in the direction of the dog, then turned back to face the doll. "William Manigault, I have a message from your sister, Julia. Can you speak to me?"

The temperature of the room dipped sharply as a small pinprick of light appeared on the turret of the dollhouse and then began to grow and shimmer, gradually shifting into a column of light that hovered between the floor and the ceiling next to the dollhouse. General Lee whimpered, then shot out of the room, his tail firmly planted between his back legs.

"William? Is that you?"

The light began to take on a human form, with arms and legs visible, and then a head, tilted at an odd angle. His suit was in the style of the nineteen thirties, his neatly combed hair parted in the center, his body solid enough to be confused with a real person except for the fact that he glowed.

"Do you see him?" I asked quietly, turning my head slightly in my mother's direction.

"Yes," she whispered. "He's the one I saw in my dream."

Go away.

I felt the words rather than heard them, the menace behind them palpable as a sheet of icy wind blew at me, strong enough to move my hair.

"Your sister, Julia, wants to hear from you. Is there something you want to tell her?"

Stop her.

I stood and felt my mother stand next to me. She reached for my hand and grabbed it tightly. "We are stronger than you," I said out loud.

No, you're not.

My mother's hand squeezed mine.

"Is there something you want to tell your sister?" I asked again. "She wants to talk with you."

Stop her.

I had to force my jaw to stop trembling as the temperature continued to drop. "What do you want her to stop?"

She knows. Only misery awaits if she does not stop.

"Why are you still here? Is there something you need to see finished before you can move on?"

He turned his head and I could see a dark welt of black and blue on the side of his neck. I recalled the dollhouse figure of William, and the fractured line of glue that had replaced the head back on the neck. *He will not let me.*

"Who, William? Your father?"

Stop her. It will only get worse if she does not.

"What happened to you, William? I think Julia wants to know, to give her peace. Can you tell me that?"

What could have been a laugh rumbled through the darkened room. *She knows.*

"Knows what?"

The light began to flicker and diminish, absorbed into the inky blackness like oxygen in fire.

"Wait!" I stepped forward, my mother moving with me, our hands still clasped. "What about the letter? The one Julia keeps in the Santa box. What is it?"

A spot in the center of the shrinking light brightened briefly. *She believes it is proof of innocence where there is none. Let her believe it. Make her stop.*

"Stop what?" I asked again, but the light was gone, the temperature of the room already returning to normal. I fell back onto the sofa, mentally exhausted and frustrated. "Well, that was a big bunch of nothing."

My mother, who'd moved to flip on the overhead chandelier, paused in the doorway leading to the foyer. "Not exactly."

I smelled the smoke as I walked quickly to join her. We both saw the smoldering bag sitting on top of the Chippendale console. The central portion appeared untouched, but the folded edge glowed with red, the color fading and intensifying as if the bag breathed.

Thinking mostly of the furniture, I knocked the bag to the heart-of-pine floor and stamped my shoe down on the smoldering edge again and again until no red showed and the sole of my Bruno Magli sling-back was crusty with paper ash.

I stared at my mother, the smell of burning paper heavy in the air. "Great. That went well. I think we really pissed somebody off— probably Harold. And I really, really don't like it when he's angry."

My mother bent down to pick up the bag. "I know, sweetheart. But you did well, and you deserve a quiet evening to yourself. Go draw yourself a bath and have a long soak. No more ghosts tonight."

As soon as the words left her mouth, the radio in Nola's room burst into life at high volume, the words to "I'm Just Getting Started" so familiar to me now that I had them memorized.

"Or not," I said as I wearily climbed the stairs, recalling with envy my previous life, when the voices of the dead were something I easily ignored.

I struggled to simultaneously close my umbrella and make it through the door at Ruth's Bakery without getting wet or dropping my purse and briefcase. A strong hand reached through the door and took the umbrella from me, allowing me to get inside. I turned to thank my benefactor, whose broad-shouldered back was to me as he carefully folded my umbrella and leaned it against the wall beside the door. My prepared smile dropped as Jack turned around to face me, his expression showing that he wasn't surprised to see me. Or all that happy, either. He looked like a boy who'd been sent to the principal's office, determined to act contrite despite his reluctance to be there. "Good morning, Mellie."

I glanced over at Ruth, who stood behind the counter, her eyes sparkling as she surreptitiously smoothed her hair and fixed the collar of her shirt. If her skin weren't so dark, I'd bet she was flushing, too, and I couldn't help but wonder whether *anyone*, besides Nola, was immune to Jack.

"What are you doing here?" I asked as I approached the counter for my morning order of doughnuts and cappuccino that Ruth usually already had bagged and ready by seven thirty for me.

"I thought this was a public establishment," Jack said as he sat down at one of the two parlor-style tables.

I looked up from where I'd been digging in my purse for the coupons I pulled every week from the unread Sunday newspaper for Ruth and saw that she was scowling at me.

"Where's your manners, girl? This gentleman's been nothing but pleasant and you're being unkind. I know your mama taught you better."

I thumped the coupons on the counter to circumvent the finger wagging I was sure was coming next.

"That's all right, Ruth," Jack said as he stretched his long legs beneath the table. "I'm used to it."

I dug back into my purse for my wallet and beamed a smile at Ruth, who was doing weird things with her eyebrows and pointing to the fourth finger of her left hand and jerking her head in Jack's direction.

I squinted, trying to figure out what she was trying to tell me. She did it again, this time her movements more exaggerated.

"No, I'm not married, Ruth," Jack said from the table behind me. "Mellie's aware of that fact, and I've had to rebuff her advances on many occasions. I'm just happy that I've remained relatively unscathed with all limbs attached and most of my clothes still in one piece."

I wasn't about to give him the satisfaction of arguing, so, facing Ruth again, I asked, "Is my order ready, Ruth? I have a staff meeting this morning and I need to be sugar-and-caffeine-fortified to sit through it."

She pursed her lips, her whole body radiating disappointment in me. "No, and it's going to be a while, so you might as well take a seat. I'm working on this gentleman's order first."

My raised eyebrows were wasted on her, as she didn't even bother looking up at me as she slowly and deliberately began to fold a flat pastry box into shape. Sighing, I retreated to the other table adjacent to

Jack's, ignoring the second chair at Jack's table that he kicked out in an apparent invitation to sit.

After dumping my purse and briefcase in the facing chair, I turned to Jack. "So, really, why are you here?"

"I told Nola I'd bring her breakfast, and you told me she likes Ruth's powdered-sugar doughnuts. I need to ask her more about Bonnie, so I figured I'd take your advice and try a little bribery to soften her up first. I'd planned to have a discussion with her the other night, but we were having such a good time that I didn't want to spoil the mood by bringing up her mother."

Nola hadn't volunteered any information as to what she and her dad had done, so I assumed they'd spent the whole day watching *Twilight* movies on DVD and eating popcorn. If I really examined my conscience I would admit to feeling a little left out, imagining that the three of us hanging out together might be more fun than the two of them doing something and me organizing Mrs. Houlihan's spice rack by myself.

"What did you do?" I found myself asking.

"I took her down to the Spoleto Festival. I'd bought some tickets to see *The Gospel at Colonus* at the Gaillard Auditorium and she loved it. She's got pretty eclectic tastes when it comes to the creative arts, and I figured Spoleto was the perfect place to take her."

He was right, of course. The Spoleto arts festival in Charleston was a yearly event that attracted national attention and poured thousands of visitors into the city for a two-week period. I'd never attended any of the concerts, plays, or art shows, choosing instead to avoid the crowds and carry on with business as usual. But I could only think now how fun it would have been to be with Nola and Jack.

"I'm glad she had a good time." I glanced at Ruth, who was now, with excruciatingly slow movements, curling ribbon with the sharp edge of a pair of scissors. For Jack's box of doughnuts. In all the years I'd been coming to see Ruth on a daily basis, I'd never seen even a scrap of ribbon.

I turned back to Jack. "Did you find out who that Rick Chase person is? I haven't heard Nola talking on her phone with him again, but that could just mean that she's being careful not to do it in front of me."

He drummed his fingertips on the table. "Yeah, I did. Besides being Bonnie's last boyfriend, he's also the guy who wrote that Jimmy Gordon hit—the one they're playing on the radio all the time."

"'I'm Just Getting Started'?" I asked. "That's the song that's always playing when Nola's radio turns on by itself. What's that supposed to mean?"

Jack shrugged. "I just think it's a little too coincidental for Nola to hate this singer whose song has a connection, although a distant one, to Bonnie. I want to ask her about it, and also find out whether 'my daughter's eyes' means anything to her."

"Please let me know if you find out anything—anything at all. It will help me approach Bonnie, if I can ever get her to stay long enough so I can speak with her."

"Do you see her a lot?"

I nodded. "Quite a bit. Mostly around Nola, or in Nola's room in the corner where she keeps Bonnie's guitar and her music. And her backpack and teddy bear. Her teddy bear wears a USC football jersey; did you know that?"

He shook his head. "What's the number on it?"

I thought for a moment. "You know, it's funny you mention that. The shirt looks like a normal college-issue jersey, but the number looks hand-stitched. And there's no name on it, either. Like Bonnie bought a generic jersey and then sewed on the numbers herself."

I glanced over at Ruth, who was moving so slowly I was getting ready to volunteer to come behind the counter and help. "While we're talking about Bonnie, I wanted to ask you something. Was she a very maternal sort of person when you knew her?"

He looked at me strangely. "I wouldn't have called her maternal—I mean, we were in college, not many chances to show a maternal side. But she was always very caring and concerned about others. Always put other people before herself. I think that's one of the reasons why she left without telling me about Nola. She wasn't being selfish; she just didn't want to saddle me with a wife who didn't want to be married or stay in South Carolina." He looked thoughtful for a moment. "But she must have been a great mother. Despite her failings, she must have done something really right to make Nola as strong as she is." He tilted his head. "Why do you ask?"

I told him about the incident in the Circular Church cemetery, and how it appeared that Bonnie had stepped in to protect me. He opened his mouth to say something, then closed it suddenly. "Never mind," he said.

"No, tell me. What were you about to say?"

A half smile lifted his mouth. "I was about to say that I think you and Bonnie would have been friends."

"Why do you think that?"

He shrugged. "For the same reason you and Sophie are friends, I guess. But also because she would have looked at you as one of her projects—somebody who needed changing."

"Who says I need changing? I think I'm perfectly fine the way I am."

Ruth appeared by Jack's table and placed the beribboned box in front of him. "I'm not taking sides here, sir, even if you're right. She's a regular customer."

Jack had the gall to laugh and slid back his chair as I continued to sit there trying to find a suitable response that ran along the lines of Ruth's comment, yet without the personal affront.

"Thanks, Ruth. I know my daughter will love them." He zipped up his jacket and turned up the collar to prepare to step outside and into the deluge. He slid on a red USC baseball hat and picked up the box, holding it under his arm like a football. "Oh, one more thing. While I was researching Rick Chase I Googled the Manigault family name and found their family plantation in Georgetown County where the developers are getting ready to clear the land."

I jerked my head up. "How did you know about that? Yvonne said you hadn't been to see her since the first time you asked about the Manigaults."

"Nola. She hears a lot more than she lets on. Anyway, Yvonne must have mentioned something about environmental protestors, which piqued Nola's attention, and Nola then told me. I found out something very interesting about the main house that burned to the ground." He paused for effect. "Guess what year it burned?"

I frowned at him for a moment before I remembered the conversation I had with Yvonne about what a bad year Julia had when her brother disappeared and her fiancé died, followed in quick succession the following year by her parents' deaths. My eyes widened. "Nineteen thirty-eight?"

"Bingo."

Slowly, I said, "And there're no such thing as coincidence."

"Nope."

Our eyes met for a long moment before I spoke. "So what happens next?"

He put his hand on the doorknob. "That would be your call, Mellie." He waved to Ruth, then opened the door. "See you around," he said, before shutting the door behind him.

I turned to Ruth, who was concentrating on rolling over the top edge of my doughnut bag. I paid her for my doughnuts and coffee, then left the store without my umbrella, my mind too busy trying to figure out whether Jack had been referring to the Manigault's dark family secrets or something else entirely.

CHAPTER 21

I closed the back door leading into my office building from the parking lot as quietly as possible, trying to escape Charlene's notice. I was craving peace and quiet and was not in the mood for Charlene's effusive morning chipperness or yet another invitation to join her in a child's pose, whatever that was. And I certainly didn't want her confiscating my doughnuts and cappuccino again. Neither did the rest of the office.

I had successfully made it into my office and was placing my cup and bag on my desk when a noise behind me made me turn around quickly, my purse tipping my cup but not knocking it over. Charlene stood next to a small table in front of the window, where a small fishbowl now sat with two goldfish swimming laps. A plastic sunken ship and pebbles lay scattered on the bottom in some bizarre re-creation of an underwater disaster.

Propping my hands on my hips—mostly to block Charlene's view of my breakfast—I pierced her with what I hoped was my "you'd better have a good explanation" look, something I'd been perfecting with help from both Nola and my mother. "Can I help you, Charlene?"

"No, ma'am. Just doing my job," she said in her heavy Southern drawl. "I've been studying feng shui for the office, and it says that every office should have a water feature or aquarium to promote success. I couldn't find one of those tabletop fountains, so I got this. Living creatures and water give you rejuvenation and calm, and I thought you could use both. You just have to give them a pinch of this food twice a day and clean out the bowl once or twice a week." She beamed broadly. "You're welcome."

"Did Sophie put you up to this?"

"Dr. Wallen? No, ma'am, she did not. I thought of this all by my-self." She beamed again. "Although when she called and I told her about it, she sounded tickled and said you'd love it."

"I bet she did." I looked at the fish, wondering whether I should name them before I dumped them into the nearest fountain. There were plenty in my neighborhood. "Thank you," I said, hoping she recognized dripping sarcasm when she heard it. "Is there anything else?"

She tried to peer behind me, but I kept turning my body to block her view. "You have a message that I pulled off the voice mail from last night. It's from Rebecca Edgerton."

I spotted the pink piece of paper poking out from under the grease-stained doughnut bag and suppressed a groan. I'd been happily avoiding her calls to my cell phone, procrastinating making a return call and the inevitable irritation that always seemed to accompany my conversations with my cousin. "Great. I suppose she wants me to call her back."

"Actually, she said she'd be dropping by at eight o'clock this morn-ing. She said she needed to talk to you about something urgent."

With my curiosity piqued, I slid the note out from under the bag, still making sure Charlene didn't have a full view of my desk. "It just has her name." I looked up at Charlene for an explanation.

"Well, I knew I'd be here when you got in and could just tell you."

I looked at the clock and suppressed another groan. I had exactly five minutes to wolf down my doughnuts—Rebecca had inherited not only the propensity for being early, but also the sweet-tooth gene, and I was not in the mood to share.

Charlene took a step toward my desk and I gently took hold of her arm. "Thank you, Charlene, but I'd like to get a few things organized before she arrives. If you could send Rebecca back when she gets here and hold my calls, I'd appreciate it."

She started to say something about moving the furniture in my of-fice to open up the energy flow, but I'd already shut the door. Running around to my desk, I shoveled in the first doughnut and was about to take the first bite out of the second when Rebecca tapped on my door and stuck her head around the corner.

"Good morning, cousin!"

I took a quick swallow of my cappuccino to wash down the dough-nut and shoved the second one in the top drawer of my desk, then stood. "Hello, Rebecca. What a nice surprise." She kissed me on each cheek, then sat down in one of the chairs that faced my desk.

She looked . . . pink. Her flawless skin was tinged with natural pink on her high cheekbones, which matched her bright pink lipstick and nails. Her pink jacket was fastened with a huge black patent-leather bow belt, and her ears held tiny matching pink bow earrings. It was like looking at a huge stick of cotton candy—pretty to look at but too much would make you sick.

"I just got your message," I said, trying to get right to business so she wouldn't linger too long. I didn't exactly dislike Rebecca, but I didn't necessarily like her either. My ambivalence to a blood relative, regardless of how removed, could be because of how she'd at first kept hidden from me who she was and her motives for getting to know me. At least, that's what I chose to believe, because I couldn't imagine hold-ing a grudge against my own cousin just because she was dating Jack. After all, she'd first dated him long before I'd met him, even before his engagement to the late Emily.

"Nice aquarium," she said, indicating the fishbowl. She crossed her legs, the top one jiggling up and down.

"Thank you," I said, stilling my own leg and not wanting to say any more that might encourage conversation. I still had my second dough-nut to eat before the staff meeting, after all. I raised my eyebrows to encourage her to get on with it.

"How's Nola doing?" she asked.

"She's doing great. She doesn't complain anymore when it's time to go to Julia Manigault's for her music lessons, and we're pretty sure she'll be starting at Ashley Hall as a ninth grader in the fall. Other than that, she's become a whiz at texting, and she and Alston Ravenel are addicted to *Say Yes to the Dress*. And, speaking of which, Sophie has asked Nola to be a junior bridesmaid in her wedding. Even better, Nola loves the dress Sophie selected for her to wear."

"Of course," Rebecca said.

That was exactly what I'd said, too, when Sophie told me, but I didn't think I'd said it in the same derogatory tone. I really had been pleased that they were in accord, since I was still trying to work up the courage to tell Sophie that I'd rather walk down the aisle wrapped in cellophane than wear the concoction she'd created for me.

Rebecca continued. "Although I think Ashley Hall is a little too close, don't you think? There are some great schools in the Northeast that would be better at accommodating Nola's . . . style."

I bristled. "Actually, that's the great thing about Nola. She's definitely different, but she's different because it suits her, not because she's trying to shock anybody. Even better, she's a genuinely good kid with a great head on her shoulders. Granted, she's still a teenager, but we haven't killed each other yet, so I'm guessing that's a good thing. And Jack wants her close by. I mean, he's missed the first thirteen years of her life. I don't think he wants to miss another second." I leaned forward, enjoying myself. "They're getting along so well right now that I'm thinking Jack's on the verge of asking me to help him find a bigger place so Nola can move in with him permanently."

She frowned, and when she caught me watching her she smoothed her forehead. I noticed that the frown lines didn't completely disappear, and I felt a moment of pure happiness. Rebecca was a few years younger than me, but she always made me feel much older when I was standing next to her.

"So," I said, clearing my throat, "what was so urgent?"

She shook her head as if trying to clear it of unwanted images. "Yes. Right." She smoothed her pale linen skirt over her knees. "I was wondering whether Jack had mentioned his next book idea to you."

"You mean his book about Louisa Vanderhorst and my house on Tradd Street?"

She shook her head impatiently. "No. And although he refuses to see it, I think that book will never see the light of day. He'll be able to keep his advance money, but I don't think his publisher has any plans to publish it."

I folded my hands on top of my desk to give them something to clutch other than Rebecca's neck. "Why would you say that? Have you heard anything definitive about his publisher's plans? I mean, why would they pay him all that money, and get excited about a book, and then just pull the rug out from under the entire project?"

She gave me a delicate shrug, but her eyes didn't meet mine. "I don't know. But I think we need to be practical here. Jack keeps beating his head against the proverbial stone wall, and I think it's time he moved on. Found another project in which to immerse himself so he's not focused on this particular little roadblock."

"Having your publisher pull your book without explanation is more than a roadblock, Rebecca. Surely you, as a writer, can understand that."

With a patient smile she said, "Of course I do. But the point I'm trying to make is that Jack needs to move forward. Start that next book. Get himself far enough along that he can look back at all of this and see it as a learning experience. Maybe even put enough distance between him and his current publisher to sell the Louisa book to somebody else." Pressing her palms against the edge of my desk, she whispered loudly, "Surely you've noticed that he . . . hasn't been himself lately."

I wasn't about to get into a discussion about Jack and his state of mind with Rebecca. Leaning back in my chair, I glanced at my watch, making sure she saw me. "So what has any of this got to do with me, and why would you say it was urgent?"

Her face became serious. "Because you and I both know what his next book should be about."

I felt the first stirrings of unease. "We do?"

She nodded. "Think about it, Melanie. It should be obvious."

When I still didn't say anything, she prompted, "A sunken boat, a skeleton on board, an old portrait of a woman with an heirloom necklace . . ."

I slapped both palms on top of my desk. "Absolutely not. That's personal and very private family history. I'd prefer it not to be known that an ancestor was a murderess."

"It was an accident, for crying out loud."

"Yes, but who's going to believe that, seeing as how my great-grandmother then conveniently inherited everything that should have gone to the dead woman?"

"I could help with the PR. Explain how, even though your great-grandmother wasn't really a Prioleau, your family eventually married back into the Prioleau family to make you rightful owners of the house on Legare Street."

I was shaking my head the entire time she spoke.

Ignoring me, she pressed on. "We could even go on book tour with Jack—think of the crowds the three of us would attract! And Jack's already done all of the research, so it would be so easy for him to just—"

"No!" I hadn't meant to shout, but at least it shut her up. For the moment. "Absolutely not. Especially since it would mean dragging out that little 'speaking with the dead' element of the whole story, since it really couldn't be told without it. I like my career too much to see it end because people think I'm crazy. Besides, the story's just too . . . sordid for public consumption. You know how people in this town are—we'd never live it down. And not that I have any immediate plans, but what if I have kids? How will that cloud hanging over them affect them?"

"Well, that's not very likely, is it?" Her expression was very matter-of-fact, as if she really hadn't meant for that dagger to go straight through my heart.

"No, probably not. But even your children would bear the stigma."

That, at least, seemed to reach her. She shut her mouth and sat back in her chair. "I hadn't looked at it that way. But you might be right." She began to chew on her lower lip, her eyes staring off into space at something that wasn't there. "What if I have a daughter and she's not allowed to make her debut at the St. Cecilia ball because of it?"

I clenched my hands tightly together, resisting the urge to throttle Rebecca. I could imagine the headlines then, proclaiming things like, "Blood Will Tell," or, "Descendant of Murderess Commits Murder." Forcing my voice to remain soft, I said, "Jack's a smart and resourceful guy. He's working through this thing, and sooner or later he'll find a new project to get excited about and move on. But not before he's ready."

Rebecca rolled her eyes to the ceiling. "I just don't think I have that kind of patience."

I bit my tongue, resisting the urge to remind her that it wasn't all about her. That Jack's career and sense of self-worth were a heck of a lot more important than his ability to make her happy all the time. I wasn't an expert on relationships by any stretch of the imagination, but I'd figured out long ago about how the effort percentages in a relationship fluctuated according to need, and zero versus one hundred all the time didn't cut it. But there was just no way I was going to give her relationship advice. Not that she'd listen, anyway.

Instead, I asked, "Have you mentioned your idea to Jack?"

She nodded. "He wouldn't hear of it. Said it would be taking advantage of a friendship, and then basically everything else you just said." She studied me closely for a moment. "Are you sure you won't—"

"Positive. Now, I hope you don't mind, but I've got some work to do before my first appointment." I stood and came around the desk, just in case she needed physical encouragement to leave my office.

She picked up her purse, then slid it onto her shoulder as she stood. "By the way, did you know that we're related to the former Kate Middleton, current bride of Prince William? On our grandmother's side. My mother did all the research and found that out. She was very disappointed when we didn't get an invitation to the royal wedding."

I raised my eyebrows, having no idea how I was supposed to respond to that. Luckily, she didn't notice and continued talking. "Also, speaking of invitations, I was wondering if you'd sent one to Marc. He mentioned he hadn't received his yet, so I was just hoping it had maybe gotten lost in the mail."

I hadn't sent him an invitation. I'd actually addressed one to him, then put it aside. For one thing, I knew he was having his own party at his beach house for Carolina Day, and I'd never expect him to forgo that to come to my birthday party. For another, I just wasn't sure I wanted him there. With me. In that dress. Once the clock struck midnight and I turned forty, there could be no telling where my desperation might lead.

"Did he say something to you?" I asked, trying to buy some time.

"Yes, actually, he did. He seemed hurt."

"I'll ask my mother," I said, feigning concern. "Ask her to make sure he's on the list and that his invitation has gone out." I took a step forward to encourage her to do the same thing and move toward the door.

We were halfway there when she stopped again. "I had another dream about your mother and a baby last night."

I stifled an impatient sigh.

"Only you were there this time, and you were barefoot and wearing the most ridiculous outfit."

She had my attention now. "Was it white and gauzy—and worn over a leotard?"

Her eyes widened. "Exactly! Do you actually own something like that?"

"Not yet. It's my maid of honor dress for Sophie's wedding." Our eyes met. "Oh, my gosh—do you think Sophie might be pregnant?"

"It's possible. It would make sense that your mother would fuss over Sophie's baby, since she's almost a second daughter to her. Why don't you ask Sophie? And let me know so I can stop dreaming about babies. There are other things I'd much rather be dreaming about."

She took another step before stopping again. "And I'd suggest praying for rain on Sophie's wedding day so you can wear a raincoat over that outfit. It's your only hope."

"Thanks, Rebecca, for the advice and for stopping by today. It's always good to see you."

She kissed both my cheeks again. "And if you change your mind about Jack's book, let me know."

"Of course," I said, watching her leave.

I turned back to my office and caught sight of the fishbowl and tried to feel calm and rejuvenated. When that failed, I returned to my desk drawer and took out my slightly smushed doughnut and ate it as I wondered about the vagaries of fate that had made Rebecca Edgerton my cousin.

A delivery van from a local music shop was idling at the curb in front of my mother's house when I pulled into the driveway. I ran up to the door, where a man holding a guitar case waited, impatiently ringing the doorbell.

"I can get that," I said as I reached the front door.

"I'm looking for Jack Trenholm."

"He's not here, but that's his daughter's guitar that he'd taken in to be repaired. I can sign for it."

"Are you his wife?" he asked.

"No, but I live here with his daughter."

"So this is your house?"

"No, actually, it's my mother's. . . ."

"Never mind." He put the guitar down and thrust a clipboard at me. "Just sign at the bottom."

I did as he instructed, then watched him leave before opening the door and bringing the guitar inside. I heard the music the moment I touched the guitar case, the same haunting melody I'd heard before, strummed on guitar. I turned my head, trying to decipher where the music was coming from, but each time I did, the music changed direction, too, as if it were being played in my ear as a private concert.

I dropped my purse and briefcase in the empty foyer. "Hello?" I called out, just in case. I knew everybody had gone out—my parents and Nola—to the Trenholms' for dinner, and they must have taken General Lee, too, because he was nowhere to be found. Unless he was in the kitchen hiding, and ignoring me for leaving him alone.

Slowly, I climbed the stairs with the guitar and went to Nola's room, thinking I'd surprise her by placing it on her bed so she'd see it when she first walked in. Pushing open the bedroom door, I felt Bonnie before I saw her, the way normal people feel somebody looking at them when they step into a crowded room. I watched the breath stream from my mouth in a small puff.

"Bonnie?"

The corner of the room where Nola's backpack and teddy bear were stacked shimmered with a bright white light. The pile of sheet music that Nola had anchored to the nightstand with three large books on top shimmied and swayed, the edges of the paper flapping like angry birds.

"Bonnie?" I said again. "I know you're there." I waited for a moment and, when she didn't disappear, I took a deep breath. "I can help you. I *want* to help you. I know you're reluctant to speak to me directly, but we're on the same team here. And I really want to help you, for you and for Nola."

The soft sigh filled the room like the hum of an ocean's wave. *Nola.*

I placed the guitar on the bed, being careful not to look directly into the corner of the room from where I felt her watching me. "She's doing well, and she and Jack are getting along much better now. You wanted that, I know. That's why you sent her here."

I'm so cold.

I nodded in acknowledgment. "You were a good mother, Bonnie. You can look at Nola and see that. And she's going to be fine. But it's time for you to move on. I could help you if you let me."

I don't want to be cold anymore.

"Then tell me, Bonnie. What do you want? What do you need to know?"

The word, when it came, seemed to fall from the ceiling like rain, soaking me in all of its meaning. *Forgiveness.*

My eyes stung at the enormity of the word. "She might not realize it yet, but I know Nola's forgiven you for leaving her. But she feels you left because she wasn't enough reason to stick around. She doesn't understand why you left her."

She's better off without me. I didn't want her to suffer any more because of me.

"Nola loves you. You know that, right? She's just very angry and confused right now. But that never changed."

Tell Jack . . . Her voice began to fade as her light flickered.

"Tell Jack what?"

I'm not very strong. I can't . . . tell you . . . everything.

"Tell Jack what?" I repeated, feeling her slipping away.

Tell Jack . . . I'm sorry. Tell him . . . Nola . . .

I looked at the corner of the room and saw Bonnie, her face and hair clear, the rest of her already vanishing. "What about Nola?"

Just . . . Nola. He knows. He knows how . . . to find my daughter's eyes.

She shrank into a tiny spot of light. I shook my head, not understanding any of it, and still with a thousand questions. "The other day at the cemetery. Why were you trying to protect me?"

The pinpoint of light disappeared, taking with it the icy cold but leaving behind the soft sound of a guitar being strummed, and the unmistakable sound of a woman laughing.

CHAPTER 22

I awakened to the sound of Nola's screams. I bounded out of bed, General Lee close on my heels, nearly colliding with my mother in the hallway outside Nola's bedroom. Without pausing to knock, I pushed the door open, relieved to find no resistance.

General Lee whimpered, waiting in the hall as my mother and I entered the room. The blinds were still closed, but in the dim early-morning light I could make out the shapes of her furniture and Bonnie's guitar leaning against a chair. Nola lay curled on her bed in a fetal position, the bedclothes tossed on the floor. Her hair was stuck to her head with sweat, her breathing rapid, her eyes closed as her head thrashed from side to side.

"Nola?" My mother flipped on the overhead light, then sat on the bed next to Nola. She then held the sleeping girl's head still while she put her other hand on Nola's forehead. Turning to me, she said, "She's burning up. Go get a glass of water from the bathroom."

When I returned my foot accidentally nudged Bonnie's guitar from its precarious position against the chair, making it wobble. For the last few nights, I'd heard Nola strumming on it, very quietly, as if she didn't want anybody to hear. I'd recognized the first few measures of the song that seemed to constantly be playing in the back of my mind, but she always stopped early, as if she didn't remember what came next. I'd also recognized what sounded a lot like "Dancing Queen," but decided to keep that to myself.

I placed the water on the nightstand as my mother gently rubbed

Nola's back, using a soothing voice to awaken her. "Open your eyes, Nola. It's just a bad dream. Open your eyes and they'll go away."

Nola's eyes shot open, the pupils so dilated that it was hard to see them in the ocean of dark blue. "Stop her," she said, her voice hoarse. "They want me to stop her."

I handed my mother the water glass and watched as she held it to Nola's lips. "Drink this. It will help wake you up and then we can talk."

Nola sat up and blinked as if trying to focus, then took two big gulps of water. My mother moved the glass away as Nola raised her hands to her face and smoothed back the damp hair that stuck to her skin. "What happened?" she asked, her gaze darting back and forth between my mother and me as if she were just now registering our presence.

"You had another bad dream," my mother said. "You screamed and Mellie and I came to see what was wrong."

I took a step forward and something hard and rigid cracked under my foot. Lifting my foot, I saw the dollhouse figure of William Man-igault prone on the floor, his head bent at the now familiar, yet un-natural angle. "Dang it," I said. "I stepped on one of the dolls and broke it. Don't worry; I'll fix it—I've become quite the pro with glue. But you shouldn't leave them on the floor."

Nola's eyes were wide. "I didn't."

I met my mother's eyes for a brief moment. "Where did you leave it?"

"Downstairs. In the dollhouse. And I know that for sure because yesterday, when Alston was here, we were redecorating all the rooms again and had all the figures set up doing their own thing. William was on the piano in the living room."

My mother tucked a strand of hair behind Nola's ear. "Can you re-member what the dream was about?

Nola shook her head. "No. I don't . . . I can't . . ."

"Here, hold my hand. It'll make it easier."

Tentatively, Nola slid her hand into my mother's, grabbing it tightly as they both closed their eyes.

"Tell us what you see," my mother said, her voice strained as she struggled to hold her hand steady.

"It was . . . William. William and his father. They don't like each other very much. William was playing the piano, but it made his father angry. I don't know why. It sounded . . . It was beautiful. It doesn't make sense. . . ."

Nola opened her eyes, but my mother squeezed her hand. "Keep going," my mother commanded gently.

Nola closed her eyes again and I watched as her eyes moved back and forth under her eyelids. "Then they were at the house—not the doll-house, but the real one, on Montagu Street. They weren't dolls, either, but real people. And Miss Julia was there looking like she does now—really old. They were waiting outside the door to that creepy Santa room as if they weren't allowed to go in, or maybe they just didn't like it. But they wanted her to hear them, so they were shouting really, really loudly and they were saying, 'Stop it. Stop it now.' She was either ignoring them or really couldn't see them or hear them, because she acted like they weren't there. And then . . ."

She began to shake and my mother placed her arm around Nola's shoulders. "Shh. You don't have to say anything more."

Nola swallowed, her eyes still closed. "I have to. It's important, I think. And it's the part that scared me the most."

My gaze met my mother's again and I could tell that she already knew what Nola was going to say. Not wanting to be left out, I prompted, "What happened next, Nola?"

"They weren't talking to Miss Julia." Her eyes popped open, her gaze panicked. "They were talking to me. In the dream, I was lying here in my bed and they were standing next to me, yelling at me. Telling me to stop her." Nola began to cry. "I didn't know what they were talking about, but I was too scared to tell them. I think that must have been when I screamed, because I don't remember anything else after that."

I was no longer looking at Nola. My gaze had traveled to the bedside table, where her cell phone and an open copy of *Seventeen* magazine lay, the facing page dog-eared in the corner. But what caught my attention was the dollhouse figure of Harold Manigault, who stood on the corner of the table, facing Nola's bed.

"Let me guess. You left Mr. Manigault in the dollhouse, too?"

Nola nodded. "In the library at his desk."

I thought for only a moment before I picked up her iPhone from the table. "Can I borrow this for a second?"

"Sure. What for?"

I said it out loud before I could talk myself out of it. "I'm going to call your father. I think he and I need to pay another visit to Miss Julia. Since they're now involving you, this has suddenly become very personal."

Jack drove like a bat out of hell from Legare Street to Montagu Street, making me wish that I'd taken my own car and met him there. But I hadn't wanted to get there early to face alone any of the house's residents—dead or alive; nor did I want to arrive after Jack. I knew he'd never get violent with a woman, but since this whole matter involved his daughter, I had no idea what to expect. At the very least, I didn't want to have to pay to replace a dozen smashed ceramic Santa Clauses.

Our conversation in the car was stilted and awkward, as I tried to pretend that everything was the same between us as it always had been, and Jack didn't even try. I kept giving him surreptitious glances from the corner of my eye as we careened around corners, trying vainly to remember the time before he was a part of my life.

He wore what I secretly referred to as his "casual writer" uniform of loafers without socks, khaki pants, and a light blue button-down oxford-cloth shirt rolled up at the sleeves. It was before noon, but he was clean shaven and had his shirt tucked in and wore a belt. I couldn't help but wonder whom he was trying to impress, knowing with all certainty that it wasn't me.

He wasn't smiling behind his sunglasses as he held open my door before sprinting across the street and up the porch steps to ring the antique doorbell of Julia's house. Dee Davenport was already pulling open the door by the time I made it to the bottom step.

She smiled brightly when she spotted Jack, dimples showing in both chubby cheeks, until she spotted me and her expression quickly changed into a frown. "Did you have an appointment?"

Jack took a step forward, his hand resting on the door so she couldn't close it. "Hello, Dee. How are you this morning? That shade of pink sure suits your fine coloring." He turned back to me. "Have you ever seen such a peaches-and-cream complexion as Miss Dee has?"

I stepped up on the porch to stand behind Jack, smiling and nodding in agreement. "One of a kind," I said.

Jack turned back to Dee. "I'm sorry that we didn't call first, but I was really hoping we could have a few moments of Miss Julia's time to discuss something very important."

Dee hesitated. "She's not ready for visitors right now, but if you want to come back later . . ."

Jack took a step closer so that he was now standing in the door's threshold. "Actually, later might not work. I know my daughter is scheduled for her lesson at one o'clock, and I'm afraid I can't let her come if I don't speak with Miss Julia first."

I could almost see the weighted scale moving up and down in Dee's head, measuring Julia's wrath against Jack's charm. Apparently, Jack's charm won out, as Dee stepped backward, allowing us into the dim foyer. "I'll go see if she's ready. . . ."

"We'll follow you," Jack insisted with a bright smile aimed at Dee.

With her forehead creased with worry, she led us down the now familiar route to the back of the house. Tapping on the door, she said. "Miss Julia? Are you decent? I've got Mr. Trenholm and Miss Middleton here, and they say they need to see you right away."

Jack reached around Dee and knocked more loudly. "If you don't let us speak with you now, I'm going to leave and get the dollhouse and bring it back here and let you deal with the unhappy spirits you tried to get rid of seventy years ago."

There was no response from inside as Jack and I shared a glance, and I had visions of the Bates Motel and a long-dead woman in a wheelchair. I jerked back at the sound of the latch turning, the door swinging inward.

Julia Manigault, with her white hair out of its tight bun and now unfurled down to her waist, glared at us from the door opening. Even stooped over and wearing a high-necked nightgown with a gray shawl around her neck, she still appeared formidable enough to make me take a step back.

"Didn't Miss Davenport tell you I wasn't available? I never take callers before noon, and I resent this intrusion."

"And I do apologize, Miss Julia," Jack said with appropriate contriteness. "But Melanie had a conversation with William that we thought you should know about."

I looked at him in surprise, having expected him to strong-arm his way into a conversation and not move the focus to me.

Julia stepped back and I saw that she leaned on a heavy-knobbed cane. It was definitely a man's cane, with a large silver eagle's head at the top, and I realized it had probably been her father's. As we walked into the room, I noticed that the sofa had been made into a bed with a pillow and blankets, leading me to believe she spent all of her time in this peculiar room. I remembered her telling me that her father didn't like the room and would never go inside, and wondered whether that was the reason she rarely left it.

We sat down in the same uncomfortable horsehair chairs that we'd sat in before, and faced Julia, whom Dee had settled into her wheelchair with a blanket thrown around her knees. "So what did William tell you?" she demanded, her dark eyes boring into mine.

I glanced at Jack to be sure he really wanted me to lead this discussion and was answered with only his raised eyebrows. Clearing my throat, I turned to Julia. "Please understand that when I speak with spirits, it's rarely completely clear what they are trying to say. We can only try to interpret what we hear to make sense of it."

She leaned forward. "So what did he say?" she asked again, as if I hadn't spoken.

"He said, 'Stop her.' And that misery would follow if you didn't stop. Does that mean anything to you?"

She shook her head but didn't meet my eyes.

"Are you sure?" Jack asked, his voice gentle.

This time she met his eyes and shook her head. Turning back to me, she said, "Is there anything else?"

"Not exactly . . ."

Julia leaned forward, her dull eyes brightening with hope. "What was it?"

"Actually, it wasn't anything he said." I paused. "His head . . ." I tried to think of a tactful way to say it. "His head was bent at an odd angle, with lots of bruising on the neck. Like his neck was broken."

She blinked several times but didn't say anything.

I pressed on. "Could your father have hurt him? Hurt him accidentally, even, but enough to kill him?"

She shook her head vehemently. "No. I know my father didn't kill William." She looked at us, her eyes defiant. "I have proof."

"The letter in the box?" It was only a guess, but the surprise in her expression told me I was right.

"How did you know about that? Did William tell you?"

I figured my source wasn't as important as the content, so instead of answering, I said, "William told me that the note was proof of innocence where there is none. Does that make sense to you?"

Her eyes went blank; her mouth slackened.

"Would you like some water?" Jack asked, already standing and moving toward a tray with a glass and a pitcher of water. He poured her a glass, then pressed it into her hands. She stared at it for a moment as if trying to remember what to do with it before raising it to her mouth.

I pushed on, trying to recall everything William had said to me. "I might be wrong with this, because he didn't say this exactly, but it seemed that he was telling me that you know something, but you're not seeing it, either intentionally or not."

Julia pressed her lips together, then took another sip.

Jack sat forward. "That last night that you saw William and you heard him with your father. What were they arguing about?"

She looked down at her hands, fisted in her lap. "The same things they'd been arguing about ever since I could remember. William was . . . sensitive. Not like our father at all. He enjoyed music and poetry, and time spent outdoors was to admire nature, not shoot at it. He and my mother were close, and they would spend hours together reading to each other. He was brilliant on the piano, until my father made him stop. He bought William a gun and told him that hunting was a more gentlemanly pursuit. William hated that—almost as much as I, because my father forced me to learn the piano. I was good, but never with the talent William had, and I suspect my father knew that, which was why he pressed me so hard to be better."

An unnatural grin lit her face. "I could outshoot, outrun, and out-hunt my cousins and my brother, and I think it turned my father into a cruel man. A year after I came back to live with my family in Charleston, my father bought us horses for Christmas. A beautiful black stallion for me and a small spotted pony for William, just to prove a point."

"And your mother allowed that?" I asked, fearing I already knew the answer.

Julia gave us a bitter laugh. "My mother had no opinions one way or the other. She was what they called 'delicate.' I'm not sure what that meant, other than that my mother couldn't face any unpleasantness. She stayed up in her rooms most of the time." Julia pursed her lips, as if trying to eradicate the bitter knowledge of her father's malice. "My father's cruelty subsided when Jonathan entered our lives."

"Your fiancé?" I prompted.

She nodded. "William met him the first year they were both at Clemson and started bringing him home for holidays and school breaks." She smiled wistfully. "He came from a family with ten children, and I think he enjoyed the quietness here." Her eyes met mine. "He was everything William wasn't—good at riding and hunting and math and . . . all those male pursuits at which William had always failed. We made plans of taking over my father's business empire and running it together when my father retired. I know my father had wanted that for William, but he had no head for figures."

"So when you and Jonathan fell in love and wanted to get married, your father approved."

Julia nodded vigorously. "And so did William. My father's focus shifted to Jonathan, and we were all relieved. My father didn't even notice William anymore, and William didn't care. Having Jonathan in our family was like an answer to all of our prayers."

"So what changed?"

Her face went ashen, her hand trembling enough to slosh water out of the glass. I took the glass from her as Jack stood. "I'll get Dee," he said, already halfway to the door.

She held up her hand and shook her head. "Not yet. Please. I'm not finished. I need . . . I need to know."

I knelt by the wheelchair and took one of her hands in mine. "Let me see the letter. Maybe what William was saying will make sense to me."

Jack came and stood next to me. "They're attacking Nola in her dreams, and I suspect the same thing happened to you, which is why you got rid of the dollhouse. You told Nola to keep the doll figures of your father and brother separated, because they didn't like each other. But they were getting along until that last argument before William disappeared. You know something you're not telling us, don't you?"

Julia glared up at Jack. "My father did not kill William, if that's what you're thinking. I have proof," she repeated.

The last word was barely a whisper, and I recalled again what William had said to me. *She believes it is proof of innocence where there is none. Let her believe it. Make her stop.*

"Then let us see the proof, Miss Julia," Jack said. "They will not leave you—or Nola—alone until this gets resolved. Mellie can help them find peace. Don't you want that?"

Her hands began to tremble on the arms of the wheelchair as bright spots of pink marred her pale skin. "No! They've not given me a moment's peace in all of these years. Do you know what that's like? To turn off your lights and feel them there? *I* want peace."

"Then what did you want to talk about to William?" I asked, my knees aching from kneeling.

It took her a long time before she finally answered. "Forgiveness."

"For what?" Jack pressed.

With a stubborn set of her jaw, she said, "My father did not kill William."

"Show me the proof, then," I said, slowly standing. Jack took my elbow and helped me up.

I spotted the small box that Jack had described to me on the bookshelf behind Julia. I retrieved it and handed it to Julia. She looked resigned and didn't bother asking how I'd known.

"Open it," she commanded. "I don't have the strength."

Regretting my own vanity at having left my reading glasses at home yet again, I handed the box to Jack. He gave me a knowing grin as he lifted the lid and peered inside before pulling out a small folded piece of paper. After replacing the lid, he opened the well-worn letter and began to read:

Dear Sister,

As you no doubt have already realized, and perhaps have known for some time, it is time for me to go. I can no longer live under the same roof as Father, as you well understand. It has not been easy for me with him, nor for you, I would imagine. Life is intolerable the way it is, and I must make the choice to change it. I suppose I have you to thank for my realization, although I doubt the result was what you expected. But that is what happens when we spill a secret—the results are not always what we planned. I am sorry for any hurt that my leaving will cause you, but it cannot be helped, as I am sure you will become aware. I want the best for you, and you will realize that in time.

I doubt I will see you for a while, if ever. I will not pass judgment; nor do I expect judgment to be settled on me.

William

Jack lowered the letter. "He was planning to leave of his own free will, and didn't expect to return or stay in touch."

I took the letter from Jack, then folded it up and returned it to the small box, going over the words in my head and Julia's request that I ask William to forgive her. "What secret was he referring to?"

"You must go now," she said. She slumped to one side, her hand pressed to her chest.

Jack immediately left the room to find Dee while I took her hand again. "Was the secret the reason William argued with your father? Is that why you need his forgiveness?"

She didn't answer, and I had to stand back as Dee entered carrying a pill bottle and another glass of water. "Miss Julia needs to rest now. Please go."

Jack took my arm and led me down the hallway and out the front door. I didn't stop walking until we were a block away and out of sight of the turret, feeling unseen eyes on my back.

Jack followed without question, then turned to face me when I stopped. "She's guilty about something; I just don't know what," he said.

"But she doesn't want us to know, and her father and brother aren't happy that we're asking questions, either."

"What about Anne, her mother? Have you tried to contact her?"

I shook my head. "My mother did, but as in life she's overwhelmed by her husband. If we want answers, we'll need to go to the source."

"You tried before, and all you got was William telling you to stop her, and a burning bag filled with dolls. And agitated ghosts who want to get Nola involved in whatever this is all about."

I nodded. "We need to get the dollhouse away from Nola. Teenagers always have too much energy so that they draw the spirits to them."

"We could move it to my loft. Dead people don't bother me, and it will give Nola an excuse to come visit more often."

"That's a thought." I smiled, remembering the conversations Nola had with Alston while they were messing with the dollhouse, and thinking how foreign it would all be to Jack. "I'll mention it to her and she can let you know."

"Anything more from Bonnie?"

I frowned. "Not really. She said something about 'my daughter's eyes' again and then . . .'" I stopped, not sure how to put the last part into words.

Jack cocked an eyebrow.

"When I asked her why she'd intervened in the cemetery, she answered by laughing."

"Really?" He rubbed his hands over his face, and I noticed again how tired he looked. "I had a conversation with Nola about Jimmy Gordon. Seems it was Rick Chase who introduced them. Rick, Bonnie, and Nola went to Jimmy's studio, where he was recording his first album. They left Nola in the waiting room for most of it, but apparently Jimmy, Bonnie, and Rick spent about an hour together in an office with Jimmy's producer."

"I'm guessing they were making a deal about Jimmy recording Rick's song 'I'm Just Getting Started.'"

"Probably. Although that still doesn't explain why Nola would have such an intense dislike of the man."

"She's a teenager," I said. "They usually don't have reasons for most of their feelings."

He jerked his head in the direction of his Porsche. "I'll go get the car, since I'm getting the feeling you don't want to have to walk in front of the house again."

"That's all right. It's not far and I'm going to walk, clear my head a bit and think."

He stared at me for a long moment, and even though I was sure he wasn't all that interested in what I needed to think about, I blurted, "Thank you for not listening to Rebecca about writing your next book about Rose Prioleau and the Legare Street house."

"She mentioned that to you?"

"Yeah. She wanted me to talk to you and tell you it was okay by me."

"And is it?"

"I'm assuming you know the answer to that or you'd already have the book written and sold."

He smiled his old smile for a moment, and I felt the familiar sensation of my chest constricting. "So you agree that I'm not such a bad guy then?"

He'd taken a step forward, his eyes steady on mine.

"I never thought that, Jack."

His eyebrows knitted. "Funny. Because you always act as if I have some contagious disease. Like right now. I take a step forward, and you answer with a step backward. I thought you had me confused with Marc Longo or something, so I just wanted to ask to make sure."

Not wanting to have this conversation again, I turned around and started walking back toward home.

"What do you want for your birthday?" he called out.

I stopped but didn't turn around. "I'm asking for donations to be made to the Preservation Society. Sophie made me." I turned to face him. "Does this mean you're coming to the party?" I wanted to kick myself for sounding like such an eager high schooler.

He shrugged. "Maybe."

I turned around again and started walking. "Whatever," I said, not wanting him to know how his admission that he might be there had made my knees a little wobbly. "Give me a wave across the room if you get there."

"I'll try to remember," he said, followed by a chuckle that I pretended not to hear.

CHAPTER 23

I reclined like a banana republic's dictator in my mother's chaise longue in her room, while a young woman from my mother's beauty salon polished my toenails in "Femme Fatale" crimson and another worked on my manicure. The makeup artist and hairstylist were both due to arrive in a few hours and already I was exhausted. And frustrated. My mother had confiscated my BlackBerry, my laptop, my Daytimer, and even my pedometer that I used to gauge my productivity while away from my desk.

Across the room hung what I referred to in my mind with a capital letter as the Dress. I'd procrastinated too long in finding a replacement, so I was stuck with no other choice but to wear it. I hadn't tried it on with a turtleneck underneath it, but as I stared at the plunging neckline I wondered whether I should have.

My mother sat next to me in an identical chintz-covered chaise, except her head was relaxed against the back of the chair as if she were enjoying herself. By contrast, my manicurist had to keep unfurling my fingers from digging into the armrests, and straightening my curling toes.

"Relax, Mellie," my mother said for the third time, her eyes closed, as if she could sense my tenseness. "This is supposed to be fun, remember?"

"Yeah. So is bungee jumping, but you don't see me doing that, do you?"

Ignoring my response, she said, "Your contractor, Rich Kobylt, stopped by earlier."

I groaned. "What now?"

"Oh, come now, Mellie. It's not always bad news."

"From him, actually, it usually is."

"Well, not this time. He said his workers and all their equipment will be removed by eleven o'clock this morning and won't return until Monday. That should give the caterers plenty of time to set up and clean up without getting in the way of the construction workers. Rich even wrapped a black tarp around the uncovered foundation to make it easier on the eyes, and Nola and Alston have volunteered to decorate the tarp for the party."

I sat up suddenly, earning a tight squeeze on the wrist by the manicurist. I sent her a look of apology before turning back to my mother. "Please tell me you gave them some parameters on what it should look like."

She actually looked affronted. "I did no such thing. They're very creative girls, and I'm sure whatever they come up with will be fine—and certainly better than staring into the dusty hole beneath your house. Now, stop worrying and relax."

The manicurist pried my index finger off the armrest to slap on another coat of polish while I made a conscious effort to rest my head on the seat back.

"Anyway," my mother continued, "Rich said that it's safe to use the kitchen entrance to gain access to the downstairs bathroom for guests. We will also have two discreetly hidden high-end Porta-Johns for the gentlemen at the back of the garden. I won't bother to mention what Chad and Sophie suggested we do instead for a more environmentally friendly solution."

My head jerked up again.

"Don't worry; I told them no. Besides, your father would never consider that for his garden. Nor do I think it's legal."

Feeling my jaw beginning to ache, I forcibly relaxed it and rested my head again on the back of the chair.

"Rich did mention something about the pipes he uncovered, but he said he'd wait to talk to you about that later."

I closed my eyes, trying to block out the image of large amounts of cash flying out the windows of my Tradd Street house, and a tarp-covered foundation as the backdrop to my fortieth birthday party. I'd suggested we have the party in my mother's garden instead, but both she and my father had dissuaded me, saying that it would mean more to me to have the party at my own house: the house that I'd brought back to life in more ways than one. Just because it was empty of furnishings and the foundation was torn up wasn't enough reason to move venues, according to them. Besides, my father insisted, it would be a testament to his skills as gardener to transform the workspace into an art form. I hadn't been allowed into the garden to see what he'd done, but from the puffed look of pride he gave me every time I asked, I imagined it was something good.

There was a tap on the door, followed by Sophie sticking her head around the corner. "Is it safe?"

I grinned. "Come on in. But if you stay too long, my mother will have you crimped and painted and stuffed into some hooker dress before you know it."

My mother frowned at me while I tried to surreptitiously study Sophie's figure for any sign of a bulging abdomen. Rebecca's dreams about a baby had me curious, but not curious enough to ask Sophie outright and embarrass her. And me. I figured if she were expecting, she'd tell me. I could only hope that if it were true, I'd be one of the first to know. I was still smarting at the indignity of finding out about her engagement with everybody else. Being BFFs—as Nola called us— should mean priority notification.

Sophie caught me looking and held her arms out. "You like it? It's a tablecloth I found at a garage sale, but since I'm so handy with a needle and thread, I thought it would make a cute summer dress. I found this piece of rope in my trunk and voilà! I had a belt."

I kept the smile on my face as I took in the red-and-white-checked pattern of the fabric, the stitching done with multicolored thread— presumably leftovers from previous jobs that she didn't want to waste— and the deep scissored vee for the neck and armholes. I couldn't imagine even ants at a picnic finding it appealing. Unfortunately, it also fit like a belted tablecloth, making it virtually impossible to ascertain whether she was actually female, much less pregnant.

Luckily, I was spared a response when Nola appeared behind her. I glanced at the small Meissen clock on my mother's dressing table. "Aren't you supposed to be at Miss Julia's right now?" She'd been going about three times a week, at her own suggestion. Jack had been too surprised and happy to question her motives. I remained suspicious.

"Dee Davenport called and canceled, and also wanted me to tell you that Miss Julia won't be at the party tonight."

Sophie held up the newspaper. "And I think I know why."

The manicurist glared at me as I tried to reach for the paper. Sending her yet another apologetic smile, I said, "You're going to have to read it to me."

Sophie opened the paper and then folded it over to the section she needed. Clearing her throat, she read:

Human remains of two individuals, thought to be a male and female, have been found by a Cobb Homebuilders construction crew during the clearing at Belle Meade plantation in Georgetown County. There is no indication how long the bodies have been there, but preliminary reports indicate they are not recent burials. No headstones were immediately apparent.

The remains were discovered behind the ruins of the main house that burned in 1938 from a lightning strike. All construction has been halted until it is confirmed that there are no further bodies buried in the vicinity and the remains are identified and reinterred elsewhere.

Sophie crumpled the paper as she lowered it. "That's the property you said Julia Manigault is selling to Cobb, right? I actually picketed the place before the judge ruled in the developer's favor, and didn't even realize it was hers. But I'm guessing the news isn't sitting well with her right now."

Nola sat on top of my mother's bedspread, almost jumping up and down with excitement. "I bet one of those environmental groups moved some bodies just to stop the construction. I mean, everybody's seen *Poltergeist,* right? Who wants to live in a house that used to be a cemetery? You get all those spooky people coming out of your closet and then green slimy stuff dripping down your walls." She turned to me, her eyes wide. "Why don't you go out there and talk to those dead people and find out who they are?"

Both the manicurist and pedicurist stopped in midbrushstroke and turned in unison to look from Nola to me and then back again.

I forced a laugh. "Right. Like that wouldn't scare me to death. Besides, I think those kind of special effects are only in the movies." I shot her a warning look. "Anyway, my mother's got me booked for the rest of the day for various procedures." Glancing over at my mother, I asked, "What's next on the agenda?"

"Well, I wanted you to try on your dress one last time to see whether any small alterations need to be made. I actually thought we could sew a little more . . . bulk in the bodice area to fill it out a bit more."

"I'd be happy to do it for you," Sophie volunteered.

"No, but thank you," my mother and I said in unison.

While my mother pretended to cough, I said, "I appreciate it, but I think we've got it covered. All I want you to do is get yourself dressed, and then you and Chad come to the party and have fun."

Her face sobered. "But I *am* dressed for the party."

If crickets had been present, we would have heard them chirping.

"Kidding!" she said, earning a howling laugh from Nola and a relieved sigh from both beauticians and my mother. "Sorry—couldn't resist. I did get a party dress. Not as hot as yours, but Chad likes it."

That did nothing to reassure me, but it had to be better than a tablecloth. "Great," I said, smiling. "I'll see you later, then. Thanks for bringing the newspaper or I might never have known."

"I know. That's why I brought it." She placed the rumpled copy on top of the bed. "Come on, Nola. I'll drop you off on Tradd Street so you can finish your mural." Turning back to me, she said, "Wait till you see it. It's awesome."

I wasn't convinced, but I smiled anyway. "Can't wait!"

I felt a hand on my shoulder and looked up to see the manicurist pushing me back against the seat. "Try to relax, Miss Middleton. It's more enjoyable that way."

Pressing my head into the cushion, I said, "This is as relaxed as I get."

I heard her sigh as she forcibly straightened my pinkie again, then gave it another swipe with the polish brush.

✤

Despite the fact that the distance between our two houses was only a
few blocks and we could have been driven by my father, my mother
insisted that we have a chauffeured limousine to take the three of us and
Nola to my house on Tradd Street. Only Nola's presence prevented this
from being a trial run for my wedding day. Or, as was most likely the
case, a substitution.

I could almost smell the scent of flowers through the closed windows of the limo as we pulled up to the curb in front of my house.
Unable to wait for the driver to open my door, I rolled down my window, breathing in the perfume of hundreds of summer blooms. There
were clusters of them everywhere—on the front gates, atop the garden
wall, wrapped around the piazza railings, and dropping from window
boxes. An arbor had been constructed inside the garden gates, entwined
with transplanted purple clematis, for each guest to walk through. From
what I could see beyond the gates, the brick paths and hedges, and even
the fountain, showed no signs that a construction crew had been anywhere near the house. Only my bank account knew the truth.

My father sat next to me in the limo, and I reached for his hand and
squeezed, knowing he was personally responsible for the transforma-
tion. Gardening had become his passion when alcohol had ceased to be,
and I'd found the joy it gave him contagious. "Thank you, Daddy," I
said, leaning over and kissing him on the cheek. "I can't believe you did
all of this! It's just . . . stunning."

He patted my hand. "I can't take all the credit, you know. Louisa
Vanderhorst planned the rose garden and the fountain, and Loutrel
Briggs designed the rest. All I've done is clean up a neglected garden
and tweak some of the older designs."

"And raid all the florists in Charleston," my mother added. "He
wouldn't dream of actually hiring a florist for the party. Insisted on
doing all of it himself." She beamed at him, her face radiating a different
kind of passion, and for a moment I was torn between admiring the
deepening of their relationship and being nauseated by it. They were
my parents, after all.

The chauffeur opened the door and helped me, and my dress, out of
the limo. Nola scrambled out next and I looked at her, grudgingly admiring her outfit. She wore a simple Lilly Pulitzer shantung sheath in a

pale lilac that set off her complexion and eyes beautifully. Amelia had purchased it for her, but Nola completed the look with the purple Converse sneakers Jack had given her. A gauzy purple scarf was wrapped around her neck, with a big saucy bow tied off center. As my mother had pointed out before, Nola's style might not be mine, but it suited her, making it a perfect complement to her unique personality.

As the chauffeur helped my mother out of the car, Nola whispered to me, "Who's Loutrel Briggs?"

I quickly tried to come up with a way to explain who the late, great landscape architect was into words Nola would understand. "He's a dead guy from New York who designed many of the most beautiful gardens here in Charleston in the nineteen twenties. It's a big deal if your house has a Loutrel Briggs garden."

She scrunched up her nose. "What kind of name is Loutrel?"

Looking down at her, I said, "What kind of name is Nola?"

She snorted, earning a concerned expression from my mother as she and my father moved to stand with us as the limo drove away. Nola spotted Alston, who'd arrived early with Sophie and Chad, and ran to join her.

I pulled my shawl tighter around my shoulders, yanking up the knot that held it together over my chest. "I feel like I'm naked," I said.

"You look fabulous, Mellie," my mother said, tugging at the knot to loosen it. "It's too warm for this, and you'll want your guests to admire your dress when you greet them. I'll hang on to it in case it gets too cool for you after the sun sets, but I've instructed the band to play until midnight, so hopefully the dancing will keep you warm."

Raising my eyes to the sky in resignation, I allowed my mother to remove my shawl.

My father gave a low whistle. "Did you pick that out for her, Ginny?"

"I sure did. And I'm sure you agree that she looks gorgeous in it."

"Well, of course. But I wish I'd come prepared with a bat to prevent a stampede."

I glanced at him doubtfully. "The only stampede will be a stampede of one as I hightail it back to Mother's house to get a sweatshirt to cover myself."

I let out a shriek as I felt my mother's knuckle dig into my back between my shoulder blades. "What was that for?" I said, turning to her with a scowl.

"Just reminding you to keep your shoulders back and stop slouching like you're embarrassed about what God gave you. You're tall, slender, and beautiful. Now stop sulking and go work that dress. Jack could be here any minute."

She sent me a knowing glance, then walked into the garden toward one of the tents that had been set up for food, and began giving last-minute instructions to the catering staff. I looked at my father, who just shrugged before following my mother. He called over his shoulder, "We'll join you back here in about twenty minutes to help greet your guests. In the meantime, go have some punch and try to relax."

It wasn't until he'd said the word "relax" that I realized my jaw was hurting from clenching it. I spotted the tent where a bar had been set up along with a large silver punch bowl and cups. Although I'd never been much of a drinker, I did love sweets, and the pink, frothy punch bubbling inside the punch bowl made my mouth water. I ladled a large serving into a cup and drank it down in two gulps before pouring myself another. I just needed something to settle my nerves before I could face people while wearing the Dress. I was about to walk away before I decided on a third cup, telling myself it had nothing to do with the possibility that Jack might be there.

I heard a low wolf whistle and turned abruptly, nearly spilling the pink punch down the front of my dress. I watched as Sophie and Chad approached. At least, I assumed it was Sophie, since the woman with Chad had Sophie's wild and curly dark hair and was wearing Birkenstocks.

"Dudette!" Chad said, giving me a quick hug. "You're like one of those Amazon women but with clothes on."

"Thanks," I said. "I think."

"Sophie! I love your dress!" I couldn't believe that those words were actually being strung together and coming out of my mouth.

"Thank you," she said, making a little twirl to show off her navy blue satin Empire-style dress, complete with bow front and center. "It's

Lanvin, 1961. I figured after getting a secondhand wedding gown that used clothing was really the most eco way to go."

I stared at her, speechless for a moment, trying to understand how Sophie could make couture eco-friendly.

Sophie continued. "Nola took me to an at-home trunk show for Library: Archives of Fashion—a company run by a local woman who travels all over the place finding old stuff. Do you really like it?"

I nodded, then stopped as I reached her shoes. "I probably would have suggested something different for your feet, but it's definitely a start. You look great," I said, hugging her. "And thanks for coming early to help my mother. She won't let me do anything, so please direct all questions to her. I'm just here to be eye candy." I didn't bother to blush, figuring it was the punch that made me say it.

My mother turned from where it appeared she was rearranging cocktail napkins and called for Sophie and Chad. "Duty calls," Sophie said. "Go ahead and try those soy grits with vegan biscuits at the food tent. To die for."

I watched them walk away, then poured myself another glass of punch, determined to sip it slowly as I wandered around the garden, smelling the tea olives and admiring the lavender-colored creeping heliotrope that my father used as a summer fill-in for his parterres, and watching the last-minute preparations with a sense of remove. A small dais had been set up for a band in front of a hastily constructed dance floor that had been set above the brick patio to keep women's heels from getting stuck in between the pavers.

Remembering the mural, I turned toward the back of the house to get a view of Nola and Alston's artwork on the black tarp before everybody else did, not really sure what to expect. I started to laugh, probably from relief. Instead of the LA gang graffiti I'd imagined, the girls had managed to paint what looked like a wall of brick where the original bricks had once been but had been temporarily moved during the foundation work. They'd even painted clusters of Louisa rosebushes to make it more realistic. As the evening got darker and people had more to drink, it might even look like the real thing.

Nola and Alston walked by, both of them furiously texting on their phones—hopefully not to each other—and I called their names. "Nice work, girls," I said, giving them both a thumbs-up. Their fingers paused long enough to wave, then continued their texting without skipping a beat.

My smile faded as I spotted Rebecca's red Audi pulling up to the curb and I realized it was almost time for people to start arriving. I slugged back the rest of the punch and set my cup down before approaching the flower-filled arbor. I watched as Marc got out of the driver's side of Rebecca's car and moved to the passenger side and helped her out.

My heart beat sluggishly with a suspiciously sunken sort of feeling. If Rebecca was bringing Marc, then Jack must have decided not to come after all. I waited under the arbor as they approached, Marc looking handsome in a white dinner jacket and bow tie, and Rebecca as beautiful as ever in a pale pink silk gown with lots of sparkles and a halter top, her blond hair piled high on her head. I grudgingly admitted that they made a very good-looking couple, but I couldn't understand why they were here together.

Marc looked up and saw me, then stumbled, making Rebecca frown as she also spotted me underneath the flowering arbor. A smile quickly replaced her frown as she reached me, air-kissing me on both cheeks.

"You look so cute tonight, Melanie." Turning to Marc, she said, "Doesn't she look just adorable?"

For the first time since I'd met Marc, he seemed to be at a loss for words. His jaw was moving and his mouth opened and closed a few times, but no words came out.

With a little nudge from her elbow into his ribs, Rebecca continued. "That is just the sweetest dress. I think I saw that exact thing in the Sears window when I was there to buy a part for my washing machine. It's amazing what you can find in that store!"

Marc's eyes remained fixated on the bodice of the dress, to the spot where the plunging neckline ended in a deep vee. "It's . . . very nice, Melanie. Very nice." His voice sounded strange, like his bow tie might be too tight.

"'One fairer than my love? The all-seeing sun ne'er saw her match since first the world begun.'"

I twirled at the sound of Jack's voice and found him standing directly behind me. He also wore a white dinner jacket, but instead of a tie, he wore the shirt with an open collar, his tanned chest dark against the bright white of his starched shirt. His chin and cheeks hinted of a shadow, and his hair was a little longer than I was used to seeing it. Marc scored more points on the GQ scale, with his impeccable grooming and outfit, but Jack was off the charts in pure animal sex appeal. He placed his hand on my hip, then drew me closer for a proprietary kiss on my temple. "Happy birthday, Mellie."

I was glad my mother had taken my shawl, because even without it I was pretty sure I could feel myself melting. "Thank you," I said, my voice breathless.

"Quoting torrid romance novels, Jack?" Marc asked, a smug smirk hugging his lips.

"Actually, that would be Shakespeare, from *Romeo and Juliet*. Perhaps you've heard of it." Jack continued to stand where he was with his hand on my hip, my right side pressed up against him. I didn't think to move away.

Rebecca looked surprised and a little embarrassed. "I didn't expect to see you here, Jack."

Jack sent her and Marc a languorous perusal. "Apparently. Guess it's not too hard to find a date replacement who owns a dinner jacket in this town."

Rebecca at least had the decency to look repentant. She took a step toward Jack. "I'm sorry. I just . . ."

Marc took her arm and gently pulled her back. "Don't waste your breath, Becca. Come on; let's go get a drink." He leaned in and gave me a lingering kiss on my cheek. Pulling back, he said, "Happy birthday."

"Thank you," I said, feeling the wetness on my cheek as he walked away with Rebecca.

"Want this?"

I turned to see Jack holding up his pocket square.

"Thanks," I said, gently dabbing at the wet spot on my cheek so I wouldn't mess up the painstakingly applied makeup that had taken nearly two hours. Folding it neatly, I tucked it back into his jacket pocket, then clasped my hands behind my back, not knowing where else to put them. "You came," I said.

"Yep. I got tired of fielding calls from my mom, your mom, Sophie, and Nola. I figured it would just be easier to show up. Didn't want to be looking over my shoulder for the next week, waiting for the dart to hit." His old smile brightened his face. "Besides, you mentioned there would be lots of food. Didn't want to miss that."

I blushed, remembering that time at his condo when I couldn't shut myself up. "Yeah, there's that. And Nola is here, and your parents are coming, too."

"Well, I hope you don't mind my coming over here to chat instead of just waving from across the canapés, like you suggested."

My blush deepened. "There is no need to remember and repeat everything I say, all right? But, yes, I'm glad you interrupted my conversation with Rebecca and Marc. I don't think I've ever met two more annoying people."

A dark shadow passed behind his eyes, and for a moment I thought he was going to say something. When it looked like he was about to turn away, I blurted, "Is everything okay?"

"If you mean between Rebecca and me, it's over. It has been for a long time. I guess I was just waiting for her to make the first move."

"You mean *she* broke up with *you*? Has that ever happened to you before?" I tried to keep the giddiness and relief out of my voice.

"Once or twice." He smirked, but his eyes remained somber.

I paused for a moment. "But there's something else that's bothering you," I said, wishing I knew why it was so important that he tell me.

"I heard from my agent today."

My eyes widened. "That's good news, right?"

"Depends. If you consider being able to keep a sizable advance without having the book published, I guess you would call it good news."

"What do you mean, they're not going to publish it? Did they have a problem with it? I mean, you've got a huge fan following waiting for that book."

He shoved his hands into his jacket pockets, trying to look nonchalant. "Yes, well, apparently another author beat me to the punch with a very similar story that they thought would sell better."

I digested that for a moment. "But they still want your next book, right?"

He snorted. "What next book? I've been so engrossed in finding out what was going on with this book that the next idea isn't even a twinkle in my eye yet."

Our eyes met and I knew we were thinking the same thing. "No," he said before I could say anything. "I'm not that desperate that I'd write a book that would make your family hate me."

I rolled my eyes. "Please. Like my mother could ever hate you."

He gave me an odd look. "Just your mother?"

I was about to retort when I noticed that his gaze was fixated at about the same spot Marc's had been. "Did you really get your dress at Sears?" he asked.

I raised my eyebrows. "No." I cleared my throat, not sure whether I was supposed to block his view or offer to twirl to give him a better look. Instead, I reverted to what I'd always relied on and what I prided myself at being good at—the business at hand. "Did you see today's paper?"

He raised his eyes to mine, an amused smile on his lips. "About the bodies found on the Manigault property? Yeah, I did. I was thinking I needed to go down there and have a look. For curiosity's sake. And then go back to Julia and ask her to come clean with everything she's not telling us."

"Can I go with you?" I said the words without thinking, but was rewarded with his Jack smile, the one he used on the back cover of his books that made the female population think crazy thoughts.

The air between us lay heavy with the scents of flowers and his cologne and something else, too. Something I couldn't name, but something primeval that saturated the earth and the space between us. I imagined the air trembling around us, wrapping us in its cocoon, where the past was forgotten and all that mattered was Jack and me. And I could have sworn that somewhere behind the tall, spindly cedars, where the sun's rays had begun their first retreat, I heard my grandmother's voice saying my name. Not as a scold, but more as a reassurance.

"Has anyone told you how beautiful you look tonight?"

I focused my attention on Jack again and thought for a moment. "Not in those exact words. But somebody did quote Shakespeare to me."

He smiled again, his face very close to mine, and I was pretty sure it was the punch that made me close my eyes and lean forward.

"Mellie!" My mother's voice carried from across the garden as she and my father approached. "Your guests are beginning to arrive. Let's go welcome them."

My parents greeted Jack before placing me between them as we turned in unison to greet the first arrivals, my boss, Dave Henderson, and his wife, Robin. I glanced over my shoulder to see whether Jack was calculating what almost-kiss number that had been, but he'd disappeared into the garden, leaving behind only the lingering scent of his cologne and an unsettled feeling somewhere inside me at about the same spot where my plunging neckline ended.

CHAPTER 24

Darkness crept unannounced into my garden. Thousands of twinkling lights had been strung through the crape myrtles and their garnet-hued blooms, around the thick trunk of the large oak, and through all the hedges, creating the illusion of stars in a sky of green. The garden sparkled like a Ferris wheel, my head spinning accordingly as I chatted and laughed and danced, all the while aware of Jack nearby but never close enough.

The band, dressed like members of the Rat Pack, kept dancers on the dance floor all night long, playing standards from just about every decade, representing the wide disparity in ages of the partygoers. Chad was a surprisingly good dancer and happily moonwalked to Michael Jackson's "Billie Jean" and danced a superb shag with me to the Tams' "Be Young, Be Foolish, Be Happy." The only time the band began to lose dancers was when Nola and Alston put in a request for "Why We Thugs" by Ice Cube. I was the only person over fourteen to actually recognize the song, because I'd heard it played so many times blaring from Nola's room. To save the day, I suggested ABBA's "Dancing Queen" and sent a triumphant look in Nola's direction as dancers returned to the dance floor. She responded by rolling her eyes.

Marc asked me to dance twice. His moves were more practiced than natural, but he was an adequate dance partner and certainly nice to look at while I was facing him in close proximity. Both times, Rebecca sought Jack out and brought him to the dance floor. I found I couldn't look at them, and not because I was afraid of a dance-off between the two couples, but because seeing the two of them was too painful despite the fact that I knew they were no longer a couple. I did look long enough to notice that Jack was a great dancer, with none of the awkward moves most white guys felt compelled to display on a dance floor, and I found myself wishing, just for a moment, that I were the one being twirled under his arm, that it was my waist his hands touched.

Just when I thought I couldn't eat any more or drink any more punch, the band began playing the familiar and cringe-worthy strains of "Happy Birthday" as an enormous cake lit with an alarming amount of burning candles was brought out on a large tray by two of the caterers and placed on an empty table festooned with Louisa roses from my garden.

I stood before the cake as everyone sang to me, and I looked around at the array of familiar and beloved faces, feeling as truly close to happiness as I'd ever felt. Even the backdrop of my old house with its wounded foundation couldn't put a ding in that emotion and might, if I'd admit it to myself, actually be contributing to my overall sense of satisfaction.

But as I thanked the people around me and hugged my mother and father, I became acutely aware that despite all that I had to be thankful for, a void hovered somewhere on the periphery of my awareness, like a vague scent that, no matter where I turned, continued to elude me. I'd always known it was there, but had always assumed that once my mother and father were reconciled into my life, it would go away. And although it didn't seem so dark and deep anymore, it was still there— the thing in the closet I didn't want to see.

"Are you all right?"

I turned and found myself looking up into Jack's very blue eyes, and like puzzle pieces my world suddenly slid into focus, with all the lines and curves fitting into their proper grooves. I took a step toward him, and instead of my falling into the abyss, as I'd always imagined, my foot met solid ground as my hands gripped his arms. "I'm fine." I smiled like a giddy teenager. "I'm great, actually."

He looked at me strangely. "Because it looked like you were having an out-of-body experience."

I threw back my head and laughed, bursting with knowledge but unsure what to do with it. "I think I was."

Reluctantly, I let go of Jack to face the bandleader, who was asking for everyone's attention again.

"Without further ado, I'd like to introduce Miss Nola Pettigrew and Mrs. Ginnette Prioleau Middleton in a duet to honor Miss Middleton's fortieth birthday."

I winced at the public announcement of my age before being propelled forward by the crowd to stand in front of the stage. Nola sat with Bonnie's guitar across her lap, and my mother stood next to her holding a microphone. A soft breeze in my hair and the distant strums of the now-familiar tune told me Bonnie was near, but I didn't see her. It was as if she knew this was Nola's moment to shine in the spotlight, and was content to remain in the shadows. With a hesitant smile in my direction, Nola held the guitar closer and began strumming.

When I recognized "Fernando," one of my favorite ABBA songs, the tears welled in my eyes. I knew what it cost Nola emotionally to play her mother's guitar, but to play an ABBA song in public must have been devastating to her.

And then Nola and my mother began to sing, their harmonizing so tight the notes seemed to come from a single voice. The garden quieted as everyone focused on the stage as the music and singers became as much a part of the night as the sky and the moon and the lights that twinkled above us in the trees. A soft hush fell over the crowd as the last note drifted into the darkness and then was followed by a deafening roar of applause and shouts of "Brava, brava."

I turned to say something to Jack, but he was gone. I looked back to where Nola and my mother were leaving the stage and spotted Nola allowing her father to hug her and kiss her cheek. They gave each other identical smiles and my heart did that squishy thing in my chest again. I tried to walk toward them, but too many people were stopping me to wish me happy birthday and ask about Nola. I could only watch from the corner of my eye as Jack kissed my mother's cheek and shook my father's hand before heading out of the garden gate. By the time I finally reached Nola and my mother, he was gone.

I stifled my disappointment as I hugged them. "That was amazing— both of you. And, Nola, wow. I know how hard that must have been for you, which makes your gift that much more special. Your mother would be very, very proud."

She looked at me and her eyes were wet. "Do you think she'll move on now? That's why I did it. I figured if she could see that I was okay, she could move on. I didn't want to be the reason she's hanging on."

I looked into the eyes of this brave and beautiful girl with the unique name and purple sneakers and wondered how Jack had gotten so lucky. "I hope so."

I stepped back to make room for other guests to congratulate the singers and found myself bumping into Marc Longo. He grabbed my elbow to steady me, and then didn't bother letting go. He took a sip of amber liquid from a glass and looked down at me. "I saw our friend Jack leave. He must have gotten the news."

"News?"

"Yeah, about why his publisher is pulling out of his contract."

Something inside me stilled. "How would you know about that?"

He gave a short laugh, then took another swallow from his drink before giving me a considering look. "Who do you think wrote the book that got his booted out? Think about it—I'm a direct descendant of Joseph Longo. My publisher recognized that I was more bankable, since I have the insider's take on the whole sordid tale. And it's got it all—lust, greed, and murder. That's the title, by the way. Kind of catchy, don't you think?"

I stared at him for a long moment, the sounds of the crowds around us oddly muted. "You wrote a book about my house and what happened in it, even though you knew Jack was writing one, too."

His smile was all smugness and self-satisfaction. "Hey, he got the girl. I figured it was a fair trade."

I was shaking my head, trying to negate everything he was telling me, and thinking he should add the words "deceit" and "prevarication" to the title. "Does he know it's you?"

Marc finished his drink, then shrugged. "Not yet. But after his conversation with his editor today it should click pretty soon. I don't think our Jack is going to be very happy with me." He winked. "Or you."

"Me?"

With a smirk, he said, "He's going to think you knew it all along. Seriously, Melanie. I can understand how Jack didn't figure it out. But you're a pretty smart cookie. Even he won't believe that you didn't know, or at least suspect."

I wanted to slap the smug smile right off of his face, but I didn't want to waste another minute. All the pieces were going to fall into place for Jack, and I needed to be there when they did. If he wasn't drinking already, I had little doubt that this would be the one thing that could send him over the edge.

I turned on my heel, in search of my mother, but the sound of Marc's laughter made me retrace my steps. "You know why I didn't want to go out with you again? Because you make love like you dance— like you've been practicing by yourself too long, so a partner's just superfluous."

He stopped laughing as I rushed past him, spotting my mother by the tree swing and reaching her before she could head toward a cluster of people who were calling out to her. "Mother, I have to leave now."

"But we're just serving the cake! What's wrong? Are you ill? Too much punch?"

I shook my head. "It's Jack. I think he might be in real trouble and I need to go to him."

She didn't hesitate. "Then go. I'll make your excuses and take care of things here, and I'll ask Chad to meet you out front to take you wherever you need to go. Call me if you need anything."

"I will." I kissed her cheek and hugged her tightly. "And thanks for tonight. I know I complained a lot, but I'm glad you did it."

"You're welcome. I just hope that it made up a little for all the birthdays I missed."

I kissed her cheek again; then I left the lights of the brilliant and fragrant garden behind me, stepping out into the darkness to find Jack.

⤴

It was a lot harder driving in my gown and heels than I'd imagined, or I would have changed clothes after Chad dropped me off at my mother's house to get my keys and purse. I'd been happily ignorant of any knowledge of where Jack spent his time away from me, but now I silently cursed my own stupidity, as if knowing where he was and imagining what he might be doing would somehow solidify or define my feelings for him. As if not knowing had mattered at all.

With surprising clearheadedness, I drove to the one place I knew of—his condo in the French Quarter. The building had garage parking, so I couldn't drive around looking for his car. Instead, I found a parking spot on the curb a block away and toddled to his building on my high heels. I earned a few admiring glances from male passersby as I concentrated on not turning an ankle, and wished again that I'd thought to change.

Taking a deep breath, I pressed the intercom button and waited for Jack to answer and allow me entry. I waited for at least a minute, until I lost patience and pressed the button again. As I stood there holding my breath, a couple exited the building. Looking appropriately grateful, I pointed at my purse as if to indicate a lost key, then thanked the man as he held the door open for me. Maybe not changing clothes hadn't been such a bad idea after all.

Humming the tune to "Fernando" to still my jumping nerves, I rode the elevator up to Jack's floor, going over in my mind what my plan B would be if he wasn't in his condo. Or if he was there and just wouldn't answer his door. Or if he did actually answer his door. I drew a blank on all three scenarios, wondering how somebody who had her shoes and their monthly polishing schedule on a spreadsheet could show up at a man's door at nearly midnight without a thought as to what should happen next.

I stared at his doorbell and held my breath until I began to feel dizzy. Then, before I talked myself out of it, I pressed it hard with my index finger, making sure I could hear it inside before letting go. I waited for what felt like an hour but was probably just a minute or two before I raised my hand to press again, my progress halted by Jack's door opening.

He stood inside the open door, his jacket off, his shirt unbuttoned and untucked from his tuxedo pants, the suspenders hanging against his legs. His feet were bare, his blue eyes dark as they regarded me with surprise and something else that looked a lot like apprehension.

I struggled not to purr or growl or whatever large female cats did when they came upon a gazelle or something equally tasty on the African plains. I closed my eyes to block out the vision, blaming my absurdity on all the punch.

"What are you doing here, Mellie?"

His question was innocent enough, but some underlying meaning lay couched behind it.

"You left the party early. I wanted to make sure you were all right."

He stared at me for a long moment. "You could have called."

An unseen door shut somewhere down the hall. "Can I come in?"

He didn't step back or open the door farther. "Why?"

I felt icy cold suddenly, remembering the last time I'd shown up by myself unannounced on his doorstep and found Rebecca in his bedroom. My voice seemed to rise in pitch. "Are you alone?"

He almost smiled. "I'm alone, and I'm tired. Can't this wait until tomorrow?"

"No. It can't." I wasn't sure which part of what I wanted to tell him was more important than the other, but either way I didn't want to wait. "Please—let me come in?"

His eyes slowly drifted from my face downward, past my chin, hovering on my chest, then dipping lower until he brought his gaze to meet mine again. "Are you sure you want to come in, Mellie?"

Lightning bolts of heat were flung through my veins, and I expected to smell something smoldering. I knew I could turn and run, something I was overly familiar with. Or I could disobey what the logical part of my brain was telling me and walk forward into a place that was uncharted and couldn't be organized on a spreadsheet. Maybe it was the fact that I was now forty years old and tired of feeling like I'd missed out on something important, or maybe it was the punch. Either way, I found myself pushing on the door until Jack let go and stepped back.

I stood in the entranceway and watched as Jack locked and bolted the door, then turned to me warily. "Can I get you anything?"

I wasn't thirsty, but I needed something to keep my hands busy while I told him what Marc had said. And I wanted to look and see whether I found any evidence of alcohol. It wasn't necessarily that I didn't trust him. It was more because I'd grown up with an alcoholic father and learned it was always better to find out for myself.

"Just water, please. If you have it."

He sent me an odd glance as he headed to the gleaming kitchen and took out a glass from the cabinet. He put crushed ice and water in it from the refrigerator door, then handed it to me. I took a sip, needing to cool off more than anything, especially with him standing so close and watching my lips as they touched the glass.

"Why are you here, Mellie?" he asked again, his voice very, very soft.

I wanted to tell him then about Marc's book, and how I hadn't known until tonight, but I hesitated. I knew how devastated he would be, and how it would make whatever was zinging between us right now stop.

I swallowed, wanting, too, to tell him what I'd figured out earlier, something I was afraid to name. It was still too new and too delicate to be allowed out in the open, especially when I was unsure of his feelings toward me. Instead, I said, "Because I was worried about you. About what you might do. I know how disappointed you must be about your book being pulled." I looked back at him, searching for some sign that he knew about Marc's book already, that he'd managed to put it all together.

Instead, his face darkened, but neither one of us stepped back. He didn't raise his voice, but his words were measured and very succinct, as if he wanted to make sure I understood. "Do you really think I'd start drinking again? That I would do that to Nola—my daughter? You asked me that same question when we were on the Battery, and I swore to myself then that I'd had enough of you and your lack of trust and faith in me." He swiped both hands through his hair. "To answer your question, no, I haven't started drinking again. I'd love to have a drink right now—several, in fact. But the truth is, I love Nola more."

I blinked my eyes rapidly, trying to stem the tears his words had made form in the backs of my eyes. There was so much about Jack Trenholm that I didn't know, hadn't bothered to see because I'd been too scared to look deeper, too scared to realize that Jack might be the one person worth jumping into the void with.

I took a sip of my ice water, startled to find my hand shaking, and searched for the right words to say. "I'm sorry I doubted you. I shouldn't have. But I know what it's like to be hurt and to face it alone. I thought maybe you could use a friend."

He stared at me for a long moment, his eyes hard. "I don't need a friend." He took my glass and put it on the counter, then placed both hands on my face, cupping my jaw. "I need you."

All I could do was breathe, to try to understand the word "need," to know the meaning in every bone. His lips hovered over mine for precious seconds until they touched, tentative at first, like a bee discovering a new flower. And then I was pressed against the counter, his lips hard on mine and my arms trying to pull him closer. I opened my eyes, feeling dizzy and afraid I might pass out and miss whatever was going to come next.

Jack pulled back, his eyes darker than I'd ever seen them. "What's wrong?"

I shook my head, trying to clear it. "I might have had too much punch. I'm feeling dizzy."

His lips lifted in one corner, as if he were trying not to smile. "The pink punch at the party?"

I nodded, wondering why he was trying to get specific at a moment like this.

I felt the laughter rumble through him. "I was drinking it all night. So were Nola and Alston. It was nonalcoholic."

I blinked very slowly, wondering how I'd found the courage to knock on his door without any spiked punch. Without thinking first, I said, "Then why do I feel so dizzy?"

His smile faded as he brought his face close to mine again. "Is that all you're feeling? Because I'm feeling a lot more than dizzy." There was no initial hesitancy this time as his lips met mine, the edge of the granite counter digging into my back as he crushed my body against him. My mouth opened under his as I began to feel less dizzy and perhaps more of whatever it was that Jack was feeling.

His lips drifted down my neck, leaving a hot, damp trail to my collarbone, and jelly where my knees had once been. His hands reached behind me to cup my bottom as his teeth did dangerous things to my earlobe and sense of reality.

"Did your mother really buy you this dress?" he said into my ear. My body shuddered as his warm breath danced across the damp skin of my neck.

"Yes." I somehow managed to get the word past swollen and seemingly paralyzed lips.

"Have I ever told you that your mother is a very, very smart lady?"

I gasped as his hands smoothed their way up my back until his fingers found the zipper to my dress. I reached up and took his hand in mine, stopping him. "What are you doing?"

He was breathing very hard and looking just a little annoyed. "Exactly what I thought you wanted me to be doing."

The familiar need to control the situation struggled to emerge from the slush that had become my brain. "Maybe we should talk about this first. What . . . this . . . would mean for you and me. For us. I know of too many couples who jump into bed together for all the wrong reasons, and then she gets hurt or he gets hurt, or they find out they shouldn't be together anyway, or that the way she flosses in bed annoys him, or the way he leaves hair in the sink makes her want to kill him, so they grow apart and wonder what it was they saw in each other in the first place. And then it's awkward at parties and bar mitzvahs or wherever they run into each other. . . ."

His hand covered my mouth. "Mellie?"

"Hmm?"

"Shut up. Please."

I frowned, then nodded.

Lowering his hand, he said, "For once in your life I want you to stop thinking. Enjoy yourself and don't think about anything except how good I'm about to make you feel."

If it were possible for people to self-combust, I'd be a smoldering pile of red silk burning a hole in the wood floor of Jack's kitchen. I felt dizzy again and realized I needed to breathe or I'd pass out. Our eyes met and I knew that words weren't necessary anymore, that everything we'd already said since the time we'd first met nearly two years ago had led up to this moment. All that wasted time.

He reached for the zipper again, but this time I didn't stop him. He slowly lowered it down the length of my back, his eyes never leaving mine even as the sleeves of the dress dropped from my shoulders, revealing the very skimpy and very red bra I'd picked up at Bits of Lace on King Street as a last-minute addition to my ensemble.

I opened my mouth to tell him that tonight was about more than making each other feel good. I thought of how I'd felt standing in my garden, when I'd realized how, despite all my efforts to the contrary, he'd somehow managed to breach the wall I'd constructed all those years ago on the day my mother left me behind.

His hands stopped removing my arms from the dress. "Mellie? No talking anymore, remember?"

I closed my mouth and nodded, unable to find any words at all as the dress slid to the floor. Jack reached behind me and hoisted me up, leaving me no choice but to wrap my legs around him. Not that I would ever tell him, but I'd had dreams just like this, and not once had any of them compared to the feel of Jack Trenholm in the flesh through just the thin silk of lingerie.

Our mouths met again and I closed my eyes, aware of him carrying me a short distance. When I felt soft cushions beneath my back I opened them again in surprise. "The couch?" I asked.

"For starters," he mumbled against the soft skin between my breasts.

My hands pushed at his shirt until Jack sat up and pulled it off along with his undershirt, throwing them onto the floor. He'd just begun to work at the straps on my bra when he suddenly stopped. Lifting his head, he met my eyes. "Just one question."

I propped myself up on my elbows, wondering—since this was my life, after all—whether this was the moment he was going to tell me he was gay. Or a woman. "What?"

He thought for a moment, as if trying to get the words right. "The dead people you see, you know when they're around, right? Like right now—you would know whether or not we're completely alone."

I relaxed back against the cushions again. "Not that I have a lot of experience as far as that's concerned, but yeah, I'd know." I reached up for him, my hands on his bare shoulders. "And right now, it's just you and me."

He looked relieved as he lowered his head to mine again and kissed me with surprising tenderness. I sighed, seeing thousands of twinkling lights behind my closed eyelids, and imagining a word softly whispered from very far away. *Finally.*

CHAPTER 25

I awoke before dawn with the familiar feeling of a warm and fuzzy body in the bed with me, except this particular body wasn't quite as fuzzy and had only two legs instead of four. And was a lot more fun to sleep with.

Jack's hand traced slow circles on my bare hip under the sheet, and I became aware of his rising interest in continuing our energetic pursuits of the previous evening. My body tingled in places I hadn't known existed, and my heart hummed with a new and unfamiliar rhythm, giving me the odd compulsion to sigh and laugh and cry—all together. For the first time since my mother had abandoned me, I was content where I was, my head not already spinning and going down the lists of everything I needed to accomplish for the day. I was with Jack, and that was all that mattered.

I wanted to lie there forever, cocooned in the darkness where no words were needed, where I could show Jack what I felt without complicating everything with those infamous three little words. It wasn't that I didn't want to be the first to say it, or even that I was unsure of Jack's feelings toward me. My hesitation had more to do with having to tell Jack the news about Marc and his book, knowing that I couldn't tell him one without telling him the other.

I turned to face him, to try to read what was in his eyes, but his face was in darkness, backlit by the glowing numbers on the bedside clock. I was almost relieved, unsure of how I could look him in the eyes without blushing after the previous evening. It was the perfect moment to tell him what I'd discovered about Marc, and to let Jack know that I was on his side, that I would be there to help him through this. And that if he needed help in making voodoo dolls or concocting elaborate dismemberment schemes where nobody would be permanently maimed or go to jail, I'd consider assisting him.

Instead, my gaze settled on the clock behind him, the glowing readout indicating it was almost five thirty in the morning. My head jerked up off the pillow. "Crap." After kissing Jack quickly on the lips, then flinging the covers off, I began to scramble around the room, and then into the hallway, dining area, living room, and kitchen, searching for my clothes and shoes, shyly holding up a pillow from the sofa as a modesty shield.

Jack stretched lazily in the bedroom doorway, completely naked and apparently finding my running around without clothes oddly exciting. "What's the rush, Mellie? Didn't you take today off? I thought we could spend the day . . . inside. Where you won't need your clothes." He gave me a long and appreciative look. "And why bother hiding behind a pillow? I've seen everything already." His smile was smug and not a little self-satisfied.

I was very tempted to stop my search and return to Jack's bed and ignore the rest of the world a little longer. Instead I snapped my bra off of the floor lamp behind the sofa and struggled to put it on as I searched for my underwear. "Jack, as much as I'd like to, I've got to get back home before everybody's up and sees me coming in wearing what I wore last night. Especially since my mother knows I was coming to find you when I left the party."

I found my dress in the kitchen and was stepping into it when Jack joined me, standing behind me and kissing me on the back of my neck and shaking my resolve. "You're forty years old, Mellie. I'm sure your mother will understand."

I turned in his arms and kissed him, feeling how eager he was for me to stay. "What about Nola? What's she going to say?"

His eyes widened. "You've got to hurry." He whipped me around and began zipping my dress. He ran back to his room while I went in search of my purse, and returned wearing shorts and a T-shirt and carrying both of my shoes. He held them up like trophies. "Sorry it took me so long. These were in my bed for some reason."

I blushed, remembering how they got there. "Thanks," I said as I took them from him and began to put them on.

"I'll drive you."

I shook my head. "That'll look worse if somebody sees you dropping me off. Besides, I have my own car."

He put his hands on my hips and drew me toward him. "So when can I see you again?"

"Tonight?" I bit my lip, embarrassed at how eager I sounded.

Jack grinned. "As much as I appreciate your enthusiasm, I'm afraid I can't. My mother's been begging for me to join her on a weeklong buying trip to the Northeast, and since I don't have the excuse of working on a book, I should go. She doesn't like going alone, and my dad needs to stay behind to manage the store. Who knows—maybe I'll find my next book inspiration while I'm gone. My mother already cleared it with yours regarding coverage for Nola if you weren't available."

I tried to hide my disappointment. "So when will you be back?"

"Next Thursday. It'll give us something to look forward to." He kissed my neck again, making me sigh. "And there's always the phone."

I nodded, thinking of everything that remained unsaid between us, and knowing that none of it could be said over the phone. "Jack—" The alarm on my phone chirped, interrupting me.

As I fumbled with my purse to pull out the phone and turn off the alarm, Jack asked, "What's that?"

"My alarm. I always wake up at six o'clock, so I set my phone alarm to go off fifteen minutes before my bedside alarm goes off."

He stared at me for a moment before responding. "That must be a 'Mellie-ism,' so I'm not going to ask for an explanation."

"A 'Mellie-ism'?"

"That's what Nola calls all of your idiosyncrasies. Like how all of the clocks in your room and your watch are set ten minutes fast. Or how you stick labels on the inside of your drawers to show where everything goes. Mellie-isms." He kissed me on my forehead. "I think they're cute." He reached over and grabbed his keys off the kitchen counter. "Come on—I'll walk you to the car. I'm not in the mood to explain the birds and the bees to Nola this morning."

I allowed him to lead me out the door. And as he kissed me good-bye at my car I did my best to convince myself that what I needed to say to him could wait just one little week.

&

My feet seemed to float above the ground as I went about my daily routine the following week. I was very careful to hide my emotions from everybody else, feeling it only fair until I'd told Jack, but Charlene wanted to know where I was getting my facials now, and my mother and Nola had each scolded me for putting the coffee grounds in the refrigerator and the milk in the pantry. Twice. Only General Lee seemed to have guessed the truth, and had taken to sleeping at the foot of my bed instead of on the pillow next to me, as if he understood that particular place was being held for somebody else.

My work schedule was busier than usual, and I closed a record three times in one week, earning me my regular—and coveted—top spot on the seller's chart in Dave Henderson's office. Jack and Amelia were apparently just as busy, as associates in the antiques business wined and dined them from Boston to New York. Our phone conversations were brief, as if both of us were aware that a profound yet unacknowledged change had occurred in our relationship. We were explorers in uncharted territory, using blank maps. And I kept waiting for him to tell me that he'd discovered the truth behind his canceled contract, and each day that he didn't I felt more and more guilt about keeping it to myself. Still, I convinced myself that telling him over the phone wasn't an option, and that I would tell him face-to-face as soon as I saw him again.

For the first time in my life, I had both of my parents to consult with about a major decision, but I knew what they would tell me, and I didn't want to disappoint all three of us by going against common sense and reason. I recognized that I was acting like a coward, but the thing between Jack and me—whatever it was—was still too new and fragile to take such a blow. Like a person staring down a tornado, it seemed I was waiting until the last minute to seek shelter, hoping against all odds that it would veer off course and avoid me completely.

The only thing that was clear to me was that the dollhouse had to go. The feud between William and his father had escalated since the discovery of the graves on Manigault property, and Nola seemed caught between them as they haunted her dreams, using her as a conduit to continue past arguments, tossing her bedclothes and anything else in the room into disarray. Mrs. Houlihan was threatening to quit, and Nola walked around with dark circles under her eyes. I'd had enough.

On the morning Jack was scheduled to return to Charleston, I was awakened from a sound sleep by a shuddering rumble of thunder. General Lee dived under the covers as my eyes popped open in time to see a flash of lightning illuminating the room and a human figure standing next to my bed.

A cold hand touched my arm and I bolted to a sitting position. Thunder growled as continuous bursts of lightning flashed through the room like the end of an old-fashioned film reel, the figure leaning toward me seeming to do so in slow motion. I dug my heels into the mattress, pushing myself away until my head collided with the headboard. I tried to meld into the wood as the figure leaned closer, and in the next burst of lightning I found myself staring into two wide eyes. Two very familiar wide eyes.

"Nola?" I could barely hear my voice over the thunder.

Her hand squeezed my arm with surprising strength, and when she spoke, it wasn't her voice that came from her mouth, but something much deeper, and darker, and not of this earth.

Lightning illuminated her very pale face, her eyes appearing hollow in the shadows. "We told you to stop her. And now you will pay." The hand tightened on my wrist, cutting off circulation to my hand.

"Nola!" I shouted, trying to snap her out of the trance or whatever it was she was having.

"There is nothing you can do now to save her. You should have listened."

I struck out with my other hand, colliding with the nightstand and making the lamp wobble. "Nola—wake up! You're dreaming; wake up!"

The temperature dipped, and I sensed a pervasive light in the room that had nothing to do with the storm raging outside, yet the overhead chandelier and lamps remained dark.

Nola. Wake up. It's just a dream.

It was Bonnie, her voice light and melodious. Nola lifted her head and I could see her eyes in the odd light as she blinked several times. Slowly, her gaze drifted to me and then to where her hand gripped my arm. She let out a cry and then covered her face with her hands.

The light dimmed and then vanished. I struggled out of the bed-clothes, hampered by a squirming General Lee, who was trying to do the same thing, and fumbled for the switch on the bedside lamp. I stood and reached for Nola, holding her in my arms as she wept.

Her words were punctuated by sobs. "It was William and his father, and they were so angry. At you! He wanted me to hurt you and I couldn't stop—" A choking hiccup cut off her voice.

"Who, Nola? Who wanted to hurt me?"

"The father—Harold. William was angry, too, but at something else. I think he was angry with Miss Julia, something about letting things go too far. And how it was all her fault."

I patted her back and waited for her crying to subside. "It's all right, Nola. It's not your fault—I know you wouldn't want to hurt me." I tried for a light note. "Unless I made you sing ABBA in public again."

Her cheeks wobbled in an almost-smile and I knew I'd hit my mark. I set her away from me, my hands on her shoulders as my mind tried to organize what I had to do next. "I want you to try to get some more sleep—but you can stay in here with General Lee. It's almost dawn, so I'm going to go ahead and get dressed, and I'll send my mother in to stay with you if you're still asleep when I leave."

She swallowed as her shoulders relaxed, and a look of relief settled on her face.

"I'm calling Chad first thing and having him bring a friend to move the dollhouse to your dad's condo until we figure out what to do with it—please let him have your key when he gets here. I've got an open house this morning on Daniel Island, but then I'm coming right back here. Should be around eleven thirty, so if you could be dressed and ready to go by then, we're going to head over to Miss Julia's."

Her brows knitted. "What for?"

"To tell her I figured out what 'stop her' meant and find out why

Julia's asking for forgiveness. It's time to put a few spirits to rest." She nodded, our understanding that she'd never allow herself to be left behind not needing to be spoken.

I didn't mention that I was afraid to let her out of my sight, afraid that William and Harold might not leave her alone until we found all the answers. Or that her mother was still here, hanging on for reasons that continued to elude me.

∞

Nola and I stood at the front door of the house on Montagu Street, watching water drip from the old eaves and listening for the sound of approaching footsteps from inside. Nola rubbed her hands over her arms, and I saw gooseflesh despite the warm temperature. "It's weird," she said.

"What is?" I asked, ignoring the obvious answers of "this house" and "its ghosts."

"I always have this creepy feeling when I'm outside the house and in the hallway. But never in the music room or in the Christmas room—which are pretty creepy but in a whole other way."

"That actually makes sense," I said. "Julia told me that her father didn't like Christmas and won't go into that room. And the music room . . . well, I guess that only William goes in there, since he was the one who enjoyed playing the piano. Then again, William isn't the most peaceful spirit, either, is he?"

She shook her head. "No. But I've . . . felt him in the music room. Like he enjoys listening. I've felt cold spots, but none of the bad feelings that I get in other parts of the house. Like right now, when I feel like we're being watched."

I nodded, not wanting to tell her that I'd seen the man in the turret as we'd approached, the man I was pretty sure was Harold, and how my skin had been prickling ever since we got out of the car.

Dee Davenport opened the door, leaving only enough of an opening to stick her head out. "Miss Julia isn't well. I've had to set up a hospital bed for her in the back room. I'm afraid she can't see anyone right now."

I wished Jack were there, to charm himself in. Instead, I had to rely on my own devices. "This is very important, and I promise we won't be long. Please tell her . . ." I thought for a moment. "Please tell her that I know what William and her father were trying to tell her."

She narrowed her eyes suspiciously. "Her brother and father have been dead a long time."

"I know. Just tell her. She'll know what I'm talking about."

Dee jutted her chin in Nola's direction. "Why's she here?"

Nola took a step forward, causing Dee to narrow the gap between the door and doorframe. "Because I wanted to tell Miss Julia how the party went. She wanted to know."

I looked at Nola with surprise. She hadn't mentioned any of that to me. I watched as she regarded Dee with a sweet, almost angelic smile. Apparently, the ability to charm people into giving her her way was an inherited trait.

Dee considered us both for a long moment. Finally, she said, "Hang on; I'll go check."

We waited while she closed the door; then she reappeared a few minutes later. As she closed the front door behind us, Dee said, "You've got fifteen minutes—tops. Miss Julia doesn't need a lot of excitement, all right?"

We nodded and followed Dee to the room that was denied the cheeriness of the Christmas season due to the presence of the shriveled woman in a high-necked nightgown, who now lay reclined in a metal-framed hospital bed. A folded newspaper lay on top of the blankets at her feet, and an oxygen tank sat next to her, its rubbery tubes running up her nose.

Her eyes brightened when she spotted Nola, then shuttered as her gaze settled on me. She motioned for Dee to leave, and with a sigh Dee placed a small hand bell on the table by the makeshift bed. "Ring if you need anything." She shot serious glances at Nola and me, as if she expected us to force Miss Julia into a foxtrot or something equally strenuous.

"Why are you here?" Julia asked, her voice gravelly, like she hadn't used it in a while. Nola sat on the edge of a chair that had been pushed against the wall to make room for the bed, but I remained standing.

"William and Harold paid a visit to Nola last night and shook her up pretty badly. They were blaming me for something, saying that it was too late for you, and that I would pay. They were talking about the construction on your property in Georgetown County, weren't they? That's what they were trying to stop—what 'stop her' meant. Isn't it?"

Her expression gave nothing away.

"I'm assuming you know that the remains of a man and a woman were found buried on the property. Do you have any idea who they are or why William and your father didn't want them found?"

A Santa clock on the mantel chimed the hour. "You should try to be more informed, Miss Middleton. I'm assuming you haven't read yesterday's paper yet." She indicated the paper at the foot of her bed, while I made a promise to myself to start reading the paper from now on.

I picked it up and discovered it had already been turned back and folded to an inside page, where the pictures of a burned-out shell of a large house were shown together with yellowed photographs of Julia's family. Squinting so I could see, I scanned the article, reading information that I already knew and had been printed in the previous article. Then my eyes stopped, stumbling over the words and making me read it twice before I understood what it was saying. For Nola's benefit, I read out loud:

> The remains discovered during the land clearing last week have now been identified as those of two males, despite women's shoes, corset bones, and jewelry being found with the remains of one of the bodies. Authorities are using DNA samples of a Manigault relative to determine whether there is any relationship to the deceased. Judging from the style of shoes and jewelry, preliminary reports indicate that the remains may date back to the nineteen thirties.

I lowered the paper, then raised my eyes to meet Julia's. "Could one of them be William?"

She shook her head, her forehead creased. "I don't know. I don't! But I can't believe it's William. He told me he was leaving in his note. Why would he have gone to Georgetown, where people knew him?"

"I don't know. None of this is making any sense to me. We need to know who's buried in those graves before we can even guess."

Julia's eyes closed, and I watched the shallow rise and fall of her chest. "I suppose we'll know something for sure rather soon. It was my DNA they took last week."

I considered her for a long moment. "If one of the bodies isn't William's, then why would they not want you to clear the land?"

Her mouth compressed in a firm line. "My father would never want scandal to touch our family—regardless of whose bodies those are. He always placed the family's reputation above all else." She grimaced, an awful, ugly expression on her wizened face. "That's how I always knew exactly how to hurt him."

I knelt by the side of her bed so I could look in her face. Quietly, I asked, "Is that why you needed William's forgiveness?"

She shrank from me. "Why are you asking me all these questions? I don't know anything!"

Angry now, I forced my voice to remain calm. "Because your brother and father are using Nola to express their anger, and we need it to stop. Now. I can also assume that you'd like some semblance of peace. And the only way I can figure out how to make any of that happen is if we deal with whatever it is that's keeping their spirits earthbound." I leaned closer to her and felt some satisfaction when she shrank back. "So why did you need William's forgiveness?"

She closed her eyes, and I watched as her fisted hands slowly opened like she was letting go of a long-carried burden. "Because I told my father things I shouldn't have." She opened her eyes but stared at a spot behind me, seeing something I couldn't.

I waited without speaking, afraid she'd stop.

Julia's gaze traveled to Nola, then back to me. "I can't . . . I can't tell you."

I leaned forward and very quietly said, "If this was just about you and your family, I would leave now. But it's not. Nola is an innocent victim of their maliciousness, which means that both she and I are now involved. So I guess we're going to have to sit here and wait until you tell us the truth, regardless of how painful it might be for you." I touched her hand. More gently, I said, "You need peace, too. Let me help you find it."

She closed her eyes again and took a shuddering breath. She didn't speak for a long moment, and I began to worry that Dee would come back before I'd had the chance to learn whatever secret Julia Manigault had been holding on to. Finally, in a voice so quiet that I had to lean toward her to hear, she said, "I told my father that William liked to dress in our mother's clothing and then go out wearing it." She turned her head away, but I wasn't sure whether it was from the shame of exposing William's secret or because of what William did. "He always made sure he went to places where he wouldn't be recognized. But I knew—had known for years. I always saw everything."

Her gaze reverted to my face as she searched for my reaction.

I kept my expression neutral. "Why did you wait so long to tell him William's secret?"

Her chest rose and fell again in another shallow breath. "Because my father was writing his will, and had left everything—the businesses, the property, everything—to William. William, who could recite pages of poetry from memory but couldn't add simple sums. I was the smart one, the one with business sense. I could have built an empire if he'd just seen beyond the fact that I was female. I thought that with Jonathan at my side it would make sense for us to run everything, and let William do as he wanted. We'd all be happy that way. I needed to make my father see."

Tears brimmed in the old lady's eyes, and I felt the weight of guilt carried for over seventy years. "That's why they argued that night," I prodded. "That's why your father killed him." I waited for Julia's reaction, to see whether I'd come close to the truth.

She shook her head, agitated. "But I have the note from William. My father couldn't have killed him." Her voice was desperate, as if she wanted me to agree with her truth. I remembered her brother's words to me, and chose to allow the truth to be what she wanted it to be. *She believes it is proof of innocence where there is none. Let her believe it.*

"If it is William's body buried at the old plantation, do you have any idea who the other male might be?" I asked.

She shook her head. "I don't know. Please. Stop." Her hand reached out for mine and I took it.

I patted her hand, hoping to offer reassurance. "I'll do what I can.

They're both very angry right now—I don't know whether they'll talk to me, but I'll try."

She squeezed my hand. "Thank you."

She dropped my hand, then reached for Nola's. Nola stood and came to grasp it.

"I'm sorry if my family is giving you trouble. You're young and strong. Fight them."

Nola nodded. "I'll do my best."

Julia studied her closely. "How was your performance at the party? I wish I could have been there."

"I think I did okay. People seemed to like it."

"She was amazing," I interjected. "People were astounded that someone so young could have that much talent."

Julia's forehead creased. "And that 'Fernando' song, did people like that?"

Nola grinned. "Yeah. They actually did, believe it or not."

I glanced at my watch. "We should go. Jack should be home any minute now."

To my surprise, Nola leaned down and kissed the old lady's cheek. "Thank you, Miss Julia. And when you're feeling better, can we continue our lessons?"

"Of course," she said.

My eyes met Julia's, her expression one of pleading and something else, too. "It's my fault William can't rest in peace," she said. "Please, please find a way to give him rest."

I nodded, then led Nola to the door. It wasn't until we'd reached the porch that I realized what the other look in Julia's eyes had been; she was saying good-bye.

CHAPTER 26

The first thing I noticed when I drove up to my mother's house on Legare was Jack's car parked across the street. The second thing I noticed was Rebecca's red Audi parked behind it. The third was Rich Kobylt, my contractor, and his exposed posterior standing at the front door and getting ready to knock. His truck was in the driveway, blocking my way.

I parked in front of Jack, calling to Rich as I exited the car and approached with Nola.

"Hello, Miz Middleton, Miss Nola," he said, hoisting up his pants.

"Hi, Rich. What's wrong?"

He scrunched up his face at me. "Why do you always ask me that?"

"Because it's usually true. I hope the house didn't topple over after the party." I looked closely at his face to see whether I'd come anywhere near the truth.

"No, ma'am. The house is fine and we're already back at work. However . . ." He scratched his head. "I just thought you should know that there's been a photographer and a video guy out there all morning. They said it was for a book cover and promotional video. I thought it was for Mr. Trenholm's book, so I didn't think it was a problem, but then when Mr. Trenholm showed up . . ."

Dread clenched my throat. "Jack was there?"

"Yes, ma'am. Asked them why they were there, and when they told him he got real mad and told them to leave. Caused a real scene. I tried to call you, but your phone must be off, 'cause it kept going right to voice mail."

I'd turned it off when we'd gone to speak to Miss Julia and forgotten to turn it back on. I tried to keep my voice calm. "Did he say anything to you?"

"No, ma'am. And I was mighty happy about that, too. I'm glad it wasn't me he was angry at." He hiked up his pants again. "I figured you might be here and I wanted to let you know."

I forced a smile. "Yes, thank you, Rich. I appreciate it."

He tipped an imaginary hat. "Well, then, I'd better get back to work. Foundation won't fix itself."

I said good-bye, then averted my eyes so I wouldn't have to watch him walk away.

"Why would Jack be so uptight about people taking pictures of your house?" Nola asked.

"Oh, Nola. I didn't want him to find out like this."

"Find out about what?"

My eyes met hers. "You're going to find out eventually, so I guess it's better that I tell you now." I paused. "Marc Longo wrote a book about the mysteries surrounding my house—the same subject as your dad's—except since Marc's related to one of the families involved, the publisher decided they'd rather publish his book."

Her eyes widened, reminding me so much of Jack's that I had to look away. "And you knew this and didn't tell him?"

"I was going to. But I didn't have time, and I wanted to wait so I could tell him in person."

She crossed her arms. "When?"

"Today," I said softly, realizing how lame and stupid all my reasons for waiting suddenly seemed. Having that pointed out by a thirteen-year-old was both humbling and humiliating.

She sat down on the front steps. "I don't think I want to see this, so I'm just going to hang out here for a while until the coast is clear and I can run up to my room. I don't think I can handle an angry Jack and Princess Pink at the same time without hurling." She squinted up at me. "I don't think he'll hit you, but if he does I wouldn't blame him."

"Thanks, Nola." I looked down at the steps, tempted to sit next to her, or jump in my car and drive anywhere, maybe cross-country, rather than go into that house and confront him.

Nola must have seen my hesitation. "If you can face mean dead people, you can do this, Mellie. He might even forgive you."

"Or not," I said as I took a deep breath and climbed the rest of the steps before opening the front door. The house was silent, making me think that maybe the cars outside weren't Jack's and Rebecca's, and I could go upstairs to my room, turn on my phone and call Jack, and tell him everything. I'd almost made it across the foyer to the steps when I heard my name called.

I turned to see Rebecca in the doorway leading into the parlor, wearing a soft pink linen suit, her blond hair loose on her shoulders. Her pale eyes were wide. "I hope you don't mind, but I had another dream last night that I needed to tell you about in person, and I ran into Jack. We thought we'd wait until you got back."

She leaned forward as if to get a better look at me, and her eyes widened further. "Oh," she said, raising her hand to her mouth. I was about to ask her what she thought she was seeing when Jack appeared in the doorway behind her, his eyes dark and cool.

"Mellie," he said, his voice doing nothing to thaw the coolness of his eyes. "How nice to see you again."

My heart lurched in my chest as I recalled the last time I'd seen him: when he'd kissed me good-bye and his eyes held so many promises. The eyes I saw now seemed to belong to a different man.

"Welcome back, Jack." I wanted to add, *I missed you,* or, *I'm finding it difficult to get through my days without you,* but held back, and not just because of Rebecca's presence. The unspoken truth hovered close, negating anything else I could have said.

Rebecca looked between Jack and me before returning to scrutinize me again. "I guess what I wanted to tell you can wait—I see you two need to talk." She disappeared into the parlor and returned with her purse. "I already explained to Jack that you didn't know about Marc until the night of the party—that Marc deliberately kept you in the dark."

I had to hand it to Rebecca. Regardless of how she actually felt about me, I was still family, and she was trying to do her part to smooth things over. As if they could be. "I'll call you later." She gave me another odd glance before tapping her way across the foyer to the front door.

I faced Jack, blushing as images of our night together flashed through my head. "Can I get you something to drink?" This wasn't how I'd imagined his homecoming.

He didn't answer. Instead, he said, "Tell me that you haven't known about Marc for almost a week without telling me. At least tell me that you didn't know before we slept together. I've been waiting here for over an hour to hear it from your lips."

I took a deep breath, knowing I couldn't evade the truth any longer. "I did know. He told me right before I left the party. It was one of the reasons I came to see you that night."

He stared at me for a long time, as if trying to translate what I was saying into a language he could understand. "For a pity party? Is that why you came? To make me feel better?" He laughed bitterly. "I did say that to you once, though, didn't I? That going to bed with you would make me feel better. I never expected you to take me up on the offer."

I took a step toward him, then stopped. "No, Jack. That's not it at all. I wanted to tell you, but then things between us . . . progressed. And then you left, and I kept telling myself it could wait until you got back."

He shoved his hands in his pockets. "That's all I needed to hear," he said, and began walking toward the door.

I took a step toward him. "Please, Jack. Don't go. I know what I did was stupid—I've been beating myself up about it every day. I just . . . Please let me explain. I didn't want to hurt you."

He faced me, his eyes hard. "You've got a funny way of showing it. Knowing you, you were probably waiting for me to figure it all out by myself so you wouldn't have to be involved at all. Tell me I'm wrong."

I almost lied. But even I was beginning to understand how the truth served warm was a lot easier to digest than a lie served cold. "I'm sorry, Jack. Please believe how sorry I am. Just give me another chance. I know now how important the truth would have been, and I was going to tell you. . . ." Even I cringed at how clichéd and pathetic my words were. I closed my mouth, certain that anything I said wouldn't bring him back. I had lost him the moment I'd entered his apartment that night with the secret I wasn't convinced I would share.

"I'm done with you, Mellie. With all the craziness you put me through. I thought the other night was the start of something new between us, but I guess I was wrong. There's a level of trust that's not there, and I just can't get past it. Life is way too short." He opened the door, then paused, looking back.

"You said telling me about Marc was one of the reasons you came over that night. What was the other?"

I bit my lower lip, tasting tears I wasn't aware I was shedding. I looked down at the floor in front of his feet. Very quietly, I said, "I wanted to tell you that I love you."

He didn't move for a long moment, and I closed my eyes, waiting for him to answer. Finally he said, "I'm sorry."

I didn't open my eyes again until I heard the door close behind him.

I stared at the two unnamed goldfish making their endless laps around their glass bowl. I hadn't found the energy to figure out what to do with them, or even to name them. I thought one looked a little thin, so I dropped an extra pinch of food into the top of the bowl, watching as the plumper one snatched the first gulp before swimming away in victory. The smaller one sidled up to the last flake and was opening its little fish mouth before the bossy one swam by and snatched it up, too. I couldn't even find the energy to scold it.

For three weeks I'd been walking through life as if in a coma. I couldn't sleep, couldn't eat, and couldn't focus on anything. For the first time in my career, my name slipped from the top seller's chart in Dave Henderson's office and I couldn't even care. My parents, Nola, and even General Lee handled me with care, not jostling me too much with questions or speculations or the need for walks. Nola even brought me doughnuts at all hours of the day, concerned that the same box had languished in the pantry for more than a week. I'd taken a bite for her benefit, then thrown the rest of it out after she left. It was odd to feel hungry but have no appetite, something with which I'd had no previous experience.

The only bright spot was that Jack wasn't asking for Nola to move back with him. I assumed the reason was because the dollhouse was now parked in his spare bedroom. Regardless, I was glad. I'd miss her—

even her wild music and eye rolling—when she was gone, and I didn't think I could take another loss so soon.

A knock sounded on the door and I leaned back in my chair. "I'm not here."

Sophie walked into my office and stopped when she saw me by the fishbowl. "You look awful."

"It's good to see you, too," I said, rolling my chair back to my desk, then laying my head on top.

"Really, Melanie, I've never seen you look this way. You're . . . puffy."

I turned my head away. "Maybe I've been crying."

"Yeah, well, I can see that. But it's more than your face. Check out your feet."

I'd figured the heat of summer coupled with my now advanced age had been making my shoes tighter. I lifted my head and looked down at my swollen feet, where my ankles were definitely approaching cankle territory.

"Who cares?" I said, my voice sounding almost as pathetic as I felt. "It's probably from all the salt tears I've been swallowing."

"I think you're probably dehydrated. Have you been drinking your water?"

I moaned in answer.

Sophie plopped herself down in one of the chairs on the other side of my desk and scooted it over so I had a better view of her and her hair, which was beribboned in about fifty or so plastic bow-shaped barrettes. I realized how bad I was feeling when I caught myself thinking that her hair looked cute. "You haven't returned any of my phone calls, and Charlene swears she's been giving you my messages."

I sat back in my chair and yawned. All I wanted to do was sleep and cry, and sometimes I even managed to do both simultaneously. "Sorry. But I've already told you everything, and there just isn't anything else to talk about."

"Actually, there is. But first, I'm going to kidnap you and do something fun."

I closed my eyes. "Does it involve sleeping?"

"Not necessarily, but it does involve things that as my maid of honor you're supposed to be taking care of."

One eye popped open. "Like what?"

"We're going to Charleston Place and having a spa day."

I sat up, trying to picture Sophie in a white robe and spa slippers. "Really?"

"Really. And trust me—after seeing you, I realize a spa day will be as much for you as it is for me."

I looked at my desktop computer and BlackBerry—neither of which I'd turned on yet, even though I'd been in the office for nearly two hours—and weighed the misery of staying at the office and ignoring calls against lying in a dimly lit room with soft music while somebody slathered my face with cream. With a heavy sigh, I said, "Whatever."

"I appreciate your enthusiasm." She stood and grasped my arms to help pull me up. "I've invited Nola, and she's waiting outside in my car. I invited your mom, too, but they called her this morning to fill in as docent at the Nathaniel Russell House."

I blinked at her. "My mother's a docent?"

"Since last month. I told her she'd be a shoo-in, and tourists love her. I'm sure she's mentioned it to you."

I searched my fuzzy memory of the last month in vain as I followed Sophie out of the office like a lemming, too tired to tell her I'd figured out that she'd decided I was going even before she'd asked.

I loved Charleston Place, the venerable stately hotel and upscale retail mecca on the corner of Meeting and Market streets. In my life before Jack, I'd loved to come shop at the Anne Fontaine store and the other beautiful boutiques that lined the marbled halls, and I frequently brought clients for breakfast or lunch at the elegant Palmetto Café. I'd even shared a few celebratory dinners at the four-diamond Charleston Grill, with its amazing dessert menu.

Today the aromas of the restaurants made me wrinkle my nose, despite the persistent hunger pangs, and I barely paused before the glass windows of my favorite shops. I even took off my shoes before we reached the elevators to take us up to the spa. It was either that or force Sophie and Nola to carry me. I thought halfheartedly about heading down to Bob Ellis afterward and demanding they fix the shoes that seemed to be shrinking daily.

I allowed Sophie to arrange my treatments—including a heavenly

Ultimate Bliss, where two therapists worked their magic on a simultaneous facial and foot reflexology—and a manicure-pedicure. My spa aesthetician, Leah, was young, trim, and perky, and tried to be diplomatic about the deplorable condition of my skin and feet. I hadn't so much as touched a bottle of lotion or pumice stone since my birthday party. But despite her gentle manner and assurance that forty was the new thirty, I burst into tears as I tried to explain that I'd always taken care of myself and had prided myself on my good skin until just recently, when I'd found my heart shattered with nobody to blame but myself.

Leah was very comforting and reassuring—making me think that aestheticians probably had to take psychology classes, too—and told me she'd have a bag of free samples waiting for me when I left, to make me feel a little better. She handed me a tissue as I thanked her, then escorted me to what I referred to as the decompression room, where robe-clad ladies waited between treatments.

Sophie and Nola were already there, their toenails and fingernails painted in matching neon purple. I sat down in a wicker chair across from them, my skin and feet feeling great, but my heart still bruised and shrunken. I blinked twice at Sophie's feet. She wore the brown rubber spa flip-flops, giving me the first non-Birkenstock view of her feet since I'd met her. Her feet were small and slender, with straight, even toes. She could have been a foot model. I had known her for so long, yet had never realized how pretty her feet were. For some reason, the thought brought a fresh wave of new tears, and I had to press the tissue to my eyes.

The two of them whispered to each other for a moment before Nola spoke. "I haven't had any more music lessons. Miss Julia's in the hospital."

"Oh, no," I said, as fresh tears threatened to spill. "That's terrible. What's wrong?"

Sophie answered. "She's having trouble breathing on her own. I guess mostly because she's old. Dee said that the doctors can't believe Julia's still hanging on. It's like there's something holding her here."

They both looked at me as if I held all the answers. I quickly shook my head. Ever since Jack walked out of my life, I hadn't even been able to see spirits, like dead people were shunning me, too, for being so stupid. "I can't. I can't see them anymore."

Nola spoke up. "Maybe you're not trying hard enough."

I glared at her, and she jutted out her chin as if I were the one in the wrong. She continued. "Remember that newspaper article that mentioned how the Manigaults' plantation house had been hit by lightning and that's why it burned? Well, Sophie took me to see Miss Yvonne at the Historical Society to see if we could find weather records or news reports from that same geographical area and time. We found a little article about a church supper that evening in the neighboring town where the sky was clear and everybody was counting stars."

"It was apparently in the middle of a drought," Sophie added. "It hadn't rained for five straight weeks."

I felt a small stirring of interest. "So if there was a fire, it probably wasn't lightning."

Sophie shook her head. "Nope. But it would certainly be a great cover-up. If you destroy the reason anybody would be visiting the plantation—namely the house—you get rid of the chance of anybody discovering two new graves."

"I'm guessing Harold Manigault paid somebody to print such a blatant lie about the lightning. Looks like everything is pointing to intentional deaths. Has there been any identification yet on either body?"

Nola nodded. "That's why Miss Julia had to be taken to the hospital. When they called to tell her about the DNA results, she stopped breathing and had to be resuscitated. She's been in the hospital ever since."

"It was William, wasn't it?"

"Yes," Sophie said. "But they have no idea who the other male is."

"And you think that's why Julia's hanging on, to find out?"

"Well, partly," Sophie said. "She's still looking for William's forgiveness for something. But maybe that can't be given until we know the whole story."

For the first time in three weeks, I felt a glimmer of the old me. Turning to Nola, I asked, "Since we moved the dollhouse, have you had any more dreams?"

She shook her head. "No, but we still can't find the dog figure, and General Lee keeps acting like he's playing with another dog."

I raised my eyebrows. "I'm not going to even try to pretend I understand what that's about."

"But someone keeps messing with my music and my mom's guitar."

I looked at her gently, but didn't say anything.

"I'm guessing Mom's still here, too."

"Yeah. I think you're right," I said.

She looked at me, her eyes pleading. "Can you help them, Mellie? Not just Miss Julia, but my mom, too? Your mom said she'd help, but she can't do it without you."

I looked at Sophie and frowned. "Is this what today's spa trip was all about? An intervention?"

They both shrugged. "Does it matter?" Sophie said. "We miss you, and there are spirits who need you. Maybe if you turned your focus outward, you might heal a lot quicker."

I was angry that I'd been so manipulated, that somebody else was telling me how to run my life when I'd done such a good job of it. Until recently, anyway. I knew, in the shriveled place that used to be my heart, that they were right, and that I didn't want to live my life feeling the way I'd been feeling for the past three weeks. Mostly I was angry that I'd let somebody else figure it out for me.

I stood, trying to muster as much dignity as a person could while wearing a robe and flip-flops. "I'll think about it. But I don't think I can help. They don't want to talk to me, and to be honest, I'm tired of trying." I swept past them. "I'm going to go get changed."

I felt them watching me as I left, the all too familiar sting threatening to explode yet again into another torrent of tears and self-pity.

CHAPTER 27

I reached into the doughnut box, my fingers hitting only cardboard. I tilted the box toward me, surprised to see it empty. There'd been half a dozen doughnuts when I'd sat down only an hour before. I still had no appetite, and I hadn't tasted anything for weeks, but a persistent and gnawing hunger never seemed to abate, regardless of what I put in my mouth.

The wall-mounted TV flickered images of Mrs. Houlihan's favorite soap opera, whose storyline was about a woman with amnesia who had accidentally married two men and didn't know who the father of her baby was. I was vaguely aware of my mother sitting across the kitchen table with her arms crossed over her chest, regarding me with a frown.

"When was the last time you combed your hair?"

I reached up to pat my hair, realizing too late that I'd probably just dusted my head with powdered sugar. I caught sight of the sleeve of my nightgown, stained with spilled coffee and something that looked a lot like toothpaste. At least that meant I'd brushed my teeth at some point. "I don't remember," I said, slumping further in my chair and wondering if it would be impolite to get up and see what else might be in the pantry.

"Do you think you might get dressed anytime soon?" she asked.

I thought for a moment. "Probably not. I'm on vacation." When I'd asked Dave Henderson for a couple of weeks of vacation, he'd nearly fallen out of his chair. In all the years I'd worked for him, I'd yet to take a real vacation, much less two weeks' worth.

"Jack called."

I sat up in my chair. "When?"

"Yesterday. On my cell. He only wanted to speak with me."

"Oh." I slumped back down.

"He said the activity in the dollhouse has increased. Every night things get rearranged or thrown out. But there's one new thing that he wanted to ask me about."

I feigned noninterest by shrugging.

"The mother figure, Anne, keeps ending up in the same spot outside the house. Right next to the place we kept finding William. Do you think she's trying to tell us something?"

I thought about my promise to both Julia and Nola to try to find out what had happened to William and why he'd ended up in an unmarked grave. It stirred my conscience just a little bit. I nodded. "She's always been silent, bullied by her husband or son to remain quiet. Why would she be taking a stand now?"

"I've been wondering the same thing. Maybe the discovery of William's body has given her a certain kind of leverage or freed her somehow. Maybe an emerging truth is giving her strength." She paused. "I mentioned that I could go over there and hold the doll figures again and see what I can find out."

I shook my head. "You know you shouldn't do that alone."

"I wasn't thinking I'd be alone."

I stood. "No way am I going back there. I . . . No. Never."

My mother stood, too. "Sweetheart, you and Jack have to talk and work this thing out. I'm not saying this to be mean, but you're pretty pathetic right now."

My throat closed a little, and I was afraid I'd start crying. Again. I swallowed. "I told him I loved him, Mother, and all he said was 'I'm sorry.' I think we've done all the talking we're going to."

She momentarily closed her eyes, as if summoning strength. "Regardless, you've got to get on the other side of this, and wallowing here in your nightgown is not going to make it happen."

I was silent, the TV blaring a detergent commercial. I picked up the remote and flipped it off. General Lee barked and began chasing his invisible friend around the table. He circled twice, then ran to the back door, stopping himself in time before colliding with the door. He sat up and whimpered, then began to paw at the wood. I moved to pick him up and he actually growled at me. Startled, I straightened.

"He's probably desperate for a walk," my mother said. "Besides being let out in the garden to do his business, I don't think he's had any exercise in weeks." Her gaze drifted to my swollen ankles. "A walk would probably do you both good."

I sighed heavily, knowing she was right. "Fine. Let me go throw some clothes on and I'll be right back. But you're coming with me in case we run into anybody I know. You can tell them I have the plague or something so they don't get too close."

"All right. But please brush your hair. And some lipstick would help, too."

I was about to glare at her when the TV popped back on with no picture, just sound. "I'm Just Getting Started" blared loudly, making General Lee renew his efforts to exit the door. I hit the "off" button on the remote and then tried the actual television, but the sound continued. Finally, I pulled out the cord, an unnatural silence filling the kitchen.

"Look what I found," Nola shouted as she raced through the doorway, holding up the dog figure from the dollhouse. She stopped when she spotted me with the television cord in my hand.

"Where was it?" I asked, feeling as if I already knew the answer.

"Stuffed inside the shirt of my teddy bear. I have no idea how it got there."

General Lee whimpered at the figure, then threw himself at the door again, his small body making a thumping sound against the wood.

My eyes met my mother's. "They're not going to leave me alone, are they?"

My mother shook her head. "No. And neither are we. You can either come willingly, or we can drag you kicking and screaming. It's up to you."

"I'll take the dog for a walk, but that's all I'm committing to right now," I said. "I need to get dressed—could somebody please let the dog out before he messes on the floor?" I didn't wait for a response as I headed out of the kitchen.

"You might want to try to drag a brush through your hair while you're at it," Nola called out to me.

My eye rolling was blocked by the closed door.

When I returned, I found Nola, my mother, and General Lee on the sidewalk, the dog nearly choking himself on the leash because he was straining so hard to follow something the rest of us couldn't see. I could make out the brief flash of a tail, but the rest was invisible even to me.

"He won't go potty, so I'm thinking he wants to take a walk," Nola said. "We were just waiting for you."

"Thanks," I said, taking the leash and nearly losing my balance as General Lee shot forward, his agenda known only to him.

"What are you wearing, Mellie?" my mother asked.

I looked down at the bright blue velour sweat suit as if I were seeing it for the first time. "Something I borrowed from Charlene. She said it was appropriate vacation attire."

"Isn't it a little warm to be wearing velour with long sleeves?"

I nodded, already starting to perspire. "You know how cold-natured I am. I'll be fine." I didn't want to tell her that it was the only thing I could find that fit me. I was so bloated, and everything else seemed to be too tight. As Jack and Sophie had long predicted, the days of eating everything I wanted without gaining weight had come to a crashing halt. I knew that turning forty had been a bad idea.

At least my mother either pretended not to notice or didn't see the flip-flops on my feet, something I never wore in public except on the rare occasions I made it to the beach.

"Where are we going?" Nola asked, sounding breathless as she jogged to keep up.

"I'm not sure, but he seems to be following his invisible friend." I stubbed my toe on a crack in the sidewalk and stumbled, cursing under my breath at the absurdity of wearing shoes without any kind of support or toe protection. "It's best just to follow."

We continued our brisk pace, and I was relieved that he wasn't heading in the direction of the Circular Church and its cemetery. When we crossed Broad Street to Rutledge, I had a pretty good idea of where we were going.

"Hey, this is the way to Miss Julia's house," Nola said.

"I think you're right." I glanced at my mother, who was delicately mopping her brow with a tissue she'd pulled from her purse. I was sweating like a horse but wasn't about to admit it by asking whether she had another one.

When we were still a block away, the hair on the back of my neck rose, an almost refreshing cold wave of fear racking my body. My mother stopped and I did, too, General Lee continuing to pull on the leash.

"Do you feel that?" she asked.

I nodded as our eyes met.

"This might not be . . . good."

"Is it ever?" I asked.

She didn't smile. "I have a feeling that if we go any farther, it will be too late to turn back. And if you turn back, I'm going to have to turn back, too, because I can't fight whatever is there by myself—it's much too strong. So you have to decide now whether you're going to see this thing through and let Julia die in peace, or go back to your wallowing as if your life is over. Right here, right now, you need to decide that your gift is something that will always be there, and will transcend even the disappointments in your life. It has always been that way for me, and I hope it will be for you, too."

I stood, staring at her while I dripped sweat in my velour sweat suit, feeling as ridiculous as I looked and wondering whether all of life's big decisions happened when one was least prepared. I looked down the street in the direction from which we'd come and saw Nola with her arms crossed, her face expressionless.

She'd changed so much in the last few months. She was still a teenager—I supposed we'd have to wait about seven years for that to change—and she was as comfortable in her own skin as she'd always been. But she didn't seem so alone anymore, or so lonely. If I didn't think she'd argue with me, I would almost suggest that she was feeling as if she belonged in Charleston now, with her father and the ragtag family that had come together to see her through. Despite all of that, I could still see the stricken little girl who'd arrived on my doorstep, the girl abandoned by her mother and not knowing why. My own heartache didn't seem so bad in comparison anymore.

Looking beyond Nola to the street behind her, I couldn't see Bonnie, but I could hear the tune I'd begun to associate with her, the song that seemed to come from inside my head. I felt the pull of my old life, but now more as a memory than a necessity. Maybe by turning forty I had traded in my metabolism for wisdom. Or maybe it was just time for me to grow up.

"Come on," I said, allowing General Lee to leap forward and following at a slow jog. It was one thing to capitulate; it was quite another to admit to being wrong about so many things in such a public way. My mother didn't say anything, but I caught her exchanging a glance with Nola and heard the slap of hands, as if a high five had occurred behind my back.

Nola spotted the yellow caution tape first as we neared the old Victorian house, starting at the curb and marking off the entire side yard on the turret side of the house and going all the way to the back property line. A backhoe loader sat in front of a large hole, a pile of dark earth parked next to it. The yard was deserted, the equipment turned off, and as we stood staring and wondering what to do next, Dee Davenport came out of the house, running faster than I thought a person her size could, and carrying something in her hand.

"Miss Middleton—you must have read my mind. I was just trying to call you!"

General Lee stopped pulling at his leash, as if whatever he was chasing had gone, then lay down at my feet. "What's going on, Dee?"

She pressed a pudgy hand against her chest as she paused to catch her breath. "We had a water pipe burst in the yard—we're thinking it's from the roots of that big oak tree by the side of the house. Anyway, when they started digging they found bones."

"Bones?"

Dee nodded. "Not human, fortunately. But dog bones—the whole skeleton. The skull was cracked—probably the cause of death."

I looked down at General Lee, sleeping off his exhaustion, and was glad he hadn't heard what Dee said. "That's awful. But why were you calling me?"

She held out a rectangular wooden box, similar to others I'd seen at Trenholm's Antiques. It was a Victorian glove box, used to store ladies' gloves. "Because they found this, too. Not buried with the dog, but nearby."

I handed the leash to Nola and took the box. "But why are you giving this to me? If it was found on this property, it belongs to Miss Julia."

Dee nodded, her cheeks flushed with exertion, her hair stuck to her forehead with sweat. "I know. I just came from the hospital, where I showed it to her. And she asked me to give it to you."

I stared at the box as if it held spiders or other crawling insects. "What's in it?"

"Letters. I showed them to Miss Julia. She said you and Mr. Trenholm would know what to do."

My eyes smarted at the mention of his name and I quickly blinked. With a glance at Nola and my mother, who both gave encouraging nods, I opened up the box, revealing a pleated pink silk interior lining that cradled a small stack of letters. The envelopes were crisp and brittle, faded to yellow. There was no writing on the outside, the flaps torn unevenly, as if the person opening them had been too impatient to find a letter opener.

"Go ahead," Dee said. "Miss Julia wanted you to read them."

Handing the box to my mother, I took the top envelope and opened it carefully. The handwriting inside was small and precise, done in all capital letters, and definitely written by a male. My eyes scanned to the bottom of the page, searching for a signature, and found only the initials JCW. I thought hard, wondering whether I'd run across a name that fit the initials.

"Jonathan Crisler Watts," Nola volunteered, reading over my shoulder. "It was in one of the newspaper articles we got from Yvonne at the Historical Society."

"She's young and still has all of her brain cells," my mother said, indicating Nola. "Just be thankful she's here and move on."

With a brief glance at my mother, I turned back to the letter and began to read out loud.

"'Darling, last night's passion and the feel of your bare skin against mine, the touch of your golden hair under my fingers—'" I broke off, then continued to scan the rest of the letter, my cheeks heating at the mixture of Victorian romance and erotica.

"What does it say?" asked Nola, reaching for the letter that I'd shielded from her view after the first few words.

"More of the same," I offered as explanation. I placed the letter back in the envelope, then picked up the next and opened it, the letter revealing yet another enraptured Jonathan waxing poetic about soft blond hair and making improbable rhymes with the words "desire" and "rapture." I examined the rest of the letters and discovered them all to be pretty much the same.

I closed the box and took it back from my mother. "I don't understand," I said, turning to Dee. "Why would Julia want me to see these letters from her fiancé?"

"Because Miss Julia says she's never seen them before. She's old, but she's still as sharp as a tack, with a good memory. She'd remember if she'd read them."

"So would I," I muttered. I thought for a moment. "But somebody read them, and somebody buried them. But who?"

"That poor dog," my mother said. "Why would somebody hurt the dog?"

"Maybe he died by accident and they buried him here," Nola suggested.

"I'd like to think so," I said. "But I think there has to be some connection, since he's haunting the dollhouse with the other family members. And the head on the dog figure had been damaged, too."

General Lee whimpered in his sleep, and I bent down to scratch him behind his ear. Looking up, I said, "Nola, look at the house and point to the spot that corresponds to the place where you found the figure of William and the dog on the floor outside the dollhouse."

She faced the house and walked to the side by the turret. The whole side yard seemed to pulsate with energy, a black cloud visible to only the lucky few, hugging the air surrounding the turret. I refused to look up, knowing what I would see.

Nola stopped about ten feet away from the turret and approximately five feet from where the hole gaped open. "About right here."

My mother crossed her arms over her chest. "So let's say William fell—or was pushed—from the turret window. If the dog were outside, he would have barked. Assuming William didn't end up on the ground by his own devices, whoever was here with him would have wanted to silence the dog in the quickest way possible."

I nodded, thinking hard, feeling the shifting of all the pieces as they tried to find their way into the correct slots of a puzzle with pieces that seemed to be not only two-sided, but had no edges. I opened my mouth to say something, then stopped, the image of the Manigault family portrait I'd seen printed in the newspaper flashing in my mind.

I turned back to Dee. "Where was the box of letters found?"

She pointed to a spot near where the dog's bones had been found. I turned to my mother. "Isn't that about the same general area where Jack said he keeps finding the Anne doll?"

She nodded. "Sounds about right. Maybe she's the one who buried the letters."

I shook my head. "None of this makes any sense." Turning back to Dee, I said, "And you're sure Julia said she'd never seen them before, and had no idea how they got buried in the yard?"

Dee nodded. "Right. But why would somebody hide letters to Julia from her own fiancé?"

I took a deep breath and raised my eyes to the turret as a certain knowledge settled on me as clear as the image of the hollow-eyed man watching us from the window. "Because those letters are from Jonathan. But they weren't written to Julia."

CHAPTER 28

I finished stowing the pick and hoe I'd borrowed from my father in the trunk of my car. I knew he would have come with us if I'd asked, but I also knew that despite his new open-mindedness, enough doubts existed that might work to drain the energy my mother and I might need. It would have been nice to have a few more muscles to help with the digging, but I wasn't about to ask Jack, and my mother had had the good sense not to even suggest it.

"Where's Nola?" I asked as I watched my mother walk toward me. She wore walking shorts and sneakers—something I'd never seen her wear, much less thought she owned—and I wondered whether she might be just trying to make me feel better about my own fashion choices. Or lack thereof, I thought, as I looked down at the mom jeans and loose Greenpeace T-shirt Sophie had given me. *Oh, how the mighty have fallen.* Accepting clothes from Sophie, purchased from Goodwill, no less, had taken a major attitude adjustment. Not as major as I'd expected, though; I didn't seem to have much attitude left.

"I drove her to Jack's early this morning. It seems the two of them had an outing planned, so Nola couldn't come with us."

I'd slept until ten o'clock, something else I'd not done since infancy, and had apparently missed Nola's announcement and departure.

"Oh. I guess I didn't need the third shovel then." My disappointment seemed way too keen to be about a shovel, but I didn't want to examine my feelings too closely because then I'd start crying. My mother was already looking at me funny.

"It's always good to have extras," she said as she opened the passenger door and slid in.

We spent the next hour and a half on our drive to Georgetown fighting over the radio buttons—me hitting the seventies station trying to get an ABBA song and her angling for the classical station. It made me wish I'd never asked for the satellite radio upgrade. Eventually, I plugged my iPod into the stereo so that we were forced to listen to my playlist, which was comprised of a lot of ABBA and the rest eighties dance music. I made no apologies, realizing that it wouldn't be enough for my classically trained opera-singing mother.

Highway 17 is a lonely stretch of highway that runs through Charleston and along the coast. We passed place-names familiar to me— Sullivan's Island and McClellanville, both towns in which I'd spent summers and other vacations with my sorority sisters from college. While I'd been at the University of South Carolina, my father had continued to move around with the army, so for vacations and holidays I preferred to borrow a home and family wherever I could find them. Not that I would have chosen to visit with him anyway, having long since gotten over the need to be his caretaker.

As we approached the historic city of Georgetown, my mother unfolded a large and wrinkled AAA map circa 1989. "The turnoff should be coming up here on the right."

"You know, I have a GPS. All you have to do is plug in the address. . . ."

"Those things are never right. Besides, I doubt any GPS could find it. It's an abandoned homestead where nobody has lived for decades. That's why Yvonne couldn't give us a street address."

"Mother, it uses a satellite. Anything that exists can be seen. . . ."

"There it is," she said, almost chortling. "Nothing like good old-fashioned map reading to get you where you need to go."

"Avoiding technology just means you're getting old," I said smugly as I turned onto an unpaved road, effectively silencing her.

Dust erupted under the tires, seeming to swallow up the road behind us. The car bumped over rocks and small limbs, making me wish I'd taken my dad up on his offer to borrow his truck. The old-growth pine forest loomed thickly over us, blocking out much of the sunlight and giving me the impression of being inside a cathedral. None of which did anything to soothe my nerves. With grave digging on the agenda, I hadn't really expected anything would.

"What if somebody sees us?" my mother asked.

It had occurred to me to bring ski masks and something to hide my license plate, but I'd dismissed these ideas as being products of watching too many *MacGyver* reruns on late-night TV, my company during my recent bout of insomnia. Still, my being caught digging up a grave would look really bad when reported in the Charleston papers. Especially if they included a photo of me in my mom jeans.

"I don't think we have anything to worry about," I said. "Yvonne checked the records and verified that the house and property have been abandoned since the nineteen fifties, when Jonathan's parents died. One of his brothers in north Georgia inherited it, but nobody's lived here since then."

"So we're trespassing," she said.

"Yes. But that would be the least of the charges if we're caught." I pressed down on the brake, stopping the car. "If you want to turn back, speak now."

I followed her gaze out the back window of the car, to where all we could see was a swirling haze of orange-colored dust, and then to the sides of the narrow road with ditches leading down into the forest. She looked at me. "I think we're beyond that now. Don't you?"

I nodded, knowing she was right in more ways than one. I pressed my foot on the gas pedal, moving the car forward with the oddest feeling of being glad that there was no turning back.

The Victorian farmhouse, when we finally came upon it in a clearing, appeared to be waging its last stand against the encroachment of the forest. It was exactly how I had pictured it—with the peaked roof, large deep porch, and the straight lines of the porch supports straight out of a book of Americana. This style of house probably existed in most regions throughout the country, calling to mind large families and chickens in the front yard. Not murder and empty graves. The only difference between my mental picture and what I saw before me was that the house seemed even more abandoned and forlorn than I had imagined.

No glass existed in the windows, allowing for gaping holes through which one could see collapsed ceilings and fallen walls. A large tree poked through the roof, the dislodged slate shingles half-embedded in the ground below where they'd fallen, as if in testament to the violence of the storm that had thrown them there.

I put the car in park and turned off the ignition. "I'm assuming the family cemetery is out back."

"That's what Yvonne said." My mother faced me. "You don't like cemeteries very much." It wasn't a question.

"Nothing good ever happens while I'm in one."

She took my hand and squeezed. "Remember, we're stronger together. Don't forget that."

I squeezed back, then let go to exit the car. We stood in the deafening silence filled only with the background drone of thousands of unseen insects. I could smell the nearby marsh and the ubiquitous Lowcountry pluff mud, a scent I'd loved from the very first whiff. People say that's how you can tell a true South Carolinian—if they don't wrinkle up their noses at the unique smell of rotting vegetation.

"Do you feel anything?" she asked as we faced the desolate house whose yard seemed to be swallowing it whole, with weeds that grew through the slats in the porch floorboard.

"No. Not yet, anyway. Maybe there's no reason for them to be here."

My mother regarded me. "Or maybe we haven't given them a reason yet."

I swallowed heavily, trying to focus on the task at hand. I unlocked the trunk and handed a shovel to my mother, then took out the pick and another shovel for me. We were rounding the side of the house when I heard the distinct sound of a car door slamming.

I started and stopped. "Oh, no—somebody's here!" I quickly calculated how long it would take us both to run to the car and back out over the long gravel drive, before looking over at my mother, whose expression wasn't registering alarm or even surprise. Instead she actually looked apologetic.

Anger quickly replaced my fear. "Are you expecting someone?" I asked, moving ahead slowly while my suspicions rose, then were confirmed when I heard Nola's voice.

"They're here," Nola announced, just as my mother and I rounded the corner to the back of the house.

Jack and Nola stood by his pickup truck, each holding a shovel. All we needed was a couple of pitchforks to reenact a medieval witch hunt.

"What are you doing here?" Jack and I asked simultaneously.

We looked at Nola and my mother, both of whom suddenly looked very, very guilty.

"Mother! What were you thinking?"

Very calmly she approached us. "I was thinking that we needed Jack's help. Nola agreed."

Nola stepped between Jack and me. "And it would be nice if the two of you would make up. I feel like that dude on *The Bachelor* trying to choose between the two of you. It's just *wrong*."

Jack was staring at me, his expression one of confusion. "What happened to you?"

You, I wanted to say, but didn't want to give him any more power over me. I couldn't meet his eyes, remembering the humiliation of our last encounter. I stuck out my chin. "I'm on vacation. This is what people wear on vacation."

The old familiar smirk lifted half of his mouth. "On a retirees' cruise to Cancún, maybe. Where did you get those clothes?"

I tried to be offended but couldn't. Even if Jack wasn't mine, it was good to know he was still Jack. Regardless, I didn't think either "Sophie" or "Goodwill" would be acceptable responses. Instead, I pulled together the last shards of self-respect and asked again, "Why are you here?"

"For the same reason you are, I'm thinking." He slid a glance at his daughter. "Nola told me about Julia's letters. She'd heard enough to be able to let me know what was in them. But, being the intelligent person that she is, instead of telling me what she already knew, she allowed me to reach the same conclusion you apparently have—that Jonathan was the other body buried with William."

Curious enough to forget my humiliation and the stabbing pain in the vicinity of my heart that came each time I looked at him, I asked, "What made you think that?"

He scratched the back of his head. "Well, his death from influenza in 1938 was too coincidental. First William, then the house fire, then Jonathan—all in the same year. There was no influenza epidemic that year, which doesn't really mean he couldn't have died from it; it's just that his death was too . . . neat."

"And there's no such thing as coincidence," Nola said, beaming.

"Fast learner," Jack said, rubbing the top of her head as if she were a little kid. Frowning, as if he were trying not to show too much interest, he turned to me. "What about you? How did you figure it out?"

"The letters waxed poetic about the beautiful blond hair of the person Jonathan wrote to. According to the Manigault family photos that I've seen, Julia's hair was dark brown. William's was blond."

"Ah." He nodded. "Anyway, Nola acted appropriately surprised when I told her about my conclusion and casually mentioned that if we could find Jonathan's grave and discover it empty, we'd have a pretty good guess as to who was buried alongside William Manigault. I imagine she even convinced Yvonne not to tell me she'd already given you the same information on where to find Jonathan's grave when I met with her yesterday."

Nola focused on a rock on the ground in front of her with scholarly intensity.

Jack and I stood facing each other, our eyes not exactly meeting. "Well," I said, "glad to have my conclusions collaborated. But I think Nola, my mother, and I can handle it from here on out. After all, none of this concerns you."

My mother stepped forward. "Let's not be so hasty, Mellie. Jack's already here, and we could really use his considerable muscle to help with the digging. It will make it go twice as fast."

As much as I wanted to contradict her, I knew she was right. An extra set of arms would make it all go so much faster—even if they were Jack's arms. I figured that maybe I could work with my back to him so I wouldn't have to look at him. Or hear him breathe, which would bring back way too many memories. With a heavy sigh that sounded a lot like Nola, I said, "Whatever."

"No."

The three of us turned to stare at Jack.

He crossed his arms. "No," he said again. "I think Mellie should ask me nicely. As she pointed out, this has nothing to do with me. If she wants to borrow my muscles, she'll have to ask."

I felt my mouth drop open. "There is no way in . . ."

My mother spoke up. "My sciatica is really acting up, Mellie. I don't think I'm going to be much help with the digging. Which would leave only you and Nola. And she weighs about eighty pounds soaking wet. So before you make any hasty decisions, please think about it."

I tried to imagine doing all that digging by myself, and couldn't get past the part where I'd need to break the surface somehow. Just thinking about it depleted my energy reserves, not to mention the time issue. The fear of discovery was never far from my mind.

I took a deep breath and sighed deeply. Looking at a spot behind Jack's shoulder, I said, "Would you please stay and help us dig?"

"Since you asked so nicely," he said, with a hint of a smile lingering in his voice.

I slid my gaze to meet his, noticing again how blue his eyes were, and how they weren't mocking me but appeared instead to be searching mine. I looked away, for the first time not able to even guess what he might be thinking.

"Then come on," I said, hoisting a shovel and pick, then marching past Jack.

"Nice jeans," he said as I walked by, giving me a couple of ideas of what I could do with the pick and shovel besides digging.

Just as Yvonne had described, a small family cemetery lay situated behind the house, down a rock path that had been rendered almost invisible by tall weeds. A rusty wrought-iron gate surrounded the clearing with its small number of unkempt tombstones, their rounded tops made visible only by the shifting breeze.

"What is it with you Middleton women and family cemeteries?" Jack asked.

My mother raised her eyebrows and I knew she, too, was recalling the last time we'd been in a cemetery together as we'd tried to put the spirit of Rose Prioleau to rest. We'd come very close to having it all end in disaster.

"Except here I'm not feeling anything," I said. "Like all the spirits here are resting peacefully."

"Or aren't here at all," Nola added.

I hoped she was right.

We fanned out through the overgrown cemetery, reading fading inscriptions on the old grave markers. There were only about a dozen, and it didn't take long for Jack to find it. "Over here," he called, indicating a white marble marker in the shape of a cross. "Just has his name—no birth or death dates. Maybe Jonathan's parents didn't want their lie to be imprinted on a cross."

We stood in front of the marker and stared at the flat expanse of dirt and grass that grew over the grave. Jack reached for the pick and I handed it to him, more grateful that he was there than I wanted to admit, and not just because of the added muscle. Still, I couldn't look at him, and each accidental glance was like the slow peeling of a Band-Aid off a wound that wouldn't heal.

"Move back," he instructed. "I'll start and then we can all take turns scooping out the dirt. We're going to go about six feet long and six feet deep, and if we work fast we should have it done in a couple of hours."

"Can you make it faster?" Nola suggested. "I've got plans tonight. With Alston," she added hastily.

We stood back as Jack hoisted the pick and let it fall, and the first tremor of fear began at the base of my neck. I glanced at my mother and saw that she'd felt it, too.

"You'd better hurry, Jack," she said. "I don't think we'll have two hours."

His gaze traveled from my mother to me, and I knew he was remembering our last cemetery digging, too. He raised the pick above his head and drove it into the earth, and I felt the ground trembling softly below me, as if we'd awakened something that should have been left asleep.

We watched until Jack had obliterated the weeds and grass that had grown on top of the grave, loosening the soil enough so we could begin digging. I picked up my shovel. "I'll go first. The faster we dig, the less time we'll have to feel the pain."

Because of the small space, my mother, Nola, and I took turns standing on the opposite end from Jack. He continued to dig throughout, changing sides with us so he could even out the depth of the hole.

The hot sun beat down on us, and I found myself wishing I'd thought to bring water. In my old life, I wouldn't have left anything to chance. In my new life, I found I could barely remember what I needed to do in the next half hour.

"Are you all right?" my mother asked.

I blinked at her, my eyes stinging from the dripping sweat, and realized that I was seeing double. "Just . . . a little hot," I said.

She took the shovel from me. "Go sit over there in the shade next to Nola and cool off. I can do this now."

"But it's my turn. . . ." I stopped protesting, knowing that if I didn't sit down sometime very soon, I'd end up facedown in the hole.

I sprawled next to a sweating Nola, her face and hands smeared with dirt and probably looking a lot like I did. If somebody came upon us now and demanded to know what we were doing, it would be very hard to prove our innocence.

I hadn't been sitting down very long when the sound of metal hitting wood traveled up out of the grave. My mother and Jack stopped. "We're barely at four feet, but I think I found a coffin," Jack announced. His shirt was soaked in sweat, but he hadn't removed it. I'm sure it was more for my mother's benefit and Nola's, but I was very, very thankful. If the heat didn't make me pass out, that surely would have.

"I can finish this," he said, then helped my mother out of the grave. She came and sat down next to us in the shade of the pine tree while we watched Jack.

He used his shovel to remove the dirt from the top of the coffin, then tossed it aside to grab the pick. "Just in case it's not empty, I want you three to stay where you are for now."

I wanted to protest, but I didn't think I could have moved to a standing position even if I wanted to. He raised the pick once more above his head, and let it come down with a crashing, splintering sound. He moved back and brought the pick down two more times, using the broad-sided portion to pry away what was left of the lid.

He turned to face us. "You might want to come see this."

Nola and my mother stood. I waited for a moment, focusing all of my energy on becoming vertical again. Using the trunk of the tree for support, I pulled myself to a stand, then joined the others.

Slowly, the three of us leaned over the edge of the gaping hole, staring inside at a splintered pine coffin, its lid demolished enough to reveal several large rocks lodged into packed dirt, filling the narrow space. We let out our breaths in a simultaneous exhale.

My mother shook her head. "I don't understand. Why would Jonathan's parents hide their son's murder and give him a false grave?"

Jack wiped his hands on the front of his jeans. "I'd bet a lot of money that they didn't know he was dead. That they were led to believe that he'd run off with William."

I nodded. "From what I know of Harold Manigault, I think he waited to find out if what Julia had told him about William was true. I mean, he must have known that Julia was jealous about William's inheritance, and he must have had his doubts. I think William was planning to leave, but wanted to see his lover one more time. So he got dressed up and that's when his father confronted him. The argument must have been brief—or nonexistent—since the fact that William was wearing his mother's clothes was evidence in itself, and in a fit of anger, Harold tossed William from the turret, killing him, either intentionally or not.

"I'm not exactly sure how the rest of it played out, but somehow Harold found out where William was meeting his lover, and waylaid Jonathan. Can you imagine his shock in finding out it was his future son-in-law? I have to imagine Jonathan's death was no accident."

"No, definitely not," Jack said. "I think he threw both bodies in his truck and drove out to the family plantation, where he buried the bodies, then burned the house so nobody would go back and accidentally discover the graves. To keep Jonathan's parents quiet, I'm guessing he told them that William and Jonathan had run off together—which would have been a huge stigma back then and would, in effect, silence them—and to save face, they faked Jonathan's death—even had a funeral for him. Either way, he was gone from them forever."

"Poor Julia," my mother said, shaking her head. "To have blamed herself for William's leaving all these years."

Nola's brow furrowed. "But then why would William's ghost try and stop Julia from discovering the graves? Wouldn't he want his death avenged?"

I had been staring at the coffin, listening to them speak, but seeing instead a dark night of violence and loss. And feeling William very close by. His presence wasn't threatening, and before I could ask him why, I suddenly understood. *Stop her. It will only get worse if she does not.*

"He was trying to protect Julia," I said. "He wanted her to believe that Jonathan had gone to his death loving her instead of allowing her to live with the knowledge of the worst kind of betrayal."

Nola kicked a clod of dirt into the coffin. "Miss Julia said her mother and William were really close. I bet Anne hid the letters after William disappeared to keep Harold from destroying them. I bet she saw Harold kill William, too—that's why they had to cart her off to the loony bin after he died."

I turned to my mother. "What are we going to tell Julia?" This was the part I had no experience with, and wasn't really sure whether or not I wanted to. "She's dying. She might need to know the truth so she can rest in peace."

Nola rolled her eyes. "I don't need another doll chasing me around. I vote we tell her."

A heavy gray cloud covered the sun, casting us all in heavy shadow. We looked up to see that everywhere else the sky was blue. But the insects were now eerily silent as a wind materialized, pushing at us with sudden intensity.

"We need to go," Jack said, his voice urgent but calm for Nola's sake. But my mother and I were remembering another cemetery not that long ago where an angry spirit tried to take her revenge on those of us who sought to right an old wrong.

"Yes," I said, leaning down to pick up a couple of shovels. "I think a storm is coming." Spots formed in front of my eyes and I stumbled. My mother took my arm. "Are you feeling all right?"

"Just a little bit of heat exhaustion, I think. Would you mind driving?"

"Not at all. Just go sit inside the car and turn it on so you can get the air-conditioning blasting. I'll worry about collecting all the tools."

"Hurry," I said without argument, squeezing her hand while examining the black cloud above us that seemed to be lower in the sky now, pressing the oxygen out of the air. "I think we've upset Harold. Julia told us that appearances were everything to him. Even now, after all this time, I don't expect he's going to be thrilled about the world seeing his family's dirty laundry."

She squeezed my hand again. "We're stronger than him. Just keep saying that to yourself and I'll be right with you."

I nodded, not completely sure I believed her, then watched her walk back to where Jack and Nola were refilling the hole. I wasn't feeling well, whatever strength I possessed depleted. I supposed that was a natural by-product of heartbreak, but I wouldn't know, having never experienced it before now.

I sat in the car, then reached over to turn on the ignition, blasting the air-conditioning in my face. I spotted a water bottle, warmed from the sun, sitting in the cup holder. Not caring that it wasn't ice-cold, I reached for it, then lifted my head to gulp it down as my gaze locked onto the rearview mirror.

The bottle froze halfway to my lips, the water splashing into my lap. The eyeless face of Harold Manigault stared at me from the backseat, the rotting smell of death and decay making me gag. *I am stronger than you,* I tried to say, but the lie stuck in the back of my throat. I had nothing left to fight him with, and my mother was out of sight, and I was inside the car where even my screams couldn't be heard. And he knew it.

I warned you to stay away, but you wouldn't listen.

I reached for the door handle and tugged on it, but it wouldn't budge. Frantically I scrambled for the door lock, realizing even in my panicked state that it was already unlocked. Cold, dead fingers wrapped around my neck, the cloying smell of dead flesh gagging me, making it even harder to breathe as something pressed hard against my windpipe.

I had no hope of winning this battle, even if my mother by some miracle returned. There was nothing to fight for, no reason not to give in. I knew I was giving up too easily, but couldn't make myself care. I gasped for breath, my body slumping into the driver's seat as bright stars of light appeared in my eyes, obliterating my vision.

I thought for a moment that I could hear music—Bonnie's song— and I wondered if this was what death must really be like, with music playing and utter peace. I felt no pain anymore, just my body and bones melting into weightlessness as I listened to Bonnie sing, louder now than I'd ever heard it before. It was like she was singing in my ear to make sure I heard it clearly.

Then suddenly I was floating outside of my body, looking down at the roof of the car, feeling more at peace than I ever had. And the music was there, too, louder and louder but so exquisitely beautiful that I didn't care. I turned my head, trying to capture the words I'd never been able to understand before.

My mother shouted and I saw her looking upward, and she was seeing me spin higher and higher above the car. I wanted to tell her that it was okay, that I was fine going where I was going, that it was beautiful and peaceful and that my heart had finally stopped breaking. She ran to the car and tried to open each door, and in my mind I heard her say, *I am stronger than you,* right before she started crying. She was on her own, without my help, and she knew it wouldn't be enough, just as I had.

Then I saw Jack and Nola running toward the car and Jack had the pick in his hand. He raised it against the back passenger window, the shattered glass splattering the car seat and the dirt outside like teardrops.

He reached into the driver's seat and tried to open the door from the inside. The music was so loud now that I almost didn't hear Bonnie's voice. *Nola needs you. So does Jack. And you need him too, in more ways than you know right now. Go back. Go back and find my daughter's eyes.*

I looked down at my weeping mother and Nola, and at Jack, who was frantically trying to reach me and get me out of the car. I allowed myself to feel, just one more time, and the pain around my heart burst anew, pressing through my chest, reminding me that I was alive. *Yes,* I whispered, no longer sure that the absence of pain was enough reason to let go of the tenuous hold on life. *And you need him too, in more ways than you know right now.* I needed to know the answer to that, realizing that I never would unless I returned to him. And to my mother and Nola and the rest of my life.

The pressure on my windpipe ceased immediately, and I began to fall through the sky, the cold air hitting my face as I fell back to the car and into the body of the woman slumped on the front seat. The passenger seat door was yanked open and I heard Jack call my name. I tried to reach for him and call his name, but my brain wasn't communicating with the rest of my body.

"Mellie," he shouted, his voice hoarse. "Somebody—call nine-one-one. Hurry!" I felt something warm and moist on my forehead and knew that he'd kissed me and that everything was going to be all right now. I heard Bonnie singing again, each word clear as tinkling bells, and I wanted to laugh out loud.

"Jack," I finally managed.

"Oh, thank God," I heard him say. "Don't say anything—conserve your energy. They're sending an ambulance."

"Jack," I said again, fighting the sleep that threatened to overtake me. "I know . . ."

"Shhhh," he whispered as he held me tightly in his arms.

I finally managed to open my eyes. "Listen," I said, wondering if he could hear the music, too. Lifting my head slightly, I said, "I know where to find my daughter's eyes."

Feeling confident that I'd said all that I could, and that Bonnie would keep me safe, I allowed myself to let go of consciousness and fall into a deep and dreamless sleep.

CHAPTER 29

I awoke with Jack's name on my lips, opening my eyes with a start as I remembered all that had happened. Bright fluorescent lights and the antiseptic scent of the room would have been enough to tell most people they were in the hospital. For me, it was the lost souls lining the walls of the room and peering through the glass window on the door that told me where I was. I hated hospitals.

"She's awake."

I turned at the sound of my mother's voice just in time to see her let go of my father's hand. They both stood at the side of the bed, my mother's cool hand pressed against my cheek. "Mellie, sweetheart. How do you feel?"

I thought for a moment, wiggling my toes and fingers, moving my arms and legs. "I'm fine, actually. I feel great. I think that's the first real sleep I've had in a while." My stomach grumbled. "What time is it?"

"It's a little past five. You've been out since Jack pulled you from the car this morning."

I shook my head. "It seems like weeks ago. And I'm having the oddest craving right now for a piece of coconut cream pie from Jestine's."

My dad took my hand. "I'll go get it for you. Anything you want, just ask." I thought I saw moisture in his eyes but he quickly blinked it away.

I squeezed his hand, grateful that both of my parents were there but painfully aware of the one person who wasn't.

"Thanks, Dad. And, um, see if you can buy an entire pie."

He at least knew me well enough not to blink. "Done," he said, leaning down to kiss my forehead. "I'll bring it to your mother's house, since I don't expect they'll keep you overnight. I'll be back to help her bring you home."

I smiled my gratitude, my stomach growling again in agreement as I watched him leave. Then I turned to my mother. "Has anyone told Julia what we found?"

She shook her head. "After I got you settled here, I called Dee to let her know. But Julia slipped into a coma this morning—about the time we were digging Jonathan's grave. They don't expect her to awaken."

An inexplicable sadness settled on me. "So all of that was for nothing?" I shook my head in disgust, trying not to think about the trauma of the morning.

"I think it's too early to tell, but I doubt it was for nothing."

I closed my eyes, trying to accept what she was telling me, then opened my eyes again as I recalled that I was in the hospital. "Why am I here?" I asked, noticing for the first time the needle in my hand and the IV fluid drip by the bed.

A look I didn't recognize passed over my mother's face. "You were severely dehydrated. At least, that's the medical explanation for why you passed out. But I saw Harold Manigault in the car with you, and then I saw you—" Her voice caught. "You weren't fighting, Mellie. You weren't even trying." A fat tear rolled down her cheek.

"I'm sorry, Mother. I . . . couldn't. I had nothing to fight with, and . . . there was nothing left to fight for." I turned my head away, not wanting to see her face as I told her the rest. "It was so much easier to just . . . let go."

She pulled her chair up to the side of the bed and grabbed both of my hands. "That was Harold's doing, filling your mind with his poison." She closed her eyes. "Promise me you will never do that again. That you will always fight. You *are* stronger than them. Even without me—although there was a reason your strength was drained today. But you should always fight. Especially now . . ." She stopped.

"What?"

She looked at me, that odd expression on her face again. "Is there something you need to tell me?"

I remembered Bonnie then, her music. Her words. *Go back. Go back and find my daughter's eyes.* "Yes," I answered. "Bonnie saved me. She's the one who helped me come back." I burst out crying for a bunch of reasons I couldn't name. "I'm sorry," I said, blotting my eyes with the edge of the sheet. "I don't know why I'm so emotional these days."

My mother gave me that look again, as if she were waiting for me to say something. When I didn't, she said, "We are sometimes given angels when we least expect them. And that's not the first time Bonnie's interceded on your behalf, either."

I shook my head. "No—she saved me in the Circular Church cemetery, though I don't know why she feels protective of me. Maybe because of Nola, and how I'm sort of her surrogate mother now."

My mother sat back in her chair and actually rolled her eyes. "Mellie, I've always considered you to be an intelligent woman. Surely you can figure out why Bonnie feels the need to protect you. Or why you've been so teary-eyed lately."

I glared at her. "Other than my heart being brutally ripped from my chest, no, I can't imagine why."

She sighed heavily. "Mellie, your feet are swollen. You're weeping all the time. Your pants and skirts feel tight. You're exhausted all the time but can't sleep. You're craving coconut cream pie. Are any of these things ringing a bell?"

Little pinpoints of light erupted in the back of my head as I stared at her blankly, unable to process something my brain was trying to tell me. My mother actually rolled her eyes *again*.

She leaned forward, her eyes intent on mine. "Did it ever occur to you that you might be pregnant?"

I continued to stare at her blankly as my mind sluggishly tumbled through my mental calendar, checking off the number of days since my birthday party, resisting the inevitable conclusion that I kept reaching regardless of the different paths my brain tried to take. At least because of a lifetime of irregular periods I couldn't claim complete stupidity in not recognizing what was probably the most basic of all biological changes in a woman's body. And the whole time my mind was shouting at me, *No! No! No! No!*

Taking my numbed silence as a reason to keep talking, she continued. "Before administering treatment to an unconscious woman of childbearing years, they're required to do a pregnancy test." She paused as I held my breath. "It came back positive."

I continued to blink rapidly, unable to make my tongue and mouth work in a collaborative effort. Finally I managed, "Pregnant? But how could that happen?"

My mother closed her eyes and took a deep breath. "Sweetheart, I know I wasn't there for your growing-up years or for when the time was right to have the birds-and-the-bees talk. But you're forty years old. I sincerely hope that even without my being there you have somehow managed to figure out where babies come from."

I felt myself blushing. "But I'm forty. I can't be having a baby at forty! And I'm single." This last word was hissed.

She took both of my hands in hers. "Mellie, older women are having babies all the time now. We'll just make sure that we get you the best prenatal care. And I'm sure that as soon as Jack knows . . ."

I shook my head, the tears coming so hard now that I didn't bother wiping them up with the sheet. "No. I don't want him to know. He can barely stand the sight of me right now."

"That's not true. And this could be the thing that brings you two together." She squeezed my hands and smiled brightly. "I'm going to be a grandmother! And I know your father and Jack's parents will be so happy, too. We all love Nola and try to spoil her as much as she'll let us, but having a baby to spoil from the beginning, well, those are two lucky grandchildren, is all I'm going to say about it."

"But I don't know anything about being a mother!"

She smiled again. "Most pregnant women say the same thing. But you, Mellie, are an excellent mother. Just look at Nola. Since the moment she turned up on your doorstep, you've known exactly the right mixture of guidance and affection to offer her. I think you can take most of the credit for her somewhat smooth adjustment to her new life. It's not been perfect, but I don't think any mother-child relationship is supposed to be. That's what makes it so special."

She squeezed my hands again, and when I looked into her eyes I saw that she was crying now, too.

I felt a small glimmer of hope that she might be wrong. "When

Bonnie saved me in the Circular Church cemetery, I hadn't . . . um, Jack and I . . . well, there was no reason for her to be protecting me."

My mother gave me a patient smile. "As much experience as we've both had with spirits, surely by now you realize there's so much more we *don't* know. Maybe she knew in advance where you and Jack were heading. Or maybe it was because of Nola and your relationship with her. We can only guess."

I sat up suddenly. "Oh, my gosh. Nola! Where is she? I need to tell her. I'd die if she found out from somebody else or figured it out before I could tell her. I'll tell Jack first, though. Promise."

I was already pushing for the call button so I could get a nurse to unhook me and discharge me when my mother took my arm. "You need to stay here and rest, Mellie. Everything else will work out."

There was something alarming in her tone of voice, and I stopped trying to get out of bed to look at her. "Where's Nola?" I asked again.

"It's all being taken care of, Mellie. Jack has everything under control."

"Has what under control? What's wrong?"

I pulled away from her and began dragging my IV toward the door. Seeing that I was serious about leaving, she moved to block my way. "Nola's missing. Jack dropped her off with Mrs. Houlihan at my house before coming to the hospital to check on you. Mrs. Houlihan says that after Nola ate an early dinner she went upstairs to get her mother's guitar and then left without a good-bye. She did leave a note for Jack, however, saying she needed time to take care of something for her mother. The good news is that she left her backpack, which makes us think that she's telling the truth. Jack's handling it and doesn't want you to worry."

Go back and find my daughter's eyes. I was already trying to peel off my hospital nightgown. "I need to find him. I can help. And I have something important to tell him."

My mother frowned meaningfully.

"Okay," I said. "Two things, although not until I know for sure about the second thing—pregnancy tests have been known to give false positives. And if you go get a nurse to come help me speed up the discharge process, I promise to stop by a drugstore on the way and pick up a home pregnancy test so that I'm absolutely sure before I tell Jack."

She pursed her lips, then nodded. "And at least a bottle of water. Promise me. You need to keep hydrated."

I started ripping off the tape that held my IV needle in place. Watching me, she said, "Stop that before you hurt yourself—I'll go get a nurse."

"Hurry," I shouted after her, then headed to a chair where my clothes had been neatly folded. With a shudder, I shook out the mom jeans and began to put them on, pressing my hand against my abdomen and feeling the truth I wasn't yet ready to accept. Bonnie had saved my child and me. The very least I could do was repay the favor.

I let my mother drive, wishing I had Amelia behind the wheel instead. Amelia would have taken stop signs and other traffic indicators as mere suggestions and gotten us to Alston's house in half the time. I'd had my mother call Jack to suggest he find out from Alston anything he could about Nola's recent Facebook activity. I wanted him to assume that I was still in the hospital. Dealing with my mother trying to discourage me from leaving the hospital was bad enough. Besides, I wasn't sure Jack would even want me near.

We arrived at Alston's house at the same time Jack did. I wanted to run to him and put my arms around him and assure him that everything would be all right. But he made no move in my direction and instead I found myself fumbling with my purse.

"Shouldn't she be in the hospital?" Jack asked, facing my mother.

"She thought she could help. She cares a lot about Nola and is sick with worry. If I didn't bring her myself, she would have found another way."

"Unless Nola told her where she was going, I don't think she can help."

"She says—"

"Stop it," I interrupted. "I can hear you, you know."

My mother at least looked embarrassed. But Jack just looked angry, albeit an angry Jack who was under a lot of stress. He still wore his dirt-covered jeans and shirt, his hair spiked around his forehead as if he'd spent a lot of time running his hands through it. "You shouldn't have come," he said, and for a moment I wondered whether he'd guessed my secret. "I need to know that at least one of you is safe."

My heart melted a little, and it took all of my strength not to throw myself at him. "I feel fine." I held up a water bottle my mother had forced me to buy at the drugstore along with a pregnancy test—which I did not hold up. "I promise to keep hydrated. And there's no way I could stay in bed while knowing that Nola is out there somewhere and might need me."

He took a deep breath to argue, but I interrupted him. "I don't know whether this will help, but I figured out what Bonnie's been trying to tell us about 'my daughter's eyes.' It's a song—the song I've been hearing since Nola walked into my house. She's asking us to find it—the music. She must have written it and then hidden it for some reason."

We began walking up to the Ravenels' front door. "Why would she hide it?" my mother asked. "Don't songwriters want their music to get out there?"

"Only if they get paid for it," Jack said.

I wanted to ask him what he meant when the front door was pulled open by Alston. "Hello," she said. After closing the door behind us, she asked, "Is my mother expecting you? It's my parents' date night, so they're not here."

Jack smiled, but I could see his anxiety in the pulsing of his jaw muscle. "Actually, we're still looking for Nola. When I spoke with you earlier you hadn't seen her, but I was wondering whether maybe since then she might have called."

She hesitated just for a moment. "I tried calling her about thirty times, figuring she'd answer a call if it was from me. She finally called me back about an hour ago."

Jack inhaled sharply. "I asked you to call me if you heard from her."

Alston's bottom lip trembled. "I know. But she said she was here in Charleston and not to worry, that she was just taking care of something and would be back home tonight. She told me not to tell you because you would just want to interfere. I figured it was okay to wait and tell you because she's okay."

Jack closed his eyes and I could tell he was trying to keep his temper in check. "Do you have any idea what sort of thing she needed to take care of?"

Again, she hesitated.

I stepped forward. "Please, Alston. We're all worried about Nola and we need to find her to make sure she's safe. Has she used your computer recently?"

She began to cry. "Please don't tell my mom. She'll kill me. I promised her that I wouldn't break my promise to you to not let her use it. But when Nola was here yesterday I left her alone in my room while my mom made me fold a load of laundry downstairs. When I got back, my laptop was in a different spot. And when I used it later it was on the Facebook home page, and I knew that's not where I was the last time I used it."

"She didn't say anything about it?" Jack asked.

"No. And I didn't ask. It was like we were both keeping the same secret so we wouldn't get in trouble."

"It's okay, Alston," my mother said as she put her arm around the young girl. "We understand you're trying to protect your friend. But we need your help now. Can you go get your laptop and let us see whether we can find out anything?"

She nodded eagerly. "I know her Facebook password, if you think that will help." She was already running upstairs.

When she returned she led us to the kitchen, where she placed the laptop on the table, the Facebook home page already showing. She sat in front of it and typed something before Nola's home page filled the screen. Her profile picture surprised me; it was a photo of her, Jack, and me at my birthday party that Alston had taken using Nola's iPhone. I felt the now-common prick of tears in the backs of my eyes and quickly blinked them away.

"Can you go to her messages?" Jack asked.

Alston nodded and made a quick click to the message page, where a single name appeared: Rick Chase. She clicked on it and a string of messages, the last one from the previous day, ran down the screen.

Jack cursed under his breath and leaned forward to read them.

Alston vacated the seat. "Sit here, Mr. Trenholm, so you can see them better."

Jack sat and began scrolling through the messages. Without looking up, he said to Alston, "It doesn't look like she's been using Facebook since I told her not to—at least until last week. I'm guessing that's why you know her password—so you could let her know when she had a new message?"

Slowly, Alston nodded. With her gaze firmly glued to the floor, she added, "The last time she spoke with him on the phone, she told him to message her on Facebook, since you wouldn't have access to that."

"But what would they have to talk about?" I asked, leaning forward and squinting but still unable to read the screen.

"Bonnie," Jack said. "And the untitled song she was working on when she died." He leaned forward, his finger hitting the down arrow button harder than necessary. "According to his messages, Rick apparently has it and wants to give it to Nola, but first he wants to hear her play it for him on Bonnie's guitar. He's coming to Charleston."

He was silent for a while as he continued to read. "Damn," he said, pushing back the chair with sudden force. Glancing at his watch, he said, "They were supposed to meet at the John Calhoun statue in Marion Square half an hour ago." He stood, then turned to Alston. "Call me if you hear from her; do you understand? No matter what she says, call me."

"Yes, sir. I promise this time I will." She blinked rapidly, but not fast enough to stem the flow of tears that poured down her cheeks. "Is Nola going to be okay?"

I squeezed her arm and gave her a reassuring smile before racing after Jack, who was striding quickly out of the house toward his car. I followed while my mother hesitated. Calling out to Jack, she said, "I'll go back to the house and wait there in case she comes home. Let me know if you need backup and I'll send James."

Jack nodded, then sent a glowering look in my direction. "Go with her, Mellie."

"As if," I said, using my favorite Nola expression as I opened the passenger door of his car and stepped inside.

CHAPTER 30

The first bubble of nausea hit me as Jack's car crossed Broad Street. I wasn't sure whether it was the breakneck speed and two-wheeled turns as he hurtled down Meeting Street that started it, or the two Twinkies I'd bought at the drugstore because I'd been so hungry. Either way, I found myself with my eyes closed as I prayed I wouldn't throw up in Jack's Porsche.

I swallowed heavily, then turned to Jack. "What did you mean—about songwriters only wanting their songs out there if they're paid for it?"

"I found something out about Mr. Chase. I flew up to New York last week to have a little discussion with my agent before firing him. As a parting gift, he got me in touch with an old friend of his who's an agent in the music business who happens to know Jimmy Gordon's agent. He made a few calls for me and I got three minutes on the phone with Jimmy himself."

I sat there for a moment, trying to digest the Twinkies and what he was telling me at the same time. "What did he say?"

"That when he met with Bonnie and Rick, it was because she was the known writer of 'I'm Just Getting Started.' Just her. No partner or anything. Jimmy wasn't even aware that Bonnie wasn't getting credit for it after he recorded it."

"So how come the song is credited to Rick Chase?"

Jack sped through a red light, narrowly missing a cluster of women carrying shopping bags. "Think about it. Bonnie was an addict. Rick would supply her until she was barely coherent, maybe make her sign papers giving up her rights to the song. I think that's how he stole it from her. From Nola." I watched him swallow. "He probably killed her, too. In a way. The disappointment and sense of betrayal she must have felt when she heard the song on the radio and knew she hadn't received any credit for it must have devastated her."

I swallowed down a ball of nausea. "Poor Bonnie," I said. "And poor Nola. All this time thinking it was Jimmy Gordon who stole her mother's song. Rick must have fed Nola some story to make her believe that—you don't have to look very hard on the Internet to find the writer of a song. But Rick must be feeling some guilt. Don't you think that's why he wants to give Nola the new song—so that he can make it up to her?"

Jack shot me a look. "The guy's a slime bucket, Mellie. My guess is he doesn't have the song but thinks Nola does. He lied that he had it to get her to meet him. I bet he's planning to take it from her."

"But she doesn't have it, or at least doesn't know she does." I thought for a moment. "He's come all the way from California. What do you think he'll do when he finds out she doesn't have it? Maybe we should call the police."

Jack responded by pressing harder on the accelerator. "I can get there faster."

I closed my eyes, not wanting to register how fast we were going. "Why would Rick ask her to bring the guitar?"

"Knowing what I know about him, he probably wants her to sing it while he videos her on his phone or something so he can re-create it. That's assuming she even knows it."

I looked at him, my eyes wide. "She knows it—or at least part of it. I've heard her singing it in the shower when she thought nobody was listening. But she sings the same part over and over, like she doesn't know what comes next." I paused for a moment, remembering. "It's haunting, and beautiful. Sort of Joan Baez at her best. Bonnie sings it, too."

He sent me a sidelong glance just as the light turned red on Calhoun. Instead of stopping, he sped up to make it through the intersection, narrowly escaping being clipped by a delivery truck. He slid into a spot just vacated across from the Francis Marion Hotel, and we both raced from the car toward the iconic statue inside the square.

The park was almost deserted, the outline of the old statesman on his column highlighted by the bruised sunset sky. As we approached the square white granite base we didn't see anybody. We slowed, looking down the other paths in case Rick and Nola were heading away from the statue.

I heard the quiet crying first and reached for Jack's arm in alarm. "Over here," I said, pulling him to the other side of the granite. We stopped suddenly, our eyes trying to make sense of what we were seeing.

Nola sat in the grass with her back against the white granite, her knees drawn up to her chest, her head lowered as her shoulders shook with each sob. Bonnie's guitar case lay nearby, splayed open, the remains of the guitar sprinkled over the ground like confetti in front of the crying girl. The neck had been separated from the body of the instrument, the soundboard crushed flat, as if somebody with a large foot had simply stepped on it. The broken strings sprang up in spindly, wild abandon, splattered over the splintered, pale wood like petals from a dying flower.

"Nola!" Jack rushed to her side and knelt in front of her. "Are you all right? Did he hurt you?"

She shook her head without lifting it.

Jack placed his hand gently on the back of her head. "Tell me what happened. I promise I won't get angry—I just want to know the truth."

She sniffed, then raised her head. "He didn't hurt me. But . . . but look what he did to Mom's guitar. It's ruined!" She began to sob again, her young world seemingly in as many pieces as her mother's instrument.

Jack gathered her in his arms and she didn't protest. "It's okay, Nola, as long as you're all right. We can get another guitar. It won't be the same, but it's replaceable. You aren't."

She pressed her face into his neck and put her arms around him as she cried harder. Jack patted her back as if he'd been comforting her hurts since birth, and I had to turn away so I wouldn't start crying, too.

"Where did he go?" Jack asked.

Nola looked up, wiping her eyes with the heels of her hands, and I noticed she wasn't wearing any makeup. She shook her head. "I don't know. He left after he broke the guitar."

Jack ran his hand through his hair, turning his head as if trying to determine the direction in which Rick Chase had fled, and I could tell he wanted to go after him. Instead, he looked back at Nola and his face softened. "Don't worry about that jerk—I'll deal with him later. But why was he here?"

With a loud sniff, Nola said, "He kept asking me for the music my mom and I were working on when she died. He wouldn't believe me when I told him I didn't know, and that we hadn't even finished it. All I know are the first couple of lines—but I didn't tell him that. I'm not *that* stupid. Especially after he told me that he was the one who sold 'I'm Just Getting Started' to Jimmy Gordon."

"He admitted it?" I asked.

Nola nodded. "He was proud of it. Said my mother wanted more time with the song to make it better, but he knew it was ready to be a hit, so he made Mom sign over the rights to him, the fu . . . stupid jerk. He told me Mom wasn't interested in the money anyway, so what he did wasn't so wrong. That she should have been happy that he was responsible for making the song so popular." She started to cry again and Jack folded her in his arms. "I'm so stupid. He came to see me the night Mom died, and he told me that she'd been afraid she was going to jail on drug charges and had asked Rick to put the song in his name so that any money it earned wouldn't get confiscated. The jerk even said that he was going to give every penny to me. But then he said that Jimmy Gordon had cheated us and was making sure we weren't going to get paid. And I believed him. I'm such an idiot." Fresh sobs erupted as she buried her face in Jack's neck.

Jack smoothed the hair on the back of her head. "No, Nola. You're just young, and Rick Chase took advantage of that. And he's the only idiot here thinking he's going to get away with it."

I bent over to pick up a piece of the guitar, trying to hide a wave of nausea. "Why would he do this?"

With another sniff Nola said, "I think he was trying to find the music—like Mom had hidden it in there, since I said I didn't know where it was and that the guitar was the only thing of hers that I took with me. He didn't find anything, though. He just . . ." She hiccuped loudly. "He picked it up and swung it against the bottom of the statue just to make sure." Her face wore a mask of abject despair, the tears dripping down her cheeks.

I sat down next to Nola and Jack with my back pressed against the granite, hoping the stone held enough chill to tap down the building nausea. "The song is called 'My Daughter's Eyes.' Did you know that?"

Nola turned her tear-streaked face to me and shook her head. "How do you know?"

I smiled softly, pressing my hand against my stomach. "Bonnie kept telling me to find 'My Daughter's Eyes.' I didn't figure out until today that she was talking about a song. She's been singing it to me for some time now." I closed my eyes and swallowed. "And I've heard you singing parts of it. It's beautiful—especially when you sing it. I'd really like to hear you sing the whole thing."

Nola started to cry again. "I don't know it. I only worked on the first verse with her and the melody line. If she finished it without me, she must have worked on it while I was at school or something."

"But when you were packing your things to come to Charleston, did you find any part of it?" Jack asked.

"No. I remember looking for it, and when I didn't find it I figured she thought it was garbage and had thrown it away." She squeezed her eyes tightly, as if trying to stem the flow of tears. "Like our lives together," she added quietly.

Jack pulled her closer and kissed the top of her head again. "That can't be true, Nola. I knew your mother, and I know you. There might be a thousand reasons why she did what she did, but I know that's not one of them."

I pressed my hand against my forehead, my skin clammy and beading with sweat now. I closed my eyes, remembering the night Jack had brought the scared yet defiant Nola to my door with everything she owned in a small backpack and her mother's guitar. Bonnie had been there, making sure that Nola was going to be okay. I faced them, glad for the dim light of dusk that would hide any green tinge to my skin. "I've known from the start that your mother loved you. She didn't destroy that song. I know she finished it, and I know it's even better than that song Rick stole, because I've heard it dozens of times and it gets more and more beautiful each time I hear it. Your mother named it 'My Daughter's Eyes' because it's her legacy to you. She's hidden it from Rick in a place she knew you could find it. Someplace we haven't thought to look."

We were silent as we considered the possibilities, the only sound that of passing cars on the nearby street.

Finally, Nola spoke. "Dad? How did you know how to find me?"

I watched Jack swallow slowly and I realized he'd heard the word "Dad," too.

"Facebook," he said, his voice stern.

She groaned. "I'm in big trouble, aren't I?"

"You could say that. I might ground you for life—I haven't decided yet." He hugged her tightly and kissed the top of her head. "I was sick with worry, you know. Promise me that you will never do anything so stupid again. That you'll talk to me first and we can come up with a plan of action together."

She nodded, then looked up at me. "Why is Mellie with you? I thought you weren't speaking to each other."

Jack glanced in my direction. "You know how she is—can't stand to be without me. I didn't have the heart to leave her behind. She's worse than General Lee with that sad puppy-dog face she does. I couldn't take it."

Nola giggled while I pressed my back against the stone, searching for any remaining coolness. Jack was spared a searing look from me by another wave of nausea. Swallowing it back, I said, "What he meant to say is that I care about you, Nola, and I wanted to make sure you were okay." I closed my eyes, trying to picture floating, weightless clouds and a cool stream. Instead I found myself seeing Nola again the night Jack brought her to my house, the guitar, and her backpack with the improbable face of a teddy bear poking out of the zipper.

I sat up, my head sloshing in a dizzy swim. "How long have you had your teddy bear?"

Nola frowned. "Since I was born. Mom bought it when she was pregnant with me, and I never spent a night without it. She named him

Wolfgang, but he's always been Wolfie to me." She swiped a hand across her eyes. "Why?"

Without answering her, I said, "So if you were to travel anywhere, or move to a new place, you would take Wolfie with you? And your mother knew that?"

Nola nodded. "Nobody knew that except my mom. The other kids would beat me up if they knew."

"And the new lettering on the jersey—when did she do that?"

Squinting in thought, she said, "About a month before she died, but she didn't tell me why."

I looked at Jack, but he was already standing. "Come on," he said, reaching for Nola's hand and pulling her up.

"Where are we going?" Nola asked.

They both turned to me as I struggled to a stand, leaning heavily on the statue's base. "I think I know where your mother hid the music." Then I turned around and emptied my stomach into the grass under the watchful eye of old John C. Calhoun.

Except for the sound of Jack's quick calls on his cell phone to his parents and mine to let them know we'd found Nola and everything was all right, it was oddly silent. I'd felt much better after throwing up and was now lying back as much as a person could in the reclined front seat of his Porsche while Nola was curled up in what space remained in the backseat. It had taken a lot of convincing to persuade Jack not to take me back to the hospital; I told him it was a Twinkie-induced stomach upset and nothing more.

My parents met us on the front porch of my mother's house. As they helped Jack extricate Nola from the backseat, I ran inside and up the stairs. As I stood outside Nola's room, my skin erupted in gooseflesh as the hair rose on the back of my neck. The stairs creaked and I turned to see Jack and Nola looking at me.

"Is she here?" Nola asked.

I nodded, then tilted my head toward Nola's room, indicating that they should follow me inside. Cold air blasted my face as I pushed open the door, the light from the windows diffused by the condensation on the glass. The corner of the room shimmered with a pulsing glow, stronger than I'd seen it before, as if Bonnie had gained strength through our understanding.

I faced her, and she didn't disappear but stared steadily back at me. "Thank you," I whispered. "For saving me—twice."

She smiled, her light even brighter now. *You know why.*

Jack hesitated in the doorway, holding Nola back.

"It's okay," I said. "Bonnie's waiting for us."

Slowly, they entered. Jack moved toward the bed, where Nola had left the backpack, the top of the bear's head visible through the open zipper. Leaning over, Jack lifted Wolfie from his prison and held him toward Nola and me. Reading her expression, Jack said, "Don't worry, sweetheart. I'll cut at the seam, and I promise to have it repaired."

Still frowning, Nola nodded. Jack reached into his front pants pocket and pulled out a Swiss Army knife. After gently pushing the small football jersey up over Wolfie's face, he held the teddy bear facedown, then eased the knife into the back of the neck with what looked like practiced precision. Once again, I was reminded of Jack's military experience and his past that I knew so little about.

Jack looked up and met my gaze. "These stitches are definitely handmade, and they don't match the machine-made stitches on the rest of the bear. I think that's why she changed the jersey numbers—to draw our attention to the bear."

Nola sucked in her breath and turned away as Jack began to slide the knife down the seam that went from the neck to the bottom of the bear. When he was finished, he placed the bear on the bed, the fuzz-filled wound gaping open.

Slowly, Nola looked back at the scene of the crime, her eyes wide. "Can I do it?" she asked.

Jack nodded as Nola stepped toward the bed and very gently began pulling small tufts of fuzz from the opening in the seam, laying each white ball neatly on the bedspread. The fourth time she stuck in her hand, she paused. "I feel something—up here in the head." She pulled out one more small tuft, then reached her hand in one last time and pulled out what looked like several sheets of paper folded into a tiny, fat square.

We watched as she slowly unfolded three sheets of lined paper with black marks indicating musical notes, and a spidery handwriting—Bonnie's, I thought—under each line of music. Nola began to hum the first part of the song, so familiar to me now, but then stopped. "These aren't the words we wrote together." Her voice shook. "I can't . . ." She held out the music to Jack.

Clearing his throat, he began to read.

In my daughter's eyes, I see the best part of me,
The me with courage and strength and possibilities,
The me unscarred and free,
The me I always wanted to be,
In my daughter's eyes.

Jack looked up, his eyes moist, as a cool breeze rattled the papers in his hand. "It's . . . amazing. And she's talking about you, Nola. It's all about how she felt about you, how she loved you."

I watched as Bonnie moved in Jack's direction, then leaned toward him, pressing her lips against his cheek. His hand shot up to his face. "I just . . ." He stopped, a half smile lifting his mouth. "She's really here," he said.

I lifted an eyebrow in his direction before turning to Bonnie. "Are you ready to go now?" I watched as she became brighter and clearer. I could see how beautiful she was, and how Nola, despite her resemblance to her father, also had her mother's clear, high forehead and pixielike chin. I'd tell that to Nola later, because I knew she'd need to hear it, to remember it when she had her own children.

Forgive me.

I knew her words weren't for me. I reached out my hand and brought Nola forward. "She's asking for your forgiveness. She needs it to move on."

Nola stared at the corner of the room where Bonnie watched us. "I feel her. I can't see her, but I feel her." Bonnie moved closer, and I watched as she kissed the top of Nola's head, just as I'd seen Jack do.

Nola lifted her face, a small smile on her lips. A strand of dark hair stuck to her wet cheek, and I gently brushed it away. My abdomen seemed to swell slightly as a wave of certainty descended on me, making me wonder whether impending motherhood made all the vagaries of life suddenly clear and understandable.

I put my arm around Nola. "You're feeling her love for you—a mother's love. That will never die. Even after she's gone, you will always know it's there. But she's finished here. She knows you are loved and taken care of, and that you've found her legacy for you. It's time to let her go."

Nola continued to stare straight ahead, as if she could actually see Bonnie. "Can she hear me?"

I nodded.

She faced Bonnie's corner again. "I was so mad at you. But I understand now. I just wish you'd told me everything. I could have figured it out for both of us, but you didn't give me the chance."

I'm sorry for all the hurt I caused you. But never doubt that I loved you and that I always will.

I pulled Nola close, my arms around her as Bonnie's light fell on both of us like a shimmering cocoon. "She wants you to know that she's sorry, and that she will always love you."

"I love you, too, Mom. I never stopped." Nola clenched her eyes tight. "And I forgive you. I do. I think I'll still be mad for a long time, but I forgive you."

The light brightened even more, separating itself from Bonnie, concentrating in a tall column that stretched from the floor to the ceiling, like a door had opened somewhere to a place of startling brightness. Bonnie looked at me, a question in her eyes.

"Step into the light, Bonnie. It's okay to leave now. Nola will be all right—I promise."

With a last glance at Jack and Nola, she moved closer to the column of light, then turned back, her gaze directed at me. *You'll be a good mother. But be vigilant. Not all earthbound spirits are lost, and they search for those of you who would take their power.* She looked at Nola, her eyes full of love, and then back to me. *Thank you, Melanie.* Her head turned slightly, as if she could hear something I couldn't. Then, with a small, secret smile, she said, *Good-bye.*

She turned back toward the light and stepped into it, the light suddenly diminishing into a tiny pinprick before extinguishing itself completely.

CHAPTER 31

A ringing phone awakened me abruptly. Opening my eyes, I was dis-oriented for a moment, having been dragged away from yet another dream where I sat waiting for the pregnancy test to show a blue line. Again. I'd taken five in the last two days and had even made a spreadsheet to indicate whether I shook it or turned it upside down or flipped it over, and noted what time of day I'd taken the test. Despite the elaborate worksheet, the conclusion was always the same.

Today, Sophie's wedding day, would be the day I'd tell Jack. Or else my mother would. I'd tried to explain to my mother that I was just waiting to be sure, not willing to put Jack and me through the drama if I were wrong. Or be forced into telling Nola that her father and I were bad examples. But even I had to admit that I'd run out of time. If I needed to prove to Jack that I learned from past mistakes, I couldn't wait any longer.

I sat up, listening as the phone continued its shrill ringing and trying to remember whether there even was a phone in the room. General Lee jumped off the bed and ran to the antique dressing table across the room, then placed his front paws on the small chair in front of it.

"Thanks, buddy," I said, rubbing my eyes. "Could you answer it, too?"

I felt his noncommittal stare across the darkened room. Shuffling toward the dressing table, I groped for the receiver and held it to my ear, belatedly remembering my mother removing the cord at my request. The only phone calls I ever received at night were the kind I didn't want to answer.

The air inside the phone crackled and popped the way international phone calls had sounded before satellites. When the hair on the back of my neck stood on end, I knew this phone call was coming from a little farther away than just another country.

"Grandmother?" I spoke quietly into the phone.

The voice, when it came, arrived like a burst of cold air, a tiny spot of sound in the swirling atmosphere. *Burn the dollhouse. They won't bother you anymore.*

My eyes opened wider. "Julia?" If I was speaking with Julia on a phone that wasn't connected, it meant that the two of us no longer existed on the same side of life and death. I felt an inexplicable sadness at the passing of this woman I barely knew.

He thinks his secret died with me, that his precious name bears no blemish. But William and Jonathan need justice. The truth needs to be told. The world needs to know that murders were committed and who was responsible.

I nodded into the phone, understanding dawning on me, and I almost smiled. "Yes. It does. I'll make sure of it."

And Emmaline—tell her to keep practicing.

"I will. I don't think it will be that hard to do now."

I heard only empty air for a long moment, and I thought she'd already gone. Then, so quietly that I had to press the receiver tightly to my ear, I heard, *Let Dee know I wrote a new will and hid it behind the hall mirror. I left something for you. And Emmaline.*

Panic gripped me as I imagined restoring yet another old house. I started to protest, but her voice came through once more, even fainter this time.

You are stronger than you think. You'll have cause soon to remember that.

The static cleared and I was left holding a dead phone. Something small and faint stirred low in my abdomen, taking my breath away as I considered how life and death coexisted in a never-ending continuum. I closed my eyes and stood in the dark for a long time, thinking about Julia's passing and her last words to me. Then I reached for my cell phone and hit the memory button to call Jack.

❧

I stood next to Sophie, rearranging the flowers in her hair. Her mother, an older version of Sophie, including the worn Birkenstocks, had left to go fuss at the florist for not using sustainable flowers. I couldn't block out the mental image of Sophie covered in plant stems and roots while guests at the reception were given tiny spades to replant them.

I stepped back to admire my work and felt the now familiar sting of tears threaten to spill over and mess up my carefully applied makeup. At my recommendation, Sophie had gone to a salon for the first time in her life and had them straighten and smooth her hair so that it fell in thick, luxurious waves halfway down her back. She looked beautiful, especially in the antique wedding dress, and even if wedding guests might be confused when they saw her hair, when they spotted the bride's bare feet they'd know they were in the right place.

Pinching the waistbands of the two pairs of Spanx I wore to hold in my abdomen, I tugged them higher. My leotard and togalike sheet that passed for my bridesmaid's dress left nothing to the imagination, and doubling up on the Spanx had seemed the only alternative. My stomach rumbled, causing both Sophie and Nola to stare at me, but I continued to fuss with the white blooms in Sophie's hair as if I hadn't heard it, too.

"You look drop-dead gorgeous," I said to Sophie, resisting another surge of emotion that would make me hug her and start crying again. She'd started to flinch each time I said something, and I had to focus on keeping my hands folded tightly in front of me.

"Thank you," she said, eyeing herself critically in the full-length mirror in the bedroom of a friend's house on Folly Beach. A barefoot wedding on the beach had seemed the perfect setting for a barefoot bride and groom. And wedding party. "I do like the hair. I'm just not sure about the makeup."

"You can take it off after the ceremony. But you want to make sure that we can see your eyes and lips in all the photographs. I know you don't think so, but it does look very natural. You're just aware of it because you've never worn makeup before."

"Which is totally weird," said Nola, moving to stand next to me. We wore identical outfits, yet on an almost-fourteen-year-old it looked cute. I just looked like the Michelin Man trying to dress like a girl. I felt like exploding biscuit dough in a can. I wanted to cry again, thinking of the biscuits and vegan gravy that were waiting at the reception.

"You look beautiful, too," I said to Nola, who wore only a sheer pink gloss on her lips and a single coat of mascara. With her dark hair and pale skin, she looked like an angel in the white leotard and toga, but I'd never say that out loud, because despite recent changes, she was still a teenager. Surprisingly, a new serenity had found her since her mother's crossing over. I suppose forgiveness and letting go would do that to a person, like emptying a suitcase filled with rocks that one had carried for a long time.

She shrugged, but I noticed her cheeks pinkening. Her phone buzzed and she looked at it and read a text message. "It's from Dad. He and the colonel are finished with the bonfire and will be here in about five minutes."

Sophie raised her eyebrows.

"Julia Manigault died late last night—I confirmed with Dee Davenport," I explained. "But I had a conversation with Julia early this morning. She told me to burn the dollhouse, and I called Jack, since the dollhouse was at his condo."

Nola straightened her shoulders. I'd thought we'd get a lot more resistance from her when I told her what we'd planned to do with the dollhouse, but she'd accepted it and had even been enthusiastic. A haunted dollhouse with evil dolls can do that to a person.

I continued. "Jack couldn't do it by himself, so he called my dad. He wanted to call Chad, but I talked him out of it, seeing as how you probably didn't want your groom reeking of woodsmoke on his wedding day."

"No, I probably wouldn't," Sophie agreed. "Where did they take it?"

"Jack has a friend here on Folly Beach who has a fire pit in his backyard. They burned everything, including the dolls." I glanced at Nola. "Except for the dog, which has somehow gone missing again."

Nola studied her screen closely, as if reading a text, although I hadn't heard it ping with a new one.

Sophie's forehead puckered. "But if you don't send them into the light, where will they go?"

"I don't think Harold's going into the light, if you know what I mean. But the others are free to go now. Their secret is no longer holding them here."

Sophie lifted her long skirt and stepped down from the step stool that had been set up in front of the mirror. "It's just a shame that the truth will never be known."

I smiled. "Actually, that might not be the case. I'll keep you posted."

There was another tap on the door and Nola opened it. "It's safe," she said, and opened it wider.

Jack stuck his head through the opening without stepping inside the room. He gave a low wolf whistle when he saw Sophie. "You're the most beautiful bride I've ever seen," he said, stepping forward to give her a light kiss on the cheek. Even Sophie wasn't immune to his charms, and I watched as her cheeks flushed pink. She flapped her hand at him. "I bet you say that to all the girls."

He winked and she flushed a little deeper. Turning to me, he said, "You said you needed to see me right away. That you had something important to tell me."

I nodded, then glanced at Sophie, who was raising her eyebrows. I hadn't told her my secret, and not because I was trying to get back at her for not telling me about her engagement. Jack needed to be first, then Nola. I hadn't moved beyond the first two.

"I'll be right back," I said to Sophie and Nola as I headed for the door, Jack following.

Sophie glanced at the clock on the bedside table. "You only have about five minutes, so be fast. I'll send Nola out to get you."

Being careful not to touch Jack, I led him to the door and out into the small, deserted hallway that led to the other bedrooms. I'd thought briefly of waiting until after the wedding to tell him, wanting more time, or a bit of sand and ocean instead of plain, white drywall in the background, as befitted such an announcement. Or at least something that would offer me a soft place to fall if the need arose. But even I knew it was time.

I looked up into Jack's face, at his incredibly blue eyes and the way they were crinkling at the corners as he gave me one of his old and familiar smiles. The events of the past week had erased much of the animosity that had been between us since my confession about Marc, but

I knew, too, that he hadn't put his hands on my arms, and that his expression remained controlled. I'd told him I loved him, and he'd responded by saying he was sorry. I opened my mouth to speak, and faltered, then listened as different words poured from my mouth. "What's going to happen to Rick Chase?"

He sent me an odd look before answering. "I've got a couple of army buddies in the LAPD who are going to make Rick's life a little difficult for a while. No unpaid parking ticket will go unnoticed, no sliding through stop signs. But that's just until the private detective I hired finishes digging up a little dirt Mr. Chase left behind in Missouri. Domestic abuse, unpaid child support, allegations of trying to pass bad checks. He'll go to jail at some point. Not for what he should be jailed for, but at least it's something. And when he hears 'My Daughter's Eyes' on the radio, I hope it hurts really, really bad."

"Me, too."

He looked at me expectantly, and my knees started to wobble. Again, I stalled. "Julia Manigault wants her story to be told so that there's justice for William and Jonathan. I think she meant for you to tell it, to write about it for your next book."

He stared at me for a moment, as if not completely understanding. "But she's dead. How did you . . . ?" He stopped and I watched as his shoulders relaxed. "That certainly wasn't expected. I don't know what to say. Thank you, I guess, would be a good place to start."

I nodded, almost hearing the ticking of an unseen clock. "I've already spoken with Dee Davenport, and once Julia's estate is settled, she'll give you access to any family papers to assist you." I paused, then found myself staring up at him with frozen lips.

"What's wrong, Mellie? Is there something else?"

I wanted him to touch me, to let me know that he still felt . . . something. But although we stood less than a foot apart, close enough that I could smell the woodsmoke on his skin, it seemed as if he were miles away from me.

Nola opened the door to the bedroom. "Sophie says it's time, Mellie. Her dad's waiting outside."

I looked at her in panic. "Tell Sophie just one more minute." I didn't wait to see her go back inside. Turning back to Jack, I took a deep breath. "I'm pregnant."

There was a brief pause, and then he leaned close to me, as if he'd suddenly gone hard of hearing.

"I said I'm pregnant."

I wondered whether this was what the Tower of Babel had been like, with people talking to one another without anybody understanding what they were saying.

"I'm going to have a baby," I said, wondering if it was the word "pregnant" that was confusing him.

He blinked several times, his eyes revealing a separate emotion each time, none of them I could interpret, because my own vision was suddenly blurry with tears.

Jack continued to stare and blink at me. "But how could you be pregnant?"

"Pregnant?" Nola's voice ended our staring match.

We both turned to find Nola and Sophie in the doorway, their expressions almost as shocked as Jack's. Nola pressed her hands against her eyes, as if trying to block out a mental image. "Dad! I mean, really. Haven't you heard of birth control?"

Sophie took Nola's arm and began walking down the hallway to the stairs. "As much as I'd like to hear the rest of this conversation, Melanie, I've got a wedding to go to. I'll be outside with my dad and Nola, waiting for you. You've got two minutes."

When I turned back to Jack, he no longer looked like a man tied to the railroad tracks as a train approached. Instead, he closely resembled the old Jack of the sparkling eyes and wicked grin, the Jack I'd fallen in love with despite my best efforts not to.

He placed his hands gently on my shoulders. "A baby. Wow." His thumbs brushed my bare skin, making my blood zing through my veins. "I don't know what to say."

I love you, I wanted to prompt, but instead I remained silent, blinking back the tears that lately always seemed to be hovering. I stood still for another moment, waiting, then pulled back, feeling the reluctant slip of his hands as they slid from my shoulders. "I have to go," I said, taking a couple of steps backward before turning and heading in the same direction as Nola and Sophie.

"Marry me, Mellie."

I stopped suddenly, the change in movement making my head spin. Of all Jack's responses I might have imagined, this particular one hadn't even grazed the surface.

I turned to face him, admiring again the face I adored, the smile that came to my dreams more often than I cared to admit. But my overriding thought was of Bonnie, and how she'd left him while pregnant with Nola, certain of the knowledge that he would tie them both down because of an ingrained sense of duty that would make him do what he believed to be the right thing regardless of his true feelings.

My breath caught in the back of my throat. "No, Jack. I can't."

He took a step forward, then stopped. "What do you mean, 'I can't'? I thought you said you loved me."

I stood staring at him for a long moment, wanting him to fill the empty space with the only three words that would make me change my mind. I swallowed down my disappointment. "I do, Jack. I don't think I'll ever stop. But I can't marry you."

Before I could start crying again, I turned and fled down the corridor, then out into the bright sunshine of a late-summer Charleston morning.

THE END
To be continued . . .

Karen White is the *New York Times* bestselling author of fourteen previous books. She grew up in London but now lives with her husband and two children near Atlanta, Georgia. Visit her Web site at www.karen-white.com.